DRAGONLORDS OF DUMNONIA

Dragon Sun

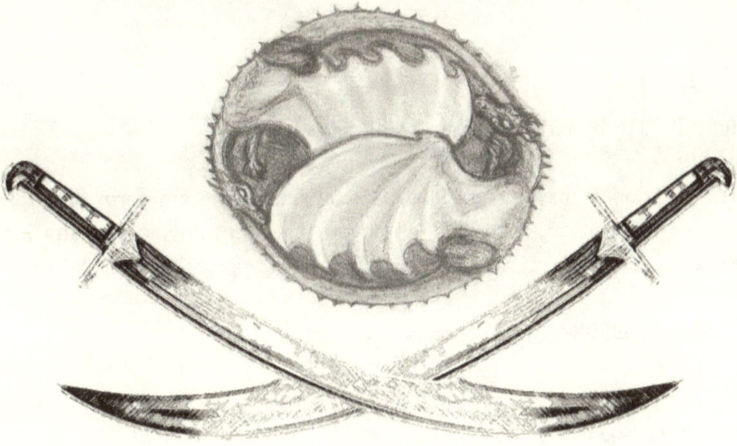

LINDA A. MALCOR

ISBN: 978-0-9969908-9-9

Story Merchant Books
400 S. Burnside Avenue #11B
Los Angeles, CA 90036
http://www.storymerchant.com/books.html

Cover & interior formatting by IndieDesignz.com
Dragon Cover Illustration & interior illustrations © 2016 Laura Cameron
www.lauracameron.net

The Anvil

Dragon Sun

For Scriptorium 101

Contents

Shashtah Climbing the Anvil

Chapter 1:

The Anvil

A good day's journey by caravan outside the King's Camp rises a great plateau called the Anvil. Aside from being an excellent landmark for travelers, the Anvil has the distinction of being the site of some of the most secret rites of the Dumnonian Dragonriders.

**—from *Arcane*
by Shane of Corin**

SHASHTAH AWOKE TO THE UNPLEASANT sensation of being turned upside down and dangled in the air by his ankles. His festive white aba ballooned around his head, entangling his arms and sending his Dragonprophetess, Tphah, into a fit of giggles. The pleasure of her mirth cascaded through their Bond, offsetting the pounding of his hangover, so he wasn't in a completely rotten mood by the time he struggled free from the entrapping robes.

Katrell, the great Bronze Dragon of Kashon, the newest Dragonlord of Dumnonia, relaxed the pinch of his agile talons just enough so he could shake Shashtah out of his soft leather, desert boots.

"Umph!" Shashtah grunted as he landed unceremoniously on the sand. At least his reflexes remembered to tuck and roll so he only sustained a few minor bruises from his fall. He squeezed the pleasantly-cool grains of sand between his toes. His solid-colored, amber eyes, without pupils or whites, darkened against the early morning glare as he squinted at the two Dragons who loomed over him.

Burnished hides covered with pure bronze scales glistened beneath the deep blue, cloudless sky. Tough, translucent leather wings, which sprouted from their sides, lay furled against their powerful bodies and muscular legs. The wicked metal spikes, not unlike enormous thorns, protected their neck- and backridges on either side of the flat spot where their necks joined their shoulders. Whiplike tails perfectly balanced their serpentine necks. Tphah's wedge-shaped head was more tapered than Katrell's, suggesting that she might be much faster than the older Dragon, who was not quite as large as Shashtah thought he should be. Humor sparkled in their solid amber eyes. Their pointed, equine ears swiveled toward him with fascination as the flaps of their nostrils opened and closed. Their forked tongues flicked briefly over their armored lips, tasting his scent. Natural shapeshifters, able to transport across enormous distances instantaneously and communicate telepathically with their own kind and their chosen Riders, they were two of the most magical, wondrous and precious creatures Shashtah could imagine, and he was deliriously happy that their only living Prophetess had agreed to Bond with him.

"A simple 'Good Morning' would have sufficed," Shashtah protested good-naturedly as he pawed the sand from his layer-cut, neck-length mane of blue-black hair. Using the leather thong Tphah had given him when he had Bonded with his first Dragon, the Council Leader and Prophetess Tkai, he retied the draping cloth of his keffiyeh across his forehead and over his slightly pointed ears, concealing them out of habit. A former caravaneer, his Otherworldly eyes and hairless skin had never bothered his Daethian customers because they were used to seeing elves. For some reason he had never understood, though, his ears, which were neither rounded like a human's nor sharply pointed like an elf's, disturbed them, so he took care to hide the trait even when he was several rotations' journey away from the land of the Dragonslayers. Silently, he said a prayer of thanks to his god, whose golden orb was just peeking over the horizon, for the new day and for his trader-developed habit of wearing his shirt, trousers and belt beneath his ceremonial robes. He could easily have looked as naked as he felt before the Dragons' magnificent eyes.

Tphah puffed out her armored chest with pride at his readiness for the day's trials in spite of the long night of feasting.

Katrell cracked his jaws in the draconic version of a grin. "That's 'Good Morning, sir!' to you, Trainee!" he barked in the metal-scraping tongue of the Bronze Dragons.

Shashtah saluted by bringing his right fist to his left breast as he half-seriously snapped to attention. "Good Morning, sir!" he shouted in the same language. The speech of the Bronze Dragons still felt strange in his mouth, but at least it no longer left his throat as raw as it had when he first arrived in the King's Camp. A Dragonheart—half-Dragon, half-Dumnonian—and a Prophet of the Light, Shashtah's life had been turned as completely upside down as Katrell had just turned his body since he had Bonded with Tkai. He wrenched his thoughts away from the painful memory of his first Dragon's death and tried to concentrate on what Katrell was saying.

"Tphah informs me that you know your way around on the ground pretty well from your years of running caravans to southern Daethia," Katrell said in a voice that sounded all-too-innocent.

"Yes, sir!" Shashtah shouted, beginning to regret his own instructions to Katrell during the happy oblivion of the Bonding Feast to be harder on him than he had ever been on a new Dragonrider. Shashtah hadn't gone through the Training with Tkai, and she'd died in part because of his lack of skill at living with a Bond Partner. He wasn't about to make the same mistake with his precious Tphah.

Sensing Shashtah's thoughts, the young Prophetess crooned her reassurance.

"Tphah, don't interrupt!" Katrell chided. "I have to give him his instructions, and then return to Camp. It's my Rider's first day as a Dragonlord, and we have our own kind of Training to go through, otherwise he'd be here now."

"He's here," Kashon said in an already weary voice as he trudged up the side of the dune. The Dragonlord was magnificent. His night-black hair, which escaped in wisps from beneath his white keffiyeh, which was held in place by a simple golden agal, framed honest features that could never beguile. A lifetime of deep hurt mingled with a child's trust and playfulness in his dark amber eyes. His shirt and trousers clung elegantly to arms and legs, which were powerful enough to wrestle a Dragon's humanform to the sand. The only thing that betrayed his high office was the dragon-shaped ring on the middle finger of his left hand.

The perfect Dumnonian male . . ., Shashtah caught himself thinking. He quickly shoved the thought aside.

"The mess Dameth left me can wait until I send off my first Pair of Trainees." Kashon grimaced at the name of the Dragonlord whose century had been entrusted to his command only the night before.

"Did you get any sleep?" Shashtah asked.

Kashon favored him with a lopsided grin. "Katrell tells me I did. I don't feel like it." He looked at his Dragon. "Where were you in the instructions?"

Katrell turned his attention back to Shashtah. "Do you know where the Anvil is?"

Shashtah called to mind the blockish outline of the anvil-shaped plateau.

Another view of the famed landmark began to overlay his.

"No!" Katrell ordered. "No transporting yet!"

The second image disappeared, and Tphah hung her head in shame.

Kashon pinched the bridge of his nose between his thumb and forefinger. "Tphah, how is Shashtah going to earn the callouses and scars he needs to be a proper Dragonrider if you cheat during the Training?"

"I'm sorry," Tphah replied. "It won't happen again."

"See that it doesn't!" Katrell slapped his tail against the sand.

"Yes, sir!" Tphah bared her throat to both of them.

Shashtah narrowed his eyes as he caught her movement. *So young. Only a Stripling. She should still be in their care, not Bonded to a sunstruck nit of a Dumnonian—*

"No cheating for you, either," Kashon ordered, staring unblinkingly at Shashtah. "The skills and scars need to be real, not altered by magic. That means no shapeshifting."

Shashtah bared his throat. "Yes, Dragonlord."

"There will be times you'll be certain we're trying to kill you." Kashon's voice softened, taking on a wry tone. "That's not the object of the Training. We've all survived this. You will, too."

Shashtah grabbed Kashon's left hand and kissed his ring of office in the traditional gesture of fealty. "Our lives are in your hands, Lord." The magic of the Bond between them, almost as deep as that shared by a Rider and Dragon, stirred.

Kashon closed his fingers tightly around Shashtah's. "I know I'm your Dragonlord. I know I can't treat you differently than I do the other members of our century. Yet I don't want to lose your friendship."

A smile curled across Shashtah's lips. "You won't, Lord. You won't."

"I need to go." Kashon reluctantly released Shashtah. "Katrell will handle most of your Training. I'm up to my ear tips in things that have to be fixed before we rotate up to the frontline. I'll come when I can." With that, he slapped Shashtah affectionately between his shoulder blades and walked, perhaps a little too quickly, into the King's Camp.

Katrell cleared his throat. "I'll meet you at the Anvil with water at midday."

Taken aback by what the Dragon had said, Shashtah protested. "But that's a full day's journey from here!"

Something unreadable flashed through Katrell's eyes. "Then I suggest you run. Tphah will fly cover to make sure you're not attacked along the way." With that he shifted to his humanform, a darkly handsome Dumnonian man in his mid-thirties, picked up the discarded aba, wrapped it around Shashtah's boots, and strode after Kashon.

Shashtah looked at his bare feet.

:*You heard him.*: Tphah launched herself into the air. :*Run!*:

Shashtah took off over the sands, heading toward the rising sun. He was good at running, since he'd spent a great deal of time fleeing from one thing or another over the years. His bare feet propelled him quickly over dune after dune until he found the caravan trail that lead to the Anvil. He slowed his pace and lengthened his stride, settling into the steady rhythm that he knew he could maintain for several candlescars. The trail led across a wadi, a stone-strewn valley that flooded perhaps once every ten winters during torrential winter rains. Shashtah tried to remember whether or not the wadi had flooded in recent winters and found, to his chagrin, that he was not entirely certain what the current year was. He'd spent so much time flitting around Centuria over the last half decade, following orders from its political and divine leaders, that mundane concerns like rotations and years had rather gotten away from him.

:*The nineteenth year of the reign of Shaharadesh. The Feast of Shadows. I can even tell you the day, if you really care.*:

:*Which you know I don't.*: Shashtah drew the clean, odorless desert air deep into his well-conditioned lungs. The trail turned rockier as it passed between two bluffs. In an effort to preserve his feet, he skittered to the right of the path, where there were fewer stones. As the sun climbed ever higher in the sky the sands would grow hotter and hotter until they blistered his soles. Without his protective boots he was going to be in considerable pain by the time he reached the Anvil.

:*Don't think about future hurts,*: Tphah cautioned from her aerial vantage point. :*Concentrate on what you're doing now.*:

Shashtah tried, but concentrating on the present had never been one of his better skills. To be honest, he wasn't very good at concentrating at all. A thin film of sweat coated his entire body, cooling him and actually making it easier to move. His calves and thighs began to feel a little tight, but it was nothing unmanageable. *Yet.* As Shashtah skirted another dry river bed it occurred to him that flying in circles above his head would be something of an endurance test for Tphah, too.

Tphah's laughter rippled through his mind, giving him a small burst of speed. :*Both Dragon and Rider go through the Training! I'm not to sit idly by while you do everything alone. How could I understand the way you hurt if I were not hurting, too? I need to be able to stay in the air all night if the Dark One's forces want to fight that long, and you need to have legs strong enough to remain astride me. Riding a Dragon from dusk until dawn is a lot different than riding a camel or a horse.*:

:*Yes. I have a lot farther to fall if I slip off.*: Shashtah ducked as Tphah swooped down at him, narrowly missing his head with a swipe of her tail. :*Sorry,*: he apologized, not completely contrite.

The trail left the sand and cut across an immense kavir. Ragged places at the edge showed footprints where generation after generation of caravaneers had brought their herds to lick the salt from the long-dried sea. Cracks, widened and mutilated by pickaxes, sparkled in the sunlight where the traders had cut blocks of salt to carry to the neighboring country of Daethia.

The unyielding, flat surface caused Shashtah's knees and ankles to ache as his feet pounded the ever-hotter ground, yet the sting of the salt in his wounds made him press harder to clear the terrain. His keffiyeh grew heavy with sweat beneath his leather thong, and runnels of perspiration dribbled into his eyes. He tried to wipe the moisture from his face and lick it to reclaim the water he was losing, but the effort slowed him so much that he gave up his attempts. His linen shirt adhered to his skin, and his sweat-drenched trousers began to chafe his thighs.

By the time Shashtah reached the middle of the kavir pain stabbed through his ribs with every breath. His lungs burned as he filled them repeatedly with the hot, dry air. His feet, though, quickly became his greatest concern. When he hit the wadi on the far side of the kavir, he'd have no surface skin left on his damaged soles. *Then what do I do?*

:*You're doing fine,*: Tphah encouraged him. :*At your current pace you should make it to the Anvil in time to meet Katrell.*:

Shashtah knew the lie for what it was, but he didn't contradict her. He'd figured out many wingspans ago that Katrell would simply find another way to deny him water if he made the run on time. Kashon had told him once that the Training began with spending half a rotation under his Dragon's wing, and now Shashtah understood why. This part of the Training wasn't for him; it was for Tphah. She had to learn how to care for an exhausted, injured Rider with heat prostration and severe dehydration, and he was the lucky volunteer who was going to teach her.

:*Don't think! Just run!*:

:*I need to think about something or I'm going to fall on my face and throw up!*:

:*Then Katrell will have you healed, and we'd get to do this all over again tomorrow.*:

Shashtah winced at the idea and ran on. He could sense the strain in her wings as she fought to keep her immense, armored body aloft above the slow-running Dumnonian. All she wanted to do was land and rest. Yet she was forbidden to do either until he reached the Anvil.

Somewhere around the middle of the second wadi Shashtah stopped looking down. He knew his feet had been sliced to a bloody mess, and there was nothing further he could do to save them. His best hope was to stay on the caravan trail, not get lost, and pray Katrell would be waiting for them at the end of the run with a solution to the problem. Shashtah could see the Anvil in the distance, rising abruptly from the surrounding, sand-dusted flatlands, but there was no sign of Kashon's Dragon. :*Where's Katrell?*:

Tphah's exercise-dulled mind stirred out of an insubstantial daydream. :*I'll check.*: She coaxed her exhausted wings into carrying her to a greater height.

Shashtah thrilled as he watched her fly: a great, gleaming, wondrous creature, impossibly graceful in the air, her metal hide glowing beneath the merciless sun like molten bronze. *About as hot as molten bronze, too*, he mused, remembering when he'd made the mistake of flying over open desert at midday on Tkai. The memory of his first Prophetess welled within him, suddenly drowning all thoughts of present pain. His fury at her gruesome death at his own hands hadn't diminished nor had his sense of agony at the knowledge that his own incompetence as a Dragonrider had led to her capture. True, he'd been severely—and quite justly—punished for that error by the Council of Ancients, and true, he'd partially redeemed himself by joining with the Elven King and Lord Criton of Daethia to punish the Dark One for causing Tkai's death and the deaths of so many other Centurians over the course of millennia. But Shashtah's sorrow at the loss of Tkai still wracked his soul, a festering wound that would never heal and that only abated from time to time beneath his fierce passion for Tphah.

The Prophetess, bleating her distress to the desert winds, soared toward him. :*Katrell's on the other side!*: she wailed. :*He says I must make you climb over the Anvil. He says Kashon needs him, and he can't afford more delays!*:

Shashtah's clenched his teeth and swallowed what little moisture was left in his mouth. His pace began to falter, but he ran on. :*Surely you didn't think the Training consisted of a one-day journey from the King's Camp to the Anvil?*: he reasoned, trying to calm her into a state where maybe, just maybe, she could help him.

:*But you hurt!*: Tphah emphasized her mental protest with a nerve-shredding wail.

:*So do you,*: Shashtah returned silently, grateful for their telepathic Bond. He doubted he could have spoken aloud even if she'd been close enough to hear him. :*You think we're the first Pair to endure this? You think Katrell made this torture up just for us? Every Dumnonian who's flown on a Dragon has succeeded at this test—except for me, and look how that turned out. Even Dameth, before he grew old and fat, passed the Training. Do you want me to fail where he did not?*:

Tphah roared in rage at his reference to the detestable former Dragonlord.

Shashtah drew on her anger to run the last wingspans between him and his goal. He reached the base of the Anvil and started to climb. Exhausted muscles and bloody feet betrayed him. He almost fell. Sweat blinded his eyes. His lungs protested his every breath. :*Tphah, you have to show me where to put my hands and feet.*:

Silence filled his mind at first, then he began to see the cliff through her eyes.

Tphah strained to hover somewhere behind him. Her first attempts to find the path up the cliff would've been fine if he were in his dragonform. But he wasn't allowed to shapeshift, and his wordless frustration finally refocused her draconic mind to think in Dumnonian terms about what he could and couldn't convince his battered body to do.

Shashtah finally hauled himself onto the top of the plateau. It took every bit of his flagging courage to stagger to his feet and stumble over the seemingly countless wingspans to the opposite rim.

Mind numb with weariness, body scraped and bruised, muscles strained beyond their limits, Shashtah concentrated more on breaking his fall than on climbing down the side of the Anvil that was hidden from the caravan trail. His torn feet finally hit the ground. He turned and collapsed near where Katrell nestled in the shallow sand.

Katrell eyed him dispassionately.

"Can . . . Tphah . . . land . . . now, . . . sir?" Shashtah rasped, somehow remembering to use the language of the Bronze Dragons as well as the proper form of address.

Katrell bugled his answer at the skies.

Tphah landed inelegantly just far enough away from Shashtah he could sense the heat from her metal scales.

Shashtah had the distinct feeling that neither of them wanted to move again as long as they lived.

"You're late," Katrell commented in a toneless voice.

Shashtah laughed. "I expected . . . to be, . . . sir!"

"Insolence will cost you your water for the day!" Katrell declared.

Shashtah stifled a fit of hysteria. "Yes, . . . sir!"

Tphah was too exhausted to protest aloud, but her eyes clouded with dismay.

"Now, the next trial," Katrell said in a deadly still voice. "Strip!"

Groggy from overexertion, Shashtah fought to push himself to his knees. Clumsy hands fumbled at his shirt and finally pulled it off over his head, yanking his keffiyeh off with it. His belt came off a little easier as movement assuaged the cramping in his muscles and concentration began to clear his head.

"Hurry up!" Katrell fretted. "Kashon needs me!"

Shashtah winced as he staggered to his bloody feet, unlaced his trousers and peeled them away from his damp, chafed skin. He dropped them beside his shirt, belt and keffiyeh. Then, clad in nothing except his own sweat and blood, he stood before Katrell. A zephyr caressed his body, drying the perspiration from his flesh. In an odd way he actually felt better now that he was out of his clothes, even though his trader instincts told him he had fewer brains than sand to stand naked beneath the blazing sun.

Katrell jerked his head toward Tphah. "Mount!"

Shashtah hobbled over to his Prophetess.

A riding harness melted into existence out of Tphah's armored skin.

"No shapeshifting!" Katrell ordered.

The harness disappeared.

Shashtah turned back to Katrell, dismayed. "Then how . . . am I . . . supposed to . . . climb?"

Something unreadable glinted in Katrell's amber eyes. "Figure it out! Everyone else has."

Shashtah smiled, absurdly pleased with himself for breaking through the Dragon's studied composure. *Poor Katrell! I shouldn't bait him. This is hard on him, too. He can't possibly enjoy hurting us.*

Tphah twisted her head around to look pointedly at him.

Shashtah glanced from the hard ledge of her lower lip, to the broad, flat surface of her muzzle. :*Bless that great, powerful neck of yours! Could you give me a lift?*:

Tphah blinked her transparent, inner eyelids in response.

Shashtah climbed onto her lower lip. He gripped her right nostril with his left hand and started to raise his right foot.

:*Hold still,*: Tphah warned him just before her great forked tongue flicked out and ever so gently cleaned the sand and dirt from his bloody foot.

Shashtah placed his cleaned foot on her armored lip and hung there, dreading the climb.

:*Other foot.*:

Seeing that Katrell was not protesting at the ministrations, Shashtah let her care for his wounds. When she finished, he hauled himself onto the top of the searing hot metal of her snout. He imagined that he could hear his torn feet sizzling as he let her lift him to his intended perch. Then, before he could think about what he was doing, he eased himself onto her back and wrapped his right leg around the spike at the base of her neck. He braced his left leg against her side and rocked back slightly onto his buttocks, making sure his groin was clear of contact with her armored skin. He heard the heat of her metal plates burning his hairless flesh, but the warmth initially felt good against the tightening muscles of his legs. Satisfied he was not going to scorch anything too important, he placed his hands on his thighs for better balance.

"Hold still!" Katrell warned just before the pain hit.

Shashtah resisted the urge to pull away as Tphah's hide branded him.

" . . . skin will tear if either of you moves, and the scars won't form properly," Katrell was saying when Shashtah's brain finally overrode the pain. "Then I'll have to take you back to Camp and have you healed so we can do this all over again tomorrow."

Shashtah clenched his teeth and dug his fingernails into his palms, determined to endure the pain as he wondered exactly how many ways there were for him to be sent back to the beginning of the Training.

"You will burn enough to mark your flesh for life," Katrell went on, "but not enough to cause any serious harm."

:*I do not want to know what Dragons mean by "serious harm,"*: Shashtah griped to Tphah. :*This is not what I thought Kashon meant by the scars Dragonriders have.*:

:*Your body must be adapting to the pain,*: Tphah said, relieved. :*You're calm enough to joke.*:

:*Or hysterical enough.*: Shashtah found that by holding extremely still his nerves would go numb against the damaging heat and that the pain would almost vanish.

"Don't relax," Katrell warned. "The last thing you want to do right now is fall. Tphah, talk to him. Keep him alert. Kashon needs me. I'll return at dawn." With that he leapt into the air, gave a powerful flap of his mighty wings and was gone.

"DAWN?" Shashtah shrieked after him.

:*Don't panic!*: Tphah warned in a thoroughly panicked tone. :*You'll be fine. I'm here to protect you.*:

Shashtah made the mistake of looking down to see where the skin of his legs adhered to her hide. His stomach lurched, and he looked away. :*Forgive me if I'm not convinced.*:

Tphah sent a wave of patience oozing through their Bond. :*Listen to me. Your wounds will attract predators—*:

:*Oh, thank you so much for pointing that out!*:

:*Stop joking, and listen. I'm too big and my hide is too tough for them to hurt me. When they try to attack you, I can reach them with my jaws. There's nothing out here so large that I can't kill it with a single bite—that's what I've spent much of the last five winters learning how to do. Fresh meat means blood that you can drink and food for me. All you have to do is sit still and stay awake.*:

Shashtah ran the fingers of his left hand through his damp hair. The Dragons never remembered that he was a caravaneer and that, unlike most Dumnonians, he hardly ever ate meat. His draconic father, Garesh, had slaughtered his entire camp, including Shashtah's mother, to save them from being turned into undead blood-drinkers by the Vampire King, Eschlend. Shashtah's stomach revolted at the memory of staggering out of the desert after his first mission into the Dark One's stronghold, Mount Cinnamar, and finding that carnage. Perhaps that horrible experience was why he usually stuck to a meager diet of bread, fruit, vegetables, nuts and an occasional piece of cheese. Whatever the reason, he didn't share the Dragons' taste for blood. *Well, I'll deal with that when the problem presents itself.* He gazed at the sun through his darkened, desert-adapted eyes. His God's bright disk was well past its zenith. In two more candlescars it would drop behind the plateau. :*Katrell's right. Keep talking with me. Make sure I don't get addled enough to fall. And keep an eye out for those predators! I don't want to become something's dinner.*:

Tphah's pleasure with him filled his soul as she obediently traded him story after story about her years at Dameth's court and her Training with Kashon and Katrell for tales of what he had learned running caravans.

Around twilight Shashtah realized that she had stopped talking. :*Tphah?*:

:*Hold on!*:

Shashtah's hands convulsively gripped her neckridge, and he pressed his injured legs even tighter against her, realizing as he did so that her hide was finally cooling off.

Tphah twisted beneath him, and her head darted to one side.

A startled yelp preceded the sound of bone being crushed in dragonjaws.

Shashtah opened his eyes—only then realizing that he had closed them—to see the corpse of a lioness dangling obscenely from Tphah's mouth.

:*Drink quickly! I need to eat!*:

Shashtah felt her hunger through their Bond and her urgency now that she had tasted the blood of her kill. He tilted his head back and let the life essences of her victim pour into him. :*Never tell Garesh about this.*:

:*Why? He's had Riders before. He knows what happens during the Training.*:

:*Long story,*: Shashtah replied in a tone that left no doubt that it was a story he was unwilling to tell. :*Go ahead. Eat. I've had enou*—: Before he could finish the thought, Tphah swallowed the remains of the lioness whole. Shashtah wiped his lips with the back of his left hand. The still-hot blood called to other memories in him, including a half-forgotten lonely hunt in wolfform through the Northern Wastes when he should have been with Tkai.

:*Katrell said he can only kill small things like jackals when he's on the ground and has a Rider on his back.*: Tphah's forked tongue flicked over Shashtah, cleaning away all traces of the lioness's blood.

Shashtah laughed affectionately. :*You're the best Dragon ever, and you take excellent care of your Rider.*: The skin of his damaged legs pulled as her hide continued to cool. From what he could see of his injuries, he knew he would indeed bear the marks of her scales until the day he died. :*One way to match the body of a Dragon to the body of a Rider after a battle.*:

Tphah swung her head around and stared at him.

:*I'm sorry,*: Shashtah apologized. :*I've been a bit morbid since Tkai*—:

:*Dragonheart.*: Love and reassurance washed through him at the whispered word. Tphah had been the first Dragon to call him by that name, the first to see exactly how much dragonblood flowed through his veins. :*I'm glad I'm the Dragon and you're the Rider,*: she teased, trying to change his mood. :*I doubt I'd have had your courage if Katrell had asked us to go through the Training the other way around.*: Her tongue darted out, making sure that his raw feet were still clean.

:*Could he have done that?*: Shashtah asked, truly worried. He doubted he could have borne even the thought of injuring his new Prophetess so soon after having killed Tkai.

Tphah's laughter sent shimmers of light tumbling through his mind. :*Who knows? The Training is a secret ritual for a reason. Would you have had the courage to sit, unprotected, on my back at midday if you hadn't been exhausted beyond thinking, conditioned to follow Katrell's orders, and reassured that others had survived the trial many times before?*:

:*Probably not,*: Shashtah admitted.

:*Besides, there's probably no protocol for it. Very few Dragons have borne a Dragonheart.*: Tphah's eyes sparkled with pride in the growing darkness as she finished grooming him, not unlike the way a mother hunting dog would clean a favored pup. :*It certainly would've done no good, either, to inform you that you beat every other Rider Katrell has Trained by over two candlescars on that run, and he Trained quite a few Riders before Kashon. He spent most of the day fretting about how he was going to make it out here in time to meet you.*:

:*You can hear Katrell worrying all the way out here?*:

Tphah's transparent inner eyelids slowly blinked in an attempt to hide a dark thought that she kept to herself. :*All Dragons can talk to each other from anywhere they please. Some, like Katrell, feel things too deeply to be any good at shielding their thoughts. You could probably hear him, too, if you were in your dragonform.*:

:*Don't tempt me! I'm not supposed to shapeshift.*:

Tphah hung her head, contrite.

Shashtah absently regarded his scarring flesh. :*This is why only Dumnonians can become Dragonriders, isn't it.*: There was no question in his thought. :*Many of the things we do would kill an elf or Daethian.*:

:*Our traditions would kill a Dumnonian, too, if your blood wasn't mixed with ours.*:

Shashtah silently thanked the Light that he was half Dragon. He'd been undergoing the ritual for less than a day and he was already wondering how, even with mixed elven- and dragonblood, normal Dumnonians survived the Training.

:*They have their Dragons,*: Tphah commented, as if that explained everything.

:*Eavesdropper.*:

:*Only when you want me to be.*:

They continued to talk, sharing their memories, fighting together against their weariness. Somewhere in the middle of the night Tphah's hide cooled adequately in the chill desert air that Shashtah's skin pulled completely free from her. Although the rest of his body began to shiver as the temperature continued to drop, he found that the ever-colder touch of her scales actually eased the burning sensation of his damaged skin.

At dawn a light mist drifted over them. The dew condensed on Tphah's metal hide, and he licked up enough of the water to moisten his lips and tongue. The precious liquid refreshed him and gave him enough strength to call out a hoarse greeting when Katrell arrived in the skies overhead with Kashon.

Tphah echoed his cry as the Dragonlord and his Bond Partner landed nearby.

Kashon still wore serviceable clothing. A plain but deadly scimitar hung against his left leg, and his sand-colored desert cloak, secured by a golden scarab brooch, draped around his shoulders. He grabbed a medical kit from Katrell's harness, dismounted, unpinned his cloak and spread the garment on the sand beneath Tphah's left wing. He tossed the kit beside it.

Katrell raised his clawed forepaw, deftly plucked Shashtah from Tphah's back and set him gently on the cloak. "Lie down," he ordered just before Shashtah's abused body prostrated itself.

Kashon quickly opened the medical kit and knelt beside Shashtah. He examined his patient as Katrell shifted to humanform and inspected Tphah. "I have bad news for you," Kashon said as he finished tending to Shashtah's shredded feet. "You're going to live."

Shashtah chuckled, almost choking on the potion that Kashon held for him to drink. "Do you always try to kill off your Dragonriders on their first day?"

"You're the first one I've Trained, remember? Kashon grinned. "Did Tphah feed you?"

Shashtah rolled his eyes. "If you can call almost drowning me with a lioness's blood feeding me."

Kashon let out a whistle of appreciation. "Katrell didn't tell me that."Tphah preened her left wing with pride.

Kashon flashed an unreadable look at Katrell. "You'd better watch out, friend, or you will be the only Dumnonian in history to gain weight during the Training." He pulled a jar of ointment from the kit. "At least she remembered to clean you off afterward."

"Her memory will always be better than mine." Shashtah relaxed as Kashon slathered the ointment over his burns somehow without making contact with his damaged skin. He felt a prickling sensation from power that was not his own. *He's using magic to keep from touching me,* he decided.

:*Katrell says Dameth wasn't so gentle with Kashon.*:

:*I doubt he was.*: Shashtah thought darkly. "I take it each Dragon has a unique pattern of scales?"

Kashon gave him a quizzical look. "You didn't know?"

"And you brand every Rider with that pattern?" Shashtah eyed his Dragonlord uncertainly. "Why?"

"How else could we sort out the bodies?" Kashon asked in what Shashtah supposed was a very reasonable tone as he continued his work.

Tphah lowered her head to the sand near Shashtah's face and whimpered.

"Ach!" Shashtah protested, clamping his hands over his ears. "Hush! Before we all go deaf!"

Tphah's forked tongue flicked out and lightly brushed across Shashtah's lips as she fell silent.

Kashon hid a grin as he gathered one edge of the cloak in his powerful grip. "Katrell, give me a hand."

Katrell took the other side of the cloak and helped Kashon move Shashtah as close as they could to Tphah's left side. "Now comes the easy part." He snatched up the medical kit, dropped his brooch into it and rose to his feet. "All you have to do is lie there for about half a rotation until you heal. Tphah will cover you with her wing, so you'll be quite safe. She can feed you, and if there's any real trouble, she can shout to Katrell for help. I have to get back to listening to all the complaints my Riders and their Dragons accumulated under Dameth. Not that I can do anything about them, but I owe it to them to listen."

Shashtah smiled at his friend. "Thank you for finding the time to tend to me personally, Lord."

Kashon laughed. "We'll see if you're still so grateful in half a rotation. Sleep well!" He stepped out of the way so Tphah could cover Shashtah tightly with her wing.

:*Can you sleep, too?*: Shashtah asked Tphah as he bunched the cloak up comfortably under his own head.

Tphah's answer was a mental snore.

Kashon Battling Dameth

Chapter 2:

Mother Nature

The Bronze Dragons are the most maternal in nature of all the draconic species. The nurturing instincts of both the males and the females can be frustrated by taking away the Dragons' eggs as soon as they are laid and having the Dumnonian ruler, rather than the draconic parents, raise the young. This has the double advantage of teaching the Hatchlings to look to the monarch as they would normally look to their parents and of accustoming them to being cared for by Dumnonians.

The adult Dragon's frustrated instincts can be redirected toward its Rider by rendering the Trainee helpless soon after the Bonding and entrusting the Dumnonian solely to the Dragon's care. During this time the Dragon must not be allowed to shapeshift so that only its draconic instincts are invoked. Done properly, this additional Bonding of Dragon to Rider will ensure the durability of the magical connection between them even under the most adverse forms of stress.

—from *The Dragonlord's Handbook*
by Corin of Daethia

THE TOUCH OF TPHAH'S FORKED tongue washing his beardless face tugged Shashtah out of the oblivion that had embraced him. For some reason he was on his knees and leaning over the edge of Kashon's cloak. Tphah's sturdy wing still shielded him from the desert sun, but she had raised it slightly to allow him fresh air from a gentle tradewind and to make room for her armored snout as she crooned her concern.

Slowly Shashtah realized that he was trying to retch and that he'd been doing so for quite some time. The absence of any overt signs of the activity on either him or the sand beside the cloak where he had managed to lean his head brought back the memory of Tphah's tongue flicking over his cheeks and mouth. His sides protested almost as loudly as the burns on his legs and buttocks as he heaved again. :*Argh! Did you have to eat it?*:

:*The poison won't harm me.*:

"Poison?" Shashtah exclaimed aloud as he tried to catch his breath.

:*The potion Kashon gave you,*: Tphah explained matter-of-factly as her tongue washed his face again.

Shashtah realized he had a headache. :*Why in the name of the Light would Kashon poison me?*:

:*So I could take care of you,*: came Tphah's puzzled reply. :*That's why I couldn't give you anything solid to eat last night: I didn't want to have too much of a mess.*:

Shashtah glared at her accusingly. :*You thrice-cursed, gravel-brained, beetle-infested wyrms! Just feeding me blood was going to make a mess! I'm not used to eating meat! You—!*: Another heave interrupted his curse. :*I thought Kashon gave me a healing potion! Between my feet and the burns, I'm surprised I'm not half dead!*:

:*But you're a Dragonheart. If the Training doesn't kill regular Dumnonians, it can't kill you.*:

Shashtah moaned inwardly as his body fought to bring up nonexistent fluid from his completely empty stomach. :*I suppose the ointment Kashon put on me is designed to make the burns scar, too.*:

:*It will make them heal faster and thicker than normal skin. Don't you want people to know you're my Rider?*:

Shashtah tried to force his protesting body to relax. :*Do you mean to tell me that you Dragons and that sadistic excuse for a Wizard who formed our Bond have been able to trick every Rider who has ever lived into submitting voluntarily to this torture?*:

:*Not everyone. You didn't go through the Training with Tkai,*: Tphah reminded him almost viciously. :*Look what happened: She couldn't remember to stay with you. A Dragon who has nursed a Rider through the Training will never forget.*:

Shashtah groaned. He felt his nausea subside and allowed himself to stretch out on the cloak. :*How much more of this Training stuff is there?*:

:*Enough that most Riders aren't willing to go through it twice.*:

:*In other words, I don't want to know.*:

Tphah relented. :*The Training usually lasts about three rotations—depending on how well the Rider listens to his Dragon and rests between trials.*:

Shashtah looked at Tphah through half-closed eyes. :*Don't worry about me. Moving is the last thing on my mind.*:

The sound of a broadsword bashing against a shield startled Shashtah out of a nightmare and sent a shiver down his spine. His sleep-fogged brain strained to make sense out of the clamor and failed. He tried to rise, but Tphah's thick leather wing held him pinned tightly against her armored side.

Suddenly elven laughter drifted through the cacophony. "Sorry to wake you, Shashtah!" the voice of Juel, Elven Lord, called in the Dumnonian tongue. "Or if you can actually sleep through this, you're in worse shape than I thought! Katrell said Tphah's fussing about not having anything but fresh kills to feed you and how too much raw meat is making you sicker you should be. So I volunteered to drop off some dates and elven bread on my way back to Tor. I've left a skin of water out here, too."

Shashtah groggily imagined the combatants redoubling their efforts. Judging by the sound both parties wore plate mail and great helms. He wished he could cover his ears, but he couldn't move his arms.

Juel's laughed again. "Tkai always said there's nothing fiercer on the face of Centuria than a Bronze Dragon hatching a new Rider. Too bad you Dumnonians can't find a way to throw that temper against the Dark One. I bet that would knock a few millennia off his unholy life!" With that he apparently left because the battle stopped.

Tphah relaxed her wing slightly and poked her snout under the edge. :*Are you all right?*:

Shashtah pushed himself up until he was gingerly balanced on his hands and knees. :*What in the name of the Dark One is going on out there?*:

Tphah's eyes glittered with delight. :*I chased off the Elven Lord. I didn't think you'd want him to see you like this. Was I wrong?*:

Shashtah did his best not to laugh, knowing full well that no one could chase Juel anywhere he didn't already want to go. :*No.*: He tried to peer around Tphah's massive head. It seemed to be twilight. :*Pass me that food and water, and I'll tell you how to get a bed for a copper a night in Krillion. Deal?*:

:*Once a trader, always a trader,*: Tphah quipped, cracking her jaws in a draconic grin. Her head vanished from sight and two talons holding a single piece of elven bread took its place.

Shashtah decided not to say anything about her failure to give him the rest of the food. He relieved her of the bread and waited patiently for the appearance of the waterskin. *Good thing there is no easy way for her to ration my water.*

:*Promise not to drink too much?*: Tphah pleaded.

:*I promise,*: Shashtah said. :*I've been through Cinnamar countless times on camels, six times on horseback, and four times on foot. I know how to make a skin of water last a rotation.*:

Tphah's talons reappeared, gently holding the waterskin.

Shashtah took it from her and loosened the top. He squeezed a thimbleful of the precious liquid into his sour mouth, rinsed, and swallowed. He sealed the skin tightly and set it at arm's length from him as he turned his attention to the bread. :*Thanks.*: He passed the time while he slowly chewed the nourishing morsel, mentally regaling her with a tale about one of his many visits to Krillion, the City of Thieves. He followed that with a lecture about the respective grammars of the Krilliac and Elvish tongues, including notes on variations among the dialect of the Dumnonian language spoken by traders, the language that was used at the King's Camp and the cant that the dragonless warriors used to communicate with the variety of fantastic creatures who served as their followers—and fell asleep himself as soon as she began to snore.

Tphah fanned her left wing in long, gentle strokes high above Shashtah's head, carefully keeping him in the shade and providing a soothing breeze to offset the midday heat.

Hovering on the edge of dream and awareness, Shashtah yawned and stretched, noting with some dissatisfaction the tightening of his damaged skin.

Tphah's head was immediately under her wing with him, her amber eyes darkened with concern. :*Katrell suggests you try a few of the basic Ban-kai stretches—if it doesn't hurt too much to do them and if Garesh taught you the Battle Dance.*:

Shashtah laughed. :*Don't worry so! I'll be all right. I've been hurt a lot worse than this. Remember when you found me in the desert after that Demonlord tried to flay me?*:

:*Yes. But Kashon used magic to heal you then.*:

:*I'm a lot tougher than you think I am,*: Shashtah assured her. He dutifully proved his point by spending the better part of a candlescar reminding his skin how to move with his muscles. When he finished, he rolled onto his right side and leaned against her armored body with a sigh. :*Pity we can't shapeshift. Your humanform is a lot softer than your dragonform.*:

:*But less shady,*: Tphah commented philosophically. She nudged him gently with her snout. Alarm flashed through her amber eyes as his burned skin inadvertently came into contact with the cloak. :*I'm sorry! I didn't mean to hurt you!*:

Shashtah slapped her muzzle affectionately—causing his hand to sting. :*Stop it! I'll be fine.*:

Tphah's eyes brightened slightly. :*Katrell says you can sit on me for a while in the morning and evening if you like.*:

Shashtah did not really "like", but Tphah was so anxious he agreed.

That evening, when Tphah lifted him to his perch, Shashtah found that her armored hide was actually delightfully soothing to the touch. His scarring skin shaped itself easily to her scales, and he sat comfortably for quite some time, admiring her, as she snoozed beneath him.

Shashtah roused Tphah with a mental touch when he grew too chilled to maintain his vantage point.

The Prophetess quickly and carefully placed him once again beneath her wing, where her body heat kept him pleasantly warm throughout the night.

In the morning Shashtah was actually eager to climb onto Tphah's neck. He also thrilled when she offered to take him down the instant he became uncomfortable. Gone was the rancor he used to feel when Tkai eavesdropped on his private thoughts. Tphah's sense of his likes and dislikes was far superior to what Tkai's had been, and that included knowing when he truly wanted her to listen to him and when he did not.

:*That's the purpose of the Training,*: Tphah informed him on the day when he managed to stay astride her through the night, only dismounting during the worst heat of the day. :*To get to know each other so well that we don't have to think about how to work as a Pair.*:

As soon as Tphah's hide had cooled to the touch one again, Shashtah clambered onto her head and nimbly took his perch. He caressed her neckridge with a more amorous a gesture than he had felt capable of since the Training began. :*So when do I get my lover back?*:

Tphah's eyes sparkled at the question. :*You've never lost her! But we do have a few more tests to complete.*:

:*Such as?*: Shashtah asked warily.

:*Such as, can you hold your seat while I get up and walk around? I've been lying here for the better part of a rotation, and—*:

:*A rotation?*: Shashtah shrieked. :*I thought Kashon said I'd only be under your wing half that long!*:

:*You were. It's taken almost another half rotation for you to sit astride me most of the day. Katrell says it took Kashon over a rotation and a half to do that after he came out from under his wing,*: Tphah added, pride shining in her amber eyes.

Shashtah glowered. :*I imagine Kashon was in a lot worse shape than I am.*:

:*Yes,*: Tphah hissed. :*Katrell says Dameth almost killed him.*:

Shashtah ground his teeth for a heartbeat, and then shoved his fury to the back of his mind as his concern for Tphah returned. :*Get up! You poor thing! You should have said something sooner. If—*:

Tphah's laughter cut him off. :*Dragons are designed to lie atop treasure for centuries at a time. Asking a Bronze to lie on top of a Rider for a rotation or two is no hardship.*: With a grunt of pleasure she extended both of her wings, gathered her legs beneath her, and thrust her body out of the sand. :*You give up warbands to claim us. We give up hoards to claim you. We think you're worth it.*:

:*So are you. Now, walk! I'll try not to fall off.*:

Tphah balanced her long, graceful neck with her whiplike tail. She took a few hesitant steps until she was positive Shashtah would stay in his seat. Then she stretched each of her legs individually and began to pace, keeping well behind the portion of the Anvil that was never seen from the caravan trail.

Shashtah felt his legs press automatically against her as his body remembered the muscles he had used while riding camels in his father's caravan. Garesh had insisted he learn to ride those intractable creatures instead of the fleet desert horses Shashtah preferred. Furious with his father at the time, he now blessed the wily old Dragon for ingraining the skill in him.

When Shashtah remained snugly settled on Tphah's shoulders until she finished her exercise, she crooned with glee. :*Katrell says we can try flying tomorrow!*:

:*Flying?*: Shashtah asked cautiously.

:*Unless you don't feel ready,*: Tphah amended hastily. She lowered him to the ground and tucked him under her wing.

:*Do I get a harness?*: Shashtah ventured as he stretched out on Kashon's cloak.

:*Not yet.*:

:*I was afraid of that.*: Shashtah remembered his terror at Tkai's aerial antics, the somersaulting and twisting maneuvers of a Dragon long used to combat.

:*Don't be afraid, Dragonheart.*: Tphah breathed heavily, filling the area under her wing with her scent. At full force that odor could send demons fleeing into the night, but out here in the desert, alone with her, Shashtah felt the scent calling to the Dragon inside him, making him yearn for the feel of the air beneath his own wings and setting his pulse throbbing with the desire to swoop down upon the forces of the Dark One and drive every last shadow of evil from the face of the world he loved.

Shashtah shuddered involuntarily as the pungency of her breath evoked the memory of the time long ago when Katrell had carried him into battle against the Demonlord Yapada.

Remembered distress flickered in Tphah's eyes. :*You weren't Bonded to Katrell. It won't be the same with me*,: She sent another waft of her breath drifting over him. :*I won't drop you.*:

:*Prophecy?*:: Shashtah joked, and then grew suddenly sullen. The vast emptiness left by Tkai's death once again threatened to swallow him. Perhaps he should have waited longer before Bonding again. Yet the mere thought of not being Bonded to his new, beautiful, clever, powerful, loving Prophetess was too much for him to bear.

Tphah pressed her wing tightly against him, bracing him against his sorrow and filling the void of his loss with her reassuring presence.:" *We shall be like the wind, you and I. We shall howl through the night, blowing where we are not expected and carving the pattern of our souls on the face of this land.*:" Her tongue flicked out and licked the tears from his cheeks.

Shashtah smiled sadly, only then realizing that he was crying. :*I think Shane of Corin meant Daethia when she wrote that.*:

:*Shane of Corin never met you!*: Tphah's love swept through his soul, mending the emotional gashes that had been left by Tkai's death.

Shashtah embraced her muzzle with his powerful arms. :*What in the name of the Light made you want to Bond with a sunstruck nit like me?*:

Tphah's eyes sparkled with boundless affection. :*Prophecy,*: she teased, :*and the fact that you're intolerably cute when you go charging in where gods fear to tread, challenging the most powerful beings on the planet to a sword fight or a wrestling match.*:

:*I'm not that bad,*: Shashtah protested, knowing full well he was. He wiped the last of his tears from his eyes with the back of his hand and licked the moisture from his sun-darkened skin. He had turned almost the same shade of bronze that she was—except for his new scars, which were still puffy and red.

:*Do they hurt much?*: Tphah asked, unabashedly redirecting his thoughts back to the present.

Shashtah prodded experimentally at the thickening skin on the side of his right knee, recognizing her trick for what it was. :*No. They feel strange. Like they aren't part of me yet.*:

Tphah's forked tongue darted out and caressed one of the scars that ran along his left thigh. :*Then I shall make them feel like part of you.*:

Shashtah snickered as his body stirred in ways her dragonform didn't have a prayer of satisfying.

A wicked light gleamed in Tphah's amber eyes. :*Don't be so sure about that!*: she chided. And promptly proved him wrong.

With the dawn, duty called in the form of Kashon's booming voice. "Tphah informs Katrell that you're feeling alive again!" He stepped under Tphah's wing and handed Shashtah a bundle of cloth. "Put this on."

Shashtah unfolded the cloth. It was an Initiate's robe, a modified caftan: loose fitting to avoid aggravating healing burns, hooded to provide some protection from the sun and slit up the front and back for ease in riding. He slipped into the garment and raised the hood.

Tphah settled her head near Shashtah's feet.

Kashon eyed Shashtah and Tphah critically. "You both look inordinately pleased with yourselves this morning."

Shashtah lowered his eyes, knowing that he would blush like molten bronze if he looked at either Kashon or Tphah. "Dragonlord," he murmured.

"Yes," Kashon said, "and I'm afraid that means I'm out here to make your life miserable again. Katrell, get his supplies."

Katrell shifted to his humanform. As he picked up the cloak, the half-empty flask of water and the remains of the bread and dates, such an impish grin played across his face that Shashtah had no doubt who had taught Tphah how to perform the Mother's Dance with a Dumnonian while she was in her dragonform.

" . . . grew up in a dragonless camp," Kashon was saying when Shashtah finally controlled himself enough to concentrate, "and aren't used to eating meat. Most of the time that won't be a problem, so I allowed that minor change in the Training. But I suggest that once you assume your regular duties you learn to tolerate at least some of Tphah's diet. Dragons are taught to fulfill their Rider's needs as well as their own, and you'll make life a lot easier for her if you're able to share her food. I know you can summon manna if you need to, but that won't help if you get caught in a zone where magic doesn't work. It's best to expect the worst: That way you'll be prepared if the worst happens." Sensing that he finally had Shashtah's complete attention, Kashon signaled for Katrell to shift back to dragonform.

Katrell deposited Shashtah's supplies at Kashon's feet and resumed his true shape.

"All right, then," Kashon said. "Next trial: On my command mount Tphah and have her take off. Stay in this general area. Get a sense of what everything looks like from the air and how she feels beneath you. In a while I'll have Katrell start popping in and out. When you see him, you'll have five heartbeats to bring Tphah into formation off his left wing. For every heartbeat you're late, you'll have to complete that many more repetitions in addition to a number I'm going to tell Katrell. For every heartbeat you're early, he'll reduce the number that you need to complete by that much. When you've finished, Katrell will fetch me, and I'll give you the command to land. If you let Tphah land before that time or if you fall off, we try this again tomorrow. Understand?"

"Yes, Lord," Shashtah answered, more concerned about Tphah's ability to stay in the air all day after lying around for a rotation than he was about his own ability to maintain his seat when the sun reached the peak of its arc across the cloudless sky.

Kashon smiled reassuringly. "Then mount!" He hauled himself up behind Katrell's neckridge.

Tphah waited for Shashtah to scrabble onto her muzzle, and then raised him to her neckridge.

Shashtah settled himself into his place between her spikes.

When Kashon decided that Shashtah was truly steady enough to remain on an airborne Dragon, he brought his right fist to his left breast, and then thrust it skyward.

With dismay Shashtah noted that the direction Kashon indicated took them straight toward the Anvil. Tphah would have to make an almost vertical jump to avoid hitting the edge of the plateau.

:*Have a little faith, Prophet!*: Tphah laughed. :*Ready?*:

Shashtah tried to swallow, but his mouth was dry. :*As ready as I'll ever be.*:

Tphah crouched close to the sand, and then lunged into the air. Her strong leathery wings carried them high above the Anvil.

Excitement lanced through Shashtah. The knot of fear in his stomach unwound as Tphah's wings steadied their weight and she flew in lazy circles. His seat at the base of her neckridge was not as comfortable as it had been during their Bonding when she'd been allowed to shapeshift to fit his dimensions, but the long days of sitting astride her on the ground had accustomed him to the feel of her trueform, a familiarity that now gave him a sense of security he'd always lacked when flying on Tkai. He delighted in the sensation of his Prophetess beneath him, the rush of the desert wind against his bronze-colored skin, and the constant touch of her mind on his, letting him know that he was safe and that he was not alone.

A flash of Bronze to his right warned him that Kashon and Katrell had taken up position off Tphah's wingtip.

Tphah matched her wing strokes to Katrell's.

Shashtah quickly glanced at his Dragonlord.

Kashon seemed preoccupied.

Before Shashtah could ask Tphah what was wrong, she corkscrewed around him.

Stark fear sliced through Shashtah's breast. :*Don't do that!*: he shrieked as he gripped her back even tighter with his scarred legs.

Kashon shouted something Shashtah couldn't hear.

Katrell bellowed a curse in the tongue of the Bronze Dragons.

Tphah flicked her tail upward in what Shashtah suspected was a draconic version of a rude gesture, and then abruptly clapped her wings to her side, shooting them high above their Trainers. :*I will not drop you! If I'm turning fast enough, nothing can make you fall off my back.*:

:*All right!*: Shashtah conceded :*But, for the sake of my abused insides, can we take it easy and stick to the exercise for today?*:

Tphah promptly found a thermal and settled into a floating glide. :*Tkai warned me that you always daydream on dragonback. You are not going to daydream on me!*:

Shashtah glanced at Kashon again.

This time the Dragonlord nodded his approval at them, peeled away and took Katrell through a warp.

As soon as they vanished, Shashtah recalled his instructions and scanned the terrain beneath them. From their new position he could see the caravan trail that wound passed the Anvil, over the wadi and onto the kavir. His far-seeing desert eyes could even make out the second wadi and the dunes beyond which lay the King's Camp.

Tphah brought them around in a gentle circle, giving him plenty of time to take in the features of the open desert that lay to the north, east and south of the Anvil as well. Her body undulated, reminding him of the feel of a camel gamboling over shifting sands. Sunlight glinted along her armored hide as they flew, and pure joy sparkled in her amber eyes.

Dazzled by her beauty and enchanted by the power of her beneath him, Shashtah almost forgot the significance of the shiny speck circling impatiently below them. :*Katrell! He's above the Anvil!*:

:*How long has he been there?*: Tphah squawked as she caught her Rider's panic and dove.

Shashtah was too busy praying he wouldn't fall to answer her. When he finally felt her level out and pull into position off Katrell's left wing, the fury in the older Dragon's eyes told him he'd been waiting for quite some time.

Katrell bugled his annoyance before vanishing through a warp.

Dismay flooded through their Bond as Tphah flapped her wings angrily to regain an altitude where she could glide. :*He said we just added two-hundred-and-forty-three repetitions to the figure Kashon required.*:

Shashtah felt his heart tremble. He toyed briefly with the notion of asking her to land so they could just start over tomorrow, but he had a suspicion that Kashon would simply set the arbitrary number at the new total. Shashtah tried to ignore the trembling in his soul. He took a deep breath and calmed himself. :*It's all right. We'll be faster the next time.*:

Tphah's eyes whirled with her misgivings. :*We'll never be able to make up more than one or two repetitions per—*:

Shashtah spotted Katrell again. :*Up! Right!*:

Tphah arched her back and turned while trying to climb.

:*Not so steep!*: Shashtah shrieked. :*You'll break your wings! If we're late, we're late! Straighten out!*:

Tphah obeyed and climbed into position using a gentler approach—arriving at the thirteenth heartbeat.

Katrell rolled away from her and disappeared through a warp.

Tphah screamed her frustration after him.

Shashtah thought furiously as she resumed her glide. Five heartbeats were never going to be enough for them to spot and reach Katrell. At least they wouldn't be enough if they continued to fly straight. But maybe— :*Did either Kashon or Katrell forbid us to transport?*:

Tphah drifted along a thermal saving her strength. :*Only the first day, when Katrell told us not to cheat at any of the exercises. But this one can't be done!*:

Shashtah smiled grimly. :*Then we're going to have to repeat it tomorrow anyway. So why don't we try warping into position the next time we see Katrell and find out whether we're allowed to or not?*:

Tphah's laughter glittered across their Bond. :*I love the way you think, Dragonheart!*: She spotted Katrell before her Rider could respond. :*See him?*

What's the Anvil look like—?:

Shashtah gave her his picture of the Anvil as he thought it would appear from just off Katrell's left wing.

Tphah's image overlaid his, and they burst into the air less than a wingspan above the older Dragon. She dropped into position.

Katrell cracked his jaws in a grin, and then dove through a warp.

:*He says we figured that out quicker than most,*: Tphah informed Shashtah as she settled onto another thermal. :*Too bad we didn't spot him faster the first time.*:

Shashtah shrugged. :*I'm not convinced that nit of a Dragon can count. How do you feel?*:

Tphah flicked her wings experimentally. :*All right for now, but I'm going to be as blind as you were the first day by the time we finish this.*:

:*Down left!*: Shashtah shouted as his sharp eyes caught the flash of bronze against the sand.

Less than a heartbeat later they were in position and Katrell was gone.

Tphah climbed onto a thermal again. :*I wonder if Kashon will let you shapeshift tonight so you can hide me under your wing.*:

Shashtah chuckled. :*I don't think that's fair to the others who have suffered through this test.*:

:*Just thought I'd—*: Tphah broke off the thought. :*Behind us! Left!*:

Shashtah glanced over his shoulder and gave her the appropriate image.

Katrell vanished the instant her wing came into line with his.

Dissatisfaction oozed from Dragon to Rider through their Bond.

:*What was wrong that time?*: Shashtah demanded.

:*Nothing! I'm sure he didn't expect us to spot him that quickly. But he didn't congratulate me or anything!*:

:*Maybe he's getting bored.*:

Tphah flapped her wings in an irritated gesture. :*Katrell is one of the sweetest Dragons I know, but he doesn't have enough brains to get bored. It's taking him longer and longer between transports. Something is wrong with Kashon.*:

Shashtah frowned. :*I'm not feeling the slightest twinge of Prophecy. How about you?*:

Tphah shook her giant head, causing them to twist in the air. :*That's what has me—*:

:*Up right!*:

They blurred into position.

Katrell vanished before either of them could blink.

Shashtah shrugged. :*Kashon's a Dragonlord now. I suppose Katrell has other duties he has to tend to in addition to us.*: The thought sounded no better when he shared it with her than when he'd considered it himself. Katrell was indeed a wonderful Dragon, but the concept of him trying to do much more than fly into battle with Kashon seemed almost laughable. Bond Break after Bond Break after Bond Break had left him so mentally scarred that it was a miracle he'd been able to Bond with Kashon. That he'd helped Train Tphah when she was a Stripling was extraordinary. That he was taking over most of their Training was astonishing. If Katrell had other duties as a Dragonlord's Dragon . . . Shashtah suddenly felt his defective timesense settle into place. *:We're going to have a full moon in a couple of days, aren't we? The beginning of the Feast of Druids?:*

Tphah's relief flooded through their Bond. *:Of course! Dameth's century had just started leave when Kashon took over. They've been on duty in the King's Camp this rotation. They must be preparing to rotate up to the frontline! Katrell's probably overwhelmed by all the details of moving a hundred Dragons and their Riders to the Border—:*

:Straight down!: Shashtah yelped, wondering exactly how long Katrell had been shadowing them.

Tphah plunged into position, bugling her annoyance as Katrell vanished without a comment. *:He could at least take the time to chew us out. I'm positive we were late for that one.:*

:Easy, love. Katrell's not vicious. He loves Kashon to distraction and probably feels he's needed back at Camp. Yet he's taking the time to come out here and help us because we are yet another of his Rider's new responsibilities. Kashon doesn't want him to make this easy on us, but neither of them probably has any idea what "easy" is. Dameth couldn't have been anything but completely cruel to them.:

:Yes,: Tphah hissed with a depth of loathing that Shashtah hadn't thought possible. She gave several flaps with her wings, hauling them higher. She continued to fume about something she didn't see fit to share with him.

Shashtah considered trying to wheedle the information out of her, but before he could act upon the thought he spotted Katrell again. *:Back left!:* he ordered, giving Tphah the appropriate view of the Anvil.

Tphah's image overlaid his almost immediately, but before either of them realized that the transportation was complete, Katrell was gone. *:I know I shouldn't complain because you've been through so much—:*

:Go ahead,: Shashtah laughed. *:You've earned the right.:*

:I'm getting tired,: Tphah moaned.

Shashtah gingerly touched her neckridge, which was starting to shimmer with the heat. *:Light of my Life, I'm here with you. I understand. If we need to do this again—:*

:No!: Tphah banked in a leisurely circle, gliding as much as possible. *:Up right!:* she called, stirring Shashtah out of the daydream that had started to claim him.

Shashtah glanced up, readjusted his image of the Anvil and found himself already putting his left hand reassuringly to Tphah's neck as Katrell blurred out. *:Compassion, love,:* he chided as he felt fury welling beneath her growing fatigue. *:Just relax and fly. I'll watch for him.:*

Tphah's flanks heaved as she drew a deep breath and exhaled.

Shashtah sighed as he caught the smell of her scent. He sensed her amusement and pleasure at his reaction, and he smiled at himself. "Dragons on the brain!" his mother had said. She was wrong. He had Dragons in his blood. He scanned the terrain below him—slowly realizing that it was a lot farther below him than it had been before. *:Uh, Tphah? Is there a reason we're flying so high?:*

Wordless frustration preceded her whisper, which was laced with fear. *:I don't see him.:*

Shashtah scanned the Anvil, the wadi and the dunes below them again. And again. And again. *:He's not here for us to see.:*

Tphah banked around. *:But that doesn't make sense. When I ask him where he is, he says he's where he's supposed to be.:*

:Which apparently isn't here.: Shashtah rubbed his forehead. *:Is it just me or is Katrell more incoherent than usual today?:*

Tphah shrugged her shoulders, causing her body to lurch unexpectedly.

Shashtah screamed and grabbed the thorn in front of him. He screamed again and yanked his hands away from the scorching metal. *:Your hide is hotter than Tkai's ever was! Why haven't I turned into a cinder?:*

:You didn't have scars to protect you when you flew on Tkai,: Tphah replied, clearly baffled at having to explain something that should have been obvious to a Hatchling.

:Then why was I allowed to leave Dumnonia without going through the Training with her?: When Tphah failed to answer, Shashtah felt his cheeks burn from something other than the midday heat. *:You Dragons knew I'd never fly on her into battle! You knew I'd hardly spend any time flying on her at all!:*

:She told you herself that she would only live five winters after Bonding with you.:

:She didn't say that I'd only spend a few days of that time with her!:

Tphah cracked her tail. *:Would you have helped Lord Criton and the Elven King cast the spell against the Dark One if she'd told you the true price you'd pay?:*

Before Shashtah could answer her he spotted Katrell. *:Up! Right!:*

Tphah shoved aside her anger, supplied the match to his image and warped them into position.

Katrell vanished only to reappear heartbeats later in another spot.

Shashtah quickly forgot what he and Tphah had been arguing about as they blurred and flew, blurred and flew, blurred and flew until their minds became numb and their reflexes took over. Words became meaningless as he encouraged her and she reassured him. Sunlight faded to a dull red glow and finally into moonlight as they continued to fly. Shashtah was just beginning to think that they could find Katrell near the Anvil in their sleep when he realized that the dragon off Tphah's right wingtip was about half the size of Katrell, bore a strangely familiar Dumnonian on its back and boasted a hide the color of the dying sun.

Tphah answered Shashtah's mental shriek by swiveling her head to her right, backwinging and sending a bolt of magical light crackling toward the unwary intruder.

:Don't drop me!: Shashtah squeaked as the strange beast opened its mouth.

Tphah carried them into a backflip so her armored hide would shield her Rider.

Shashtah felt flames lick at his scarring skin. He gave Tphah the image of the Anvil from the opposite side of their current location.

Conditioned by candlescars of responding without thinking, Tphah provided him with the answering image. They burst into the air several wingspans away from the immediate threat.

The attackers bellowed in rage, but before they could pursue their prey Katrell, Kashon firmly lodged in his harness, materialized in front of the strange dragon's nose and spit a cloud of his scent directly into the beast's eyes.

The flame-colored dragon backwinged in surprise, nearly dislodging its rider.

Kashon's hands hastily wove an intricate pattern in the air. Magical bursts of light leapt from his fingertips and caught the scarlet-colored dragon in both wings.

As dragon and rider plummeted toward the sand the air shimmered around them, and they vanished.

Kashon brought Katrell around, set down beside the Anvil and made sure the warp that had swallowed the attackers had closed.

Several heartbeats later Shashtah realized that Kashon had dismounted and was frantically signaling for them to land.

Kashon was at Tphah's side, helping Shashtah down, almost before she settled onto the sand.

Katrell shifted to humanform and examined Tphah. "Are you all right?"

"Don't worry about me!" Tphah screeched in the tongue of the Bronze Dragons. "My Rider—!"

"My Rider will take care of him." Katrell crouched low to inspect the scorched scales on her belly.

"I'm fine." Shashtah sank to the sand and leaned against her bronze-clad side. "Let him make sure you're all right." He stared at Kashon, sheer admiration of his friend's fighting prowess shining in his amber eyes. "I'm glad you're on our side!"

Kashon grinned self consciously. He crouched beside Shashtah and verified with his own eyes that his Trainee was only slightly singed. "You're sure you're fine?"

Shashtah nodded. "Yes. Scared halfway into the Afterlife, but otherwise in one piece. What was a Dumnonian doing riding a red dragon?"

Kashon glowered. "That wasn't just any Dumnonian. That was Dameth."

Shashtah's brow furrowed. "You're certain?"

Kashon nodded solemnly. "I will never forget what he looks like in the air."

Katrell finished his examination of Tphah and moved close to Kashon. "She's exhausted—as she should be—but not harmed."

Kashon reached up and pressed his hand firmly against Tphah's metal hide. "Well done! You took excellent care of your Rider."

Tphah answered his praise with a rumble that sounded vaguely like a snore.

Kashon laughed and glanced at Katrell. "Alert Shaharadesh that Dameth's been seen riding a red dragon near the Anvil. Scramble the first watch to back up the third—I don't want anyone patrolling alone tonight. Order the second watch to get some sleep. Tell anyone who complains to pack in the morning. Whom did we trade Bakir to Amasiah for this afternoon?"

"Salene," Katrell informed him promptly.

Kashon smiled his approval at the speed with which Katrell replied. "Tell her Dragon I want the two of them stationed on the Anvil to keep an eye on us while we personally guard our Trainees. Make it sound like a special honor. I don't want to leave them out of all the action just because they haven't had a chance to drill with anyone from our century yet. And while you're at it, could you shift to dragonform and help Tphah give us a little shelter?"

Katrell snickered. "Only you would believe I could do a half dozen things at once." He took his dragonform, positioned himself nose-to-tail with Tphah and extended his left wing to prop up hers.

Kashon grinned like a child who could finally reveal a long-kept secret. He gestured at the living structure that surrounded them. "Allow me to welcome you to a Dragonrider's true tent."

Shashtah smiled appreciatively as the Dragon bodies blocked out most of the moonlight, though some still shone through their translucent wings. "Much better than canvas."

"More secure, anyway." Kashon favored him with an unreadable look as he stretched out on the sand.

Shashtah copied Kashon's example, planted his elbow in the sand and rested his head against his hand. "So what happened this afternoon that you had to trade Riders with another Dragonlord just before our century takes the frontline?"

Kashon let his breath out slowly. "I didn't think anyone would challenge me while I still had you in Training. I mean, that would jeopardize the Bonding of our last living Prophetess with her new Rider, right?"

Shashtah sat up, suddenly realizing what Kashon had said. "Someone challenged you? No wonder Katrell disappeared on us! Sands! What happened? "

Kashon folded his hands behind his head and crossed his legs, stalling as he searched for the right words. "Let's just say that I'll be exceptionally glad when you finish this bloody ritual and take Quatar and Peri off my hands."

"Great sands! Quatar and Peri!" Shashtah hit himself in the forehead with his palm at the sound of his fosterlings' names. "They were with the Elven Lord at our Bonding Feast. He probably assumed I'd hired someone to care for them because that's what he would've done. Katrell woke me up so abruptly that first morning, I completely forgot! I've been so exhausted and sick ever since—"

"I know," Kashon cut him off. "That's why I didn't mention anything about them before. I figured you have so much dragonblood in those veins of yours that your memory must be almost as bad as theirs is when it comes to Dumnonian problems. Plus you've just had a Bond Break. No one is expecting you to be thinking straight yet. It's a miracle that you are already Bonded with a new Dragon and in Training. That's the sort of thing only my nit has ever been able to do." He stared affectionately at Katrell's side for a moment, his eyes slightly unfocused and a small smile dancing on his lips. Then he grew serious and concentrated on Shashtah. "But today things got so far out of hand that I thought I'd better say something. I convinced Shaharadesh that you should be forgiven for your negligence since most Riders aren't saddled with wards until they've been out of the Training for at least five years and then they only care for Striplings. He said he'd settle things with the Council if I promised to have your hide over this. I think he meant literally, but I hope that just mentioning the problem when you can't do anything about it for at least another rotation will be punishment enough."

Shashtah sank back onto the sand, acknowledging the wisdom in Kashon's sentence on him and imagining exactly how displeased his monarch would be the next time they met. "How are my two misfits?"

"Oh," Kashon drawled, "I suspect they're still on their cots in your tent."

"What'd you do? Poison them?" Shashtah regretted the words as soon as they passed his lips. *I shouldn't be angry with him. He didn't make up our barbaric traditions.*

Something dark flashed in Kashon's amber eyes. "The thought occurred." He went on hastily as he saw the protest forming on Shashtah's lips. "The other choice was to cut off Quatar's hand—"

"WHAT?" Shashtah surged halfway to his feet.

Kashon motioned for him to lie back down. "I have everything under control. Your father will alert Katrell if any more complications arise. When you finish the Training, though, you'd better have a long talk with Quatar about the differences between Dumnonian and Elven law. Apparently in the Elven Kingdom where he grew up there's so much food that it's permissible for children to go around stealing whatever they want from other people's plates." Kashon locked stares with Shashtah. "At least Quatar was in Dumnonia when he made the mistake. He could have been in Mount Paradin where the Galantites kill thieves." He waited for Shashtah to wince, then went on. "We don't do that here because no one wants to inflict a Bond Break on a Dragon. Still, Krills and other thieves are no more welcome among us than they are among the Galantites. The Dragons think our laws are merciful. By comparison, I suppose they are. Finding someone who can resurrect someone is almost impossible. Locating a Healer who can regenerate a hand is Hatchling's play in Daethia, but such a spell is extremely expensive and the trauma of such an experience would be nightmarish. I saw no reason to put either you or Quatar through that."

Shashtah desperately wanted to tear his eyes away from Kashon's, but he could not. "What did Quatar take?"

"A couple of oranges that a trader sold to Bakir for a jambiya dipped in demon blood." Kashon's voice was unnervingly casual. "The lad at least had the good sense to share his prizes with Peri, so I had a way to modify the punishment. I argued that the Dragons should be subject to the same laws they impose on the Dumnonians unless they want to be the monsters the Daethians think they are."

Shashtah felt as if he were trying to stare down a cobra. Kashon's gaze held him paralyzed. "That wouldn't make you popular with the Council."

Kashon shrugged. "I'm already unpopular with the Council."

Shashtah shook his head slightly in disbelief. "How were you able to change the punishment?"

"Peri took the blame for half the crime and demanded that he receive half of

Quatar's sentence. There isn't anyone in Dumnonia who would expect me to cut off half of a Dragon's hand—even if Peri is a mutant. So I took the boys to my basecamp and ordered them to stay put in your tent until you personally show up to deal with them."

"But that didn't satisfy Bakir," Shashtah deduced while fighting off wave after wave of nausea.

"No, it didn't. Especially when he found out that I'd ordered my aide, Patch, to leave a little food and water inside the flap for the boys every day and to provide a chamber pot so you wouldn't have too much of a mess when you get back."

Shashtah could not decide which was worse: the story Kashon was telling or the way he was looking at him while telling it. "So Bakir challenged you for your command."

"Yes. I chose to fight him myself instead of having Katrell champion me the way Tlee used to fight for Dameth. That impressed most of the Riders who were watching, so when I won, several of them volunteered to trade assignments with Bakir. I selected Salene because her Dragon, Councilor Bahktarah, used to be Bonded to a Dragonlord. He knows his way around the frontline well enough to help Katrell if directing our century in combat proves too much for . . . one Dragon to handle."

"You should have me flogged to death!" Shashtah bitterly passed sentence on himself.

The left corner of Kashon's mouth quirked into a brief smile. "Demonlord Yapada tried that. It didn't work." He broke eye contact, paused for a heartbeat, and then flashed Shashtah an apologetic grin. "I'm sorry. I didn't want to do that. But the alternative—" Kashon let the word hang in the shadows. "I trust that once you assume your regular duties I will never be bothered with your fosterlings again."

"Never!" Shashtah swore. *Sands! How can he make me feel so horrible just by talking to me? If he weren't my friend—*

Kashon signaled for him to lie down. "Get some sleep. I'll wake you if there's a need."

Shashtah settled obediently onto the sand. He closed his eyes. *Lord of Light!* He swore silently at the amount of trouble his lack of foresight had caused his friend. *Some Prophet I make.*

Tphah stirred from her exhausted sleep, disturbed by his guilt. :*Dragonheart?*:

"I'm sorry," Shashtah said softly, unsure to whom he was apologizing.

"I know." Kashon remained silent for several heartbeats. "Sleep while you have the chance."

:*Sleep, Dragonheart.*: Tphah's silent whisper echoed Kashon's words.

Shashtah heard Kashon's breathing grow steady beside him. Lulled by the sound, he rolled onto his side, closed his eyes and coiled up like a baby Dragon inside its shell. *What was it Juel said? Something about a Dragon hatching a new Rider?* The half-memory danced behind his eyelids, but before he could resolve it, Tphah's voice slipped through his mind once again.

:*Sleep.*:

All conscious thought twirled away and with it carried Shashtah into the world of dreams.

Salene and Bahktarah

Chapter 3:

The Hard Way

The Dragonriders of Dumnonia are given to fits of stupidity: In addition to warping in large groups to remote destinations, the Riders have been seen skimming the dunes on the backs of speed-blurred Dragons, travelling so fast that the unlucky Rider who is thrown from his or her mount by the appearance of an unpredicted obstacle in the Dragon's path leaves no more than a bloody streak across the unforgiving sands.

**—from *On Dumnonia*
by Shane of Corin**

SHASHTAH WOKE TO KASHON'S GENTLE TOUCH at least half a day before his abused body would have liked.

"I'm needed at our basecamp," Kashon apologized as he straightened. "Do as many of the Ban-kai stretches as you can. You need to regain your strength as quickly as possible, just as you would if you were injured and still alone. The Dragons aren't there for us to lean on them. We're there for them to lean on us. Salene and Bahktarah will guard you, so you don't need to wake Tphah."

"Yes, Lord." Shashtah stood, stripped off his Initiate's robe and obediently began the slow, deliberate movements of the Battle Dance.

Kashon watched him critically for a few heartbeats, then jogged over to where Katrell waited in dragonform. He hauled himself up his Dragon's harness and settled easily onto his seat.

The magnificent Bronze rose beneath him.

Shashtah watched enviously until the Pair vanished through a warp, and then concentrated on his exercises. He was almost feeling alive again by the time Tphah stirred.

:*Ouch,*: the Prophetess commented as she stood up and stretched her wings. :*Where are Kashon and Katrell?*:

:*At our basecamp. I hope Quatar and Peri aren't in trouble.*:

Tphah reared on her hind legs and, balancing with her tail, flapped her wings experimentally. :*Kashon handled me for the better part of ten winters. He can handle two small boys for a few rotations.*:

Shashtah grinned as he watched her move. :*Do I detect a memory or two of Kashon becoming displeased with you?*:

Tphah cracked her tail in embarrassment. :*Let's just say I'm unlikely to breathe a bolt of light anywhere near you no matter how annoyed I get.*: She lowered herself back onto the sand. :*The boys are probably mortified enough that they won't misbehave again—at least until we finish the Training.*:

Shashtah blinked. :*You knew?*:

:*While Katrell was checking me for injuries, he apologized for being distracted during the exercise.*: Tphah extended her left wing, shading Shashtah from the sun's fierce heat. :*Actually he babbled hysterically about everything until I figured out what had happened. I love Katrell beyond life, but I'm amazed Kashon can even find his way to the latrine if that racket is going on in his head all the time. With another Dragon Kashon might have become a formidable king. With Katrell . . . Kashon needs you to become king so he'll be free to become . . . something else.*:

:*Can we worry about turning me into something resembling a Dragonrider first?*: Shashtah worked the knots out of his right calf. :*Sands! After all he's done for me, how could I have put him in such an awful position?*:

:*You didn't do it on purpose. Kashon knows that. That's why the boys are in one piece and safely in your tent.*:

Shashtah slipped back into his robe. :*Quatar is safe because Tkai's son is the bravest little Dragon who's ever graced Centuria.*: He strolled a few steps away from her, trying to catch a glimpse of the Dragonrider on the Anvil.

Tphah twitched her tail playfully at him, narrowly missing his scarred legs. :*Do I detect a little fatherly pride?*:

Shashtah hung his head. :*Pride, I suppose, is the last thing I have a right to feel. I'm fostering two bastards of the Dark One, and my incompetence at that task almost cost Kashon his Dragonlordship. He's the most intelligent Dumnonian I've ever met. How can he tolerate me? I can't find my brains with two hands in the midday sun!*:

:*Kashon's Bonded to Katrell, and he's the only Rider who's survived that match this long since . . . I doubt even the Council can remember. He relishes a good challenge. That's why you captivate him. Besides Quatar might have gotten into trouble even if you had arranged for someone to take care of him. He spent his first five winters as the ward of the Elven King. He's bound to have some adjustments to make to desert life.*:

:*If he keeps all of his body parts intact long enough for me to explain the difference to him,*: Shashtah grumbled. :*Wow!*:

Tphah hoisted her neck into the air to see what had distracted him this time.

An adult male Bronze with more muscles beneath his armored hide than Shashtah had thought possible perched on the rim of the Anvil. Astride him was a Dumnonian woman whom few males of the race would not die for. An elaborate mesh of Galantite chain worked into the semblance of a keffiyeh flowed over her long, black hair. Fierce, darkened amber eyes separated by a hawk-like nose stared out of an incredibly wise and intelligent face. Sensuous lips were pressed into a grim line as she constantly scanned and rescanned the air and sand for any hint of trouble. A Galantite mail shirt glittered over more-than-ample breasts and wrapped the sinuous body that seemed too delicate to support the muscle beneath the priceless armor. Tight-fitting trousers clung to shapely legs, and soft, desert boots encased her perfectly proportioned feet. The hilt of a deadly scimitar glittered above a jewel-encrusted scabbard that was tied securely to her left leg.

Tphah lowered her head to the sand and glared at her Rider. :*Bet she can't take dragonform.*:

:*Huh?*: His attention once more on Tphah, Shashtah sensed the jealousy seeping through their Bond. He gave a small cry, rushed for her muzzle and embraced it as best he could. :*I'll never feel about anyone else the way I feel about you!*:

Tphah breathed out heavily, surrounding him with her scent.

Shashtah swore to himself as he fought the overwhelming urge to take his dragonform and engage her in the mock battle that was the draconic version of the Mother's Dance.

Kashon and Katrell flew out of a warp above them. The Dragonlord took in the situation at a glance and started to laugh so hard that Katrell sprayed both of the Trainees with sand in his haste to land before his Rider could fall off. "Guess I should've warned you about Salene. I suspect she has her reasons for preferring to serve under a Dragonlord who's not attracted to females."

Shashtah greeted his friend with a rude gesture. "You are vicious! You know I can't shapeshift for at least another rotation!"

"Serves you right!" Kashon chortled.

Shashtah smiled at his friend, grateful that the tension between them had vanished. "I know. I deserved that." *And so much more . . .*

Kashon tossed a Dragon's harness at Shashtah's feet. "Put that on Tphah."

Shashtah picked up the leather straps and checked them for wear, a habit developed from years of loading and unloading camels on endless treks across the desert. He honestly couldn't remember what Tkai's harness had looked like other than that it had been stunning. This one, though, was spectacular. The legends of Tchang, the Founder of Tphah's House, decorated every surface. Where the straps joined, the image of a Male and a Female Bronze, lying nose to tail, hid and protected the clasp. Dragon tails and talons covered the leg braces that would hold him securely to Tphah's back if something truly horrible happened.

:They had it specially made,: Tphah commented happily. *:It's their Bonding gift to me.:*

Kashon smiled his approval at Shashtah's caution. "Most Trainees lose half a rotation's worth of food on that test."

Shashtah tossed one end of the harness over Tphah's back, just behind her neckridge, then buckled the leather straps together under her belly and across her chest. He stepped away so Kashon could check his work. "Now, Lord, why do I need to have an empty stomach for the next half a rotation?"

Kashon tensed with barely controlled excitement and concern. "There is one extraordinarily fun and tremendously dangerous maneuver that Dragons and their Riders learn during the Training. Dameth, by his impeccable timing, has given me a wonderful excuse to teach it to you myself under the pretext of guarding you. Speedflying."

Shashtah felt his heart skip a beat. "Speedflying?" He had heard of the Dumnonians and their Dragons practicing the insane feat, but he'd never known how much was truth and how much was legend. "It's real?"

Kashon nodded solemnly. "If you're going to die during the Training, this is where it'll happen, so don't take anything I'm about to tell you lightly."

Shashtah nodded his understanding. "Yes, Lord."

"One: Never try this with a shapeshifted harness." Kashon ticked off the points on his fingers. "The harness goes away, you go away, and no magic on Centuria is going to save you. Two: Only use this skill if you are physically able to. If your body fails, you will die and probably take your Dragon with you. Got that?"

Shashtah nodded gravely. "Real harness and only when physically able."

Kashon smiled his approval. "Think you can remember that while we fly in formation to an area with fewer obstacles?"

"He won't," Tphah said before Shashtah could reply. "He's a hopeless daydreamer unless we're actually doing something dangerous. I'll remember for him."

Kashon grinned affectionately at her. "I suppose you will." He jerked his head toward Tphah. "Mount up."

Shashtah climbed onto Tphah's back.

Kashon mounted Katrell and waited until Shashtah secured himself before continuing. "Once we're airborne, Tphah will have to take instructions from Katrell. We'll fly in formation for a while, then climb to the thin layer of atmosphere. From there the Dragons will go into a steep dive. When you feel the wind pushing against your chest so hard you can barely sit upright, grab the harness with both hands, take your feet out of their bracing positions and kick them straight out behind you. The rush of the wind will keep you from slamming into Tphah's back. When she gets close to the sand, she'll level out and start skimming the surface. Occasionally she'll have to use her wings, but other than that, the two of you will be moving like skyfire. Tphah will worry about rising or falling to make sure you don't hit any dunes. You have two jobs: Hold on, and don't let go. Your entire body weight will pull against your fingers and wrists. The harness is designed to make this possible, but you still have to hold on. Let go, and you die. It's as simple as that. When you get too tired to maintain your grip, tell Tphah to land, and she'll do so as quickly as she can. You need to tuck and catch yourself with your knees on either side of her backridge. You'll probably not be successful the first million times you attempt this—at least it'll feel that way. When you do make it to your knees, slip back into your proper riding position, and wait for my command to dismount. Once you're on the sand, lie next to Tphah, let her cover you with her wing, and sleep until she wakes you. She'll know when you're both recovered enough to make another attempt. Then we'll try the maneuver again and again and again until you get it right. Any questions?"

"Yes, Lord," Shashtah answered. "How many times are we going to fly between the King's Camp and the Border before I die?"

Kashon's lips curled into a sympathetic grin. "Let's hope we don't find out. And while you may be in a hurry to finish the Training, you will practice this and keep practicing it until I'm certain you're not going to kill yourself or Tphah. So, enjoy your bruises!" He abruptly brought his right fist to his left breast in the

Dumnonian salute and shot his clenched hand into the air, ordering them to rise in as near to a vertical jump as could be managed by any Dragon.

Shashtah was slightly surprised to see Salene and Bahktarah rise with them, but then he realized that this was probably part of their Training to fly with a new century. He felt the sunlight burning down upon his back, growing ever hotter as Tphah's powerful wings carried them higher and higher above the Anvil.

:*I won't drop you,*: Tphah promised, sensing his growing fear even before he noticed it himself.

Shashtah felt his deep love for his Dragon swell within his breast and spill into her mind through their Bond as she settled into position off Katrell's left wing. :*I think the object of this exercise is that I'm not supposed to drop you.*:

:*Don't joke!*: Tphah chided. :*This is serious! I don't want to lose you.*:

Shashtah tightened his grip on the leather straps. :*I know. Just jitters, love.*: His heart filled with joy as he flew with his fellow Riders, soaring high above the desert of Dumnonia.

:*Katrell wants to know if you remember your instructions,*: Tphah's voice wafted through Shashtah's mind.

:*When the wind pushes against me,*: Shashtah repeated dutifully, :*I grab the harness with both hands and kick my feet out behind me. When you start skimming the sand, I'm to hold on and not let go. When I get too tired, I tell you to land. I tuck and catch myself with my knees on either side of your backridge. Then I return to my proper riding position and wait for the order to dismount. Tell me before we—*:

:*Katrell says "Dive!"*: Tphah shouted as she lowered her snout and plunged toward the sand.

Shashtah felt his sinuses wind up somewhere around where his bladder was supposed to be before the strain of the wind against his shoulders yanked his mind back to more immediate concerns.

:*Katrell says for you to uncoil your legs now.*:

Letting go of Tphah with any part of his body was the last thing Shashtah wanted to do, but the alternative appeared to be letting the wind sweep him off her back. He unwrapped his right leg first. Then he slid his left foot from its brace. In less than a heartbeat he was flying through the air a scant hand span above her lethal spikes.

:*Relax your elbows,*: Tphah warned just before she leveled out above the sand.

Shashtah almost lost his grip as the shock hit his arms.

:*No shapeshifting!*:

Shashtah quickly suppressed the urge to spread his wings. His beautiful Prophetess had spent years learning how to do precisely what she was doing now, and his dragonform would probably wind up as dead as his humanform if he tried to imitate her without learning the skill himself.

: *This is the fun part! Just hold on, and let me do the work.*:

Shashtah had no intention of doing anything else. The wind whipped by him too quickly for him to see. The hood of his robe flew back, and his blue-black hair streamed after it. He tried not to think about the metal thorns beneath him as Tphah's body undulated, avoiding dunes, carrying him up, then down, then up again. He had a vague sense that Bahktarah was somewhere off to his left and Katrell to his right, but he was too terrified to look. By the time he realized his wrists were tiring almost beyond his ability to grip Tphah's harness, he found he was even more horrified of the idea of asking her to land.

Tphah's cried in distress as she extended her wings. She strained to slow their forward rush.

Too late Shashtah remembered to tuck his knees. A metal spike on her back caught him in the groin. As his body convulsed, his forehead and nose slammed into an equally wicked spike at the base of her neck. His chin smashed into her scales—which had the added effect of causing him to bite his tongue. His knees finally bounced into their proper position just as he started to black out. His last conscious thought was that someone had slipped a half-dozen or so swords between his chest and Tphah. Then he lost his grip and started to fall.

":*Ouch!*:" Shashtah screamed silently and aloud as feeling returned to his battered body.

"Everyone says that the first time," Kashon's voice chuckled.

Shashtah spat blood out of his mouth, narrowly missing his Dragonlord. "What on Centuria makes any of you think this is 'fun'?"

"You'll see when you get the hang of it."

Shashtah remained unconvinced.

Humor softened to sympathy in Kashon's eyes. "Tphah, you may shapeshift long enough to heal him, then I want you back in dragonform at once. Understand?"

A firm, gentle hand pressed against Shashtah's forehead and his disjointed hip. Healing light flashed over him.

Shashtah's broken nose reset. The furrows on his chest, left by Katrell's talons, knit. His hip slid back where it was supposed to be. He reached up in a desperate effort to embrace his lover.

Tphah's touch faded instantly.

Shashtah's arms closed around the armored muzzle of her dragonform. Disappointment flooded his face, followed closely by guilt as he opened his eyes and saw the longing in her amber gaze. "I'm sorry!"

Kashon's hand closed lightly on Shashtah's shoulder. "Remember the rules. Lie under her wing where she can protect you until you're both ready to try again." With that, the pressure of his hand vanished.

Shashtah heard the rustle of Katrell's wing enveloping Kashon as Tphah's sturdy appendage covered his own prone form. :*I'm sorry!*: he apologized again.

Tphah tucked her head under her wing beside him. :*For getting hurt or for loving me too much to obey Kashon's orders?*:

Shashtah hugged her muzzle as best he could. :*When this is over we're going to find a nice soft dune somewhere and not let go of each other until we have to report to the King's Camp.*:

:*Sounds nice, but I don't think that'll be possible with Quatar and Peri to look after.*:

Shashtah kissed the flap of her left nostril. :*I'm never going to be able to make this up to you.*:

Tphah let her scent drift over him. :*Quatar and Peri won't take forever to grow up.*:

:*I'll never neglect you because of them!*:

Tphah's forked tongue flicked out and brushed him lightly across the lips. :*Katrell says you're supposed to let me sleep. And I imagine even those spawn of the Dark One have to sleep sometime.*:

:*I suppose they do,*: Shashtah conceded as he relaxed his mind and joined his dreams with hers.

:*Wake up, Dragonheart,*: Tphah's mental voice called. :*I've been pretending to sleep for the last candlescar, but Katrell knows I'm awake. He's going to be angry if we don't try again soon.*:

Shashtah stirred, crawled onto her head and noted with some surprise that the full moon was shining above the barren landscape as she heaved him up to his place on her back.

"Hold on!" Kashon called from where he already sat astride Katrell. "And tuck the instant she begins to slow!"

Salene, who was perched on Bahktarah's neckridge, looked as if she had little faith in Shashtah's ability to follow Kashon's commands, but she held her tongue.

Half asleep, Shashtah did far better on their second attempt than he had on the first. This time he only took a blow from Tphah's backridge to his stomach and bit his lower lip as he tumbled over Tphah's shoulder and landed in a groaning pile on the sand at her side.

Kashon generously allowed Tphah to heal him again before he made them sleep once more.

When Shashtah took a glancing blow from Tphah's backridge to his breastbone on his third attempt, he began to wonder whether Kashon was trying to get back at him for something else Quatar and Peri had done. He picked himself up from where he had bounced onto a dune and rubbed his chest.

The doubt on Salene's face slowly transformed into speculation as she took cover under Bahktarah's wing.

:*You're doing fine!*: Tphah laughed as she covered Shashtah without healing him this time. :*We're only halfway to the Border, and you almost have the hang of this! Katrell's turning copper with envy. Dameth tortured Kashon with Speedflying for almost a full rotation before he learned.*:

Shashtah shuddered. :*Remind me to kill that fiend very, very slowly if we ever get the chance.*:

:*You'll have to get in line.*: Tphah snarled. :*Vengeful dreams.*:

The fourth time Tphah pulled out of Speedflight, Shashtah slammed his left thigh against her backridge and slipped off her right side, but the fifth time he landed precisely on his knees. He leapt from her back with a shout of triumph, only to find Kashon glaring at him from high atop Katrell.

"I didn't say to dismount, Trainee!" Kashon bellowed.

Shashtah hastily scrambled back onto to Tphah's neckridge. :*What's wrong with him?*:

:*We're almost at the Border, and he's worried about you. He needs to be certain you'll always follow his orders, even if you don't understand them.*:

:*Orders?*:

:*He told you to wait for his command to dismount when we land,*: Tphah reminded him patiently.

Shashtah hung his head. He had completely forgotten that part of Kashon's instructions since all of the other times he had simply fallen off. "Sorry." Once again unsure whether he was speaking to Tphah or Kashon.

"I have to return to our century." Kashon sounded thoroughly annoyed. "I've given Salene orders to keep an eye on you until you start the final trial."

"You mean I'm almost done?" Shashtah asked.

"Yes, and no," Kashon said bruskly. "This is the last part. See that dune over there?" He indicated a lonely mound in the otherwise almost flat land.

Shashtah nodded.

"That," Kashon informed him solemnly, "has been created by all of the Dragonriders who have gone before you. To finish the Training, you must fly to Mount Cinnamar—without transporting—and bring back a handful of sand to add to that dune. Then dismount and walk to our basecamp. Katrell will tell Tphah where it is."

"Walk?" Shashtah warily regarded his friend.

"The location is secret, and you and Tphah don't yet have enough experience to find it without accidentally opening a warp that could lead the Dark One's forces straight to us," Kashon elaborated. "When you reach our basecamp you'll have to assume your regular duties as a Dragonrider. I suggest you walk slowly if you wish to avoid fighting on the frontline this rotation. Unless, of course, you wish to maintain my friendship, in which case you'll run most of the way so I can stop dealing with your fosterlings while I'm trying to fight a war."

:*Oh, sands! What have Quatar and Peri done now?*: Shashtah asked.

Tphah answered him with a mental shrug.

Kashon's sharp eyes noticed the silent exchange. The hard line of his mouth relaxed into a smile, reassuring Shashtah that whatever was bothering the Dragonlord was not his fault. "Salene will bring you water and food and will guard you tonight so you can sleep without fear. She will take whatever supplies are leftover in the morning and bring them to me. If you can make it back to our basecamp with only your Dragon to care for you, you'll be allowed to take your place in my century. If you can't, you'll either be dead or you'll have to go through the Training again. Do I make myself clear?"

Shashtah shuddered. "Very."

"Any questions before I go?" Kashon's voice quaked slightly.

"I have to walk to our basecamp," Shashtah repeated the instruction. "How's Tphah supposed to get there?"

"That's up to her. She can fly or walk, shapeshift, or whatever else pleases her. After she crosses the Border on the return from Mount Cinnamar, her part of the Training is finished."

"Eternal Death to the Dark One!" Shashtah shouted as he gave his Dragonlord the Dumnonian salute.

Kashon's eyes flashed with approval as he returned the salute and signaled for Katrell to rise.

Shashtah watched until they vanished through a warp.

:*Dismount. Now.*:

:*Isn't Salene supposed to—?*:

:*If you aren't safely hidden under my wing when she arrives, I'll chase her off!*:

:*Jealousy does not become you, Light of my heart.*: Shashtah slid to the sand and settled into his place beneath her wing, secretly admitting that there was something tremendously flattering about having a creature as magnificent as Tphah so insanely possessive of him.

Tphah had just covered him tightly, blocking out the sun, when he heard her bugle her challenge at the desert skies.

A male Bronze answered her. "We have water and food for your Rider: dates and some bread—even a piece of cheese. The Dragonlord thinks highly of him and doesn't want him to get sick during the last part of the Training."

:*He has a point,*: Shashtah prompted.

:*You're attracted to his Rider,*: Tphah accused. :*And I'm not permitted to shapeshift to compete with her!*:

:*Just wait until I'm allowed to take my dragonform again, and I'll show you who's competing with whom. Do you really think I could ever consider another lover after having performed the Mother's Dance with you?*: Shashtah wondered how many times Kashon had had similar arguments with Katrell.

Tphah raised her wing just enough to poke her snout under it. :*I know you crave contact with a Dumnonian. All Riders do by this stage of the Training. Tkai would've let this Rider fill that need for you, but I'm not Tkai. I've nursed you and protected you and served as your companion through all the trials, and my humanform, not her, deserves to give you that comfort.*:

Shashtah caressed Tphah's muzzle and kissed the corner of her eye. :*You shall be the one,*: he promised. :*Now, will you please let the nice Pair Kashon sent give me some help? I'm thirsty, and those dates sound like the answer to my prayers!*:

Reluctantly, Tphah lifted her wing enough for Shashtah to step into the desert sun.

Salene stood beside Bahktarah, watching Shashtah with a bemused grin. At her feet was a waterskin and a pack of supplies.

"Sorry for the wait," Shashtah croaked, his thirst strangling his voice at the sight of the waterskin.

Salene snickered as she maneuvered the supplies closer to him, and then backed away to a discrete spot beneath the shade of Bahktarah's wing. "They're all over possessive during the Training. No offense taken." She eyed him critically as he took a small sip of the water and pawed through the pack in search of the dates. A blush turned her skin a lovely shade of bronze as he caught her staring. "I'm sorry. It's just that you're so different out here alone than when I've seen you before."

Shashtah selected a date. "Let's see . . . Is it the absence of children hanging all over me? Or perhaps it's the lack of light leaping unexpectedly from my fingertips and rearranging the political structure of our kingdom? Or maybe it's the bare feet?" He wriggled his toes in the powdery sand as he nibbled at the sun-dried fruit.

Salene's blush deepened. "I'm sorry," she apologized again. "I shouldn't be intruding. Normally you'd be alone while you prepared for your flight. But after Dameth showed up at the Anvil, the king insisted that a guard be placed over both of you even before Lord Kashon could ask permission for the breach in tradition. I never dreamed the honor would fall to me."

Shashtah stretched upward, feeling the date sitting like a stone in his empty stomach. "I suppose this is easier if you have a body conditioned to drink blood." He lowered his arms and rubbed the still-bruised muscles of his abdomen.

"I don't know," Salene said. "Probably just different. Somehow I doubt Corin designed this ritual to turn us into a tribe of vampires."

A shadow crossed Shashtah's face as her words unwittingly called to mind the slaughter in his family's camp. "No, I don't suppose he did." He took another small sip of water. "Any news of Dameth?"

Salene shook her head. "We don't know how he got a red dragon to accept him as a Rider let alone transport with him anywhere."

Shashtah extracted a piece of flatbread from the supplies. "Maybe he was only learning and instinctively went to the Anvil to do it. He'd just suffered a Bond Break when he was exiled. He might've lost track of time and failed to realize I'd be there with Tphah. One more day and there wouldn't have been anyone around to notice his return."

Salene raised an appreciative eyebrow. "That's pretty insightful thinking for someone who looks half-dead. I'll have Bahktarah tell—"

"I've already passed the message to Makara and Katrell," Tphah said defiantly. The Dumnonian language sounded odd in her draconic mouth.

Shashtah threw a sidelong look at Salene under the cover of nibbling on his bread.

Salene dropped in a salaam. "Thank you, Prophetess. You really didn't need to bother with something so mundane. You should be sleeping and conserving your strength for the next test. Bahktarah and I will take good care of you and your Rider."

Tphah responded by curling tightly around Shashtah, leaving him just enough room to see over the place where her snout touched her tail. She extended her wing high above him, shading him from the blistering sun.

Salene made an admirable effort to stifle a laugh at the much-put-upon look that flashed across Shashtah's face. "Eat and drink what you can manage without getting sick, and then sleep. I'll take Bahktarah aloft and fly cover. He's rested enough we can stay in the air most of the day and night. That should ensure you have a little peace as you prepare."

Shashtah silently mouthed his thanks at her, and then settled against Tphah's side.

Salene remounted.

Bahktarah lunged into the air.

Shashtah allowed himself a taste of the cheese, took another sip of water, and then decided to sleep for a while in the hope that he would be able to eat and drink more later.

Later came too soon for Shashtah. Tphah's plaintive cries roused him from his dreams.

:*It's dawn! Katrell says we have to give the supplies back to Salene!*:

Shashtah struggled to his feet and gathered the waterskin and pack, his lips flattened in a grim smile. :*As if you didn't think that was going to happen.*:

":*But I could've awakened you earlier!*:" Tphah wailed silently and aloud in the language of the Bronze Dragons.

:*Hush!*: Shashtah protested. :*You'll attract all of the fiends in Cinnamar carrying on like that! Let me out.*:

Tphah obediently raised her wing.

Shashtah saw Salene astride Bahktarah, hands over her ears, gazing warily at Tphah. He stepped forward and laid his supplies at Bahktarah's feet. "What are my orders, Rider?" he asked in Dumnonian.

Salene took her hands from her ears and removed something from Bahktarah's harness. "Catch!" she called as she tossed him a pack.

Shashtah snatched the satchel out of the air. Surprised by the heft of it, he gave her a curious look.

Salene rocked back slightly in her seat to receive Shashtah's supplies as Bahktarah's exquisite talons handed them to her. "That's a gift from our king. Strap it onto Tphah's harness between where you place your hands for Speedflying. It's an emergency kit. Hopefully you'll be able to return it unopened. Now, mount!"

Shashtah hauled himself onto Tphah's back faster than he'd planned. The tone in Salene's voice startled him. Gone was the playfulness she'd shown before, and in its place was something that made him feel like a Hatchling who was in serious trouble. He strapped the kit into place, trying not to let his fear seep through his Bond to Tphah. He had a little difficulty settling into his accustomed riding position with the extra bulk in the way, but he philosophically accepted the fact that he wouldn't be sitting upright for long.

"Listen carefully," Salene ordered in the same disturbing tone when she saw he was ready. "This is the last part of the Training, and the object is not to get yourself killed. When you get tired, order Tphah to land. She knows how to nest in the sand to make herself look like a dune. You'll be quite safe under her wing. When you're rested, have her dig you out and fly again. If you're in an area where your magic will work, use your spells to summon food and water. If you're in a zone where your magic won't work, stick it out until you get to a location where it will. Save the kit as long as possible: You may need it if one or both of you are injured in a non-magic zone and we have trouble finding you. No heroics: Just get the sand, and get back. Am I clear?"

"Yes, Rider!" Shashtah tried not to squirm.

"I'll see you when you return!" Salene gave them the signal to rise.

Shashtah felt his stomach lurch as Tphah sprang into the air. Higher and higher her wings carried them above the pile created by all of the Dragonriders who had succeeded at this ritual. When he sensed the air grow thin, he took Tphah's harness firmly in both hands. :*Dive!*: He felt Tphah plunge downward almost before he finished the command. His heart wound up in the pit of his stomach this time as the wind pushed against his breast. Carefully, knowing that Katrell and Bahktarah were no longer around to save him, he kicked out his legs and felt the rush of air lift him above the spikes along Tphah's back. He closed his eyes and held on until his wrists and shoulders complained too loudly for him to ignore. :*I need to land.*:

Tphah obediently slowed.

Shashtah tucked just in time to protect his groin. His shout of joy ended as abruptly as it had begun when he opened his eyes and realized it was night.

:Hurry! I need to dig us in so you'll be safe.:

Shashtah dropped to the sand and waited patiently while Tphah burrowed into the side of the dune. At her signal, he slipped beneath her wing and into the nest she'd formed.

Tphah lay her head beside him in the cool sand and was snoring almost before she finished covering them up.

Shashtah stood with his hand on Tphah's jaw for several heartbeats. *How many Dragons have I ridden camels and horses over, thinking they were dunes? How can I know so little about creatures I love so much?* He stroked her scales gently. *So young. So brave. So beautiful. So scared. But not alone. Never alone.*

Tphah's hunger ripped Shashtah from his exhausted sleep. *:Eat!:* he ordered frantically.

:Eat what?: Tphah asked as she dug them out of the nest. *:This is Cinnamar.:*

Dismay flooded through Shashtah. He had crossed Cinnamar enough times to know that the land had been rendered completely barren by the War and by the spell the Lord of Daethia used to keep the forces of the Dark One locked inside the only mountain on the seemingly endless plain. Not even a lizard would cross their path.

Tphah waited impatiently, ravenous light shining in her amber eyes.

The sight was too much for Shashtah. He muttered the words to a spell he'd last used half a decade ago.

A pile of not completely palatable, but decidedly welcome, manna appeared in front of him.

:Eat!: Shashtah commanded again.

:You, too.:

Shashtah made a show of eating a single piece. He marveled at the way the flaky white substance seemed to change to water in his mouth. *:I'd forgotten it did that.:*

:Good thing it does,: Tphah observed, swiping up the remainder of the meager meal with her forked tongue. *:Dragon bodies weren't designed to eat bread. If I tried, I'd probably get as sick as you do when you drink blood.:*

That's the real purpose of this test, Shashtah suddenly realized. *Just as she cared for me during the first of these trials, I must snow how I can care for her. And I'm doing as bad a job of it as I did of taking care of Tkai. Tphah wouldn't be starving if*

I ate meat. She would've been feeding us both with her prey. He tried to remember the last time he'd felt his Prophetess kill something—and failed. He had no idea how much food a Dragon needed. Perhaps not much while she was simply lying on top of him, but she'd been flying hard for several days now. *Did Katrell or Bahktarah feed her when we were at the Border? Or did they assume she'd eaten with me the way their Riders ate with them? I need to get her out of here as quickly as possible! Which means we need to get to Mount Cinnamar now!* Growing dread sent him scrabbling up Tphah's harness and onto her back. Soon they were skimming the sands again even though he had no memory of giving Tphah the command to rise.

Their life settled into a mind-numbing sequence of landing and flying that carried them deep into Cinnamar. Kashon's dire warnings about Shashtah's need to rest warred with Tphah's ravenous need to complete their mission. Dreams merged with daydreams. Shashtah had no idea if he was waking or sleeping or whether the thoughts in his head were his or Tphah's. Their roles reversed as he kept insisting that Tphah land and she kept insisting that they return to the air. So he was completely unprepared for her to invert the pattern on him.

:*Landing!*:

:*Wait!*: Shashtah shrieked. *It's too dark.* Experience from his years of raiding shoved aside the fog inside his brain. :*Is it night?*:

:*Day!*:

Shashtah caught himself on his knees as they slowed. He sensed Tphah come to a stop.

The wind, however, did not stop.

Shashtah choked on the dust that surrounded him. He raised his hood and covered his nose and mouth with the cloth. *Sands! A simoom!* He shielded his eyes with his forearm. *How can she see anything?*

Someone else's memory, perhaps Tkai's, supplied the answer from deep within him. "*Dragons use their third, transparent lid to protect their eyes.*"

Great, Shashtah grumbled to himself. *Now the voices in my head decide to start talking. They couldn't have done that when I was frying like a piece of flatbread beside the Anvil? No lessons about draconic anatomy then? No observations about how Tphah might like an addax or two while I was scarfing down dates?* Still, he wasn't completely ungrateful as he felt his slumbering powers stir. *If I'm going to accidentally blast something off the face of Centuria, this would be a good place to do it.* :*Where are we?*:

:*We're here! Quit stalling! Get the sand, and let's go!*:

Shashtah slid to the ground, absently noticing that Tphah had positioned herself so her bulk protected him from the storm. He snatched up a handful of sand.

:*Faster!*: Tphah hissed. :*I want to get you out of here before that dog-faced Demonlord gets his paws on you again!*:

Shashtah's eyes flashed with remembered pain as he turned to haul himself up her harness. Only then did the inherent problem in the mission occur to him. :*Uh, Tphah? How am I supposed to hold onto your harness with both hands if one is full of sand?*:

Tphah craned her head around to look at him, at a complete loss for words.

Shashtah inventoried his options. Magic would do him no good the instant they hit a non-magic zones. The weave of his Initiate's robe was too loose to tie the sand in his hood, hem or sleeve. The harness consisted of simple straps. The emergency kit . . .

:*You aren't supposed to open that except in case of an emergency!*:

:*If I return without the sand, we have to go through the Training again. If I try to fly one-handed, I'll die. If we sit here in indecision until sunset, the Dark One's forces will emerge from the mountain and make the decision for us—unless this sandstorm blasts us into the Afterlife first. Maybe you don't call this an emergency, but I do!*: Shashtah abruptly dropped the sand, scrambled up Tphah's harness and grabbed the kit. He slid to the ground once more as she curled around him, protecting him as best she could from the simoom. He opened the flap.

Inside was a note folded neatly atop the contents: food, water, healing potions and an empty pouch. Shashtah grabbed the message as the wind tried to snatch it from him. He squinted at the script.

"How long did it take you to figure this out?" the writing chided. "Enjoy the food and drink on your way back, compliments of your king."

Shashtah chuckled. *Maybe—just maybe—they aren't trying to kill me after all.* He filled the pouch with sand and placed it in the kit. He scrabbled up Tphah's harness and secured the satchel in place. :*Let's get out of here!*:

Tphah arced her wings and let the winds sweep her into the sky. :*Too bad we can't transport instead of flying through this—*:

Shashtah squawked, appalled. :*Kashon had a fit at the thought of opening a warp between the Border and his basecamp! I can't imagine what he'd do if we opened one between here and the Border.*:

:*Sorry. I wasn't thinking.*: Tphah climbed above the storm and glided for a moment in the clean, dust-free air.

Shashtah glanced around. The simoom was so huge he couldn't see Mount Cinnamar beneath them. *Sands! We have to get out of here!* He tightened his grip on Tphah's harness. :*Dive!*:

The Prophetess plummeted into the simoom.

Shashtah closed his eyes tightly against the abrasive winds. He felt Tphah level out and undulate beneath him. By the time they cleared the storm, he was convinced his power was once more doing something without his consent. *The simoom should've swept me off her back. We should've slammed into the ground. At the very least I should be missing most of my face.* This time when Shashtah's wrists grew tired he decided not to argue with his Prophetess. After a few abortive attempts he managed to grip her backridge between his powerful thighs and use his muscular legs to hold himself close to her thorny spine, easing the strain on his arms. He thought at first it was his imagination, but, goaded by hunger, Tphah picked up speed. When he opened his eyes just enough to verify what his prickling skin was telling him, he nearly let go of the harness in shock.

Skyfire crackled less than a handspan away from them, outlining them against the darkened sky.

Lord of Light, I'm going to die! Shashtah felt a thousand curses tangle in his throat as he realized that, once again, someone had forgotten to tell him something important about Dragons. *The mind scrambling works both ways! Her brain has started to work like mine! She's daydreaming!* He frantically tried to imagine what Kashon would do.

A single word formed inside his head like the eye of a storm: *Talk.*

:*Tphah, my love,*: Shashtah called softly. :*Please, don't panic. Just don't pick up any more speed, and when you've slowed a bit, then we can think about how we're going to stop without killing me. Okay? Tphah?*:

:*Sands!*: The oath held a world of panic.

:*I'll be all right,*: Shashtah promised, not believing the lie. :*We'll panic together later, okay? Just let yourself slow down.*:

After what seemed like an eternity the skyfire disappeared.

Tphah extended her wings experimentally.

Shashtah brought his knees up tightly to his chest and thrust his body away from her lethal backridge. By the time Tphah plowed into the top of a star-shaped dune, he was too busy praying the harness wouldn't break to notice when their motion ceased.

Katrell burst into the sky above them with Kashon. Their mouths were both open, but no sound came forth.

Shashtah glanced down at the blood that was dripping between his chin and Tphah's armored hide. :*Tphah, my ears are bleeding.*: Pain started somewhere at the base of his skull and cascaded toward his eyes. He felt an intense tremor in his soul. His world wavered for a heartbeat. Then blackness trimmed in gold shot along his entire spine, and he began to fall.

Somewhere in the darkness an annoying whine insisted that Shashtah had to wake up. :*Kashon's given you all the potions that were in the kit, and now we have to fly somewhere I can heal you. It's too dangerous for us to stay where we are.*:

Shashtah tried to sink back into the folds of the comforting darkness.

The voice returned. :*Dragonheart, we don't have time for this. We're in danger! You need to wake up. Now!*:

Shashtah filled his lungs rapidly several times. The air had the taste of cooling heat. *Night.* His eyes snapped open.

Kashon's worried face hovered just above Shashtah's nose.

:*Katrell says to tell you we need to get across the Border as quickly as we can,*: the voice, which Shashtah started to recognize as Tphah's, continued. :*Kashon wants to fly with you on Katrell, but Katrell's afraid of what happened the last time you rode on him. He doesn't want Kashon to face the Council again. They're arguing.*:

Shashtah blinked back the pain that throbbed in his head. He grabbed Kashon by his shirt front. He started to pull him closer, but then shoved him out of his way. He scrabbled along the sand until he found Tphah's head. He grasped as much of her muzzle as he could in his arms. :*Tell Katrell to tell Kashon I'll never fly on another Rider's Dragon ever again even if it kills me!*:

:*I nearly did kill you.*:

:*You didn't smear me on a kavir. You found some nice, soft sand to crash on. I'll be fine.*: Shashtah felt Kashon's hand on his shoulder and looked at him.

Kashon handed him the kit and pointed skyward.

Shashtah felt his body spring into action before he could think. He was halfway up the harness and onto Tphah's back when he realized that their century was engaging more demons than he could count directly over their heads. He secured the kit to her harness and braced himself in her straps. :*What's the Border look like from—*:

:*Kashon says you're too injured for me to try transporting with you. I'm to follow Katrell.*:

:*Follow Katrell where?*:

:*To the Border.*:

Shashtah's brow furrowed as he tried to think. :*Won't that take—?*:

:*We're almost there.*:

Shashtah watched Kashon mount Katrell and give them the signal to rise. *How is that possible? What did I do? What did we do?*

Shashtah clung tightly to Tphah's harness, fighting wave after wave of dizziness as she sprang skyward. Long after he was sure he could hold on no more, he felt Tphah settle onto a dune. He opened his eyes, freed the kit, and slid to the ground.

The sacred pile of sand rose before him.

:*Katrell says you're to add your sand to the pile. Then I'm to care for you until they get back.*:

Shashtah opened the kit, pulled out the pouch, and staggered over to the mound. Slowly, he poured his fistful of sand onto the dune. Then he turned around.

His Dragon was gone. In her place stood a sensuous woman, tears shining in her amber eyes. Scarcely two fingers shorter than him, she wore the coin-decorated headdress of a Dumnonian matron over the veil of a Priestess of the Mother. Beneath the translucent fabric, silky black hair cascaded to her shoulders, perfectly framing her exquisite face. An inky black dress covered with flecks of sparkling bronze hugged the enticing curves of her body, leaving almost nothing to his imagination. Her delicate right hand covered her mouth as her left hand removed her headdress and veil in a single, elegant motion and tossed them on the sand.

Shashtah dropped everything and held out his arms.

The woman ran to him.

Shashtah clutched her to his breast and buried his face in her hair. :*Tphah.*:

:*Dragonheart!*: The Prophetess's tears spilled onto his shirt and mixed with his blood.

:*Hush.*: Shashtah took her hands and placed them against the sides of his head. :*Nothing's wrong with me a little magic won't fix.*:

:*I'm only a Priestess, not a Healer. I don't have enough power for this!*:

:*Have a little faith, Prophetess. You've put me back together before. You can do it again. You're the only one who knows where all the pieces of me go.*:

Tphah took a deep breath and closed her eyes.

Shashtah felt his skin tingle as her magic enveloped him. His pain vanished, and he heard the cacophony of a battle only a few leagues away. "See? I told y—"

Tphah's lips pressed against his, cutting off the rest of his sentence.

Shashtah lowered her onto the sand.

Tphah wrapped her powerful arms around him so tightly he could scarcely breathe.

Then again, breathing was the last thing on his mind. He worked his hands up her body until his fingers gripped her throat in an imitation of the draconic lovemaking hold.

Tphah fought against her instincts, struggling to stay in her humanform. Her forked tongue flicked out and licked the perspiration from his cheek. :*How can you still love me?*:

:*How could I not?*: Shashtah released his hold on her throat and nestled against her breasts. Having dreamt of her humanform's touch for so many rotations, he had no desire to force her back into her dragonform.

Tphah settled firmly into her human shape. She ran her hands over him. :*Is everything where it should be?*:

Shashtah grabbed her fingers and kissed them. :*I don't know whose idea it was to turn you into a flying emergency kit for me, but that was genius! Body, mind and soul—I could never find a more perfect partner.*:

Tphah smiled as she nuzzled him. :*You know exactly whose idea it was. Only one Dumnonian is brilliant enough to come up with that plan. Of course, it helped that I knew who my Rider would be so he knew what skills I needed to have.*:

Shashtah rolled so she was under him. :*An extraordinary teacher and a perfect student. I'm the luckiest Rider ever to fly for Dumnonia.*: He pressed his lips against her mouth once more, marveling at how flawlessly their bodies fit together.

Tphah returned his kiss with the full force of the power of the magnificent Priestess she was. :*I don't care how hungry I get. I'll never risk you like that ever again!*:

Light flared in Shashtah's heart. He was fairly certain that the combination of their magic was going to blow him into a million grains of sand, but he didn't care.

"You seem to be feeling better," Kashon's amused voice laughed directly behind him.

Shashtah broke their kiss, scrambled to his feet, helped Tphah rise, straightened his robe, and turned to face his friend.

"You can hear, too," Kashon observed. "That's a definite improvement."

Katrell in humanform, a pack slung over his shoulder, stood behind Kashon in a Dragon's traditional place. His face wore the grin of someone with a secret he simply had to tell.

Shashtah realized that the sounds of the battle had ceased. "You won, I take it?"

Kashon inclined his head slightly to hide the flash of pride in his eyes. "The fiends sent to attack you didn't expect to find an entire century in their faces."

Shashtah's eyes widened. "You called up our whole century to defend us?"

A nervous laugh rattled in Kashon's throat. "The century sort of called itself up. Tphah's scream was a bit loud. Poor Katrell had to spend most of the battle arguing with all of the other centuries to keep them from showing up, too. It's a good thing we had Bahktarah with us. He and Salene are organizing the search of the battlefield so I could check on you."

Katrell could stand it no longer. He dropped his pack to the ground, pulled something rather large and bloody from it and dangled the prize in front of Tphah. "I thought you might like this."

Kashon pulled Shashtah out of harm's way as Tphah lunged at the gift. "KATRELL!" he bellowed. He shook his head. "You nit!" He led Shashtah a wingspan away from the Dragons, careful to keep his friend's back to Tphah as she greedily devoured Katrell's offering. "Was Tphah able to put you back together? Or should I send for a Healer?"

"I'm fine," Shashtah assured him.

Kashon looked skeptical.

Shashtah absently studied his blood-and-grime spattered robes. "Well, I'm at least as fine as I suppose most Trainees are after they return from Mount Cinnamar."

"I got worried a couple of days after you left when Katrell started repeating over and over again that you'd be okay. What went wrong?"

Shashtah extended his hands like a supplicant. "What went right?"

Kashon, clearly dissatisfied with the answer, waited for Shashtah to try again.

Shashtah threw up his hands. "All right! I think we got lost."

Kashon raised an eyebrow but remained silent.

"I've never traveled to Mount Cinnamar without using warps," Shashtah elaborated.

Kashon sighed. "It's a big mountain, Shashtah. At least compared to everything else in Cinnamar."

Shashtah nodded his head. "I know. But I couldn't open my eyes while Speedflying."

"First day of the Training, Shashtah." Kashon's voice dripped with exasperation. "When you can't see, you use Tphah's eyes."

Shashtah gestured at the space between them as if he were displaying a prize rug for sale. "And there we go again. No one explains anything to me until after it's become a problem. Reminding me to feed Tphah before we left Dumnonia would have been helpful, too."

Kashon froze. "She didn't eat?"

Shashtah shook his head. "No, she didn't eat. I didn't find out until we were well on our way."

"You should've returned to Dumnonia and fed her." Kashon stared at something over Shashtah's shoulder.

"Why would I have done that?" Shashtah demanded. "Every time we thought about disobeying a command, someone threatened to send us back to the beginning of the Training! Neither of us wanted to start over, so we pressed on."

Kashon winced. "I almost killed you."

Shashtah relented. "It's not your fault. I'm the one who didn't take care of Tphah. If I'd been sharing her diet, I would have known she hadn't eaten."

"And that's my fault," Kashon insisted. Words tumbled out of him like a sandslide. "With so many things demanding my attention, I hadn't finished reading *The Dragonlord's Handbook*. I shouldn't have allowed the change to your diet. I didn't think something so simple might get you killed. I should've stuck to tradition even if I didn't understand it. My Training wasn't normal, and Katrell's too muddled to remember what a normal Training is like. Tphah's never done this before, and you didn't go through the Training with Tkai. None of us knew what we were doing. I should've asked Bahktarah for help instead of just ordering him to keep an eye on you. I should've made you practice Speedflying for at least half a rotation. That way I would have been sure you and Tphah were working as a team before sending you off to Mount Cinnamar, but I knew you were in a hurry to get back to your boys —"

"Kashon!" Shashtah grasped his friend's elbow. "You're babbling like a Hatchling!"

Kashon blushed and glanced over Shashtah's shoulder again. "Katrell's having a bad night. He's worried sick about what I let happen to you and what I almost let happen to Tphah. Bahktarah tried to reassure him that I wouldn't be arrested and taken before the Council—"

Shashtah took a firmer grip on Kashon. "Pull yourself together. Tphah's fine. I'm fine. You're doing fine. You won the battle even though I've been causing you to have one of the worst turnovers of a century in the history of Dumnonia. Tell Katrell to calm down so you can collect yourself."

Kashon closed his eyes and bit his lower lip.

Shashtah ventured a glance at their Dragons.

Tphah had finished eating and was lounging beside Katrell on the sand, talking quietly with him.

Katrell stared at her, rapt.

Shashtah looked back at Kashon, who had reopened his eyes. "I don't know how you handle it."

"Handle what?"

"Once, when I was Bonded with Tkai, I found myself snapping at Shaharadesh as if I were the king. When I realized what I was doing, I thought he was going to kill me. He just looked beleaguered while Tphah roared something about how I sounded like Tkai before storming off." Shashtah grinned. "Tphah is very impressed by your ability to stand upright let alone think straight while being Bonded with Katrell."

Kashon smiled sheepishly. "I'm usually able to think well enough for both of us."

Shashtah poked Kashon in the breastbone. "And that is the truly important thing you should've made sure I understood before you sent me off alone with Tphah."

"What?" Kashon looked more puzzled than Shashtah had ever seen him.

Shashtah threw his head back and roared his amusement at the stars.

Behind them Tphah giggled.

"You really are as big of a nit as your Dragon!" Shashtah shook his head, thoroughly bemused. "You should have reminded me that the Bond works both ways. I'm a hopeless daydreamer on dragonback, and Tphah—"

Kashon's confusion turned to horror. "Goddess of War! I sent the most precious Pair on Centuria off alone to Mount Cinnamar with little more than a brain between them!"

"Yes, well, I suspect Katrell did the sending, and Bahktarah didn't object. Pairs are supposed to fly to Mount Cinnamar once they reach the Border, right? The Dragons were following tradition, just as you said you should've done." Shashtah clapped Kashon playfully on his upper arm. "Don't beat yourself up about it. It's not as if Tphah and I come with our very own Handbook. I suspect we'll have to figure things out as we go along just as you've done with Katrell."

Kashon grabbed Shashtah's hand. "I cannot treat you differently than I do the other members of our century," he said, repeating the words he had spoken on the first day of the Training.

Shashtah leaned in close so he could whisper in the Dragonlord's ear. "I think you need to rethink that policy. We aren't like other Pairs. It doesn't take Prophecy to see that we'll need a little more of your personal attention—at least until we figure out what will and won't get us killed."

Kashon pulled Shashtah into a full embrace. "I'll never risk you like that again!"

"You'll have to. You're my Dragonlord." Shashtah patted him between the shoulder blades. "I wish I could have been there for you when you needed me. I know how hard I've made your life."

"Katrell says you still won't be there for him unless we finish the Training." Tphah observed.

Shashtah startled, wondering how long she'd been standing in her place as his Dragon.

Kashon quickly released Shashtah and deftly guided him into Tphah's arms. "I'm sorry, Prophetess."

Tphah clutched Shashtah possessively. "Don't be. Katrell says my Rider is only half Dragon. He must have contact with fellow Dumnonians as well as with me and that you also need contact with fellow Dumnonians. Katrell says he's glad you two have become close friends. So am I."

Kashon blushed a beautiful shade of molten bronze.

Tphah pretended not to notice. "Katrell says you need to return to the battlefield and I need to lead my Rider to your basecamp before it moves again."

:*Does Katrell ever say anything for himself?*: Shashtah asked silently.

:*Quiet.*:

Kashon dropped into a salaam. "Yes, Prophetess." He gestured for Katrell to take his dragonform.

Katrell gave Kashon a salute that was far from serious but obliged.

Kashon's blush actually found a way to deepen. He strode quickly over to Katrell. "Remember: Tphah can shapeshift as much as she wants from now on, but you have to walk." He mounted his Dragon. "Quatar and Peri are still lying low, so there's no immediate rush. Our basecamp moves in five days, so try to make it before then." With that, they took to the air, flying back toward the battlefield.

Shashtah retrieved Tphah's veil and secured it to her head with her wreath of coins. He smoothed the silken folds until they were once again perfect. "There. Just as I've pictured you in my deepest dreams." He picked up the pouch and stuffed it back into the emergency kit. "Where is our basecamp anyway?"

Tphah gave him the image of orderly tents nestled atop massive whaleback dunes.

Shashtah thought he recognized the location from a couple of odd-shaped rocky outcroppings nearby, and his heart quelled at the distance from where he suspected they currently were. "Even if I run the whole way it can't be done before the basecamp moves!"

Tphah took the kit from him and concealed it in the folds of her dress. "I take it you didn't travel the Border much in your caravan days."

"No. Garesh avoided the Border and the basecamps. Except for once. That was the first time I saw you." Shashtah smiled at the memory.

Tphah laughed. "The fighting has been so heavy along the Border for so many millennia that there are even more permanent ground warps here than there are between the King's Camp and Daethia. Kashon made sure five winters ago that I knew where to find every one of those warps. We can make the trip in less than three days and never go faster than a leisurely walk. He just gave us extra leave."

"Of course he did." Shashtah said a silent prayer of thanks to the Lord of Light for his cherished friend.

Tphah smiled, clearly aware of what he'd just done. She lay her cool hand on his too-warm cheek. "It's all right, Dragonheart. Kashon loves us both in his own way, but his heart belongs to Katrell. He'll do everything he can to make sure you're never taken from me, and I'll never be jealous of him." She gave Shashtah a reassuring kiss. Then she wrapped her arm around his waist and, pretending not to notice how much he had to lean on her, began to guide him flawlessly over the dunes.

Patch

Chapter 4:

The Dumnonian Way

Until the end of their fifth year, the Hatchlings shall be cared for by the Dumnonian ruler. From the beginning of their sixth year through the end of their fifteenth year the Fledglings shall be remanded into the care of a specific Dragonlord for the purposes of socialization. From the beginning of their sixteenth year until the end of their twenty-fifth year, the Striplings shall be assigned to the care of an individual Dragonrider for training. At the beginning of their twenty-sixth year the young adults shall become eligible for Bonding. The ruler and the Council of Ancients may make special arrangements for the care and training of young Bronzes as necessary, but in general these guidelines should be followed.

—from *Handbook for the Dumnonian Rulers*
by Corin of Daethia

SHASHTAH AND TPHAH ARRIVED at Kashon's basecamp on the morning of the third day. The Prophetess had proven more adept than she'd promised at finding the warps, and Shashtah had discovered that he still loved dashing over the blistering sands in spite of the grueling trip to the Anvil.

Occasionally Tphah had landed to stroll with him, but she sensed his distress over Quatar and Peri and took to the sky whenever he became too agitated so he could run.

A dragonless aide to Kashon's court met them at the edge of the camp. "The Dragonlord says to congratulate you on the completion of the Training. Your orders are to spend a candlescar at the oasis of your choice so you don't scare your wards into the Afterlife when they see you, and then to report back here, claim your two miscreants and consider yourself on leave until the beginning of our rotation in the King's Camp," the woman panted with the air of someone extremely anxious to please a new—and infinitely preferred—master.

Shashtah saluted her in acknowledgment of the order. "Is it permitted for me to ask you to tell my two ruffians that I'm back and I'll be seeing them shortly?"

"No," she smiled. "But since you ask so prettily and since I have to pass your tent anyway, I'll poke my head in and terrify them for you."

Shashtah offered his thanks with a salaam. "Do you wish to tell me where my tent is now, so I don't have to take you away from more pressing duties when I return?"

She giggled. "Aren't you the polite one!"

Shashtah bowed again, even lower this time. "I would honor you even more if it were in my power, but, alas, I do not know your name."

The woman laughed. "Call me 'Patch,' because I'm good at plugging holes in supply lines and my keffiyeh is full of them!" She gestured at her much-repaired head covering.

Shashtah's right hand nearly touched the ground as he honored her with a salaam usually reserved for the royal court. "I'm deeply in your debt, Patch."

Patch's eyes flashed. "Yes, you are. But, while I must admit you tempt me sorely, I know better than to look twice at the Rider of a Prophetess." She bowed respectfully to Tphah, who regally inclined her head in a thinly-veiled threat.

"I'll remember my obligation to you," Shashtah swore.

"See that you do!" Patch grinned. "Column five, row five! The Dragonlord said it'd be easier for you to remember if the numbers were the same." With that she turned abruptly and bustled back into the camp.

Shashtah, uncertain whether Kashon was teasing him or trying to be helpful, motioned for Tphah to shift to dragonform. :*Do you know Karaif's?*: He climbed onto her back and settled his legs into her harness.

Tphah sprang into the air and gave him the image. :*One of Kashon's favorite spots.*:

:*Nice and easy this time, eh?*:

:*Yes, sir!*: Tphah piped. She spiraled around him, barrel-rolled into a steep climb and, as their images blurred together, burst into the air above the oasis, diving straight for the turquoise water.

:*Tphah! The idea of going through the Training was so you wouldn't kill me!*:

Tphah laughed as she splashed into the desert spring. :*Patch was right. You are pretty rank. Swim!*: She paused, her eyes filling with concern. :*Or don't you know how?*:

Shashtah let go of her harness, scrambled out of his wet robe, threw the garment over her back and took to the water like a pupfish. :*Wash my robe while you're waiting, woman! Or don't you know how?*:

Tphah splashed him with a swish of her tail. :*Wash it yourself!*:

Shashtah dove beneath the clear water, delighting in the feel of moisture against his dry skin. When he surfaced, the robe, as clean as it was going to get, was hanging from the top of a date palm.

Tphah, in dragonform, stood beneath it.

:*Are we going to get into a shapeshifting duel over this, or are you going to take that down from there?*:

Tphah carefully lowered the robe onto a rock near the water's edge.

Shashtah swam to where he could touch bottom, then stood up and, water glistening on his bronzed body, strode ashore.

:*A shapeshifting duel does sound like fun, though.*: Tphah shifted to her humanform with only a sheer, bronze-colored silken veil for clothing.

"Vicious Dragon!" Shashtah laughed.

Passion glinted in Tphah's amber eyes. "Last chance before fatherhood calls!" She ripped off her veil and threw it to the sand.

Shashtah leapt at her. The skin on his back shifted to scales. His fingers became talons as they closed around the steely muscles of her arms. He twisted midair so his body would break her fall as his weight carried them to the ground.

":*Dragonheart!*:" Tphah pressed her lips against his, breathing the power of the Mother into him.

Their shapes blurred between their dragon- and humanforms.

Shashtah didn't know whose instinct was guiding them nor did he care. His forked tongue caressed her cheek before his lips pressed against hers. :*I love you so much it hurts!*:

:*That's just the sand,*: Tphah laughed.

:*I can't believe how good it feels to be able to shift again! I don't understand why any of you would want to get trapped in humanform—*: Shashtah froze. Shaharadesh's voice slithered through his mind: *"A Dragon who conceives while in humanform will be stuck in that form for twenty-five winters."* He grabbed Tphah and pushed her away from him. He stared at his Prophetess in alarm. "Are you carrying fertilized eggs?"

"Why would I need to?" Tphah asked, genuinely perplexed.

"Shaharadesh once told me that he couldn't lie with Makara in her humanform unless she was carrying fertilized eggs!" Terror at the possibility that he might trap his Dragon so soon after completing the Training swept through him.

Tphah touched his face gently. "Why are fewer and fewer Dumnonians born every year?"

Instinct prompted Shashtah. "The dragonblood. And my father was full Dragon." He saw the confirmation in her amber eyes as he felt a bitter word forming on his tongue. "Am I a mule?"

:*Do you think that matters to me?*: Tphah kissed him, tears for his pain shining in her eyes.

:*No*,: Shashtah held her close, letting her wrap him in her love. :*In a way it's a relief*.: He broke their kiss and put his lips close to her ear. "People are going to be as envious of us as they are of Kashon and Katrell."

"More. You have no idea how jealous Kashon is that you can shift to dragonform as easily as he can draw a breath. It will take decades of study before he will know enough about magic to work that spell, and then it will cost him so much power that it would be sunstruck to use it on mere pleasure."

"Is that why he forbade me to shapeshift during the Training?" Shashtah asked.

"Of course not. You had to stay in humanform for the Training to work. So he gave you the order, and then made sure you had to follow it." Tphah arched her eyebrow. "You honestly didn't notice?"

"Notice what?"

"Kashon knows what it's like to live with someone who can't remember an instruction for two heartbeats." Tphah combed her elegant fingers through Shashtah's damp hair. "When we started our Training he put the same spell on you to keep you from shapeshifting that he uses on Katrell when he needs him to stay in humanform. He lifted it at the Border when we returned from Mount Cinnamar."

"Why that deceitful—!" Shashtah stopped mid-thought. He couldn't decide whether to be angry or grateful. "He really should have me flayed alive."

Tphah smiled at his mixed emotions. "I think he has another plan for you. He really is the only Dumnonian who's any good at thinking."

"Yes," Shashtah agreed.

A wicked smile curled across Tphah's lips. "But thinking isn't what I care about." The fangs of her half-dragonform closed on Shashtah's neck.

Shashtah changed to dragonform in unison with her. His wings clasped firmly against his back, he clutched at her with arms and legs as she flapped wildly in a feigned attempt to get away from him.

Tphah's tail tightened around his as she released her grip on his neck and crooned her pleasure at the sky.

Shashtah's call answered hers as the Mother's Blessing washed over them.

Tphah nipped playfully at his neck. :*You are the most splendid lover who's ever lived!*:

:*How would you know?*: Shashtah teased. :*You've never done the Mother's Dance with anyone but me.*:

Tphah curled protectively around him. :*Well, there's Katrell. But he doesn't really count. He's just my teacher.*:

:*He taught you well.*: Shashtah resumed his humanform and lay, staring at the palm fronds as they danced against the clear, blue sky. :*So I'll never sire my own children?*:

:*No. But Fate has granted you a little Prophet and a not-so-little Daethian instead.*:

:*Which is your way of reminding me I should get back to my orphans.*:

:*They're not orphans,*: Tphah cautioned. :*We can't forget who their true father is even if we don't dare tell them.*:

Memories of pain, terror and the sickening touch of the Dark One sent a shiver through Shashtah's soul. Just a few scant rotations ago his god's power, so diluted in his mortal body, had only been able to join imperfectly with the magic of the Elven King and the Lord of Daethia to lock the evil deity in agony within Mount Cinnamar. The White Wolf, perhaps the greatest Wizard of Corin, might have had the power to make the spell permanent, but the elusive Wizard had refused to expose himself to the Dark One. *With good cause,* Shashtah admitted.

:*Rinse off, and put on your robe,*: Tphah suggested, distracting him from his morbid thoughts. :*In this heat, you'll dry before we get to camp.*:

Shashtah obeyed. :*Let's go. I've been shirking my duties for too long.*: He climbed to his place at the base of her neck, delighting in the feel of her warm metal hide against his thickened skin as his scarred legs gripped her firmly.

Tphah hurled herself into the air. She glided, almost wistfully, in a circle around the oasis.

Shashtah gave her an image of Kashon's basecamp and smiled with satisfaction as almost instantaneously her image blended with his.

Shashtah paused outside the entrance to his assigned tent in a hopeless attempt to collect himself. His foster sons—one scarcely five winters old and one just a few rotations out of what should have been his mother's egg—lay inside. Gifts from a Daethian woman and a Dragon, both killed shortly after giving birth to the Dark One's sons, Shashtah doubted whether he had spent a full day with either boy before he had abandoned them in a world they didn't understand. *What must they think of the Dumnonian Prophet, the trader-turned-Dragonrider, the foster father they do not know?*

Tphah's hand pressed against arm. She smiled reassuringly. :*They're just boys. Demigods, but still boys. You remember what that's like.*:

Shashtah pulled aside the canvas flap and stepped inside.

The tent would have been spacious if Shashtah and Tphah had been the only occupants. Richly-colored rugs, woven with legends of Tchang, Tphah's ancestor and the first Dragonprophet, and his Rider, the Dumnonian king Bahakesh, covered the floor. Cooking utensils were neatly arranged near a small brazier to the left of the entrance. Just beyond the center of the tent a polished oaken couch, shaped vaguely like a throne, held embroidered forest-green cushions. Beside the throne someone—probably Patch—had placed Shashtah's pack, which held the few belongings he had managed not to lose. The absence of a chamber pot suggested that Patch had removed that on her visit as well. Two cots for children took up much of the space behind the throne, but they looked as if they could be collapsed to make a little more room.

:*Kashon supplied the rugs and tapestries.*: Tphah's amber eyes twinkled with glee. :*He and Katrell had a nasty experience with their first tent that still sends them into fits of giggles if you mention it.*:

Shashtah made a mental note to mention it the next time he had the chance, though he suspected he would forget. :*Tell Katrell to offer our deepest appreciation to Kashon.*:

:*I will as soon as he stops snickering.*:

The boys lay stretched out on the cots, faces buried in their folded arms. A small turban lay where it had fallen on the floor near Quatar.

Shashtah cleared his throat. "I hear you two had some problems while I was away."

The children scrambled to their feet. Quatar stared sullenly at the ground, but Peri rushed forward and launched his small body straight at Shashtah's chest.

Shashtah caught the dragonboy.

Peri, his shape blurring between his human- and dragonform in his agitation, twined his small body as far as it would go around Shashtah's ribs and neck. "Motherrider!"

"Not anymore," Tphah growled.

Shashtah silenced her with a put-upon look. "Hello, Peri." He pulled away just far enough that he could stare into the dragonboy's solid, nauseating green-colored eyes.

Peri's face clouded. The youngster sniffled. "The Dragonlord almost . . . cut off . . . Quatar's hand!" He buried his face against Shashtah's neck.

Shashtah rocked Peri gently from side to side. "Hush. The Dragonlord said your quick thinking gave him the excuse he needed to make sure that didn't happen. You were an extremely brave little Dragon to protect Quatar like that, and I'm very proud of you."

Peri settled into his humanform, dried his tears on the back of his wrist and licked the moisture off his hand. "You're not mad at us?"

"Sands, no!" Shashtah pegged his charges with a quelling glare. "Unless either of you is planning to take something that doesn't belong to you again."

Both boys shook their heads in frantic denial.

Shashtah smiled. "All right, then. Past's past. Let it go. We'll do everything we can to make sure you both stay in one piece the next time Tphah and I have to be somewhere else. Deal?"

"Deal!" Peri chirruped promptly.

Quatar nodded his dark head but somberly stared at the rug.

Shashtah shot an imploring look at Tphah.

The Prophetess tugged at Peri's sleeve. "How would you like to come with me and practice hunting in your dragonform? I think you can trust my Rider to look after Quatar while we're gone."

Excitement glittered in Peri's putrid-green eyes. He glanced briefly at Quatar, and then held out his arms to Tphah.

"Let's see if we can scare up something big enough to call 'dinner.'" Tphah grinned as she took Peri from Shashtah and carried the dragonboy outside.

Shashtah sensed the uncertainty and despair in Quatar. Garesh had always had a simple cure for such moods in a child. Shashtah wandered over to where his trousers, shirt and keffiyeh were folded tidily on top of his desert boots at the far side of the tent. The leather thong Tphah had given him to serve as an agal when he Bonded with Tkai rested beside his boots. His elaborately carved, brightly-colored belt lay atop the clothes. "Get undressed." Shashtah picked up his tooled leather strap, tracing the legends of the greatest heroes of the Dumnonians with his fingertips. He studied the stories for a heartbeat, then returned the belt to the pile. The clothing seemed so strange to his touch, as if it belonged to another man. *I suppose it does.* He picked up his leather thong and tied it around his head to keep his hair out of his eyes. He started to remove his

Initiate's robe, then noticed that Quatar was leaning over his throne, bare buttocks in the air. "What are you doing?"

"Getting ready for you to beat me."

"Do I need to?"

Quatar straightened and stared at Shashtah, confused. "Why did you tell me to get undressed and pick up your belt?"

Shashtah smiled reassuringly. "I told you to get undressed because Dumnonians find it a lot easier to exercise in this ridiculous heat when they aren't wearing clothes, and I picked up my belt because it's a gift I received from my parents when I left on my first mission into Cinnamar. I haven't been without it this long since they gave it to me."

"Exercise?" Quatar frowned suspiciously at Shashtah.

"You told me that you wanted to be a Dragonrider. Have you changed your mind? I could teach you how to be something else, but I thought I could start with teaching you the Ban-kai stretches."

Quatar's irrepressible curiosity overcame his misgivings. "The Dumnonian Battle Dance?"

"Yes."

Quatar bounced a dagger-length off the carpet in excitement. "Show me!"

Shashtah stripped off his robe and let it fall beside his clothes.

Quatar grew still.

Shashtah realized that the boy was staring at the hideous scars on his legs. "Oh, sands! I should've warned you."

Worried brown eyes focused on Shashtah. "Did you get those because of me?"

Shashtah hastily crouched and gripped Quatar's shoulders. "I gave myself these scars during the Training. They identify me as Tphah's Rider."

"But you didn't have scars like that when you rode Tkai."

"No. I didn't." Shashtah's eyes clouded with regret. "I should have, but I didn't go through the Training with her. That was an extremely bad decision on my part. I couldn't take care of her, and she couldn't take care of me—and because of that she died. I don't want that to happen with Tphah, so I went through the Training with her and earned these scars. Now, please. Stop worrying about the past and concentrate on the present. All right?"

Quatar nodded but stared at his toes.

Shashtah lifted the boy's chin until he was able to look into his troubled eyes. "The Ban-kai stretches are a series of movements designed to build the muscles a Dragonrider will need in combat. In battle nothing happens in a set pattern, so you can do the stretches in any order you like. What muscles do you want to work on first?"

Quatar shrugged.

"The shoulder muscles!" Shashtah declared enthusiastically, trying to recapture the boy's earlier excitement. "Good choice! Now, turn around and let me feel what you have to start with."

Quatar obediently turned his back to him.

Shashtah's hands traced the shape of the small but impossibly well-developed muscles. "Impressive. You're much further along than most Dumnonian children your age. The elves have taught you well. Now, feel my shoulders to see how a warrior's muscles should be shaped." He twisted so his back was to Quatar.

The boy's hands hesitantly touched his scar-crossed shoulders.

"Bear down, lad. You aren't going to hurt me."

The hands increased their pressure.

"The main thing I want you to notice is that I'm left-handed. This means some of my muscles are backward from the way yours will be. Now," he turned to face Quatar, "listen carefully: The Ban-kai stretches are supposed to be something fun that you enjoy and that make you feel good. If you don't like doing them, they won't work. So, when you want to stop, just tell me. I will only get mad if you need to stop and you don't say something. Understand?"

Quatar nodded again.

"Good," Shashtah smiled. "This move is called the 'Flying Dragon.' Hold your arms out like a pair of wings." He stood up and extended his arms.

Quatar mirrored Shashtah.

"Now move your arms up and down, like you're pretending to be a Dragon in flight."

Quatar gave an experimental flap.

"Slower. Like this." Shashtah waved his powerful arms gracefully in the air. "Push up, as if someone is trying to hold your arms down by sliding their hands from your elbows to your fingertips. Then drop your wrists and press down until your arms are at your sides." He displayed the exercise again with an exquisite fluidity of motion that left the boy staring at him open-mouthed.

"I can't do that!"

"If you practice as long as I have you'll be able to do all of the moves without even thinking about them. It's called the Battle 'Dance' for a reason. Now, try again." This time Shashtah knelt behind Quatar and applied pressure to his arms where he wanted the boy to imagine it. "Up and down. Up and down. Good. Now, try it by yourself."

Quatar obeyed with better results.

Shashtah stood up and tousled Quatar's hair. "Very good!" He circled until he was standing in front of him again. "Now, we repeat the move until we're both ready to drop!" He spread his arms and mirrored Quatar's movements. When the boy no longer needed to think to perform the maneuver correctly, Shashtah began to talk to take the child's mind off his growing fatigue. "Our century is on leave this next rotation. The king likes off-duty Dragonriders to travel so we can see different locations in case we need to transport there. It also eases the strain on our food supply. There are four of us in my household and twenty days. I thought we could each choose a place to spend five of those days. Where would you like to go?"

"To see Adrial!"

Shashtah hid his sudden panic at the thought of returning to Tor, the capitol city of the Dragonslayers, especially with Tphah. While the Elven Princess, Lady Adrial, might be delighted to see the boy she had raised from infancy, her new husband, Lord Criton, would probably be less than pleased to lay eyes on Shashtah since their last encounter had left the ruler of Daethia all but paralyzed with eternal pain. Then there was the not so little matter that most of the Kyondoca, Daethia's elite guard, still wanted to execute Shashtah after his misadventures in Tor with Tkai. "Wouldn't you rather go to Mount Paradin to watch the Galantites mine ore?" he suggested, hoping to spark Quatar's interest in a relatively safer destination. "Or to Krillion to see the caravans trading with the thieves? Or to Rashtar to find some barbarians? Or to the Northern Wastes to hunt for the Isle of the White Dragon?"

Quatar's eyes widened with wonder. "No one ever let me go outside the Elven Kingdom!"

Shashtah's heart lightened as he saw Quatar's imagination take over and supply a thousand other possible—and infinitely safer—destinations. "Dumnonia is not the Elven Kingdom, and Dumnonians are not elves. As the foster son of a Dragonrider you'll have more freedom than you could ever imagine. We are the people of the Desert—a harsh land with harsh laws and even harsher judges. We are free as the wind: Dragonriders—soaring high above the dunes, carrying 'Eternal Death to the Dark One.' Yet a single mistake up there—" he flicked his imaginary wings upward, "or down here," he lowered his arms, "and we can pretty much count ourselves dead—or worse. We are a poor people, living always on the verge of starvation. We have very little. Look at this tent. I don't own the canvas or the rugs or even the cots. Besides the leather strap that I use to secure my keffiyeh, the only piece of clothing that I can truly call mine is my belt." He saw Quatar hesitate briefly in the exercise at the mention of the belt, but something beyond Shashtah's control was singing through his blood in time with the chanting of his voice. Unable to stop the sermon, he went on. "Because we have so little, what we do have means that much more to us than it would to an elf. Dumnonians have three basic things that are extremely important to them. First are the Dragons. My people gave up food and comfort to sit out here on the sand, Bond with the Bronzes and soar through the skies! There isn't a Dumnonian alive who wouldn't die rather than see a Bronze miss a single meal. Even the dragonless Dumnonians and their followers spend their entire lives caring for the needs of the Dragons. I grew up in a dragonless camp, running caravans between Dumnonia and Krillion. We'd eat our fill off the trees in the Great Woods while we bargained with the elves and Galantites and Krills and Daethians for whatever our people needed most. Then we would nearly starve to death running those supplies to the oases where support personnel would pick them up and convey them to the secret locations of the basecamps along the frontline. We dreaded to take even a single bite from the packs of our laden camels for fear that a Dragon or Rider might need that food to live. We'd take inedible items in trade from the supply personnel and run them back to Daethia with nothing more than conjured manna to live on.

"Second, we have each other. Dumnonians tend to Bond with other Dumnonians almost as surely as Riders Bond to Dragons. Male or female, we don't care. Blood-related or not, we don't care. We may fight with each other, but we always fight for each other. Kashon—"

Quatar's lower lip trembled as he stood very still, dripping with sweat, his arms hanging limply at his sides.

Shashtah ceased his own movements and crouched before the boy. "Kashon and I share a Bond that is formed by mutual respect and trust and love. Because of that Bond he was willing to look after you as if you were his own son, protecting you, caring for you, and even disciplining you while I was unable to do so. If I should die, he would take you into his household the way a Dragon takes a Rider under its wing.

"Third," Shashtah's voice droned on, "Dumnonians place tremendous value on the few simple possessions they do have. Something that may mean absolutely nothing to you, having grown up in a land of plenty, may have cost a Dumnonian more than you can imagine.

"Night after night the Dragonriders fight the Dark One's fiends, often at the doorstep of their vile mountain, while the Daethians sit entrenched, defending the border of their wealthy land. You can hear the difference between our peoples in our battle cries. Which one calls to your soul? 'May the Light Save Us!' or 'Eternal Death to the Dark One!'? What do you want your battle cry to be? Dumnonians don't wait for gods to save them. We don't wait for war to come to us. Of all the peoples on Centuria, only we carry the war to the Dark One. And," he paused, watching as Quatar squirmed, "we do not take what a fellow Dragonrider and his Dragon have paid for with their blood."

Quatar collapsed into tears. "I'm sorry! I didn't know!"

Shashtah embraced the distraught boy. "It's my fault. I didn't teach you." He brushed away the child's tears and automatically licked the moisture from his fingers. Quatar's tears tasted far saltier than Shashtah's own. The boy would never be able to reclaim his own body's moisture the way a Dumnonian could. *One of many details that will make it very, very difficult for him to survive in the desert.* Shashtah chose to worry about that problem later. "There. Feel that?" He pressed his left hand to Quatar's chest and fancied that he saw a dim light flicker there. "That's a Bond forming between us."

"But I'm not a Dumnonian," Quatar pouted.

"Perhaps being a Dumnonian is not so much a matter of race as it is of attitude."

Quatar leaned his head against Shashtah's shoulder.

Shashtah held him close, letting him feel his protective love. After a while he put his lips close to his foster son's ear. "What do you say we dress, get some water and find a warm dune to lie on before our muscles get any stiffer?"

Quatar looked at Shashtah warily. "What can we pay for the water with?"

Shashtah smiled his approval. "You learn fast. That's good. You'll have to. Now, listen carefully: Dragonriders and their households are entitled to have their basic needs supplied by the king and the Dragonlords. I pay for your water with my blood—so don't be greedy. Ask for what you need—no more. Accept what you are given graciously and with profuse thanks—even if it is less than you need: It may be all someone has to give. And, when you can, pay them for the gift many times over so they can be generous to others in your name. If you become well-liked by the traders, their followers and the support personnel, if you form Bonds with them, you'll find that you don't need much more to survive." With that, he set Quatar down. "Now, get dressed." Shashtah rose, made his way across the tent and slipped into the clothes he had discarded beside the Anvil what felt like a lifetime ago. He tugged on his boots and tied his keffiyeh into place. As he tightened his belt a bit more than he used to, he grinned at the embarrassed look on Quatar's face. "Come on." He placed the turban on Quatar's head and held out his hand. "Let's see how much water the blood I've shed so far will buy."

Quatar hesitated a heartbeat, then gripped Shashtah's fingers with his small yet already powerful hand and let the Dragonrider lead him outside.

At sundown Tphah, dressed in the practical garb of a Dumnonian warrior and a pack slung over her shoulder, found Shashtah and Quatar, lying shamelessly on a star-shaped dune, half-asleep.

Peri broke free from her grasp and jumped on Shashtah's chest, startling him. "I taught Tphah how to hunt!"

Shashtah stifled a laugh. "How'd she do?"

"Okay, but she shouldn't show off so much," Peri said critically.

Shashtah lost any hope of controlling his merriment, spilled Peri onto the sand, and curled up in a fit of giggles.

Quatar scuttled out of the way. "Hey! Watch out!" He snagged his turban from where it had rolled and placed it back on his head.

When Shashtah remembered how to breathe, he ventured a glance at his Prophetess—and the look on her face sent him into spasms of mirth all over again.

Tphah's disapproving glare softened with relief. "You actually look like you might live."

Shashtah hugged Peri tightly with one arm as Quatar moved in close and demanded an embrace from the other one. "Did you save anything from this bountiful hunt for your half-starved companions? Or do Quatar and I have to fend for ourselves?"

Tphah dropped her pack to the ground. She reached inside and produced a rib from an addax, half-charred from a bolt of magical light. She tossed the rib at Quatar. "Peri said that's how you like your meat."

Quatar caught the priceless gift and bit deeply into the juicy flesh. "Uh-huh," he grunted around the enormous mouthful.

Shashtah tried not to look too queasy.

Tphah grinned and pulled out a leather pouch containing some of the largest dates he'd ever seen. "You think I'd forget so soon?"

Shashtah bowed his head. "Many thanks, Prophetess."

Tphah laughed. "It doesn't take Prophecy to figure out that you're famished!" She helped him to his feet and popped a date into his mouth. She grinned at the pleasure her gift brought him and kissed his lips as he chewed.

Shashtah swallowed, then kissed her back, enchanted at the touch of her humanform. He took the pouch from her and chose another date. "So where do you want to go while we're on leave? I told Quatar we could each pick somewhere to spend five days. I chose Krillion, and he wants to see Mount Paradin." He stuffed the date into his mouth.

"I want to see the Elven Kingdom!" Peri piped up.

Grief dulled Tphah's amber eyes. She backed away from them and shifted to her dragonform. "Do you really think the Council is going to let their only Prophetess leave Dumnonia?" she asked in ClearTalk so she would not hurt the boys' ears.

Shashtah nodded as he swallowed. "I most certainly do. If they're willing to send us into battle, they should be ecstatic about me taking you into our allies' territory while we're on leave."

Tphah nestled her armored head into the sand near his feet and breathed her scent at him. "Then I want to go to Tor."

Quatar let out a delighted whoop before Shashtah could reply, and then busily started to tell Peri for the millionth time about Adrial, daughter of the Elven King.

Shashtah knelt beside his Prophetess's head. "Dragonslayers, Tphah. Plus, I'm a dead man if the Kyondoca realize I'm there." He tried not to think about the last time he'd had a run-in with Daethia's elite guard—and failed.

"You're a shapeshifter," Tphah coaxed. "Besides, I want to see the great temples. I want to walk where Tkai walked, and I want to meet the Ruler of the Daethians who haunts your dreams."

Shashtah caressed her muzzle. "All right. We'll go to Mount Paradin first because I gave Quatar first choice. Then we'll go to the Elven Kingdom before Peri bursts. Then I'll take you to Tor. And then, if we're all still alive, we'll go to Krillion. I'm thinking of sending Quatar and Peri there on a caravan when we rotate up to the frontline."

"A caravan?" Tphah murmured, half asleep.

Shashtah nodded as he settled into the space between her folded forelegs. "That will give them some sense of my background and keep them out of everyone's way while we're not around. Plus Quatar tells me he wants to be a Dragonrider. He should start by learning to ride camels."

Laughter rumbled deep in Tphah's throat. She sobered mid-laugh and cocked her head as if listening to a silent voice. "Katrell says Patch wants to know if she can reassign some of the injured to our tent for the night."

Shashtah shrugged. "I'm perfectly comfortable, and you have two wings.

The boys will probably appreciate a night outside after all that time in our tent."

"Plus, they're less likely to get into trouble if I have them clamped safely to my sides." Tphah winked one of her inner eyelids at him. "You two! Over here!" she roared at the boys. She raised her wings.

Peri installed Quatar under one wing. "It will be all right," he assured him. He hugged his friend, and then took his place on Tphah's other side.

Tphah concealed them like a nesting dove.

Shashtah absently studied the constellations that paraded above them in the cloudless sky. Dragon, Warrior, Arrow, Sword . . . The names whispered through his mind, tangling with the memories of the hundreds of times they'd led him back to Dumnonia. He didn't want to force his way against them, away from the King's Camp. He wanted to stay right where he was. *Some nomad I make.* He shifted slightly in Tphah's loving arms and let the starry patterns carry him into the world of dreams.

King Jochia

Chapter 5:

With Friends Like These . . .

Little is known about the warping abilities of the Dumnonian Bronzes. Riders and Dragons have tried to describe the skill, but, since few possess the understanding necessary to discuss the workings of High Magic, their comments are largely unintelligible. We can assume that the skill derives from the spell Wizards use to transport instantly between locations in the material world. As with Wizards, the better known the destination, the less likely it is that the Dragon will wind up in an awkward position upon arrival. Since the Dragons have wings, they habitually aim higher than their actual goal to decrease the inherent dangers in this mode of transportation. Apparently the magic of the Bond allows the Riders to add their own experiences of how a destination is supposed to look to those of their Dragons, somehow decreasing the likelihood of an error. The type of error the Dragons and their Riders fear most is when a breakdown in communication occurs and their Bond "blurs" the images of two entirely separate locations. This can apparently result in the Bonded Pair arriving at an unknown height over a location that neither of them intended. It seems likely that Dragonriders are encouraged to travel when they are on leave so they can increase their own knowledge of the world and that of their Dragons, thus diminishing the possibility of such errors.

—from *Report on the Dumnonian Bronzes*
by Maelor of Corin

SHASHTAH AWOKE ONCE AGAIN to the unpleasant sensation of being dangled upside-down from dragonclaws. "Katrell! Why can't you ever just say, 'Good morn—?'" His protest was cut short as Katrell dumped him onto the sand. Shashtah tucked, rolled and came up in a fighter's stance.

Kashon, who stood beside Katrell, applauded. "Nicely done."

Shashtah saluted. "Thank you, Lord." He pawed the sand from his hair, retrieved his keffiyeh from where it had fallen and tied the cloth back into place. "I thought we were supposed to be on leave. Did I misunderstand your orders?" Real worry that he might have inconvenienced his friend yet again combined with a secret dread that he might have to disappoint his foster sons.

"You'd already know if you had," Kashon assured him. "Last night our century found a raiding party of vampires mounted on demon horses and hunting with hounds that breathed fire. We took out most of them near the Daethian border, then tracked the survivors back to their camp and finished them off."

"Casualties?" Shashtah asked, immediately concerned.

Kashon's face clouded. "None—yet. The Healers are working on the most seriously injured now. Kassandra's century volunteered to rotate up to the frontline early so we could pull back before we lost any of the wounded." He gave a dark laugh. "I think they really wanted to see if we missed anything. It was a tremendous haul." A rather draconic avarice glittered in his dark amber eyes.

Shashtah sensed a similar greed flooding through Tphah as Katrell gave her a mental picture of the hoard. "I wish we'd been there."

"So do I. But, since you weren't, I decided to take the time to come out here and bring you your share."

"Our share?" Tphah echoed in ClearTalk as she rose halfway out of the sand, revealing a curious boy under each wing.

Shashtah frowned. "But—"

Kashon emptied an impossibly large pile of gold, silver, gems, jewelry and magic items out of a small bag. "I instituted a new rule when I took over from Dameth in order to get rid of a lot of the gripes about who got what: We take turns choosing from the spoils on the battlefield just as we select food at a feast. Whatever is left of the big stuff when we decide to stop the distribution, we put in the Tribal Hoard. After that, Patch divides up the coins and other small pieces into equal amounts and deposits them to our accounts. You made full Dragonrider before sundown last night, so this pile belongs to you. I chose your items for you. I thought you might need your coins and gems with you rather than in your account while you're on leave. You can deposit what's left when you return."

Shashtah sank to his knees before the bounty Kashon had presented to him. "That's more than we ever made on a caravan run!"

Peri and Quatar, minus his turban, bolted forward and hovered near Shashtah's elbows, torn between their desire to see the treasure and their attempt to use his body as a barrier between themselves and the Dragonlord.

Tphah cracked her whiplike tail in the air as she trumpeted her glee. She shifted to her humanform, choosing a keffiyeh, shirt and trousers, and rushed forward to join her Rider and the boys.

At least fifty gold coins and almost twice that in silver glittered on the sand. A bright green emerald, a deep red ruby, a fiery yellow topaz and a rich purple amethyst sparkled in the light of the rising sun. A Galantite wolf with diamond eyes crouched ready to leap at imagined prey. A serpentine golden armband, fitted with a delicate spring so it would not restrict the use of the wearer's arm, challenged the desert dwellers with its blazing red, opal eyes and its carved ruby tongue. A brooch of wrought Galantite, twisted into an intricate pattern of vines and leaves, lay against a silver hair comb set with deep black jet. A ring decorated with feathers, a small magic cloak of the type the Elven Lord favored, a rather plain scarab similar to the one Kashon wore, and a liquid-filled vial—carefully marked as a healing potion—rounded out the treasure.

Kashon crouched on the far side of the pile. "You can divide it up any way you like, but I thought the ring might be useful to Quatar, since the rest of you can fly. It will stop him from landing too hard if he falls from a great height. Peri might like the cloak to keep him from being too noticeable in a crowd. The Council will probably feel better about Tphah traipsing around Centuria if she wears the scarab to protect her, and, with your talent for getting yourself sliced up," he winked at Shashtah, "that potion should come in handy." He held out the small bag. "The treasure will be easier for Tphah to carry in this." His chuckled at Shashtah's perplexed look. "I know Tphah can keep track of things, and I'm fairly certain you won't lose her."

Shashtah reached for the bag. His fingers closed around Kashon's left hand instead, and he pressed his lips to the Dragonlord's ring. "I can't possibly thank you enough!"

Katrell cracked his jaws in a dragongrin. "He hasn't shown you the best part!" He shifted to his humanform and removed something from a pack on his back. Grinning like a lion who'd just swallowed the king's favorite songbird, he held out a bundle that looked like a crescent moon wrapped in the remains of Kashon's old cloak. Carefully Katrell peeled back the fabric to reveal a magnificent scabbard, studded with diamonds and topaz, and a glittering scimitar, marked with the symbol of Shashtah's god.

Shashtah gaped. "I can't accept that!"

Kashon laughed. "Of course you can. I'm tired of you running around without so much as a camel stick! Besides, everyone in the century took one look at that blade and figured a Prophet like you was probably the only person who could wield it."

Shashtah handed the magical bag to Tphah, then reverently took the stunning scimitar from Katrell. "A thousand thanks."

"Put it on!" Kashon ordered, pure joy ringing in his deep, rich voice.

Shashtah draped the sword belt around his slender hips, tied the scabbard to his right leg, and hesitantly reached for the hilt with his left hand.

"Go on!" Kashon prompted. "Draw it! I want to see what a holy sword looks like in the hands of a Prophet!"

Obediently, Shashtah drew the scimitar from its sheath and pointed the tip at the sky. "Eternal Death to the Dark One!"

Light danced along the blade and covered them all with its glow.

Power flooded through Shashtah, warming the cold places in his soul. "It feels like a scimitar half its size!" He lowered the weapon, admiring the workmanship. Legends of the miracles of Leot, the sun god, flickered along the flat of the blade.

"It looks like it's made of gold," Katrell whispered.

"Can't be," Quatar piped up. "Gold would break."

"Maybe it's made of sunlight," Tphah suggested.

"Probably a special alloy of Galantite," Peri said. "We should ask the miners at Mount Paradin. If we ever get there. You promised Quatar."

Shashtah sheathed the scimitar, bent down and hugged Peri. "We'll leave as soon as we pack up these spoils and properly thank our Dragonlord." He reached out, plucked the scarab from the pile and pinned it on Tphah's linen shirt near her throat. "May it protect you if I cannot."

Quatar had already fished the ring out of the pile and shoved it onto the middle finger of his left hand by the time Shashtah turned back around. The boy marveled as the golden band shrank to fit him perfectly.

Peri put on his cloak and started shoveling handful after handful of coins, gems and jewelry into the magic bag.

Quatar looked at Kashon. "Would you mind if we saved as much of the treasure as we could until we reach Krillion, then buy all the food we can carry back with us?"

Kashon raised an approving eyebrow at Shashtah as the Dragonrider practically glowed with fatherly pride. "I won't mind."

The three Dragons squawked in protest.

Kashon pursued Quatar a handspan as the child flinched away. "Come here. I won't bite." He crouched and drew him closer.

Quatar shot a worried look at Shashtah but let Kashon pick him up.

Kashon balanced the boy on his knee. "That's a very generous offer, and I'm extremely pleased you made it. The Feast of the War Goddess takes place when we return for duty in the King's Camp, and our king will need all the food he can find with the multitude who will be at the celebration."

Unexpectedly, Quatar burst into tears at the praise. "I'm sorry! I didn't mean to be bad!"

Kashon hugged Quatar gently. "I know. And I know that you are going to try your very best to be a good Dumnonian from now on. Why, you are the only one among all of us who thought about using our newfound wealth to help our people!"

Shashtah grinned like a Hatchling displaying his first kill.

Quatar sniffled, wiped his tears from his face, jumped off Kashon's knee, ran to Shashtah, and embraced his foster father's leg.

Shashtah placed a quieting hand on Quatar's shiny black hair as he mouthed his silent thanks to Kashon. "Quatar, go find your turban."

Quatar scampered back to where his turban lay in the sand, retrieved the still tightly-wound strip of cloth and placed it on his head.

"You're good with children," Shashtah observed, studying Kashon thoughtfully. "Ever consider fostering any of your own?"

Kashon rose to his full height. "Now that I'm a Dragonlord, I have an entire tent of Fledglings to satisfy any paternal urges, though I leave most of their care to my staff. Our king doesn't exactly like me having anything to do with children, and I see no need to antagonize him over the matter." His dark eyes flashed in the sunlight. "Patch will make sure that your belongings are settled into whatever tent is assigned to you when you return. Unless you need to take anything with you?"

"No," Shashtah said. "I'd just lose whatever I took. There's more than enough treasure in that pouch to buy anything we need."

"So," Kashon drawled, as he tapped the toe of his right boot on the sand. "You're going to Mount Paradin. How are you getting there?" He stopped tapping.

"Well, we—" Shashtah faltered. "I mean—, I—" He hung his head. "Sands. Peri. He can't transport. I can't leave one of the boys alone while I fetch the other, and carrying both of them would be too dangerous. I didn't think."

"Fortunately I do think, and I remembered that you wouldn't." Kashon teased. "Also, lucky for you, Katrell knows how Shaharadesh teaches the Hatchlings to transport."

Katrell abruptly shifted to dragonform and leapt at Tphah. "Go!" he thundered.

The Prophetess instantly blurred to dragonform and disappeared. Within a heartbeat she was back, bugling her indignation at Katrell.

The older Dragon, who was busy rolling on the dune in a rather undignified fit of laughter, ignored her.

Kashon appealed to the heavens. "Will the two of you stop it?"

Tphah obeyed with a glower, but Katrell continued to snicker as he stretched out on the sand.

Kashon gave his Bond Partner an exasperated look, then turned to Tphah. "Where did you just go?"

The Prophetess blinked. "The Valley of Ancients."

Shashtah glanced from Tphah to Kashon. "That's where I went with Peri when my Bond broke with Tkai."

Kashon nodded. "The Valley must be tied to the magic somehow. Death and Bond Breaks produce an instinctive reaction for Dragons to transport themselves—and often their Riders—to that canyon. Apparently frightening the scales off a Hatchling causes the same instinct to function."

"I'm not a Hatchling!" Tphah protested.

Katrell examined his talons. "Compared to me you are."

"The age doesn't matter!" Kashon bellowed. "The transporting does."

Shashtah frowned. "But I transported into your tent when Corin scared me when I was Bonding with Tkai."

Kashon looked puzzled for a heartbeat, then his eyes widened and he blushed.

"You're a Dragonheart," Tphah explained. "When you're in dragonform you transport to the Valley the way Dragons do. When you're in humanform you transport to where Kashon is."

Bewildered, Shashtah asked, "Why would I transport to Kash—?"

"The place doesn't matter!" Kashon snapped, blushing even deeper. "The point is that once Dragons transport instinctively, they can figure out how to do it on purpose."

Peri handed Shashtah the magical bag.

"The problem I see with Peri," Kashon continued as he finally controlled himself, "is that either he's impossible to frighten or his mixed blood is inhibiting his instincts. He should have figured out how to transport by now."

"Maybe he just needs the right incentive." Shashtah crouched beside his fosterling. "Peri, take your dragonform."

Peri complied. The decaying green-colored dragonette, far smaller than any Bronze his age, looked quizzically at his foster father and squawked his curiosity.

Shashtah signaled for Tphah to reveal her harness. As soon as she did, he mounted her. "All right, Peri. It's up to you. Tphah and I need to go on leave. But I don't see how I can take one of you boys with me and not the other. So Tphah and I are going to transport to the Valley of Ancients. You have five heartbeats to meet us there. Katrell will keep the count. If you aren't there in five heartbeats, Tphah and I will be gone. We won't be back until the end of the rotation, so you two will be on your own out here in the desert until we return. Do you understand?"

Peri screeched.

"No!" Quatar shouted. "You promised we could see Mount Paradin!"

Shashtah shrugged. "That's up to Peri."

At Shashtah's signal Tphah leapt into the air. :*You are vicious, Dragonheart.*:

"Peri, follow them!" Quatar ordered.

The disgusting little mutant hurled himself after the Prophetess.

"ONE!" Katrell boomed, slapping his tail against the sand for emphasis, as Tphah gave Shashtah the image of the Valley and his view blurred with hers.

They burst into the air over the canyon, and Tphah quickly dropped to the Valley floor. :*Two . . . Three . . . Four . . .* : she counted silently, punctuating each number with a nervous crack of her tail.

"Five!" Shashtah called as Peri erupted into the sky with a startled shriek.

Tphah was immediately in the air again, circling the young Dragon. :*I'm giving him the image of Kashon, Katrell and Quatar on the dune outside the Camp.*:

Shashtah called the same picture to mind and said a silent prayer as three images merged in his head.

Quatar's cry of joy greeted them. One hand holding his turban in place, he ran forward. He released his headpiece and reached up to embrace the little Dragon almost before Peri had time to land. "You did it! You did it! We can go!"

Admiration sparkled in Kashon's eyes. ""You are ruthless! How did you know that would work?"

"I didn't." Shashtah slid to the ground. "I just gave Peri something to be afraid of and then put me and the Valley in the same place. I figured either his draconic instincts or his attachment to me would call him." He strode over to Kashon and draped his left arm around his Dragonlord's shoulders. "So, tell me," he asked in a low voice, "how did you get Tphah to be so completely terrified of Katrell?"

"I had nothing to do with it," Kashon said. "He has tones that can make her cower in the sand, startle into the air, or transport in utter shock. I have no idea where he learned them. Don't worry. I'm sure she'll sort herself out after a few winters now that she's Bonded to you."

"Only winters?" Shashtah glanced at his fosterlings and decided that they had settled down enough to try transporting to Mount Paradin. He embraced Kashon. "Thank you. For everything."

Kashon pounded him on the back. "See you in a rotation."

Shashtah broke away from his friend and strolled over to Quatar and Peri. "All right. Peri, I want you to fly out over the desert. Tphah will give you a picture of where I want us to go, and then you will merge your image with hers, just like you did when we came here from the Valley of Ancients. If you get lost, return to the Valley and tell Tphah where you are. We'll come back and find you. All right?"

Peri's wedge-shaped head bobbed in agreement.

Quatar started to climb onto the little Dragon's back.

Shashtah scooped up the Daethian boy. "You fly on Tphah with me."

Quatar gaped. "Fly on Tphah?"

Shashtah patted Peri's snout. He briefly considered trying to climb up his Prophetess's harness while carrying Quatar, then had a better idea. :*Give us a lift?*:

The Prophetess lowered her head to the sand and waited for Shashtah to scramble onto her broad, flat muzzle as he balanced Quatar on his left hip. She hoisted them up behind her neckridge.

Shashtah settled into place and shifted Quatar to his right thigh. He let the boy's legs dangle across his lap. "Hold on!" Shashtah warned unnecessarily as Quatar threw one arm around his foster father's neck and clamped his turban to his head with his free hand. Shashtah brought his left fist to his right breast and shot his arm skyward in a reflection of the command to rise.

Quatar squealed with delight as Tphah gave a mighty leap and slapped downward with her powerful wings.

:*Ever been to Mount Paradin?*: Shashtah inquired as they waited for Peri to join them in the air.

:*I've never been beyond the desert.*:

Shashtah's heart skipped a beat. *Kashon never took her anywhere on leave? How does he expect us to transport to Mount Paradin if she doesn't know where she's going?* He almost dismounted so he could ask Kashon what it was everyone once again assumed he knew, but Quatar was already bouncing with so much excitement that Shashtah could barely maintain his grip on him. :*That's okay,*: he assured Tphah, having absolutely no idea whether it really was. :*I've been there enough times for both of us.*: He called up his memories of multiple trips to the fabled Kingdom of the Galantites, the tumbling waterfall that was the source of the Ripon River, the intricate pulley system across the massive entrance that raised supplies from the forest floor and lowered priceless goods that had been fashioned deep inside the mountain. He had the strange sensation that another image overlaid his, an aerial view that was not supplied by Tphah. Almost before he knew what was happening, the images blurred, and they materialized in the cool, damp air over the Great Woods.

Shashtah glanced around to see if another Dragon was in the air with them. Peri flew just off Tphah's right wing, but otherwise they were alone. *Must be one of those stray memories from Tkai.* He gave the Dragons the command to land.

Tphah, Peri at her side, perched on the slope of Mount Paradin within easy walking distance to the entrance of the enormous cave.

The thunder of the waterfall made it almost impossible for Shashtah to hear himself think. :*Tphah, ask Peri to shift to humanform.*:

Apparently the Prophetess passed along the message because Peri was standing patiently, the cloak rendering him nearly invisible against the rocks, by the time Shashtah and Quatar climbed to the ground.

"Stop right there!" a gravelly voice ordered in ClearTalk as Shashtah set Quatar on the rugged slope.

Shashtah froze. "Shashtah, Dragonrider of Dumnonia, requesting permission to enter Mount Paradin to trade!"

"Shashtah?" the voice echoed. A stunted figure who looked like a petrified tree stump with a beard separated itself from a pile of boulders.

Quatar clutched tightly at Shashtah's left thigh while Peri blatantly ignored the order to hold still, rushed forward and latched onto Shashtah's right knee.

Shashtah's quieting hands pressed the heads of his charges against him. "Easy, Makkaba. You're frightening my fosterlings," his voice cracked in the Galantite tongue.

"Braver than you were the first time you saw a Galantite," the warrior crunched in the same language. "I thought Garesh was never going to catch you." The Galantite made a sound like a gale-force wind whistling through a stone chimney as Shashtah blushed. "So, you finally got that Dragon you were always dreaming about," she rumbled in ClearTalk.

"This is my second Dragon, Tphah," Shashtah presented the Prophetess with a flourish of his right hand. "I lost my first Dragon, Tkai, inside Mount Cinnamar."

Makkaba made a hissing noise like steam escaping through a fissure. "Bonded twice since I saw you last? My, it has been a long time."

"Over five years," Shashtah admitted.

"Closer to ten," Makkaba corrected. "We've extended the northern tunnels over a league since you used to meet me there."

Tphah took a closer look at Makkaba. "Friend of the family?"

"Something like that." Shashtah laughed a trifle nervously.

Tphah's head shot straight up. "Former girlfriend?" She shifted immediately to her humanform, complete with the coin-decorated headdress of a Dumnonian matron. She strode to her Rider, reached over Peri's head and grasped Shashtah's right elbow possessively.

"Ouch!" Shashtah squawked. "We grew up together, Tphah! We played in the tunnels while our parents traded! I've known her forever, nothing more. Let go! She's the daughter of King Jochia's Steward, and we need her help if we're going to get inside."

Tphah relaxed her grip, but she didn't take her hand off Shashtah arm.

A small avalanche rumbled in Makkaba's throat. "Fear not, Prophetess! That one was always too in love with Dragons to look twice at a tunnel rat like me." The Galantite guard peered at the boys, who stared with eyes as big as twin full moons at her from beneath the safety of Shashtah's arms. "So how does a Dumnonian trader wind up with a Daethian child and a mutant Hatchling in his company?"

Shashtah stroked his fosterlings affectionately. "That's a long story."

"Good! You traders are so much better at telling stories than most of the people who visit us." Makkaba eyed Peri with concern. "King Jochia will want to speak with you about the mutant."

Shashtah's eyes glittered as he scented a bargain. "Badly enough to give us four nights of food and lodging?"

"Lodging only!" Makkaba snapped. "The forest and river await your dining pleasure, you trader-spawned Krill of a Dumnonian!"

Shashtah laughed good-naturedly. "Deal!" He crouched low enough that the boys had to release their hold on him. He hefted the children into his arms. He handed Peri to Tphah and balanced Quatar on his left hip, making it impossible for him to draw his scimitar.

Makkaba noted the gesture with a wink, then trudged toward the entrance to the cave.

Shashtah suddenly heard Quatar's stomach growl over the thunder of the waterfall. "I'm sorry! I keep forgetting you're a Daethian. Here." He fished in his belt pouch with his free hand and came up with three of his leftover dates. "Eat!" He handed Quatar the fruit.

Quatar started to bite into the dried fruit, but then glanced warily at Shashtah. He twisted slightly and held out two of the dates to Tphah and Peri, who were walking behind them. "Do you want them?"

Peri gave Tphah a conspiratorial look. "No!"

"Thank you for the offer, young friend," Tphah said, doing her best to remain serious, "but we sated ourselves on our hunt last night."

Quatar, still looking troubled, glanced at Shashtah again.

The proud Dragonrider kissed his foster son's cheek. "Good lad! Go ahead. Eat."

Quatar promptly stuffed all three dates into his mouth.

Shashtah rounded a turn in the path, and the wonders of the entrance to Mount Paradin came into view.

Stone walkways ran the length of a cavern at least twice as big as the Valley of Ancients. Boats of all sizes were moored to stone wharves, loading and unloading their cargos. Elves, Daethians, half-elves, and Rashtarians bustled along the docks. No Dumnonian caravan was in evidence. Krills were noticeable by their absence. Galantite warriors patrolled the wharves and exchanged information with the guards at the entrance to the cave. Nearby more Galantites eased outbound boats onto the pulley system, lowered them to the Ripon and guided inbound crafts from the platform into the water a safe distance above the falls. Galantite children chased each other inside massive wheels that were connected to the pulleys.

Quatar forgot to chew as his eyes seized on marvel after marvel: splendid armor and weapons of various shapes and sizes, piles of gems and coins, jewelry of incredible craftsmanship, all flowing out of the mountain in exchange for wood, clothing, food and other items that could not be found in stone.

Shashtah ventured a glance at Tphah and Peri.

Both Dragons were salivating at the sight of the unbridled wealth.

Shashtah turned, faced them and tapped his foot impatiently until Tphah ran into him, nearly dropping Peri. :*Perhaps I should mention that the penalty for theft among the Galantites is death. Period. No appeal. Notice the absence of Krills?*:

Tphah apparently passed the information along to Peri since the dragonboy squawked and clutched at her neck.

Quatar glanced worriedly from Peri to Shashtah.

Shashtah put his lips close to Quatar's ear and repeated his warning.

"I won' take anythin' ever again!" Quatar swore around his mouthful of dates.

Shashtah hugged him tightly. "I know. I just wanted to warn you so you will be extra careful and help me keep a close watch on Peri and Tphah. Their instincts will be to hoard any treasures they can get their talons on."

Quatar swallowed and nodded vigorously. "I'll protect them!"

Makkaba guided them into a side corridor and led them through a network of halls and cross-passages. Eventually she opened something that resmebled a windowless cell door. She ushered them into a large, Spartan room that contained two large granite shelves, a stone table and four stone chairs. "I'll tell the king you're here." She ducked outside, closing the door behind her.

Tphah lowered Peri to the floor, surveying the room with a critical eye. "We'd be more comfortable outside."

"Yes," Shashtah admitted, "but we wouldn't get any farther than the docks. The Galantites monitor these rooms constantly. They know exactly what we brought in with us—even the contents of the magical pouch. They'll know if anything extra joins us during our stay, and they'll also alert us if anything that is supposed to be here vanishes."

"Security fanatics!" Tphah hissed.

"Wouldn't you be if you were sitting on the source of all the treasure in the known world?" Shashtah placed Quatar on one of the ledges. "I'm afraid these are the Galantite idea of beds. Usually you'll be so tired from hiking around all day, you won't mind. Makkaba should return shortly with a summons for me to appear before the king. There's no need for any of you to come with me. You'll just be bored with the politics of the Galantite court; it'll sound more like a rockslide than a language anyway. I'll arrange for someone to take you on tours of the various shafts and forges." He unstrapped his scimitar and handed it to Tphah. "See what you can find out about this—it would be rude for me to appear before King Jochia while I'm wearing it, especially since I don't know who its former owner was."

The Prophetess nodded at his wisdom. "When can we expect you back?"

Shashtah shrugged. "Talking to Galantites is a bit like talking to stones. They may pay attention to me; they probably won't. I advise against exploring on your own. Memories of my own choice to ignore my father's warning about that matter urge me to repeat his advice to you now."

A knock like a sledge hammer pounding against granite preceded the opening of the door. Makkaba poked her craggy head into the room. "The king will see you at once!"

Shashtah kissed Tphah on the cheek, whispering, "Wait here until I send a guide for you. It shouldn't be long." Then he followed Makkaba into the corridor.

"Nice little family you've acquired for yourself," Makkaba observed in her native tongue as she lead him through the twisting tunnels to the Throne Room.

"I wouldn't trade any of them for the world," Shashtah rumbled in the same language.

"How very Dumnonian of you."

Shashtah chuckled. "I am that, as we established long ago. Find anyone to replace me yet?"

Makkaba heaved her shoulders upward in what must have been a shrug. "I suppose it's amazing we miners ever have any offspring. We're all madly in love with our ore and gems and the products of our blacksmiths and jewelers. Hard for mere mortals to compete with things that last forever."

"I'm sorry," Shashtah apologized quietly.

"Don't be. You are what you are. That's what we all should be." With that, Makkaba showed him into a chamber with her best attempt at a salaam.

Magical torches lined the walls of the massive grotto served as the Throne Room of the Galantite king. Every kind of gem imaginable studded limestone columns that had been formed over centuries by carefully balancing the priceless jewels on stalagmites and setting them into tiny crevasses chipped into stalactites. Tiny brooks filled with oysters babbled happily as they flowed over veins of gold and silver imbedded in quartz, tumbling toward the spring where they would join the underground rivers that formed the source of the Ripon. An enormous throne of solid Galantite ore loomed at the far end of the cavern, and perched atop the throne, surrounded by what looked like several massive boulders but what Shashtah knew were the royal bodyguards, sat King Jochia.

Shashtah approached as close as he dared, then dropped in a deep salaam, sweeping the damp ground with his right hand. "Majesty!" he shouted in a crisp, clear voice that echoed through the grotto.

Jochia's rough-hewn face split into a grin. "So what brings the young scamp who forced me to marshal half of my miners to find him in the northeast tunnels back to my humble mountain?"

Shashtah smiled rakishly at the king. "Picked up a couple of my own scamps in my adventures and promised I'd take them wherever they wanted to go while I was on leave. My Daethian fosterling was raised in the Elven Kingdom and wanted to see how the fabled Kingdom of the Galantites compared."

"You're not planning to lose them in my mines, are you?" Jochia asked only half in jest.

Shashtah clasped his hands behind his back. "Not planning to, no. But it wouldn't hurt to send someone to show them around before they try exploring on their own."

"And how many guards do you suggest I pull away from their duties to show your Dragons and Daethian my people's secrets?" The king's solid sapphire eyes sparkled in the flickering light.

"Two should be enough," Shashtah bargained. "They know I'll personally have their hides if they get into trouble here."

"One," Jochia declared. "And I will personally have your hide if you cause me to stop production again."

"Deal." Shashtah dropped into another salaam.

Jochiah nodded at Makkaba, who backed out of the throne room and disappeared into the corridors.

Shashtah straightened, hoping the constantly shifting shadows caused by the torches hid the dread in his eyes. *:Tphah, King Jochia just sent Makaba to be your guide. Be nice. She knows more about this mountain than I ever will.:*

:Bet she doesn't know more about you.:

:Tphah . . . : Shashtah let the thought hang until he sensed her submission. He dragged his attention back to the king, realizing as he did so that he stood easily half again as tall as any of the Galantites. Lost in past memories, he'd failed to notice the height difference when he'd been talking with Makaba. *Sands! I must've grown at least two dagger lengths since the last time I was here.* "So why is the mighty Jochia bothering to bargain with the son of an insignificant trader about something I could easily have arranged with one of your dock wardens?"

The king's laugh rumbled through the grotto. "You always were a clever one. You're not just a trader's son anymore, either, Dragonrider."

Shashtah inclined his head in gratitude at the use of his new title.

"You come to me," Jochia continued, "claiming a mutant Dragon as a foster son. In my experience the Dumnonian king kills all mutant Dragons the instant he sees the eggs. How is it that this one lives?"

Shashtah took a deep breath. "Peri didn't hatch; he was born. My first Dragon, the Prophetess Tkai, the Leader of the Council of Ancients, died giving birth to him inside Mount Cinnamar. Her last request was that he be allowed to live. Even though he was a product of the Dark One's magic, I could see that his soul was unaltered by his physical form. So," he took a deep breath, "I bought his life with the pain of my own soul."

Jochia clenched his teeth. "No small price. I marvel that you agreed to such a trade. Perhaps you are the one we need."

"Need for what?" Shashtah asked, finally becoming wary.

The king squinted at him for a long time, then made a decision. "Follow me." He staggered to his sturdy feet and with an odd, rolling gait moved toward a tunnel.

Shashtah hurried after the bulky, yet remarkably agile, king.

Jochia led Shashtah through half-remembered tunnels and corridors, deep into the heart of the Dragon's Back Mountains. Guards stumbled along behind, more for form than from any real ability to protect their king if Shashtah decided to harm him. The regal Galantite had chosen to separate himself from his would-be protectors and put his person at the Dragonrider's mercy. Even though Shashtah seriously doubted that he could bring down the granite-like king in a single blow—or even in a dozen blows—he was extremely conscious of the confidence that was being shown in him and of how deeply that confidence was putting him in Jochia's debt.

Eventually Shashtah suspected he was being taken too far into the mines to return to the guest quarters by nightfall. :*Tphah, I'm going to be delayed at least overnight. I'm perfectly all right—you'll know instantly if I'm not. I'm among friends. Makkaba will know who is best to ask about my scimitar. Oh, and don't forget to feed Quatar!*:

:*Rather like having a puppy at times, isn't he,*: Tphah's voice chortled.

:*How do you know anything about puppies?*:

:*Your talking rock is here.*:

Shashtah said a prayer of thanks that Jochia's back was to him so the king could not see him blanch. :*You will be polite to her! Galantites can hold grudges as long as mountains stand. Anything you do to offend them will come back to haunt me. Don't touch anything, or I'll have to pull your thieving talons out myself before they slaughter you!*:

:*Not to worry,*: Tphah reassured him, oozing confidence through their Bond.

:*Let me know immediately if there's any trouble,*: Shashtah ordered, planning to worry anyway. They walked for several leagues, doubling back on their tracks occasionally as even the king took a wrong turn now and then. Finally Jochia led him through an illusionary wall near the end of the northern tunnel system. Shashtah stopped so suddenly the guards almost ran into him.

Dragon eggs of all sizes lay piled in alcove after alcove, chamber after chamber, and corridor after corridor behind the illusion.

"What is this?" Shashtah. "Tabo's hoard that Shantaclezad could never find?"

Jochia shrugged. "I doubt it. Look closely at the eggs. There's not a pure Bronze in the lot. Nor pure anything for that matter."

Shashtah hastily examined several shells. Each displayed signs of belonging to at least two and up to as many as twelve draconic species. "Mutants," he whispered.

The Galantite king nodded. "Every last Mother's son and daughter of them."

Shashtah frowned. "Why haven't you told Shaharadesh?"

Something unreadable flickered in Jochia's sapphire eyes. "You Dumnonians have some strange ideas about purity when it comes to your Dragon stock. We Galantites are a little more practical about the matter: Absence of flaws is one thing in a diamond, but without a flaw you'll never get a pearl. How many

Dumnonians would be left if you killed everyone whose blood was mixed with that of your Dragons?"

Shashtah narrowed his eyes suspiciously. "Why are you telling me this?"

Jochia leaned closer to Shashtah. "I knew Garesh when he was Bonded to Shantaclezad, and we both know which of that Pair was the Dragon, eh, Dragonheart?"

"My father was Bonded to Shantaclezad?" Shashtah steadied himself against one of the eggs. He drew his hand away almost instantly, as if he had been burned. "These eggs are hard! They're almost ready to hatch!" He glanced around him. The sheer number of dragonettes that were about to descend on Centuria chilled his heart. "I don't suppose the Galantites want to forget about mining and become a race of Dragonriders?"

An avalanche rumbled down Jochia's throat. "In your dreams, Dragonheart!"

"But there must be enough dragonettes in these caverns to mount half the population of Centuria!" Shashtah exclaimed in dread.

Hatred flashed in the king's sapphire eyes. "Probably the Dark One's intention. But the fiend didn't reckon with the elves capturing most of them and bringing them here."

Shashtah looked around again. "It would take decades to move this many eggs!"

"Millennia," Jochia corrected.

Shashtah shook his head in disbelief. "But Dragon eggs only take a rotation to hatch!"

"That," a crystalline tenor said in the High Tongue of Daethia, "is where I come in."

Shashtah looked up and saw a tall, wiry man walking toward them from an inner chamber.

The man's hair, originally black, now streaked with white, flowed down to the shoulders of his sapphire blue robe. A completely white beard hid half of the stranger's face. Piercing blue, Daethian eyes looked out at the world with an intelligence that Shashtah had only seen in the eyes of the shade of Corin and of the White Wolf.

"Who are you?" Shashtah asked in the same language.

The man bowed gracefully. "I am known to the Galantites as Balkar the Guardian. I keep the eggs from hatching with my spells, but we are reaching the limits of even my considerable power. I fear that the Lord of Plenty will be hard-pressed to provide food for this many new mouths if they all hatch at once."

"And you think the Dumnonians have a better chance?" Shashtah tried not to laugh in despair. Zed, the Lord of Plenty, had all the food anyone could wish for. Dumnonia had practically nothing. There was absolutely no way the desert folk could take in this many mutants even if he could convince Shaharadesh not to kill them.

The Wizard's face, unused to laughter, contracted into a smile. "I ask not for the Dumnonians' food but for their wisdom. When my magic fails—and it will—Centuria is going to need the answers to three questions: one, can these mutants be Trained; two, where can we find Riders for them who don't belong to the Dark One; and three, how can we best turn them to our advantage?"

Shashtah gave a low whistle. "A person could spend a lifetime answering such questions."

Balkar nodded. "But you seem inclined to start: You call a mutant by the name of 'foster son.' Can the mutant Dragons be Trained the way the Dumnonians Train the Bronzes? That is a question for a Dragonrider. Whom among our allies can ride them? That is a question for a Dragonlord. How can we use such a force to our advantage? That is a question for a Dragonking. Seek out the answers to each question and send them to me. I'm a methodical man, you see. I like things in order. This," he gestured at the contents of the caverns, "is about to become absolute chaos."

Shashtah swallowed hard. "When will your magic fail?"

The Wizard gave the question the consideration it deserved. "A decade. Maybe two. That's all. I've been shielding these unborn children for millennia, and even my legendary prowess with that spell has its limits."

Cobal! The soundless word formed on Shashtah's lips. *The consort of Shane of Corin! Best friend of the White Wolf! The Shield Master!* The epithets thundered through his mind. *Another Wizard returned from apparent death! How many more are in hiding? How many more have disasters waiting to happen, kept from hatching upon a dying world by powers grown frail with incredible age?*

Cobal saw the recognition in Shashtah's eyes and acknowledged it with a nod. "Corin performed the first part of this experiment by figuring out how Dumnonians and Bronzes could Bond. The second part has fallen to me, and I—" he gestured at the eggs again "—am too preoccupied to conduct it. Answer the first question for me, Dragonrider: Can your mutant be Trained like a Bronze? When you know the answer, I will still be here. Hurry, though, lest you find me in here alone."

Ten years! Peri is only a Hatchling! Panic seized Shashtah's heart as the numbers tumbled through his head. *Tphah was not presented to Dameth until she was six, and Kashon did not undertake her formal Training until she was sixteen. She is all of, what?, twenty-four now and not really old enough to be Bonded. How can Peri accomplish half of what he needs to before he's ten?*

Cobal laughed. "Someone who has cast spells with the Lord of Daethia and the Elven King is worried about Time? Oh dear, Jochia! You'd better tell your guards to stand ready. He's going to faint when he realizes he's been in here four days—"

"Four—!" Shashtah, instead of fainting, turned, shoved his way past the Galantite guards, and dove through the illusionary wall. He tucked and rolled to his feet on the stone floor of the tunnel beyond. :*Tphah! I'm sorry!*:

:*WHERE WERE YOU?*: came the mental scream.

:*Talking with a Wizard of Corin!*: Shashtah charged down the tunnel ahead of him, hoping he remembered the way through the dimly lit corridors. Something told him that Jochia and his guards would not be emerging from those caverns anytime soon, and he couldn't afford to wait. :*Are the boys with you?*:

:*No. They slipped away from me when I was talking with a smith about your scimitar. All the images I give Peri look the same to him, and I can't make sense out of the ones he's giving me.*:

:*Show me where you are.*:

An indistinct image formed in Shashtah's mind.

Too vague. She doesn't know how to distinguish one passage from another well enough for me to transport to her. Shashtah's sharp eyes spotted a gouge in the wall that looked familiar, and he took another turn. :*Go to the guest quarters. I'll meet you there.*:

:*I don't know where they are.*:

:*Ask Makkaba for help.*: Shashtah realized there were too many openings off the current passage and doubled back on his path.

:*She's not with me either.*:

:*She left you?*: Shashtah swore as he cut a corner too close and slammed his right shoulder against the wall. :*Why?*:

Tphah remained silent too long. :*I may have been rude.*:

:*Then ask another Galantite where the guest quarters are!*: Shashtah made his way up a ramp.

:*I can't. I don't speak their language, and I can't find anyone who knows ClearTalk.*: Tphah griped. :*Or at least anyone who will speak with me in ClearTalk.*:

"Dragons!" Shashtah roared and ran down yet another corridor, praying he was heading the right way. He burst into an enormous cavern and skidded to a stop. :*Can you find a cavern big enough to shift to dragonform?*:

:*Yes. Why?*:

:*Shift!*: Shashtah transformed and took wing. :*Now! The Valley of Ancients! See it?*: he asked as he imagined the steep walls of the formidable canyon.

An answering picture—complete with the massive metal bodies of the Council members perched on the rim—blurred with his.

Shashtah burst into the air over the canyon.

Tphah appeared off his left wing.

:*Peri!*: Shashtah screamed, ignoring the glares of the Council members who did indeed line the canyon walls. :*I'm flying above the Valley of the Ancients with Tphah! You have five heartbeats to shift to dragonform, get a good grip on Quatar and transport to us like I told you to do if you got lost! One, two, three, four—!*:

Peri exploded into the air just off Shashtah right wingtip, Quatar's weight in his tiny forearms sending them both plummeting toward the ground.

Shashtah immediately dove.

As Peri lost his grip, a golden light flickered on Quatar's left hand, and his haphazard descent slowed.

Shashtah landed directly below them, resumed his true shape and reached up. He caught Quatar and cradled the frightened Daethian boy in his arms. "It's all right. I have you."

Tphah settled onto the canyon floor and bugled for Peri to land beside her.

Quatar threw his arms around Shashtah's neck. "Papa!"

"Don't call me that. Especially here," Shashtah warned as he stared up at the Council of Ancients. "We're in enough trouble as it is."

Peri shifted to his humanform, picked up Quatar's turban from where it had fallen and handed it to him.

Quatar let go of Shashtah just long enough to take the turban and return it to his head. He wrapped his arms around the Dragonrider's neck again.

Tphah took her humanform as well, balancing Shashtah's scimitar in her right hand.

Shashtah crouched down and snaked his left arm around Peri, pulling him close as the sounds of a massive battle echoed off the canyon walls.

"You—!"

"—from inside—!"

"—dare risk—!"

"—Dragon or Dumnonian—?!"

"—Dragonheart must not be judged by—!"

"—guilty of—!"

"—insulted the Galantites—!"

"—in one piece!"

The Ancient Bronzes of the Council and Makara clattered all at once in their native tongue.

"Hear that?" Shashtah whispered, causing the boys to move their heads closer to his lips. "Remember how those judges hurt me the night Tkai died?" He tightened his hold on the boys. "They are trying to decide whether to hurt me or Tphah or one of you or all of us because you two didn't stay with Tphah like I told you to."

Both children instantly collapsed into hysterical tears, shrieking unintelligible promises against his shoulders. Quatar could hardly breathe through his sobs, and Peri's form blurred so badly that his tail wrapped around Shashtah's ankles, nearly tripping him onto the sand.

"BE STILL!" Makara roared.

Silence fell on the canyon.

Tphah pried Peri from from Shashtah and picked him up. "Hush," she hissed as she pressed Peri's head against her shoulder. "If you are going to be brave enough to disobey, you must be brave enough to face the consequences."

Something in Tphah's voice bothered Shashtah, and he glanced back at her. He frowned with concern at the tightness in her jaw that betrayed her fear. "Hush, Quatar! Good Dumnonians don't carry on like this. You'll lose too much water."

"I'm not . . . a good . . . Dumnonian!" Quatar hiccupped.

Shashtah kissed the child on the top of his head. "You'll learn. You'll grow wise and strong." He caught sight of the jealous look on Peri's face. He reached out, wiped away one of Peri's tears and pressed the moisture to his lips. "I held you the last time we stood here. This is Quatar's turn. Tphah will hold you this time." As soon as he saw Peri curl deeper into Tphah's arms, he ventured a look at Shaharadesh.

The Dragonking, a brilliant white keffiyeh on his head secured by a bejeweled golden agal, was watching them intently from his perch atop Makara's back. "I think you've made your point," Shaharadesh said, addressing the Council. "They look about as miserable as they are going to get. We really can't spare a tent for convalescents right now, and I would hate to call Lord Kashon off leave to deal with them when he just finished bringing us such a magnificent victory."

Makara glanced uncertainly at the other Council members.

Garesh suddenly craned his great armored head high above the Valley and howled his amusement at the setting sun. "Who but a Dragonheart could get a Hatchling that age to teleport with anything, let alone with a Dragonslayer? And floating down like some kind of insane feather—at least someone had the foresight to give the boy a magic ring! I can't wait to hear Jochia's side of this story! This is worth a trip to Mount Paradin, even if I do have to spend candlescars—or rotations—in humanform trying to talk to those walking stones!"

Slowly, the other Council members started chuckling with him.

"I'm surprised the Dragonheart didn't scare the Hatchling into the Afterlife with that roar!" a female Ancient chortled.

"Nice trick, that: transporting from three separate caverns to one location," Dameth's former Dragon, Tlee, mused.

"He didn't know it would work, and he shouldn't have tried!" another male thundered. "They could have all wound up imbedded in solid rock!"

"As if any of us can remember a time when the Valley floor rose that high!" Makara scoffed.

Tphah snaked her free arm around Shashtah's waist and leaned her head against his shoulder.

"Sounds like we'll be in the Elven Kingdom before dawn," Shashtah murmured.

Shaharadesh dismissed the Council with a wave of his hand.

The Ancient Bronzes rose into the air.

Garesh soared low, giving his tail a warning snap as he passed over Shashtah's head, then climbed high into the growing darkness before flying though a warp.

The other Council members also vanished into the desert sky.

Shaharadesh scowled at Shashtah. "That was close, Prophet. Your god must be smiling on you even as his orb sinks in the sky. Beware the Darkness, and do not press your luck!" With that he gave Makara the signal to rise.

Makara leapt into the air. She carried them into a steep climb, and then disappeared through a warp.

Shashtah set Quatar down, took his scimitar from Tphah and fastened the scabbard loosely against his right leg.

Tphah set Peri down and took her dragonform.

Shashtah scrambled onto her back and motioned for Quatar to climb up after him. "Hurry. Before they change their minds."

Quatar settled onto Shashtah's right thigh and grabbed onto his turban.

:*Easy does it*,: Shashtah cautioned as Tphah launched herself into the air too quickly. He felt her even out.

Peri shifted to his dragonform and joined them in the sky.

Shashtah gave Tphah the image of the clearing in front of the Elven Kingdom as he imagined it from a great height: massive oaks set into an impenetrable, unclimbable hedge, a large clearing before the main gates, an illusion of unbroken foliage covering an area large enough to contain an impressive castle or city but actually hiding a realm several times its apparent size, elven guards bedecked in Galantite chain mail patrolling the Great Woods nearby . . .

:*Hold on!*: Tphah warned just as Shashtah sensed that the particular chaos that surrounded them belonged to the Daethian rather than to the Dumnonian night.

Chapter 6:

By Any Other Name

Just as the Dragons take you under their wings and you take their young into your care, so shall you take the children of the dead into your households and raise them as if you were the fathers and mothers who have been taken from them by this Unholy War.

—from *The Dumnonian Code,*
by Corin of Daethia

"I BRING QUATAR, ELVEN WARD!" Tphah bugled in ClearTalk above the eerie cries that shattered the stillness of the Daethian night as she circled down toward the dozens of lethal elven arrows that Shashtah knew were aimed at them. "I am Tphah, Prophetess of the Bronze Dragons! My Rider is Shashtah Dragonheart! My companion is Peri, son of the Dragonprophetess Tkai! Send for the Elven King!"

Natural and magical creatures scurried into the forest in all directions at the sound of her roar. At the Sterrefyr, a three-day journey by caravan through the dense forest, the elves would be engaged in their nocturnal battle with the Cinnamarians. Shashtah wondered absently how the Elven Lord's troops covered the distance so quickly every night without Dragons. He shivered as Tphah carried them below the warm thermals and into the cool night air of the clearing that marked the entrance to the Elven Kingdom.

By the time Tphah landed, Peri had joined her on the forest floor and shapeshifted to his humanform. He swiftly hid under the Prophetess's protective wing.

Shashtah belatedly remembered Tkai's warning about it being unwise to transport directly to the doorstep of the Elven Kingdom.

Quatar, the Light bless him, came to their rescue. The boy, still holding onto his turban, slid to the ground and bolted toward one of the guards stationed beside an ancient oak that grew like a fence post in the midst of the massive hedge on the far side of the clearing. "Lani!" Before the guard could lower his bow, Quatar had embraced him.

"Elven Ward?" the flustered elf ventured as he identified the Daethian waif in desert clothing. He glanced from Quatar to Tphah with a look that suggested that he had never seen a Dumnonian Bronze up close before.

"Permission to dismount?" Shashtah called.

Quatar bounced up and down, tugging on the elf's tunic. "Please! Please! Please! That's my pa—foster father!" he corrected himself mid-outburst.

The elf screwed up his face in an effort to make a decision in the absence of the proper superiors. "Permission granted."

Shashtah slid to the forest floor, picked up Peri and motioned for Tphah to shift to her humanform. He hid a smile as she took a virginal and innocently beautiful shape. He settled Peri on his left hip and held out his right arm to escort her forward. As her fingers closed around his elbow, rendering him effectively incapable of physical attack or defense, he led her toward the guard. Shashtah could almost feel the tips of hidden elvish arrows follow him as he moved.

Quatar charged at Shashtah and threw his arms around his legs, nearly tripping him. "I won't let them hurt you," he promised importantly.

Shashtah favored the uncertain guard with his most charming smile. "My foster son wanted to show us where he grew up, and I need to see the Elven King."

"Do you think the king will see just anyone who comes calling in the middle of the night?" the guard scoffed.

Shashtah stammered, "N-no, but—"

The bark of the oak tree opened magically, and the Elven King, Farador, stepped into the clearing. "I will see him." His forest green cloak, held securely at the right shoulder by a flame-shaped brooch, parted slightly in front to reveal a loose-fitting white silk shirt, green-dyed leather trousers and boots, and a plain golden sash. The simple golden circlet that ringed his mane of oak-colored hair glinted in the starlight. His remarkable, glowing, solid green eyes danced with good-humor above his neatly trimmed, very non-elven chestnut beard. "Greetings, Quatar," he rumbled in his heartbreakingly beautiful voice as the bark of the tree closed behind him.

Quatar released Shashtah, who was bowing as low as he could without dropping Peri, and ran to his former guardian. "Elven King!"

Farador hefted the boy into his arms. "You've lost weight. Aren't the Dumnonians taking good care of you?"

Quatar flashed a worried look at Shashtah. "They don't have much food, and we have to feed the Dragons first. Peri's a Dragon, but he's special because he's Tkai's son. No other Dragon on all Centuria like him. He protects me and plays with me when p—my foster father is off fighting the Dark One."

Shashtah straightened as the boy prattled on. He noticed the glint in Farador's eyes as he caught Quatar's slip. He also saw the king glance sharply at the putrid green color of Peri's eyes.

"So," Farador interrupted the stream of information from Quatar, "you've become foster brother to a mutant Dragon since I saw you last. Let's get you something to eat while you tell me all about it."

Quatar's face brightened, but then grew worried. "What about the Dragons? Can they eat first?"

Farador laughed. "You can all eat as much as you like, and you don't have to wait for anyone to eat first. No one shall want for anything in the Elven Kingdom while I rule!" He placed his right hand against the trunk of the oak, and a door opened before him. He led Quatar into darkness.

Shashtah followed him with Peri and Tphah. The magical door closed behind him. His eyes strained against a darkness even his superior vision could not penetrate. His blood pounded in his ears, and his lungs could find no air. Abruptly the sound of his pulse gave way to the slow, steady, seepage of sap. His skin seemed to harden into bark, and his feet felt as if they had taken root in the ground. Absurdly he imagined he could feel sunlight beating down on him, even though he knew it was night. A nervous sickness churned in his stomach as the sensation conjured memories of the four winters he had spent in the shape of a tree beside the Northern Temple of the White Wolf, time that was lost to him forever that he should have spent with his precious Tkai. He opened his mouth to scream, but he could make no noise. A burst of magic passed through him, confirming that he was what he said he was and nothing more. The tree expelled him into the most beautiful garden on Centuria.

Shashtah remembered the Elven Kingdom from his caravan days, but it always amazed him. Flowers and trees of all descriptions grew with the same disregard for climate and season as they did in the Great Woods, only these plants shone with an inner light. Sky so blue it hurt to look at stretched overhead dotted with clouds that glistened with the light of Shashtah's god.

Sparkling brooks splashed light onto their banks as they tumbled in rainbows over glittering stones. A massive silver-blue lake stretched across the southern horizon, beyond which stood the biggest oak tree Shashtah had ever seen. Elves and woodland animals of all varieties wandered among the marvelous plants, delighting in their perfection.

"It's bigger than it looks from the outside," Tphah marveled.

Shashtah found himself unable to respond because Peri was choking him. *:Tphah, please tell Peri that I have him, and he'll be all right:.*

Tphah gave a small cry as she saw the problem. She gently pried Peri's left arm away from Shashtah's throat. "Easy. This is where Quatar used to live. It's safe. We won't let anything bad happen to you."

Peri didn't look as if he believed her, but he relaxed enough for Shashtah to lower him to the ground. The instant his feet touched the glowing grass he latched onto Shashtah's left leg and stood silently, staring at the wonders around him.

Farador laughed as he stepped out of the tree, carrying Quatar, and saw the awestruck Dumnonians. "Not my home, but the best I could do with what I had." He set Quatar down.

Quatar immediately ran to Peri and tugged at his friend's arm. "You have to see the boat!"

Peri gave Shashtah a worried look.

Shashtah smiled. "Go on. It's all right."

Peri slowly released his grip on his foster father, raised the hood of his magic cloak and allowed his playmate to lead him toward the lake.

Farador strolled after them, clearly waiting for Shashtah and Tphah to fall into step at his side. "So, who is this lovely young lady?"

Shashtah belatedly remembered his manners. "This is Tphah, Prophetess of the Bronze Dragons. Tphah, this is Farador, the Elven King."

Tphah somehow managed a salaam without breaking her stride.

Farador laughed and clapped Shashtah on the shoulder good-naturedly. "She is definitely one to set the blood pounding in anyone's veins. I wouldn't want to introduce her to other people, either, if she were my Dragon!"

Shashtah's face turned the color of molten bronze. He doubted he would forget to introduce Tphah to anyone ever again as long as he lived—though he knew he probably would. He removed his keffiyeh, tucked it into his belt and retied his leather thong around his head to keep his hair out of his eyes.

"So, what brings you and my former ward to my doorstep in the middle of the night?" Farador asked. "The spell against my nephew is holding, isn't it?"

Shashtah shuddered. "The last I had any personal knowledge of the Dark

One, he was trapped in a rather small room in the heart of Mount Cinnamar where I never want to go again!" He had started the statement in a calm voice, but he ended it with a stifled shriek that sounded hysterical even to his own ears.

Tphah put a quieting hand on his arm. "The servants of the Dark One take prisoners there and torture them to feed their god with the pain of others."

Farador's face darkened. "I'm sorry, my friend. The Mirari should never have dragged this world into a family squabble. We should have dealt with our own problems on our own plane." He ushered Shashtah and Tphah onto the boat with the boys. He muttered a magic word, and the boat glided gently across the lake.

"See! I told you!" Quatar, tiny fists on his hips, declared.

Peri glanced up at Shashtah, not amused. In fact, he still looked terrified.

Shashtah crouched so he was at Peri's eyelevel. "What is it? What's wrong?"

"Quatar and I will be alone in Tor," Peri whispered. "You won't be there like you weren't there in Mount Paradin. Someone will try to kill Quatar, and he'll have to fight him—alone." Peri threw his arms around Shashtah's neck. "I don't want to lose you again! I don't want someone to hurt Quatar!"

Tphah gave a little squawk. "Prophecy!" she exclaimed, confirming Shashtah's suspicions.

Shashtah glanced at Tphah. :*I don't understand. What's he talking about? I don't see anything.*:

Tphah stooped beside Shashtah. "Hush, Peri! It could be in a few days; it could be in many, many winters. You're too young to know the difference yet. I'm still too young to know the difference half the time! Besides, you don't know who'll win this fight-to-be. And maybe you haven't lost my Rider at all; maybe you just need him to be somewhere else or perhaps he hasn't arrived yet."

"Come on, Peri!" Quatar called as the boat touched the opposite shore. "You have to see this!" He tugged imperiously at Peri's cloak.

Shashtah watched his boys leap ashore and run toward the tree. He jumped out of the boat and lifted Tphah down beside him.

Farador joined them. "Is raising a mutant anything like raising a Bronze?" he asked in a barely audible voice.

"You are the second person to ask me that." Shashtah thought about the question for a heartbeat. "Even if I can raise Peri, I have no idea if the Council will ever let him Bond. Who knows what the future holds, though? I'm only a Prophet."

Farador laughed softly. "You are far more than that, my friend." He directed them toward the tree.

The great oak itself seemed rather unremarkable except for being tremendously large and for having ten elven guards posted around it. Like the tree in the outer hedge, the splendid oak boasted a magical door in its trunk that opened whenever anyone approached.

The Galantites should get the elves to teach them that spell, Shashtah mused. *Or maybe they taught the elves.*

The entry hall looked like a wood-lined Dragon's den.

Shashtah scanned the hall.

The boys were nowhere in sight. "Peri? Quatar?"

"Don't worry," Farador assured him. "There's nowhere they can go in here that I won't know exactly where they are." He placed his hand on a wall. The wood opened, revealing several staircases that trailed away from them. "This way." He escorted them down steps that spiraled through seemingly endless wooden tunnels beneath the twinkling illusion of a starry sky. Side passages, all glowing with a soft, warm light, forked off the main staircase like so many roots. Legends danced upon the surface of the intricately carved doors and walls.

Shashtah resisted the impulse to trace the images with his fingertips, contenting himself with naming the tales he had heard long ago around his father's campfire in what seemed like another life. The saga of the elves' flight from the Southern Continent and the building of their new home in the Great Woods. Stories of Tira, the Elven Queen, who was slain by the Dark One, buying her people time to escape from their original homeland. Tales of Laedor, Elven Prince, who had been captured in a battle at the Sterrefyr, taken to Mount Cinnamar and tortured to death. Reminders of injustices and injuries intertwined with stories of courage and self-sacrifice and the ever-present promise of hope in the person of the Elven King.

Countless elves, dressed in all the colors of the rainbow, wandered through the living maze. Every elf on Centuria called the Elven Kingdom "home." Each night, they sent out their finest warriors to defend what little was left of the good in their world. The joy that flooded through the hallways of the massive tree seemed sharply at odds with Shashtah's mental picture of the desperate army engaged in a hopeless war at the Sterrefyr, and the looks on the faces of the elves as their divine king passed among them left no doubt as to the source of that happiness.

Farador led them to a wood-lined cavern that seemed to go on forever in all directions. Stairs connected curved oaken platforms in a pattern vaguely reminiscent of a vine. Each platform varied in size and boasted solid oak tables that could seat anywhere from a single person to a hundred. Elven servers scurried everywhere, taking orders and delivering meals, but try as he might Shashtah could not detect where they went to obtain the enormous quantities of food and drink.

The Elven King escorted his guests to the table Quatar had chosen.

"Quatar, Peri, don't run off like that," Shashtah scolded. "I don't mind you going ahead a bit, but I want you both to stay where I can see you."

Quatar looked perplexed. "Nothing bad can happen to us here!"

"You told me to go with Quatar," Peri reminded Shashtah.

"I know," Shashtah admitted. "But if you get in the habit of being cautious when you don't have to, then we won't have any repeats of previous mistakes. Do I make myself clear?"

The boys nodded soberly.

Shashtah climbed onto the bench beside Peri. Tphah settled beside him as the Elven King took the seat across from her and next to Quatar.

Farador signaled for a server to approach.

The young elf, who possessed solid bright green eyes beneath a haphazard shock of copper-red hair, bowed with a rakish insolence that brought a smile to his king's lips. "Your order, sire?"

Farador turned to his guests. "What would you like? Anything is available, but be specific—we have a somewhat temperamental chef."

"Six dates and a freshly-baked piece of elven bread," Shashtah said.

Tphah gave him a look that declared him to be an unrepentant glutton. "A small partridge, freshly killed—uncooked, please."

Peri squirmed until he was under the protection of Shashtah's left arm. "A sliced peach? Quatar told me they were good. I'd like to try one."

"Aw, you don't understand how this place works at all." Quatar pegged the server with an imperious glare. "Ice milk in a dish as big as me with browned sugar syrup, whipped cream, toasted almonds and—" he paused to count, "five cherries on top!"

Shashtah gasped. "Quatar!"

Farador chuckled. "It's all right. We'll all be helping him finish that much."

"You don't understand," Tphah explained. "Most Dumnonians have only heard legends about ice milk, and the quantity he just ordered would feed the entire King's Camp! He's being sinfully decadent for someone who's supposed to be learning how to subsist on a starvation-level diet."

"He's five years old!" the Elven King protested.

"He's my foster son," Shashtah glowered. "Quatar, please order something to sustain yourself and then, because we are on leave and you want to teach us about the land where you were raised, ask for a small portion of this marvel— just enough to give us all a taste."

"But he doesn't need to worry about mere sustenance here!" Farador objected.

Shashtah's words were to the Elven King, but his amber eyes focused steadily on his foster son. "He doesn't live here anymore. He lives in Dumnonia now. Or doesn't he?"

"No, papa! Don't be mad!" Quatar scrambled under the table and tried to crawl into Shashtah's lap.

Shashtah fended him off. "A desert dweller does not ask for more than he needs."

Tphah nudged her Rider in the ribs.

Shashtah relented. "Well, maybe a little more than he needs. But he certainly doesn't demand enough to feed three centuries!"

"A small bowl of beef broth with potatoes, carrots and peas!" Quatar amended, tears of frustration welling in his eyes.

"And just enough ice-milk to give us all a taste—after we finish our other food," Shashtah added as he lifted Quatar onto his lap.

"With five cherries," Tphah added.

Shashtah gave her a much-put-upon look as the server bowed and retreated from the platform. He hugged Quatar. "Hush. You didn't understand. Now you do. I know you'll be good from now on." As he wondered just how many times he wouldhave to repeat that pledge of confidence, he noticed the jealous look on Peri's face. He traced the line of the dragonboy's chin with the back of his fingers. "You'll be good, too. I know you will."

Peri studied his foster brother. "It's just hard for a Daethian to understand Dumnonian ways." He offered his hand to Quatar. "He'll make a good Dragonrider someday."

Shashtah felt his skin prickle as Quatar let himself be guided onto the bench between them. He glanced at Tphah, who inclined her head just enough that he knew she felt it, too. *Prophecy . . .*

Farador studied Shashtah through narrowed eyes. "I'm afraid I haven't made your life easy, friend."

Shashtah shrugged. "A Dragonrider wouldn't know what to do with an easy life."

The server returned with their food. He frowned at the Dumnonians who had lined up on one side of the table against the Elven King. He retreated just out of ear shot but remained poised to intervene at the slightest gesture from Farador.

Tphah picked at her partridge as Peri sucked at his peach slices and Quatar devoured his soup.

Shashtah broke off a bit of his bread and let it melt in his mouth, never taking his eyes off the Elven King. *I wish there were a way to conjure this stuff instead of manna. It tastes so much better.*

Farador watched his former ward finish the soup. He held his tongue, even though Quatar was clearly not satisfied.

Shashtah slipped one of his dates into Quatar's mouth.

Tphah caught the movement out of the corner of her eye and snickered. "You're as bad as a Dragon Hatching his first Rider."

"Maybe," Shashtah admitted as he unabashedly handed Quatar the rest of his bread and contented himself with his remaining dates. "But if he's been looking for me in the mines of Mount Paradin for two days, I doubt he's eaten in three."

Peri gave a shocked gasp and promptly force-fed Quatar the rest of his peach.

Farador raised an eyebrow. "You got lost?"

"Not exactly," Shashtah replied. "I was with King Jochia. I should have realized I was standing in a time warp when I found myself speaking to a Wizard of Corin. I tend to lose big chunks of my life every time that happens."

The Elven King's eyes sparkled with understanding. "You met Balkar."

Shashtah nodded. "He has a big problem that is about to become our big problem. The one you referred to earlier. The power he uses to preserve the time warp is running out." He swallowed his last date, glanced over to make sure Tphah had finished her partridge, and then signaled for the server to bring the dessert.

The elf reluctantly scurried down a set of stairs.

Farador studied Peri with an intensity that made Shashtah uneasy. "What are your plans for your charges?"

"I'll try to raise them as I would any Dragon or Dumnonian," Shashtah said. "When Peri is old enough, he can ask the Council for permission to Bond with someone. They sometimes let creatures that have been magically changed into Bronze Dragons Bond with former Riders who have been careless enough to lose their first Dragon." He felt Tphah's comforting hand on his arm. "Most Riders are not lucky enough to get a true Bronze twice," he said in a husky voice. He forced himself to control his emotions. "Such Pairs do not serve in our centuries. They fly reconnaissance and help our supply personnel. If Quatar still wants to be a Dragonrider when he's grown, he might be allowed to Bond with such a Dragon. Or if he'd rather make his way among his own people, I'll return him to them."

Quatar pulled Peri close. "You are my people!"

"And I'm his Dragon!" Peri piped up.

Shashtah felt his skin prickle once more. He stretched out enough to embrace both boys. "If that's what you want, we'll work on it until you change your minds."

"We won't!" the children promised in unison.

Shashtah shot another look at Tphah, who slightly inclined her head again.
Farador saw the exchange. "Prophecy?"

Shashtah released his charges. "May—" He gasped. "Oh!"

The server returned, bearing a marvel that Shashtah only half-remembered
as a pleasant dream from his childhood. The elf had thoughtfully divided up the
portions of iced milk Shashtah had dictated into small, crystal cups with just the
right amount of caramelized sugar, whipped cream, and toasted almonds on top.
A single, glowing red cherry crowned each creation.

Farador grinned as Shashtah devoured his small serving almost as quickly as
Quatar did. Peri and Tphah were a bit more cautious, eventually deciding that
the excessively cold food might be fine for their companions but the lukewarm
cherries were more to draconic tastes.

Quatar looked mournfully at Peri's barely touched ice milk as it melted in
the little dish. He bit his lower lip and wormed his way onto Shashtah's lap again
as if the Dragonrider could somehow shield him from temptation.

Tphah leaned her chin on Shashtah's shoulder and batted her long eyelashes
at him. "Sin to let good food go to waste," she commented in her most sultry
voice.

The look Shashtah gave her would have peeled the hide off a lesser Dragon.

Tphah blurred the shape of her jaw slightly, parted her lips and flicked her
forked tongue across the end of his nose. She was back in her humanform and
holding a spoonful of her own unfinished dessert to his lips before he could
react, and when he opened his mouth to object, she shoved the spoonful inside.

Shashtah took the spoon from her and swallowed the delicacy. "You are in so
much trouble . . . " He turned to his boys. "Peri, you may share the rest of your
treat with Quatar if you wish."

Peri beamed and held out the remains of his treat to his friend.

Quatar slid off Shashtah's lap and onto the bench. He sat happily, letting
Peri feed him the ice milk while Shashtah finished Tphah's dessert.

As soon as they were done, Shashtah yawned. "Permission to stake out a
corner of your meadow and sleep for a decadent period of time? I know you
have guest rooms, but I want Tphah and Peri to take their dragonforms while
they sleep."

"Permission granted. Rest well." With that Farador rose and wandered over
to another table where a group of elven warriors accepted him into their midst
like a long-lost comrade.

Shashtah leaned backward and planted his hands on the platform. Slowly he
slid his legs out from under the table and over the bench until he was in a full

handstand. Then he tucked his knees to his chest and landed in a crouch, facing his open-mouthed boys. He grinned. "The Ban-kai stretches are useful for a few other things besides exercising."

"He's already taught me some," Quatar informed Peri importantly.

"Peri will catch up with you soon." Shashtah sent his arms into the swooping pattern of the Flying Dragon. He ended the maneuver by grabbing a boy in each arm and hauling them into the air as he rose. He balanced them on his hips, and then, without looking at Tphah, strode toward the entrance to the dining hall.

Shashtah made it all the way to the meadow beside the magical lake before he was certain Tphah had actually followed him. He lowered the boys to the grass and turned to glare at her. Without a word he gave her the signal to shift to her dragonform and cover them with her wing.

Tphah's eyes flashed as she obeyed.

Shashtah squatted in front of Peri. "Please take your dragonform."

Peri threw a jealous glance at Quatar. Reluctantly he shifted to his trueform.

"Thank you," Shashtah smiled as he caressed the ugly little dragonette, feeling Peri's thick leathery hide beneath his hand. "Lie between Quatar and me and use your wings to cover us."

Pride at being assigned the task gleamed in the dragonette's eyes. "Aw nigh'?" he ventured in ClearTalk.

"All night," Shashtah confirmed.

Peri promptly lay down on the grass.

Shashtah motioned for Quatar to slip partially under Peri's right wing while he removed his scimitar, set it within easy reach, and slid into place beneath the left.

:*Comfy?*: Tphah's voice growled in his head.

:*You weren't helping in there.*: Shashtah closed his eyes. :*If Quatar really hadn't eaten in three days, you could have made him sicker than you made me at the Anvil!*:

Tphah stifled a whine.

Quatar immediately peered over Peri's neck at Shashtah, somehow aware that the adults were arguing. "Don't be mad at Tphah, papa. I was the one who was bad."

Shashtah grimaced. "I'm not your 'papa,' Quatar. If you need a special name for me, call me 'Dragonheart,' the way Tphah does."

Tphah poked her head under her wing and filled the air around them with her scent.

Curiously Quatar did not gag or try to flee the way other Daethians would have. Instead he cuddled against his foster brother.

Before Shashtah could contemplate what that meant, Peri swiveled his head around and flicked his forked tongue into Shashtah's right ear.

"How I'm going to teach any of you to behave with you all sticking up for each other? Get some sleep!" Shashtah rolled onto his right side and covered his head with his left arm. He heard Quatar settle back into his assigned place.

A swishing sound betrayed Tphah wrapping her tail around the outside of her raised wing.

Shashtah sighed, deciding it would take too much effort to remain annoyed. Shoving his irritation out of his mind, he slowed his breathing, relaxed and let himself fall into the sleep of a warrior who was finally confident his dreams wouldn't be disturbed.

Shashtah groaned in pleasure, stretched—and startled completely awake as he felt scales that were definitely not Bronze against his side. He grabbed his scimitar and drew it. He rolled away from the monster, twisted and came up on his feet, facing his attacker.

Peri, blurring between his true shape and of a Hatchling covered with bronze-colored, fishlike scales, hobbled a few experimental steps, dragging his injured wing. He screamed in distress—an odd sound, more like the trumpeting of an elephant than a Bronze's cry.

Shashtah dropped his scimitar, leapt forward and grabbed the injured wing firmly in both hands. "Sands!" He started to shout for a Healer, but light shot from his fingertips.

The torn muscles and tendons healed.

The wing became the arm of a child as Peri settled into his humanform. He pouted at Shashtah with accusing eyes. "Ouch!"

"I'm so sorry!" Shashtah quickly checked the boy for other injuries and found none. *We'll have to treat the mutants with more care than the Bronzes. It's hard to hurt a Bronze.*

"At least you won't be hauled before the Council for hurting a mutant," a voice observed inside Shashtah's head.

Shashtah scanned the meadow.

The elven guards around the oak tree stood frozen, watching him suspiciously. Other elves in the meadow, after a few heartbeats of curiosity, continued on their way.

That wasn't Tphah. One of Tkai's memories? Or something else? "Where are Tphah and Quatar?" Shashtah asked.

Peri pointed toward the oak. "Quatar woke up and was hungry. Tphah took him to get him something to eat. I said I'd stay here and protect you. I tried to make myself look like a Bronze, but I couldn't do it right."

Shashtah into Peri's repulsive green eyes. "Do people make you feel bad for being what you are?"

Peri stared into the future. "They will."

Why is his Prophecy suddenly causing so much trouble? Shashtah contemplated Peri's all-too-Dumnonian ears. "I think I know something that will help. You're a shapeshifter—"

"I'm not a good enough to do Daethian eyes." Peri sulked.

"We can worry about your eyes later. Daethians place great value on appearance," Shashtah said, repeating a lesson he had learned long ago from Tkai. "They're used to seeing elves. You already have dark hair and green eyes—okay, it's not quite the same green, but Daethians won't realize that if you give yourself ears like the elves—a little more pointed than Dumnonian ears. You don't have to change anything else. With elven ears, the Daethians will assume you're an elf."

Peri concentrated and blurred his form. When his shape steadied, his ears had elven tips.

"Perfect! Much more effective than a green-eyed Dumnonian!" Shashtah picked up his scimitar and strapped it back into place against his right leg. Then he took Peri's hand firmly in his. "Come on! Let's find Quatar and Tphah and show them your new ears."

Peri regarded Shashtah with uncustomary caution but finally let himself be led inside the tree.

"This stretch is called 'Hatchling Rising,'" Shashtah instructed his foster sons as they stood on the deck in a bare-rock cavern with a hot spring and a stream-fed pool of much colder water. The three of them wore nothing more than a grin among them—except for the leather thongs that bound their hair.

Tphah stood watch outside the door to prevent any elves from walking in on them as Shashtah taught his fosterlings the secret moves of the Dumnonian Battle Dance. "It's a Dragon's proper place," she'd informed him when he objected to her doing something as menial as guard duty.

Shashtah decided not to argue with her about the matter. *I really need to ask Kashon what Dragons mean by "proper place."* He crouched close to the floor and hunched over with his face against his knees and his arms wrapped tightly around his shins. He slowly uncoiled and pressed himself upward until he was balanced on the balls of his feet, back arched, head tilted backward, arms extended, and palms angled toward the sky. He rotated his palms forward until they faced the ground and dropped into the "Flying Dragon" stretch. "See how the moves can flow from one into the other?"

The boys nodded dutifully even though Shashtah suspected that they had no idea what he was talking about.

"Now you try. Scrunch up in a ball near the ground," he instructed.

The boys curled up almost in unison.

That was the last thing they did together for nearly a candlescar. Peri had the balance and grace that Quatar lacked, but Quatar had the raw power needed to push through the various maneuvers and the stamina to complete fifty repetitions after Peri blurred to his dragonform and coiled up in an exhausted heap on the deck.

Shashtah, grinned with fatherly pride and nudged Peri awake mid-snore. "Come on, you. Into the hot spring before that shoulder stiffens."

The fact that Quatar was already splashing happily in the pool did more to entice Peri to slither into the spring than Shashtah's urging did.

Shashtah had just lowered himself into the soothing water when Farador, a forest green velvet robe trimmed with white rabbit fur draped around his naked frame, strode into the cavern.

Peri abruptly shifted to humanform and latched onto Shashtah, nearly drowning him.

By the time Shashtah finished sputtering, Farador had slipped out of his robe and eased his impressively muscled body into the water beside Quatar.

:*I couldn't very well stop him,*: Tphah apologized from her post in the hall.

:*I know.*: Shashtah inclined his head toward Farador. "I'm sorry. Should we leave? I don't want to inconvenience you or any of your people."

Farador splashed water at Quatar. "You aren't inconveniencing anyone. I'm hiding. I've healed most of the wounded from last night's skirmishes, and I need to recharge my powers before I tend to anyone else. I figured the one place no one would ask me to use magic for a while would be in the company of a Prophet who is capable of working miracles all by himself."

Shashtah settled Peri in front of him and gently massaged the dragonboy's left shoulder. "Recharge? I don't see anything around here that you can drain."

Farador watched absently as Quatar frolicked about the pond like an otter. "There are days I wish I could tap into a child's energy instead of relying on the magical items in the lake that is connected to these pools. We don't capture as many from the Dark One's forces as we used to."

Shashtah arched his eyebrow. "Do I hear a backhanded request for a Dumnonian caravan bearing inedible spoils of war?"

"In exchange for all the food they can carry," Farador offered.

Shashtah gaped. "You're serious? What would we have to supply in exchange for that?"

Farador shrugged. "I don't much care—so long as whatever the caravan brings is magical."

A hint of panic chilled Shashtah's heart. "You're that desperate?"

Farador grabbed Quatar in a bear hug and held him tightly until the boy grew still. "I suspect Criton is more desperate than I am. Trying to fight off the after-effects of our spell must cost him dearly."

"We're headed for Tor. After that I was going to stop by Krillion and make arrangements for a caravan to bring them something they need from Dumnonia. I suppose I can arrange for a caravan to the Elven Kingdom and another to Tor as well."

"I'd be grateful," Farador murmured. He handed Quatar to Shashtah, climbed out of the warm spring, and dove into the cool pool. He seemed a little revived when he surfaced and pulled himself onto the deck. He waved his hands in an intricate pattern. Light flickered briefly over his body, and he was suddenly dry. He winked at Quatar, then wrapped himself in his robe and strode out of the cavern.

Juel, Elven Lord

Chapter 7:

Culture Clash

It is advisable to send your Dragonriders out of Dumnonia while they are on leave. In this manner they may become acquainted with remote locations in the event that they need to transport there. They will also become increasingly familiar with the cultures and languages of your allies. On this last subject, too much knowledge about friends seems to be something of a contradiction in terms. One never knows when some small look or casual word might hopelessly offend someone who might otherwise be your greatest supporter. Dumnonian ways are not the ways of everyone on Centuria, and the failure to understand this can easily result in unnecessary and tragic death.

—from *The Dragonlords' Handbook*
by Corin of Daethia

THE DAYS IN THE ELVEN KINGDOM PASSED SWIFTLY. Shashtah spent a little while in Farador's impressive library trying to find out more about his scimitar. The Galantites had told Tphah that the blade was originally forged for Shaharadesh's predecessor, but she had had to leave in search of the boys before she could discover the weapon's special properties. Reading had never been one of Shashtah's favorite pastimes, though, so he quickly abandoned the books in favor of cavorting with his family in the magnificent gardens and pools of the Elven Kingdom and swapping stories with the elves. Quatar and Peri stifled guilty cries of joy when Shashtah docked Tphah one of her chosen days in

Tor for undermining his discipline when they'd first arrived, and even the Prophetess didn't seem too disappointed about spending one more glorious day in the enchanted realm.

When the dawn came for their departure, Shashtah carefully tied his hair over the tips of his Dumnonian ears

Tphah rolled her eyes. :*You could just shapeshift.*:

:*Which would work only as long as it took me to become so upset that I lost my shape. Which would probably be about half a dozen heartbeats. I don't have fond memories of Tor.*:

Tphah tilted her head and studied him closely. :*You're really afraid.*:

:*With good reason! You haven't met Criton. Nor the Kyondoca. Dragonslayers, Tphah. They even terrify my father!*: As Shashtah turned to take his leave of Farador, he had an idea. "Could you transport us into the palace somewhere near your daughter? I know it costs you magic, but I've been trying to figure out how to get all of us inside in one piece, and I keep envisioning one of the Kyondoca splattering me against a wall while Tphah and the boys watch."

Farador laughed, a deep rumbling sound that put everyone within earshot at ease. "You might as well ask my grandson if he could bother picking up his sword to defend me against the Dark One!" He led them to the clearing outside the main gate. With a wave of his hand, their world blurred.

When the warp closed, the Elven Princess, Adrial, stood smiling her welcome at them.

Shashtah returned the smile, noting that the Elven Princess bore little resemblance to her father. Her bone structure was as frail as Farador's was large. Her solid amber eyes could have been Dumnonian, and her flowing silver hair could have been living Galantite. She may have been effectively wed to Criton for two and a half rotations, yet she still styled her hair in the loose manner of an elven maiden instead of gathered into the intricately braided roll that elven matrons wore at the back of their necks. Her silver-trimmed, white samite gown gave her an ethereal appearance that marked her as someone not quite elven while not quite divine. *A living feather from one of Criton's wings.*

"Adrial!" Quatar squealed. He rushed forward to embrace his former caretaker while Peri, anchored firmly to Shashtah's leg, looked warily at his surroundings.

"The White Wolf's lab," Shashtah identified the chamber. A shiver ran down his spine as he remembered standing in the pristine room with Tkai at his side. Even though everything in the lab appeared more orderly than the woven rows of Kashon's magnificent tapestries, Shashtah wondered how the White Wolf could ever have found anything in it. The books covering the walls were shelved according to size rather than content. Quills, bottles of ink, sheets of various materials to write on, ingredients to cast spells—everything was precisely organized according to a pattern that must have made sense to the mind of the Wizard who had created it but that looked completely useless to the former caravaneer.

Shane's enormous spell book, still opened to an ominously blanked page, remained atop a podium in the corner to the left of the door, waiting patiently for the long-promised Great Wizard.

Shashtah marveled that warmth from the splendid brazier to his right still crept across the room even though the White Wolf had lit it millennia ago. He half expected to see the forests of Rashtar reflected in the polished oak-framed mirror with gold fittings that glittered darkly in the third corner—a magical gateway to anywhere the user had the power to focus it.

"The path is two-way, so whatever is there can come here if I leave it exposed." Criton's words—though in someone else's voice—slid through Shashtah's mind. *Criton closed the path,* another voice explained with the eternal patience of a teacher who despaired of a particularly thick pupil ever learning to think.

Shashtah tried to ignore the voices, but they insisted on haunting him from the edge of his consciousness.

Tphah restered her hand on his arm, trying to calm him.

Peri stood on his toes to peer at the vessels filled with various powders and liquids that lined the silver-trimmed shelves along the center of the massive table in the middle of the room.

Shashtah made a salaam to Adrial. "Elven Princess, we did not have time for formal introductions the last time we met. I'm—"

"Shashtah Dragonheart," Adrial finished his sentence for him. "Come." She freed herself from Quatar. "Before we accidentally lose a rotation of our lives. This room reeks of Time Magic." She escorted them into the hallway and closed the door behind them. "Your lovely companion must be the Prophetess Tphah." She held out her fragile hand.

Tphah clasped the princess's hand uncertainly as she glanced from the glitteringly beautiful elf to her Rider. "You've met before?"

Shashtah grimaced as he felt a wave of jealousy through their Bond. "Please excuse my Dragon. We've only been out of the Training for half a rotation, and she's still a bit possessive."

Adrial laughed, a delightful sound like a babbling brook that set Shashtah's blood to pounding—with fear rather than with pleasure. "I understand." She released Tphah's hand and bent to pick up Quatar.

Shashtah quickly slipped his left arm around Tphah's slender waist and pulled her close to him. "You wanted to come here," he reminded her under his breath.

Tphah mirrored his movement, drawing him closer to her than was necessary. She leaned her head against his shoulder. "Is the Lord of Daethia any better since the last time my Rider saw him?"

Sadness clouded Adrial's exquisite eyes and the corners of her mouth tugged down slightly before she controlled her features. "He's in constant agony," she said in a conversational tone so as not to frighten the children. "He doesn't scream much anymore. He usually just lies in bed staring at the ceiling. I don't think he's said more than a few dozen words since he cast that ghastly spell with my father and your Rider. I spend most of my time sitting at my Lord's bedside, holding his hand so he'll know he's not alone, but I'm not sure he realizes I'm there. Seraphe, his flying horse, is grey with worry. I let him come inside whenever possible. My Lord seems to rest a little easier when he's near. They're together now, otherwise I couldn't be here."

Tphah prompted Shashtah with a nudge. "May my Rider see Lord Criton?" she asked when he remained silent.

Adrial brushed Quatar's hair away from his face. "Why?"

"Papa can help him!" Quatar boasted. "Papa can work all sorts of miracles!"

"Quatar," Tphah growled.

Quatar blinked at her. "That's what Katrell—Oh!" The boy saw Shashtah's frown and panicked. He twisted out of Adrial's arms, dropped to the floor and threw himself at Shashtah's legs.

Shashtah hastily disentangled himself from Tphah and intercepted the boy midlunge. He heaved Quatar into the air and dangled him at arm's length.

"I'm sorry, Papa! I forgot!" Quatar squealed with dismay as he repeated the error yet again.

Tphah, Adrial and Peri all clapped their hands over their ears in protest.

"What am I going to do with you?" Shashtah asked quietly as he lowered Quatar to the floor.

"Let him call you 'Papa,'" Peri suggested as he wriggled his finger in his still-ringing ear.

Shashtah scrunched up his face in distaste, annoyed that Peri was right. "I don't seem to have much choice. It's either that or be mad at him all the time, and I don't concentrate well enough to do that."

If Quatar had been the White Wolf's panther, he would have purred.

Tphah peeled Quatar away from her Rider. She reached for Peri with her fee hand. "Come here, Dragon!" she ordered, a mischievous twinkle in her amber eyes. "Let's see what secrets these ruins hold while your 'papa' tries to help a sick friend."

Peri obediently took her graceful hand in his tiny grasp.

"Stay in the ruins," Shashtah warned. "I don't want you running into any of the Kyondoca." He turned to Adrial. "Shall we?"

Adrial inclined her head and motioned for him to follow her.

In less time than Shashtah thought possible they were standing inside the study that he remembered in excruciating detail.

Criton's too-still body lay on a cot near his bookcases. Someone had placed his sword atop his massive oak desk. His extremely exhausted and distressed winged horse stood, head drooped and his muzzle almost grazing the stone floor, beside the cot. Other than that, nothing in the room had changed since Shashtah had helped the Lord of Daethia and the Elven King cast their infamous spell against the Dark One.

"Lord of Light!" Shashtah exclaimed. "You didn't move him from this room?"

Adrial blinked at him. "But this is his room," she declared as if that explained everything.

Shashtah knelt beside the cot. He studied the husk of the winged deity whom he had first seen in all his glory in the Throne Room of Tor. Criton had become a distant memory of what he had been. Gone was his self-assurance, only a vacant stare in its place. His sky-blue kilt wrapped around his hips just the way it had the last time Shashtah had seen him. The golden armbands of the Kyondoca, magically welded to his forearms, glittered in the sunlight that filtered through the only window in the room. His great white wings, however, remained hidden. "Has he maintained his shifted shape the whole time?"

"Is that important?"

Shashtah shrugged. "I don't know about Mirari, but Dragons have trouble holding their shifted form when they're injured or upset. The fact that he hasn't blurred and his Bond with Seraphe hasn't broken suggests that there's still a part of his mind that's not insane with pain." He took Criton's right hand in his left and swore silently when no miracle occurred. "Hasn't anyone tried to do anything?"

"Nothing works," Adrial whispered. She sighed. "I see the accusation in Juel's eyes. He'd rather watch me die than tell one more child that the Dark One's forces slaughtered a beloved parent so thoroughly there wasn't even a body to bring home. He's right. If I'd mated with my Lord when Tchang first prophesied our union, then my daughter would've sealed the Paths by now. Countless beings would still be alive. But I want to live! In this world, not in the

Afterlife. This is the world I love. I look at my Lord lying there, helpless, and I know I love him, too. He's one more reason I don't want to die. How could I bear to add to the pain he's already enduring? Could you? Could you give up the fight and the people you love and your Bond with your Dragon and the thrill of soaring through the skies above Dumnonia carrying 'Eternal Death to the Dark One' in exchange for a child you would never know?"

Shashtah bowed his head. "I don't know. But my first Dragon did just that. She'd lived over a thousand winters and probably could have lived a thousand more. Yet she gave us Peri, the son of a being she detested, and asked me to slay her so she'd die by the hand of someone she loved." He rose. "I'm about to do something that may get me killed. Do you want to leave the room?"

"What are you planning?"

"Your Lord may know we're here and not be able to respond. I had a similar problem when I was under this spell. The Dark One has found a way to break the paralysis."

"How do you know what your spell did to the Dark One?"

"Because I went to the heart of Mount Cinnamar and looked!" Shashtah hadn't meant to scream. Something about being in Criton's study again summoned the terror the memory of his last encounter with the Dark One held for him.

Fury flashed like skyfire in Adrial's amber eyes. "My Lord's soul is in agony! My father said you understood how incapacitating that pain can be!"

"I do." Shashtah's heart quaked as he recalled holding Peri in the Valley of Ancients while under the spell's effects. His power stirred, using his anger to shove aside his fear. He loosened his carved leather belt, pulled it free from his trousers, and fingered it carefully. "Last chance to leave."

Adrial squared her shoulders. "I'll stay."

"As you wish." Shashtah studied Criton closely. "I'm betting that the distress cry of a winged horse is at least as loud to its Bond Partner as a Bronze Dragon's is."

"Distress cry?" Adrial echoed.

Shashtah whirled around and brought his belt down with a sickening slap on the winged stallion's sensitive nose.

The resulting chaos was immediate and complete.

Seraphe reared, backed into the desk, tried to take off, and fouled his wings on the furniture, preventing him from hitting his head on the ceiling.

Adrial startled back into the doorway, shrieking.

Shashtah rolled under Criton's cot, barely avoiding the winged horse's deadly hooves. He winced as the hilt of his scimitar bit into his right side.

Criton surged to his feet with an unintelligible screech. He grabbed Seraphe's muzzle. Light flashed from his hands and bathed the injured area in a soothing glow.

Seraphe calmed down instantly, nickered, and nuzzled his Rider.

Shashtah slid out from under the cot. He slipped his belt back around his waist while Criton was occupied with his horse. The heartbeat the Lord of Daethia picked up his sword and turned his attention to him, Shashtah dropped to his knees and, head bowed, awaited execution.

Adrial stood motionless, her hand covering her mouth.

"Why?" Criton demanded. "Why hurt a noble creature who has never done harm to anyone or anything in his life?"

"It got your attention," Shashtah replied.

Criton raised his blade to strike.

Quatar ducked passed Adrial and bolted into the room. He yelped as he saw the fatal tableau. "NO!" He rushed forward and shielded Shashtah with his tiny body. "Don't hurt Papa!"

Peri rushed after Quatar, causing Adrial to flatten herself against the door jamb. He blurred to his dragonform, squawked, and leapt across the study. He landed squarely on Shashtah's back, planted his forepaws on the Dragonrider's shoulders and hissed.

Seraphe backed into the wall near the window at the appearance of the two absurd defenders. Wings fluttering in agitation, he neighed his distress.

Tphah thrust herself into the doorway beside Adrial. She glanced at Shashtah to make sure he was still unharmed, then glared at Criton.

Criton lowered his sword, turned to face his mount, and raised his left hand.

The glorious beast thrust his head forward to be caressed.

Criton buried his face in Seraphe's silky mane.

Adrial stepped into room. She positioned herself between her husband and Shashtah and curtsied almost to the floor.

Tphah joined her Rider and offered Criton a salaam due to a king.

Criton sensed the movement and turned. His brows knitted together as he saw the women. He blurred his form and spread his wings as he took his true shape, complete with anklets and sword belt—and minus his sky blue kilt.

Quatar drew a sharp breath but held his ground as the deity turned toward him.

Criton tried to concentrate on the kneeling figure of the Dragonrider behind Adrial, between Tphah and Quatar, and beneath Peri. He lifted his sword and pointed it over Adrial's head at Quatar's throat. "I could order my guards to take the boy to a temple where Daethian orphans belong." Criton's movements were impossibly slow. His speech sounded thick with the tremendous effort to overcome great pain.

"I'm not an orphan!" Quatar protested. "He's my papa!"

Peri bugled in confirmation.

Criton feinted at the dragonette with his blade, "I could kill the mutant as he should have been slain at birth."

Peri easily avoided the blow and coiled tighter around Shashtah, covering most of the Dragonrider's body with his wings.

Criton stepped around Adrial, snatched Tphah by her wrist and forced her to rise. "I could hurt your Bond Partner as you hurt mine!"

Shashtah reached out, grabbed Quatar, and, with some difficulty, stood up, bleeding from where Peri's talons were digging into his shoulders. He stared dispassionately at Criton. "You could do all of those things. But then at least you would be causing someone else pain instead of wallowing in your own."

Adrial straightened and gently pulled Tphah's wrist and Criton's hand apart until the Lord of Daethia released the Prophetess. The Elven Princess placed her own wrist in Criton's grasp. "I'm the one you're supposed to kill."

Criton gave a strangled cry and dropped his sword. He pulled Adrial close to him and folded his wings around them, shielding their private despair from the eyes of the Dumnonians.

Tphah pried Peri off of Shashtah.

Peri, still too upset to remember how to shift to humanform, twined himself around Tphah, rendering her immobile.

Quatar glanced at Shashtah to see if the danger had passed—and saw the blood flowing from the deep gashes on his shoulders. "Peri hurt you!"

"Hush," Shashtah whispered.

Criton lowered his wings slightly so Shashtah could see his tortured, sky-blue eyes, but he kept Adrial hidden from view. "I was so sure you were the weak link. You were the only one without Mirari blood. Yet the backlash hit me. Through you, my father gave me the strength to endure, even though I don't want it. Yet you needed no such help when this spell was used against you. Why?"

Shashtah gripped Quatar tightly with his right arm and embraced Tphah and Peri with his left. "Because I want to live—no matter what. The Elven King has also chosen life. Even the Dark One, in his own twisted way, shares our passion. Perhaps you should cultivate a similar obsession."

"Yet you ask Adrial to die," Criton said.

Juel, Elven Lord, poked his head inside the doorway. "Sorry it took me so long to get here. I was going over tonight's duty roster with my lieutenant, and I didn't want him and half of the Kyondoca tagging along. Everyone still alive?"

Criton lowered his wings a little further so the elven commander could see his aunt.

"Good!" Juel declared in a ringing tenor as he stepped into the crowded study and closed the door. Extremely tall for an elf, he wore a magical, hooded cloak that draped down his back like a waterfall and made him all but invisible against the stone walls of the room. His solid violet eyes sparkled with a mischievous nature that had long ago inspired Shashtah to treat the golden-haired commander with extreme caution. Priceless Galantite chain mail, as flexible as cloth yet almost impossible to pierce, shifted soundlessly beneath Juel's violet-trimmed, dark-blue tunic. Shashtah noted that the deadly elf made absolutely no effort to hide his exquisite dagger and rune-covered, Galantite sword. Juel winked at Shashtah, crossed the room like a fine dancer, perched on the edge of the desk and pegged Criton with a glare that made Shashtah's soul tremble. "Then you can control Tor while I take charge of our Dumnonian friends. Gran'da has developed a concerted interest in their staying in one piece until he gets a particular caravan they've promised him."

"Caravan?" Criton echoed, unfurling his wings.

Adrial twisted to stand with her back against Criton's chest and pulled his arms tightly around her waist. "Slow down, Juel. You're going too fast for him."

Juel gestured at Shashtah. "Dumnonian. Go home alive," he said in a ridiculously slow voice as he pantomimed a Dragon in flight. His fingers danced in the air, drawing sparkling illusions of camels laden with overflowing packs. "Send caravan to Elven King with magic items for Gran'da to drain." He waved his hands again and sent the sparks flying off toward the Elven Kingdom.

"Ooo!" Peri crooned with delight, finally settling into his humanform.

Quatar beamed with proprietorial pride in the elf.

"Juel!" Adrial snapped. "He's not stupid! Things just happen too fast for him in this world."

Juel rolled his eyes. "Too fast? You've spent millennia marching down the aisle with him! You've now sat in the same room with him for almost two rotations, holding his hand, and that was only because he was almost paralyzed! If you slow things down anymore the gods are going to die of old age before you bear him that Great Wizard we've all been promised!"

"Juel!" Criton boomed. "Adrial will die when our child is born!"

"Which means her spirit won't be trapped on this plane," Juel countered.

"You're Mirari, a 'miracle worker.' All you have to do is find whatever plane she goes to and join her there. Unless you decide to wait so long that the Dark One runs us over and doesn't leave you anything to find. If you aren't stupid, think! Gran'ma's spirit is waiting for Gran'da on your home plane. Da's spirit is there, too. The only reason we're separated from them is that we have work to do here to atone for your Da's mistake of sending your brother to this unprotected world. Gran'da says we'll join our loved ones when we die: Our Mirari blood will call us home."

Adrial crinkled her petite nose. "I think I understood you better before you became enchanted with Dumnonians."

Juel laughed harshly. "Let's just say they've given me a more efficient view of our world for someone who's constantly winning battles and still losing this unholy War." He sobered as much as he ever did. "What about it, Criton? Are you competent enough to mind your own business if I go back to tending Gran'da's?"

Criton's mouth twisted into a disapproving smile. "Since when is meddling in Dumnonian affairs elven business?"

A deep sadness flooded through Juel's solid violet eyes. "Since I loved a Dragon and she died."

"Don't cry, papa," Quatar whispered.

Only then did Shashtah realize that tears were streaming down his cheeks. He met Criton's pain-filled gaze. "Maybe," he said in a hushed voice, "I was wrong. Maybe you were hit with the backlash because the Elven King and I already know the pain of great loss. So does the Dark One. Maybe the magic sensed that you alone didn't understand."

Criton raised his left hand.

The winged stallion trotted over to him and nickered.

Criton caressed the stallion's velvety muzzle. "I don't pretend to understand the magic of this world the way my uncle does. I'm a warrior who likes simple solutions to simple problems, and there's nothing simple about this whole mess." Criton buried his face in Adrial's silver hair. "You and Seraphe are the only pleasures left to me. I understand what has been asked of you. But I promise you this: If you give up your life, so will I. I will live only long enough to raise our daughter, and the day she assumes her powers is the day I, too, shall die."

Adrial gasped. A dozen responses tangled in her throat.

"So be it!" Shashtah heard his own voice thunder, shocking everyone in the room, including himself. "'And a warrior shall rise up from the Wasteland, and he shall bring you comfort and death!'" he quoted the ancient Prophecy of Tchang.

"Criton," Adrial whispered.

"Shashtah," Juel corrected her.

Peri started to say something, and Tphah slammed her hand over his mouth. "Mphf-mphf."

"Hush," Tphah whispered. "Now is the time for uncertainty, not Prophecy. You will learn the difference eventually."

Adrial beamed at Criton, believing that she had heard her own interpretation confirmed by the Dragons.

Shashtah decided not to disillusion her.

Criton nodded slowly. "I relieve you, Elven Lord."

"I stand relieved." Juel leapt to his feet. "Come on. Let's get out of here before he has time to change his mind."

Shashtah winced as he ushered his charges after Juel, but Criton and Adrial were too lost in each other to hear the Elven Lord's remark.

Quatar latched onto the Elven Lord, and Tphah took a firm grip on Peri, which left Shashtah free to trail behind them, trying desperately to think as they wound through the ruins of the School of Wizards. Although he dreaded venturing into the world of the Dragonslayers that lay beyond the palace walls, staying anywhere near Criton seemed like an even worse idea. *Someday he really is going to kill me.* The last time Shashtah had walked the streets of Tor, he'd done so with Tkai and under the cover of night. The Kyondoca had bound his hands and escorted him into the palace to be tried and executed for the murder of Quatar's father. He'd had no time to prevent the Kyondoca from taking Quatar's sister away to a temple as an orphan because he was too busy being splattered against a wall by the bolt Criton had sent at him from the dead warrior's bracers while Tkai looked on. At the last heartbeat Criton had decided to transport him to a jail cell and make it look as if he'd been reduced to ash. But Shashtah doubted the Kyondoca had forgotten him, and he didn't need Prophecy to show him his fate if they realized he was still alive. *Even my father wouldn't enter Tor. But Tkai did . . . Why? What did she know that my father doesn't? That I don't?* The voices in his head stubbornly refused to answer him.

Shashtah followed the others through an inconspicuous door Juel opened in the outer wall. He stared at his boot tips on the cobblestones while his eyes darkened against the light so none of the passers-by would notice the change.

Someone nearby gasped anyway.

Shashtah looked up to see who'd made the sound.

A couple of women, carrying baskets of bread, stared at Shashtah, and then scurried to the far side of the street. They disappeared around the first corner they reached.

Shashtah's mind froze with terror. *Two heartbeats outside the palace, and something's already gone wrong.*

Tphah laid her hand on his elbow. :*Relax, Dragonheart. No one is going to harm anyone in the Elven Lord's company. They're only shocked because you look like you lost a fight with a murder of crows.*:

Shashtah followed her bemused gaze to his shirt.

A trickle of blood made its way down his chest. Sweat turned dirt and dust dark on the torn fabric, blending with angry bruises and scrapes that covered all of his visible skin.

Tphah handed her Rider the healing potion Kashon had given him. "Drink."

Shashtah downed the liquid and handed the empty vial back to her. "Thanks." He felt the cuts knit together. The potion, however, did nothing to fix the rends in his clothing nor clean away the blood. *Where's Kashon when I need him?* "I wish I had another shirt."

"That I can fix." Juel waved his hand in the pattern Shashtah had seen Kashon use so many times. The grime vanished. Another gesture mended the shirt enough to pass for a well-worn garment.

"Thanks." Shashtah studied the people who continued to cross to the other side of the street to pass them. *Dragonslayers.* The word kept echoing through his mind. "We need to get somewhere a little less public."

"How about the Temple of the Light?" Tphah suggested. "I can't imagine your deity will let you come to harm in his House."

Shashtah appealed to the Heavens. "That's not what I meant by 'less public.'"

"Please, Dragonheart?" Tphah wheedled. "It's the main temple of your God. I want to see it." She favored him with a knowing look. "So do you."

Shashtah felt Quatar starting to bounce while Peri stood very still.

Juel squinted at the formidable Dragon's Back Mountains.

The impressive range still hid the rising sun, casting deep shadows across the bustling city.

"If we hurry, we can catch the sun topping the peaks," the Elven Lord observed.

"All right!" Shashtah agreed, his own desire to see the temple he'd dreamed about for so long defeating his certainty that they should be more cautious. He grabbed his fosterlings' hands and nodded for Juel to lead the way.

The temple of Leot, Lord of Light, soared above the westernmost wall of the city, not far from the main gates. The enormous domed structure, flanked on either side by comparatively unimpressive extensions that served as living quarters for the clerics in residence and offices for conducting temple business, dwarfed the other buildings around it. A golden spindle rose high above the dome, designed to be the first and the last thing in the city to touch the rays of the rising and the setting sun. Massive crystal doors had been thrown wide to admit worshipers to the service.

Juel ushered Shashtah and his family inside.

The crowd parted before the Elven Lord like sand before a dust devil.

Juel herded his guests as close to the center of the temple as non-clerics were allowed.

Shashtah said a silent prayer of thanks that, although the temple was packed, everyone was too focused on Juel to take any real notice of anyone else. He studied his surroundings as he prepared for the service to being.

Mosaics, fashioned out of Galantite, gold, silver, electrum and copper, covered the floors and the walls. The dome itself was constructed of gems of every description, set in patterns of flame and positioned in such a way that the sunlight cast tiny sparkles of colored light throughout the room. Beneath the golden spindle a diamond easily twice the size of a Dragon's egg reflected pure white light against the mosaics, showing the path of the sun across the face of Centuria, the subtle changing of the seasons in Tor, and the time of day.

As the first rays of the sun topped the mountains the tip of the spindle began to glow. It sent an intense beam of light through the diamond, toward the worshipers below.

Shashtah's skin tingled.

The High Priest stood, arms spread wide, palms upward, in a welcoming gesture. Clerics of various ranks formed a precise circle around him. Behind them, in dirt-smudged plain white tunics, knelt the wraith-thin orphans who had chosen these priests to replace the parents they had lost. The sheer quantity of children was staggering, and, if representative of the number in the other temples, a shocking testimony to the appalling slaughter the Daethians had endured in the War.

The beam of light touched the High Priest, turning his blond hair the color of the rising sun. Power flowed into him as he opened his mouth and led the clerics in a chant.

Shashtah heard his own tenor voice join with theirs. "Blessed Light shine down upon us, Warm the frozen places in our souls, Summon all the sacred colors, Wrap us now with rainbows' holy stoles . . . "

By the time the song finished, the dome was alive with color. Sunlight glittered through the gems. Quatar, Peri and Juel were almost blinded, but Shashtah's desert adapted eyes detected Tphah's scowl. He followed her stare to the kneeling children and noticed that several were using the cover of the brilliant light to hide tears of despair.

As the sun continued its unceasing journey across the sky, the light vanished and the children resumed the stony expressions that Shashtah now realized had been on their faces when he first entered the temple.

"Let us now partake of the bounty the Light has provided for us, and then return to the fields Our Lord has entrusted to our care."

"Our Lord." The words echoed in Shashtah's head. *Does he mean the Lord of Light or Lord Criton?*

The High Priest spotted the Elven Lord and signaled for him to join them.

Or Juel? Shashtah watched Juel extend his arm to Tphah.

The Prophetess let the Elven Lord escort her after the clerics and children.

Shashtah pulled his foster sons close to him and followed after Juel and Tphah, feeling more than a little awkward as he took a Dragon's proper place.

Orphans crowded onto wooden benches at one end of the immense dining hall while the clerics took their places at the grand table that occupied the other. Delicacies, many of which Shashtah could not recognize, filled priceless vessels in front of the clerics. At a nod from the High Priest, Juel settled Tphah onto a cushioned, straight-backed chair and took the seat to her right. A cleric moved to separate Quatar and Peri from Shashtah, but, at a scowl from the Elven Lord, the two boys were seated at the high table on either side of their foster father.

Shashtah, his arms draped possessively around his boys like dragonwings, stared at the orphans.

Teenagers served bowls of a thin gruel to the younger orphans, took some for themselves and settled on the floor in front of the benches. At a signal from one of the clerics, the children drank their gruel, set aside their bowls and proceeded to watch with unseeing eyes as the clerics at the high table leisurely consumed their feast.

Dragons first. The command slipped unbidden through Shashtah's mind. His frown deepened.

Juel picked absently at some grapes as he watched the faces of his guests.

Shashtah had the distinct impression that the Elven Lord was expecting something from him. He looked at the orphans, then back at the contents of the high table. The gruel would have suited him quite well. It was exactly the sort of thing he had eaten while running caravans between Dumnonia and Daethia. In fact, it was more than the caravaneers usually had to eat in an entire day. The food on the high table held no attraction for him. It consisted mainly of meat, which he detested, and everything else looked decidedly too rich. Then he heard Quatar's stomach growl. :*The children are Daethian. They aren't being honored. They're starving.*:

Tphah claimed a small chicken wing and bit off part of the skin. "I am sated." She handed the remainder to Peri.

Peri glanced from the Prophetess to the orphans, and then took a bite only slightly larger than Tphah's. "I am sated as well." He passed the remainder of the wing to Quatar.

Quatar looked from the partially eaten chicken wing to Shashtah. "Can we give those children some of our food like we do with the Dragons?"

A cleric overheard the question and glowered in disapproval. "There isn't enough for all of them, and this sort of food would make them ill."

A fierce headache gripped Shashtah. He closed his eyes and bowed his head. "This city was the home to the School of Wizards who gained their power from knowledge. Is there no one left here who can think?" He opened his eyes and gestured at the food. "Trade what you can't use for what you can use."

"To whom would you have us trade it?" another priest snapped. "You? Dumnonia has nothing to offer Daethia."

Shashtah glared at the cleric, too angry to realize that the priest had correctly guessed his race. "It's just a matter of moving food between the north and the south. The Krills would love this type of fare, and they're small so little portions go a long way."

"Krills?" yet another cleric scoffed. "You want us to trade with Krills? What food do they have?"

Shashtah gestured at the food on the high table. "The Krills can give you treasure for this food. You take the treasure to the Elven Kingdom and exchange it for the type of food you do need. Bring that food back here and use it to feed these children."

"Why would we go to all that effort?" the first cleric asked in complete astonishment.

"Because you're supposed to take care of the children." Shashtah tried not to roar, but he suspected that he'd failed.

"Like your Dragons take care of you?" the second cleric snapped. "Are you so blind that you can't see how the powerful monstrosities have enslaved you?"

Dragonslayers . . . Shashtah swallowed the knot that tried to form in his throat. "Do you think these children would enslave you if you cared for them as *The Book of Light* instructs?" He could sense the fury of the clerics rising against him, but he couldn't stop. "We take care of the Dragons because they protect us just as you should take care of these children so one day they can protect you."

One of the priests laughed. "And what, exactly, do you think these children are good for besides working the fields and breeding more warriors?"

Shashtah rose, shifted Quatar closer to Peri and Tphah, and walked over to the orphans. He spotted a particularly downcast girl of about seventeen. "Come here," he ordered.

The girl glanced at the priests, clearly terrified.

Shashtah stepped forward and took her hand gently. "Don't be afraid. I won't let anyone hurt you."

Disbelief flooded through the girl's dark brown eyes, but she let him help her to her feet.

Shashtah saw something familiar in her melancholy features. "What's your name?"

After another fearful glance at the priests, she whispered, "I'm not allowed to say."

"Why on Centuria not?" Shashtah asked.

The girl's shoulders sagged. "It's the same as the war goddess's name."

Shashtah took a closer look at her. *Impossible.* "Why would you have such a name unless you followed Her? The orphans of Daethia are raised in the temple of their choice. Why didn't you ask for the temple of the War Goddess instead of the Lord of Light?"

Tears filled the girl's eyes, threatening to spill out. "I did! But when I told the Kyondoca I wanted to be like them someday, they brought me here."

"They deliberately denied your request?" Shashtah's suspicion that he knew the girl deepened.

The girl bowed her head. "Women can't be holy warriors and fight in the elite guard. They can't even join the army! The guards said that training me to be a warrior would be training me to be an outcast among my own people, so they brought me here where I've been taught to cook and sew and work the land, and now I'm old enough to be married to a Daethian farmer, and—" A sob cut off the rest of her lament.

"Hush, Kyla," Shashtah whispered, using the War Goddess's name.

The clerics gasped in horror.

Shashtah pulled the girl close, but his efforts to calm her produced the opposite reaction. Kyla's sobs became hysterical. Shashtah closed his eyes and prayed.

:*Dragonheart!*: Tphah's mental whisper warned him just as a priest's hand closed on his left arm, and another hand tried to pry the girl away from him.

Shashtah snapped open his eyes. "No!"

"You're making life harder for her," the priest protested.

"I'm making your life harder, not hers! You've trained her to do what you think she should do, not to use the skills she wants to use!" Shashtah looked over the girl's shoulder and past the priest at the orphans. "Come here! All of you! Come here!"

Hesitantly at first, then faster as they gathered courage from each other, the children rose and surrounded Shashtah, pushing the priest away from him.

Shashtah reached out with his right hand and touched one of the younger boys. Light leapt from his fingertips.

: . . . *heal the sick* . . .: a voice whispered inside him.

He touched another child.

: . . . *feed the hungry* . . ."

His glowing fingers caressed the face of an older boy.

: . . . *carry the Light into the Darkness* . . .:

As Shashtah touched each orphan, the true reason behind their choice of temple whispered through his mind. Only Kyla had originally wanted to be somewhere else. The others simply had found hunger and despair instead of what they had been looking for in the Temple of the Light. "Go. Eat your fill from the high table." At the sound of protest from the priests a bolt of light shot from Shashtah's hand, changing the food to what the orphans needed. "There will be plenty for all. Eat."

The children were not about to argue with an obvious Prophet who was handing them exactly what they desired most. They rushed to the table.

The clerics scrambled to their feet and attempted to impose some sort of order on the chaos.

Only Kyla stayed beside Shashtah.

Shashtah ran his fingers along her jaw and raised her chin until he could look into her dark brown eyes. *Eyes the same as Quatar's.* "Do you know me? Have you seen me before?"

"Yes."

"Who am I?"

"You killed my father after the devils corrupted his body," Kyla said in a voice too soft for anyone but him to hear. "You gave my brother to the Elven King, and you let me fly with you on your Dragon. You took me before the Lord of Daethia and watched as I gave him my father's armbands. You heard him promise that one day they would be mine. When I heard you'd been executed, I gave up hope that anyone would rescue me." She swallowed hard. "Why have you returned to make me hope again?"

Shashtah brushed the tears from her cheeks and automatically licked the moisture from his hand. The salty taste startled him. *Why do I always forget that Daethians aren't Dumnonians?* He turned her so she faced the high table. "See the Daethian boy seated with the adults?"

Kyla nodded.

Shashtah put his lips close to her ear. "What name did I give your brother?"

"Quatar," Kyla answered promptly.

Quatar looked around at the sound of his name.

Kyla took a quick breath. "Is it really him?"

Shashtah smiled. "Yes, it's really him. And, if you like, I'll make you his sister again: I'll take you into my household and train you to be a warrior, just as I'm training him. He'll lead the Kyondoca one day and that will give him the power to grant your heart's desire." The Prophecy flowed from Shashtah like a ten-winter storm flooding a wadi.

"But the priests want me to marry a farmer," Kyla said bitterly.

"Do you want to marry a farmer?" Shashtah countered.

"I'd rather marry you," Kyla confessed.

Shashtah chuckled. "I don't think that would set well with my Dragon, but I think she'd be thrilled if I adopted a daughter to care for my foster sons when we're fighting in Cinnamar. Dumnonian ways are harsh. Can you adapt to them long enough to learn what you need to know?"

Kyla stood straighter. "What must I do?"

Shashtah studied her carefully. "Study well, and earn your brother's respect. If you can do these things, the Lord of Light will see that your brother grants your wish." He felt his power gathering within him and shoved Kyla gently toward the high table. "Go sit between the Priestess of the Mother and the Elven Lord. I don't think you want to be near me for a bit. Something's about to happen, and I'm pretty sure I don't have any control over it." He watched as Kyla settled safely next to Tphah and delivered his message, then he raised his hands high into the air.

A ball of shimmering light formed just above his fingertips. His lips moved, forming words that were not his own. "The Light blesses the fields of Daethia and curses the sands of Dumnonia. From the sacred fields the Daethians have summoned fear. From the barren sands the Dumnonians have conjured courage. Children of Plenty, learn from the Children of Want! Teach the Children of the Light not to hide in Darkness but to share my bounty with all. Care for them as you would have me care for you. You have been blind to my Light, but I have sent my Prophet to make you see. Eyes now open, darken my name no more!" With that the light flickered out, and Shashtah collapsed.

Silence descended on the room.

The next thing Shashtah remembered with any clarity was the sensation of a hysterical sack of grain being dropped repeatedly on his chest.

A plaintive whine resolved into intelligible speech. "Papa!"

Shashtah threw his arms around Quatar and hugged him hard enough that the boy had to stop pounding on him. "I'm all right!"

Tears that were not his own dripped onto Shashtah's face. ". . . don't want . . . to stay . . . you die . . . no parents . . . send me . . . !" The rest of Quatar's protest was lost in a hopeless garble of inarticulate sounds.

Shashtah rolled to his right so that Quatar was lying beside him on the tiled floor. He covered his fosterling protectively with his left arm. "Hush! I'm not dead, and I've told you again and again that if something bad ever happens to me, Kashon will take you into his household. You'll never have to stay here."

". . . want . . . you said . . ." Quatar dissolved into inconsolable tears.

"Hush. You're wasting water." Shashtah sat up and pulled Quatar onto his lap. He was dimly aware that Peri was at his left elbow, ready to spring to his defense and that Tphah was standing in front of him, her hands firmly gripping Kyla's shoulders. Shashtah snapped playfully at Quatar's nose.

Quatar hiccupped and grew still at the absurdity of his action.

Shashtah smiled. "There. That's better. Really, now. As if I would dream of leaving a perfectly good warrior like you in a temple of farmers."

Quatar hiccupped again as he relaxed against Shashtah, exhausted.

Juel pushed his way through the crowd and thrust a goblet of water at Shashtah.

Shashtah took the chalice and held it to Quatar's lips. "Here. Drink."

Quatar drank obediently. His hiccups eased.

Shashtah handed the empty goblet to the Elven Lord. "I have someone I want you to meet." He motioned for Kyla to come to him.

Tphah released the girl so she could obey.

"This is Kyla," Shashtah told Quatar. "She's your sister. She's going to come live with us in Dumnonia. You'll have to help me teach her all about how people live in the desert."

Tphah raised her eyebrow but kept silent.

Quatar pouted. "I'm not a very good Dumnonian."

Kyla laughed, a delightful sound. "You have to be better than I am! I've never lived anywhere except here and the Great Woods."

Quatar's eyes widened. "You lived in the Great Woods?"

Kyla pressed his nose with her forefinger. "Didn't you listen to your papa, silly? I'm your sister. Your real sister. From before you went to live with the Elven King."

Quatar regarded her uncertainly. "I don't remember you."

"Of course you don't," Kyla said. "You were a baby when our parents were killed. Your papa saved you and gave you to the Elven King. I was sent here. Now your papa wants me to come live with you so we can be a family again. Is that all right?"

Quatar looked at Peri. "Is Peri going to be your brother, too?"

Kyla glanced at Shashtah and read the need for caution in his eyes. "Only if you want him to be."

Quatar considered the thought for longer than Shashtah would have liked. "Peri's very special. He's a Dragon. The only one of his kind. I don't know if I want him to be someone else's brother."

Shashtah hid a cringe, hoping none of the Daethians had overheard.

"He doesn't have to be my brother," Kyla assured Quatar. "But if you ever want him to be, all you have to do is let me know you've changed your mind." She held out her arms. "Will you come to me so your papa can stand up?"

Quatar clutched at Shashtah's shirt for a heartbeat, and then reached for his sister.

Kyla pulled Quatar to his feet.

Tphah gripped Shashtah's hand and helped him rise.

Peri seized Shashtah's left leg.

Shashtah put an arm around Tphah, swiveling so that he faced the High Priest over the heads of the baffled orphans.

The High Priest crossed the dining hall and stood before the Shashtah. "Thank you for bringing us the Word of the Light. I fear, however, that we won't be able to change things much: We don't have the resources to care for so many."

"Start by teaching these children how to trust instead of fear the Light," Shashtah declared solemnly. "Accomplish that, and you will be amazed at what can follow." He raised his voice. "The Light is with you always—even in the Darkness you can see His visage reflected in the moon and the stars. His Truth shines upon you. Follow a new path where you can walk together in the Light so that if I pass this way again I may bring you His Blessing." He paused and lowered his voice. "And I'll see what I can do about your trading problem." With that he escorted his family out of the temple, Juel strolling in their wake.

As soon as they cleared the temple walls, Tphah threw her arms around Shashtah. "So much for keeping your presence a secret. You scared me halfway out of my hide in there!"

Shashtah chuckled and held her reassuringly as the others gathered around them on the sidewalk, oblivious to the stares from the people passing on the street. "Scared myself. But, as Tkai once observed, my power is a bit different from everyone else's. I hope no one in there figures out I didn't do that on purpose. If they think I can blow up like that whenever I feel like it, maybe the Kyondoca will think twice before trying to kill me."

Juel flashed him a rather draconic grin. "If the Kyondoca doesn't understand, I'll explain it to them."

Fairly certain that the Elven Lord didn't plan to do such explaining verbally, Shashtah nodded his thanks, hoping that no such action would be necessary. He released Tphah and turned to Kyla. "My blood is your water. Care for the members of my household, and they will care for you." He wiped the last of the tears from Quatar's cheeks. "Do you want to walk with Peri or your sister?"

Quatar held out his hand to Kyla.

Kyla's eyes shone with hope as she grasped Quatar's fingers with hers.

Shashtah reached down, took Peri's hand and placed it in Tphah's. "I'm afraid you're stuck with Tphah."

Peri shrugged as if he could think of several worse places to be. "Where are we going to get into trouble next?"

"We're not going to get into trouble," Tphah stated firmly.

Shashtah gave Juel an apprehensive look. "I assume all the temples of Tor are as in need of a visit from a Prophet as this one was?"

"Gran'da's is doing fairly well," Juel said. "His clerics have established a town in the Great Woods for their orphans. It's mostly a problem of transporting them there without opening a warp. Caravans like the ones you promised your God's clerics should solve that difficulty. There's no temple for the White Wolf; he's rather unpopular here. No one openly worships the Lord of Pain, the Lord of Shadows nor the Dark One. Daethians are too prudish to have a Temple of the Mother. But the Temple of the Lord of Plenty has plenty of orphans it doesn't know what to do with. The Temple of the Lord of Humor doesn't find the number of orphans they are dealing with funny at all. The Temple of the War Goddess—"

Shashtah saw Kyla focus on Juel's words like a hawk on prey.

"—only takes in potential warriors, and most of those children wind up dying far too young because they're sent to the battlefield before they are ready." Juel shrugged, his muscles flowing more like those of a panther than an elf's. "I don't think any of the clergy are evil. They're just overwhelmed. They don't have the Dumnonian sense of organization."

Shashtah laughed. "It must be a cold day in Cinnamar if you consider the Dumnonians organized." He glanced back at the Temple doors. "It's probably best if I get off the streets until things calm down. Let's buy Kyla something decent to wear, and then explore the unused portions of the palace. Maybe I can find that jail cell where I woke up after Criton almost killed me."

Tphah hissed.

"You're the one who wanted to see where Tkai walked with me," Shashtah reminded her a bit too sharply.

Tphah bared her throat to him.

"I'd also like to see where Tkai walked with you," the Elven Lord said wistfully.

Shashtah bowed his head. "As you wish."

Juel stood to one side as they entered the Temple of the Lord of Plenty, cleaning nonexistent dirt from under his immaculate fingernails with his dagger.

Frescoes of beings of all races frozen in a perpetual orgy covered the wine-red walls. Heavy incense failed to cover the stench of sweat and vomit. Adults reclined on lavish, pillow-covered couches that were arranged more closely together than eggs in a Dragon's nest. Children stole food freely from the overflowing plates they served their guardians, who were clearly too drunk to notice. And everything took place in eerie silence.

Kyla took one look at the interior and clapped her hand over Quatar's eyes.

"Wha—?" Quatar started to object only to be furiously hushed by the nearest clerics. He tried to pry Kyla's fingers apart enough for him to see.

Tphah, disgust plastered across her face, gripped Peri's shoulder so tightly that the mutant discretely shifted until the skin beneath her hands was covered by Bronze scales.

Shashtah wanted to tap his foot in displeasure, but something half-glued the soles of his boots to the floor. His stomach lurched. There was nothing in the chamber he wished to consume, even though an abundance of mute orphans pressed him repeatedly to accept their hospitality. As he looked at the statue of

Zed, the god of the temple, he felt pretty sure he knew where the rich feasts of his own priests came from.

Never much liked Zed. The words slipped through Shashtah's head from somewhere deeper within him than where his Bond was with Tphah. *Always in a foul mood. Perpetual hangover.*

The noiseless chaos around Shashtah made it impossible for him to contemplate who the speaker was.

An avalanche of impossibly decadent food spilled from the cornucopia in the hands of the god's statue and onto the floor. As fast as the children scooped it up and served it to the clergy and the worshipers, the feast replenished itself, each offering more outrageous than the last.

Wine flowed freely from the god's mouth and other orifices.

The children caught the gleaming liquid in chalices of silver, gold and even Galantite and passed the sacred beverage among the clergy and the worshipers.

Older girls and boys shared the couches with the adults.

Well, "share" wasn't exactly the right word, but Shashtah didn't want to think about what the right word was.

Why is everyone barefoot? Shashtah wondered.

Immediately a wave of water washed across the floor, carrying away at least some of the waste as it vanished into troughs at the sides of the room.

Shashtah stared at his now soaking boots. *How in the name of the Light am I supposed to turn these children into Dumnonians? They'll all be missing body parts if they aren't dead in less than a rotation! They won't even survive the trip to the King's Camp.*

Since when does a caravaneer think Daethians belong in the King's Camp? a voice snorted.

Shashtah ignored it and scanned the couches.

Goat-legged fauns with their horned heads cavorting through the oblivious crowd caught Shashtah's eye. He squished his way through the doorway and back onto the cobblestone street.

The others followed him.

Without a word, Juel dried them off with a wave of his hand.

Shashtah took a deep breath of the relatively fresher air. "We need to move these children to the Great Woods. The same caravans we send north to bring proper food to my God's Temple can carry children from the Elven King's temple and this one south. If Dragons don't travel with them, the traders should be able to cross Daethia without a problem—provided we can figure out a way to swap camels for horses somewhere near the Great Woods like my father did when we journeyed to Rashtar. Camels won't do well with all of this water."

Tphah looked at him skeptically. "Your father isn't running caravans anymore, who has that many horses?"

Kyla brightened. "My father bred racing horses for messengers. Several other members of the Kyondoca also have estates near the Great Woods. We could get horses from them."

Shashtah blanched. *Dumnonians temporarily trading camels for horses bred by Dragonslayers?*

Juel nodded slowly. "Add some draft horses to pull wagons with the tradegoods . . . It could work."

Only my father could negotiate that deal, Shashtah fretted. He decided to worry about the problem later.

The Elven Lord took a deep breath. "As for the next problem, I hope you find it more amusing than I do." He escorted them down the bustling street.

The colors in the temple of the Lord of Humor hurt Shashtah's eyes. Diamonds of mauve and lime-colored light danced across the stone walls that were slathered with blindingly bright yellow paint. And they weren't the only things dancing.

Children skipped, twirled, pirouetted, hopped and leapt everywhere as worshipers joined them and laughed.

A chaotic food fight dominated the room with more sustenance winding up on the floors, walls, and furniture than inside the worshipers.

Juel stood in the temple doorway, magic glittering from his fingertips as he shielded his companions from the worst of the chaos.

While Tphah and Peri looked perplexed, Quatar laughed so hard that Kyla knelt beside him and braced him against his mirth. "Breathe!"

"But it's funny!" Quatar protested. He surged forward to join the other children.

Kyla stopped him.

Quatar pouted. "You're no fun."

More cacophony filled this temple than silence had filled the temple of the Lord of Plenty. Musical riffs from panpipes twisted off into nowhere, scales remained unresolved, rhythm came and went without warning, and otherwise abusive sounds assaulted Shashtah's sensitive ears. *Lord of Light, this would be pure torture for a Bard!*

This would be a musical joke to a Bard, one of his internal voices contradicted.

The dancers tumbled, spun, and sprang with complete disregard for timing and no perceivable grace.

Shashtah expected them to slam into each other at any heartbeat. He could see why Juel thought the Dumnonians were organized if this was what he was comparing them to.

Order can hide in chaos.

Shashtah rubbed his left temple. *Same voice? Different voice? Past? Present? At least it should have enough manners to introduce itself!*

A girl of about eight grabbed Shashtah's belt and pulled him into the dance.

Half a dozen steps later Shashtah ducked just in time to avoid being hit by a bright blue clump of something that looked remotely like hummus. He took the opportunity to twirl away from the dancers and rejoin his companions at the door.

"Nice move," Juel remarked.

Shashtah ignored the praise and gestured at the revel. "What am I supposed to do about this?"

"Tkai would have known, but Criton didn't tell us how bad things were while she was still alive." Juel studied Shashtah's face. "I was hoping that showing you the problem might stir one her memories in you."

Shashtah glanced at Tphah. *Something's stirring all right. I just have no idea what—or who—it is.*

Laughter cascaded through Shashtah's brain like sands through an hourglass. *You're hopeless! Good thing you're a Prophet and not a Wizard!*

Shashtah rubbed his forehead, wishing the voices would go away. He tried to focus on the nonsensical crowd once more. "Who's the High Priest?"

"Priestess." Juel pointed at a Daethian woman who was contorting herself into positions that natural bodies shouldn't be able to take.

Shashtah threaded his way through the chaos until he reached her. "Is there somewhere quieter we can talk?"

The woman pressed herself into a stance that would have looked halfway normal if her arms and legs had switched places. "The Temple of the Lord of Plenty?"

Shashtah discarded the first half dozen comments that occurred to him and settled on "What happens to your orphans when they leave your care?"

"They join the dance troupes." The Priestess untangled herself. "You should stay awhile. You need a good laugh."

She's right, you know.

Be still! Shashtah thought furiously.

Tphah's head shot up. A hurt look crossed her face. :*I didn't say anything!*:

Shashtah winced. :*It's not you. I'll explain later.*: He gestured at the revelers.

"The children arrive faster than you can train them to join the troupes."

The Priestess smiled wryly. "One of my god's little jokes, I suspect."

Too bad they aren't Striplings. You could assign them to the Riders you don't have.

Shashtah froze as he saw the pattern. He inclined his head slightly to the Priestess. "I'll send help as soon as I can!"

The High Priestess laughed. "And I'll turn blue from holding my breath!" She filled her lungs, held her nose, and pursed her lips, causing everyone around her to cheer.

Shashtah spun back to his companions with the grace of a fine Ban-kai dancer.

Kyla cocked her head in surprise.

Peri's eyes sparkled with pride as Quatar broke into wild applause.

Shashtah took Tphah by the elbow. :*Let's get out of here.*:

As soon as they cleared the temple gates, Tphah tore her arm free from his grasp. "I didn't say anything!"

Shashtah squeezed his head between his hands. "I know. It's not you. Something's set off the voices in my head, and I can't get them to shut up."

Juel tilted his head thoughtfully. "Have you spent much time in Tor before?"

Shashtah shook his head. And promptly wished he hadn't. "No. My father refused to bring me here. When I was with Tkai, Criton kept using me for magical target practice, so we left as soon as we could. When I cast the spell against the Dark One with Criton and the Elven King, the Kyondoca—well, let's just say we were certain your grandfather was going to deliver my ashes instead of my humanform to the Valley of Ancients."

Deep, dark knowledge shone in Juel's solid violet eyes but he remained silent.

Shashtah gestured at the Lord of Humor's temple. "These clerics already have a way to deal with their problem. They just aren't focused enough to see it. The older children can travel with the Lord of Humor's Dance Troupes and learn from the trained entertainers the same way Striplings learn from Riders."

Juel nodded thoughtfully. "I'll summon the High Priestess in the morning. It's easier to talk with her in the palace."

"Can we go to the War Goddess's temple now?" Kyla asked.

Shashtah winced at his stupidity. "That's the first place we should have gone. I wasn't thinking."

A voice snorted in his head.

Knowing it wasn't Tphah's, Shashtah ignored it.

Juel gestured toward something that looked more like military barracks than a temple. "This one will makes more sense."

Shashtah saw the doubt on Tphah's face, but he let Juel guide them on.

Row after row of Daethian children, most of them males, stood in ranks before a blue-clad instructor. Their immaculate sapphire blue uniforms fit them like finely crafted armor. Behind them several rows of worshipers joined in the ritual exercises.

Shashtah watched as the orphans moved in unison, performing maneuver after maneuver that resembled the different sequences of the Ban-kai stretches.

"Come on!" Quatar shouted, grabbing Peri by the hand and pulling him forward to start a new line.

Peri flashed Quatar a skeptical look but obediently fell into place and mirrored the worshipers.

Rider Striding Left. Dragon Turning Right. Scimitar Slashing. The Dumnonian names for the stretches whispered through Shashtah's mind. He saw the disapproval in the instructor's eyes. *My boys' movements aren't sharp and clean like Daethian swords but fluid and shifting like Dumnonian sands. The Daethian way is too stiff. It's supposed to be a dance, not a drill.*

Kyla gawked at Quatar and Peri. "How do they know how to do that?"

"They practice," Tphah commented dryly.

"As if anyone's taught her the moves," Shashtah growled. He motioned Kyla forward. "The only way to learn is to try. Go ahead."

Pure joy replaced Kyla's disbelief as she stepped up beside the boys and started to copy their movement.

Shashtah watched her critically. *Not as stiff as the Daethians. Not as flexible as my boys. Somewhere in between. Not bad for someone who's never practiced. She just needs someone to show her how—*

Tphah wrapped her arm around Shashtah's waist to prevent him from taking up position beside his fosterlings. "No, you don't. We need to find the High Priest."

Juel chuckled and led them down a hall that paralleled the exercise room.

"Feeling better?" Tphah asked.

"Yes," Shashtah admitted. "There's less magic."

"Almost none," Juel confirmed. "The War Goddess presides here."

Shashtah found himself wishing he'd been more curious about Kashon's religion. "Doesn't she have clerics?"

"One." Juel said mysteriously.

Heartbeats later Shashtah found himself plastered against the far wall of an office that was about a quarter the size of Criton's, wondering why he wasn't dead.

Across the room from him stood a member of the Kyondoca. The man's impressively muscled chest and legs silently proclaimed that he could do far more than use the golden bracers that were magically welded to his forearms. A pristine black kilt circled his waist, and black leather boots protected his feet. His dark brown hair and Daethian eyes were perfect matches for Quatar's.

Tphah planted herself firmly between Shashtah and the warrior.

Juel, a bemused look on his face, leaned casually against the doorjamb, trapping them in the room. "Sol, meet my guests: Shashtah Dragonheart and the Dragonprophetess Tphah. Shashtah and Tphah, this is Sol, High Priest of the War Goddess and my chief lieutenant."

Shashtah gaped at Juel. *He's completely sunstruck! He just told his second in command that Tphah's a Dragon and I'm a Dragonheart!*

Sol's eyes shifted warily from Juel to Shashtah. "I thought you were dead, Dumnonian." His voice sounded all the more lethal because he kept it soft.

Juel fingered the hilt of his sword. "Yes, well, Lord Criton had a change of heart. I suggest you do so as well."

Sol looked like a cobra about to strike. "He killed Davit."

"I know. I was there," Juel drawled. "He's also the Lord of Light's Prophet, who saved Davit's soul. He returned Davit's bracers to Lord Criton. And he's raising Davit's son to be a member of the Kyondoca, just as Davit wished. So I suggest you leave him in one piece if you wish to remain in the Lord of Light's, the Lord of Daethia's and my good graces."

Sol hesitated for several heartbeats then shifted into a deceptively relaxed stance.

Shashtah peeled himself off the wall.

"What do you want?" Sol demanded

"Wh-what do you need?" Shashtah stuttered softly, still not convinced the lieutenant intended to spare his life.

Sol tilted his head and regarded Shashtah skeptically. "Can you teach these orphans how to live long enough to kill at least one of the Dark One's monstrosities before they become undead themselves and take their victim's place?"

"Can't you?" Tphah asked.

Sol gave a bitter laugh. "Everyone who isn't guarding our Lord or fighting at the Sterrefyr is spending his leave patrolling what's left of our country. I'm using older students to train younger ones until I have even younger ones come in and I have to send the eldest off to the frontline to make room for the newcomers—where they usually increase rather than decrease the Dark One's forces because they don't stay dead when they're killed."

Shashtah's eyes widened in horror. "You can't be serious."

"I wish I weren't," Sol said with a bitter laugh.

Shashtah silently appealed to his own deity. *What am I supposed to do about this?*

Juel flicked his fingers, sending sparkles that gathered into the shape of tiny Bronze Dragons circling around Shashtah's head.

Tphah glared at the Elven Lord. "You aren't helping."

Juel straightened and dismissed the magical images with a wave of his hand. "Oh, but I am. Don't you see it? Tkai did."

Tphah frowned for a moment. "I—" She stared at her Rider. "Oh!"

Shashtah rounded on the Elven Lord. "Seriously? You want Dumnonia to take in Daethian orphans and somehow turn children who don't belong in the desert into warriors for the Dragonslayers?"

Sol started to clash his bracers together.

Juel's sword tip hovered a hair from Sol's throat, the blade preventing the bracers from making contact with each other. "I prefer my guests alive."

Sol threw up his hands, his deadly armbands glittering in the light. "I'm not sending Dragonslayers to live among Dragons!"

Shashtah awkwardly found himself agreeing with the High Priest. "My king will never approve of this."

Juel lowered and sheathed his sword. "So we get the other members of the League of the Nations to convince your king to cooperate."

"Right," Sol barked, his harsh laugh echoing off the office's walls. "The only thing the League of the Nations has ever done is agree that we won't kill each other at the same time we're trying to kill the Dark One."

"Not true," Tphah said. "Dumnonia honors each leader of the alliance one rotation each year with a Feast. Some, like the Elven King, even attend in person. We trade with all of the nations in the League. Maybe it's not much, but it is a foundation for—"

"Working together," Shashtah said, completing her thought.

Sol shook his head in disbelief. "Daydreamers. The lot of you."

"Daethians coordinate with elves." Juel pointed southwest, toward Daethia's border with Cinnamar, the Sterrfyr River.

"And the Galantites sit in their mountain," Sol said, gesturing southeast. "The Rashtarians stay on their side of the Pass," he continued, pointing northeast. "No one has seen the King of the Forest in—I can't recall how long. And don't get me started on the Krills!"

Shashtah bristled but held his tongue.

Tphah laid a quieting hand on his arm. "Maybe the Children of the Mother can help. We understand people who are different from us very well. We can become ambassadors to connect the different races."

Juel scratched his ear and sighed. "Which will take time."

"Which we don't have," Sol snarled.

"Which is something I can fix!" Shashtah snapped. His shoulders slumped. "If I can find the White Wolf again."

"And what, exactly," Sol demanded, "do you expect us to do while you're 'fixing' things?"

Shashtah rubbed his temples as he felt his headache growing worse. His mind conjured an image of Kyla. "Use your women."

Sol gaped at him. "What?"

Shashtah forced himself to focus on the High Priest. "Our greatest Dragonlord is a woman. Shane of Corin was a woman. The Elven Queen Tira was a woman. The goddess you worship is a woman! Let your women fight for you!"

"That," Sol declared, "is going to take divine intervention."

"You're the High Priest of the War Goddess," Shashtah roared. "Ask your Goddess to intervene!" He stormed out of the room, Tphah close on his heels. As soon as he heard Juel close the door behind them, he slowed his pace and started to shake. *Lord of Light! I need to get out of this city while I'm still alive!*

Yes, you do, a voice in his head agreed.

Shashtah stood atop a grassy knoll, Tphah on one side and the Elven High Priestess on the other, watching as Kyla, Quatar and Peri joined the other orphans in target practice with their bows. Kyla and Quatar had traded their regular clothes for elven shirts, trousers and boots, and Peri had shapeshifted to match. They blended perfectly with the other orphans, although Kyla's and Peri's archery skills needed a lot of work. Quatar, however, had apparently spent a lot of time developing his talent while he was growing up in the Elven Kingdom.

Sapphire blue sky curved above them, and green grass glowed beneath their feet even though Shashtah knew they were inside a rather insignificant stone building. The single field was only large enough for one class to use it at a time. A moderate size oak tree stood in a campground adjacent to the field. Shashtah had spotted a couple of waterfalls that could be used as showers, but there was nothing like the great bathing complex in the Elven Kingdom. Juel had abandoned them with the High Priestess, assuring them that they would be safe and shielded here until he returned.

The High Priestess—whose name was virtually unpronounceable, so Shashtah had promptly forgotten it—shimmered in the mystic sunlight. With solid, sparkling silver eyes, flowing silver hair, porcelain-like skin, frosted lips, and a wispy gown that could have been woven from spider webs, she looked even more otherworldly than any of the deities Shashtah had met.

Tphah draped herself a little too obviously against her Rider.

Shashtah watched the sheer joy on Kyla's face as she engaged in the activities she'd always wanted to be a part of. "There's no chance she can stay?"

"No," the High Priestess said, regret mingling with finality in her voice. "She's too old. She'd have to go south with our older orphans. If we limit our numbers here and conserve our power, there's enough to meet our needs."

"I don't see a lake," Shashtah said. "Where does your magic come from?"

"Beneath the earth," the Priestess said absently. "It's still possible to drain some magic from the School of Wizards, but little is left after all these centuries."

Tphah's expression turned thoughtful. "I think this is the first time I've seen elven children."

"Those of us who are purebloods keep our children hidden," the Priestess explained in the voice of a patient teacher. "There are too few of us left to risk losing them to the Dark One's forces."

"There are different races of elves?" Tphah asked.

"Just as there are different types of dragons," Shashtah said quickly before Tphah embarrassed him anymore. "Sylvan elves prefer the woods. They watch over villages and such."

The Priestess smiled in serene surprise. "You've met them."

"Several times when traveling with my father's caravan." Shashtah turned his attention back to Tphah. "Then there are the elves who guard pools and streams."

"Riverfolk," the Priestess supplied.

"You saw the Elvenkind in the Elven Kingdom," Shashtah continued. "The Shadow Kith fight for the Cinnamarians. And then there are the Faery." He bowed his head slightly to their hostess. "I've never met one of you before."

The Priestess inclined her head toward him. "You've listened to the stories."

Shashtah blushed. "Many a night around my father's campfire."

"I thought Garesh had introduced you to every race on Centuria," Tphah said. "Why haven't you met one of the Faery?"

Shashtah gazed at the High Priestess, an expression akin to worship on his face. "The Faery can live much longer than the other types of elves, but most of them were killed when their homeland fell. The Elven Queen, Tira, was one of them."

The Priestess stared into the past. "I remember when she died. It seems like another lifetime."

Tphah took a closer look at the Priestess. "How many of you are left?"

"A few dozen perhaps." The Priestess sighed. "We watch over places like this, hiding from death as we prepare children to die." She locked stares with Shashtah as the archery practice drew to a close. "Our solution will work for a while, but not forever. Eventually there will be more children than there are adults to care for them. Then what do we do?"

Shashtah had no answer for her.

The Priestess waved her hand. Bows and targets vanished from the field, and horses wearing silver-covered tack cantered out from behind a hill.

Shashtah watched wistfully as elves helped his fosterlings climb onto the saddles of the nearest mounts.

The Priestess smiled as she caught the look in his eye. "Would you like to join them?"

Shashtah stared guiltily at Tphah.

Tphah laughed. "Go on! You don't need my permission."

Shashtah grinned his thanks and half ran, half slid down the hill. He grabbed the blue and silver reins of a willing white stallion and climbed onto the saddle. He dug his heels into the stallion's flanks and thundered off across the field.

The elven steed's deceptively bulky equine body rested atop lithe legs. Bred to carry more than one, often inexperienced, rider, he possessed a gait so smooth that the grass remained almost undisturbed as he ambled across the pasture. Tiny silver bells on his bridle tinkled, but no tack creaked. He breathed in silence and his coat yielded no sweat or scent as Shashtah put him through his paces. The stallion was as magnificent as Seraphe.

And he wouldn't last two candlescars in the desert. Shashtah found himself desperately missing his beloved, perfectly proportioned desert mounts.

:*I can always shift to a smaller form if you prefer to ride around on things the size of Hatchlings,*: Tphah suggested.

Shashtah laughed. :*Talons in, my love. Nothing compares to riding on you.*: He sent the stallion racing back toward her. He slowed as he heard elven instructors calling out corrections in ClearTalk as the children guided their horses in a circle. He pulled up beside Tphah and leapt to the ground. "Care to give it a try?"

Tphah stared at him as if he'd become sunstruck.

Shashtah winked at the Priestess. "Which way to your stables? It's been awhile since I've hot-walked and groomed a horse."

The Priestess gestured at a row of shrubs. "Walk directly at the hedge. The path will open for you. I must attend to my other duties. Go where you will and do as you wish until the Elven Lord returns."

Shashtah bowed his thanks, then, leading the stallion, escorted Tphah toward the hedge, regaling her with a tale about his first unfortunate encounter with a certain ill-tempered mare.

Shashtah woke up screaming. He fought to separate the horrors of his nightmare from the world around him and failed. Something pressed hard against his chest, pinning him to the bed. He could barely breathe.

"You're safe," Tphah's voice whispered in the darkness.

Shashtah didn't feel safe. He felt as if every demon in Mount Cinnamar was bearing down on him. His heart raced, and sweat covered him.

Not very Dumnonian of you.

Shashtah doubted the thought was his own.

"Easy, Dragonheart. I'm here." Healing light flickered from Tphah's fingers, slowing his heartbeat.

Shashtah could barely see in the radiance that flooded the sleeping quarters Juel had provided for them inside the Palace. His skin burned like brimstone, but he couldn't run away.

Peri and Quatar huddled under Kyla's arms as they crouched on their sleeping mats. All three looked as terrified as Shashtah felt.

Tphah tried again. "Look at me, Dragonheart."

Shashtah tried to obey but couldn't.

"Look at me." Tphah took his chin firmly in her hand and turned his head so he was staring directly into her loving amber eyes. "I'm with you. You're safe."

"That wasn't a dream," Shashtah whispered.

"I know." Tphah's fingers combed his damp hair away from his face. "I'm sorry. I should never asked you to bring me here. Just look at me."

Shashtah felt her essence reach through their Bond and curl protectively around his brain.

Tphah couldn't dismiss the magic, but her power set up a barrier between his soul and the blinding light.

Shashtah dimmed.

"As soon as the Elven Lord returns, he'll take us to Krillion," Tphah murmured. "You like Krillion, remember? You feel safe there. You've loved that city since you were a child. You told me so much about it during the Training. It's one of your favorite places on Centuria. You can enjoy all the trading you want, and you can show us those candy stalls you're always going on about."

Shashtah barely heard her over the question that repeatedly crashed through his mind like the ceaseless roar of the waterfall at Mount Paradin. The words finally broke through his lips. "Tphah, how do the Daethians slay Dragons?"

The Prophetess fell silent for several heartbeats, then gave him an honest answer. One he didn't want to hear. "I don't know."

Crown Prince Treigo

Chapter 8:

City of Thieves

To the Daethians, the Dumnonians are outcasts, mutants by virtue of their dragonblood, a race apart. Perhaps that explains why of all the races of Centuria only the Dumnonians are willing to trade with the Krills.

**—from *On Dumnonia*
by Shane of Corin**

THE EVENING WATCH WAS COMING ON DUTY as Shashtah, Tphah and the children climbed the gently rising slope on the southern side of Krillion to the only visible gate in the ramparts. The city crouched low on the highest hill in southern Daethia, less than a league north of the Great Woods and the mighty Ripon River. Barely three hundred and fifty Krills survived the destruction of their homeland by fleeing to Daethia under the guidance of the father of Treigo, the current Crown Prince of the Krills. Treigo refused to claim his father's throne because no one knew exactly what had happened to the king the last time the Krills had joined with the elves in battle against the forces of the Dark One. With too few Krills left to risk any more in combat, Treigo and his people had taken shelter in Daethia, where a new horror confronted them. Daethian law barred non-Daethians from joining the military, holding land or taking permanent employment within the country. Since the Krills had no divine ruler like Farador who was powerful enough to blatantly ignore Daethian laws, the diminutive humans turned to the one occupation that was left to them: They became thieves.

Within a decade of their arrival the Krills had "stolen" a city from the Daethians and renamed it Krillion after their homeland. Anyone entering the city could plan on leaving a forced tithe of their wealth behind. But inside the simple iron gates also lay the traders' paradise of Shashtah's childhood. The rates were fair and often absurdly low in contrast to the massively inflated prices in Tor, making Krillion a haven for caravaneers and other adventuresome souls. Anything a person wanted, be it goods or services, the Krills would find. For a price.

The instant Juel had half ushered, half shoved them through the magical mirror in the White Wolf's laboratory, Shashtah had started to feel better. He had to stop several times to wait for Tphah and his fosterlings to catch up as he trotted toward Krillion's gates. Excitement glittered in his amber eyes, and it was all he could do to keep from bellowing his name before the half-elven mercenary at the tollbooth finished hailing him. "Shashtah Dragonheart, Dragonrider of Dumnonia, son of Garesh! Tphah, Prophetess of the Bronze Dragons! Peri, Quatar and Kyla, my fosterlings!" he shouted at the bored and not-particularly-impressed half-elf.

"A gold piece for each of the adults; a silver piece for each child," the mercenary demanded.

Shashtah claimed the treasure pouch from Tphah, handed the designated coins to the gatekeeper and returned the pouch to his Prophetess.

"Pass and good trading," the mercenary said in a lifeless voice.

Shashtah ushered his charges through the iron gates. He knew Treigo well enough to be able to reclaim anything truly important that might be stolen from him or his family while they were within the city walls, and he fully intended to leave the entire balance of his new-found wealth in the royal Krill's hands to purchase the food the Dumnonians so desperately needed. The trading he intended to enjoy would be excellent.

Shops of all descriptions, just closing for the night, lined the outer wall as Shashtah and his family of misfits entered the main courtyard. The booths of two moneychangers stood in the southeast and southwest corners of the square. Shashtah ignored the stalls, knowing that the best rates were to be found at the seldom used stands in the northeast and northwest corners of the city if he had need of such services. To the left lay Thieves Row, to the right Merchant Street. Shashtah strode straight ahead through the opening in the inner wall and into Smith Lane.

The pungent scent of horses washed toward them from the stables, and armorers pounded glowing metal on anvils next to massive forges. The hiss of steam slithered through the cacophony of the ringing blows as armor, weapons and other necessities for a military life took shape beneath the practiced hands of the smiths. Daethians, half-elves, Rashtarians, even a couple of Galantites slaved over the fiery coals. But not a single Krill.

Shashtah guided his family across Knights Avenue and onto Monk Street, which ran between the Chapel of the Mirari and the Crown Jewel, the main tavern in the center of the city. He turned left onto Chapel Lane and escorted Tphah and his fosterlings through the tavern doors.

Rough wooden tables and benches creaked beneath the weight of people of all races, sizes, and professions. Mercenaries and traders—some of pure, others of decidedly mixed blood—drank, ate, gambled, told stories, and negotiated with each other for the kind of information that could only be found in a place such as this. The barkeeper and servers sported partially healed, crippling injuries that attested to their former military lives.

The lone Krill in the room was a pint-sized gent, scarcely as tall as Quatar. The little man stood on a table, avidly gambling with three Rashtarians. He wore a white ruffled shirt, black trousers and boots, a bright red sash, and a black cloak caught at his neck with a simple flame-shaped brooch. His brown-black hair glittered with red highlights from the light of the flames in the massive fireplace, and his solid indigo eyes betrayed an intelligence that few beings of any race could match.

"Treigo!" Shashtah called over the racket in the tavern.

The Crown Prince of the Krills glanced up and grinned from pointed ear to pointed ear. "Shashtah!" He dropped to the floor and slipped across the room, making no effort to hide either his phenomenal dexterity or his covetous appraisal of Shashtah's bejeweled scabbard and splendid scimitar.

Shashtah grabbed the Krill and heaved him into the air.

"You've lost weight," the Crown Prince commented drily in ClearTalk.

Shashtah set Treigo down and nodded at Tphah. "This is my Dragon, the Prophetess Tphah."

Treigo greeted Tphah with a rakish bow. His gaze lingered briefly on her scarab. "So, you finally got that Dragon you were always dreaming about."

"Tphah is my second Dragon," Shashtah admitted softly. "My first Dragon, Tkai, was killed in Mount Cinnamar."

Treigo bristled. "I remember Tkai. She shall be avenged. We all shall." He turned and peered at Quatar and Peri who were trying not to look as if they were hiding under Kyla's arms. "And who are these fine strapping boys and their beautiful guardian?" His sharp eyes took note of Quatar's ring and Peri's cloak, and he tilted his head thoughtfully as he studied Kyla, who seemed ill at ease beneath his scrutiny.

Shashtah beamed. "These are my fosterlings. Quatar and Kyla are Daethian orphans whom I've taken into my household. Peri is Tkai's son."

"Quite the handsome family," Treigo commented, patting Quatar's head.

"Put it back," Shashtah ordered with a grin.

Treigo sighed and returned Quatar's magic ring. "You're no fun."

Shashtah guffawed. "I'm an honest trader, and that amuses you more than a dance troupe of the Lord of Humor!"

Treigo conceded the argument with an elegant bow. "So, what," he asked as he hopped onto a nearby table to put himself near Shashtah's eye level, "do you have to trade?"

"It's not what I have to trade that's important," Shashtah said. "It's what you have."

Treigo put his tiny fists on his slender hips. "And what is that?"

Shashtah shrugged. "I have no idea, but we'll come up with something to make my plan work."

Treigo leaned closer, intrigued. "Plan?"

Shashtah turned to Tphah. "Wait here. I shouldn't be long."

"That's what you said in the Galantite Kingdom," Tphah reminded him.

"There are no time warps for me to step into here," Shashtah assured her.

:*You're not running off without me. You've just spent the better part of the day trying to imitate your god's orb. Kyla can watch the boys.*:

:*She's an orphan who's never left Tor. She doesn't know how to protect the boys in Krillion.*:

:*And I do?*:

Shashtah hung his head slightly. He had once more forgotten how young Tphah was and how limited her experiences were compared to his. :*Please. I'll be safe. You promised I could trade, and I can't concentrate on that if I'm distracted by the children.*:

Tphah relented. :*All right. This time.*:

:*You should be more worried about him keeping his hands off me.*:

Treigo's eyes narrowed as he recognized the silent exchange between Dragon and Rider.

"You must all be starving," Shashtah said a little too loudly. "Get something to eat while you're waiting. You don't need to haggle: The price will be fair here. Sit in a corner where no one can come at you from behind. And check everyone for missing items if a Krill comes within a wingspan of you."

Treigo gasped in mock offense. "Really! Such mistrust! And from an old friend!"

A compassionate smile flickered across Shashtah's lips. Seeing that he now had the Crown Prince's undivided attention, he dropped in an elaborate salaam and gestured toward the door. "After you."

Treigo hopped down from the table and slipped out of the tavern.

Shashtah jogged after him, amazed at how fast the Crown Prince could move.

Treigo led Shashtah through Inn Square, along Wall Road, and into Assassins Lane along the north wall of the city. He paused briefly outside a nondescript leather shop, then motioned for Shashtah to follow him inside.

Dark figures, so small they had to be Krills, stirred in the shadows, positioning themselves to guard the entrance.

Treigo directed Shashtah to a pile of skins near the back of the stall and gestured for him to sit.

Shashtah shifted his scimitar slightly so he would not damage the pelts and sank onto the soft hides

Treigo perched on a work bench. "What plan?"

Shashtah's amber eyes sparkled. "The Dumnonians have sand but need food. The Galantites have magic items but need sand. The Elven King has food but needs magic items."

Treigo's eyes narrowed. "Get to the point, trader spawn."

Shashtah ticked off the parts of his plan on his fingers. "I can send a caravan out of Dumnonia to Mount Paradin with sand, pick up magic items and take them to the Elven King, and pick up whatever you need and bring that load to Krillion. Here the caravan would pick up magic items, take them to the Elven King, pick up food there and then return to Dumnonia."

Treigo's eyes sparkled catching Shashtah's excitement. "Legitimate trade with the elves?"

Shashtah nodded. "With the Dumnonians as the go-betweens."

Treigo tugged at his beardless chin. "What's in this for the traders?"

Shashtah nailed the Crown Prince with a stony stare. "Twenty percent and a moratorium on stealing from the members of these particular caravans."

Treigo sputtered, "Twenty—!"

"If the minions of the Dark One find out the Dumnonians are running magic items from Krillion to the Elven King those traders and their followers will be worse than dead."

Treigo laughed. "But no one's concerned about taking magic items from the Galantites to the elves?"

Something dark flashed in Shashtah's eyes. "It's not the same kind of magic, and you know it. The Galantites make everything they send to the Elven Kingdom. The Dumnonians and Daethians acquire their magic items through combat. The Krills acquire theirs by," he paused, searching for the right words, "other means. The Krills are obviously not using the Galantites as a source of their . . . supplies. It doesn't take a Wizard to figure out that Dumnonians, Daethians and Cinnamarians must be . . . contributing to the cause. Some pretty powerful stuff comes off the battlefield, most of which I'm sure the Dark One doesn't want falling into the Elven King's hands." He absently fingered the hilt of his scimitar.

Treigo frowned. "It's too good a deal. What do you really want?"

Shashtah leaned forward. "My Dragonlord stumbled onto an enemy camp just before we rotated off the frontline. The treasure from that one haul made everyone in our century absurdly wealthy and added a healthy chunk to the Tribal Hoard." He lowered his eyes and examined his fingernails. "Just imagine how many more camps like that are out there, particularly on this side of the mountain—so close to you, so far from Dumnonia. Picture the possibilities, my friend, if the Krills used all that time they'd save from foraging to scout out similar camps and send word to our frontline centuries."

Treigo was in the throes of sheer and utter avarice when Shashtah ventured a look at him. "Twenty percent to the traders," the Krill agreed. "Forty to us, and forty to you." He offered Shashtah his hand.

Shashtah grinned. "Fifty to the Dumnonians, you unrepentant scoundrel, twenty to the traders and thirty to you."

"It'll be our hides if we're caught," Treigo protested.

"It'll be our blood, and the blood of our Dragons, if you're not." Shashtah shrugged. "You establish legitimate trade with the elves, make a noteworthy contribution to the war effort, and make a profit. Thirty percent is more than fair."

Treigo made a face. "Your father taught you too well. Thirty it is."

Shashtah joined palms with the Crown Prince. He grinned as the diminutive thief realized that Shashtah was literally wearing nothing except the clothes on his back and his scimitar, which Treigo had no intention of trying to touch. "Permission to spend the night in the Common Lodge?"

"Can you even afford that?"

"I have my resources." Shashtah surged to his feet. "I'm planning to purchase an obscene amount of food on our last day here. You might want to warn your . . . associates to pay a visit to the Lord of Plenty."

"Consider them warned."

Shashtah paused in the doorway of the Crown Jewel, watching Quatar and Peri doze in Kyla's and Tphah's laps. Too frightened to return to sleep after Shashtah's nightmare, both boys had spent the day in uncharacteristic silence and apparently collapsed shortly after he'd left them.

Tphah and Kyla leaned their heads close to each other, talking in voices just barely loud enough for each other to hear over the clanking of mugs and dishes and the unceasing clamor of the other patrons.

Shashtah's sensitive ears could not pick out the details, but the speed with which the women fell silent as he joined them told him that he was the subject of their conversation. He sensed Tphah's disapproval. "What is it? What did I do?"

"You need to stop abandoning me in places where I don't speak the language." Tphah shoved a piece of bread at him.

Shashtah cautiously claimed the bread and bit into it. :*That's not the real problem. What's wrong?*:

:*What happened when you left Tkai alone?*: Tphah's exasperated voice thundered in his head.

Shashtah took another bite of his bread. :*But you aren't alone! The children—*:

:*Shouldn't even be here!*: Tphah snapped. :*I have my talons full trying to keep you safe without having to worry about them, too!*:

Peri stirred.

Tphah forced herself to calm down long enough to lull the mutant back to sleep. "I'm sorry. I'm tired. Where's this place to sleep you told me about during the Training? I'd like to stay there tonight."

Shashtah finished his bread in silence. *She's right. I'm doing it again. I'm not working with her. She's too young to be Bonded, and she's saddled with a Rider who could blow himself into grains of sand any heartbeat. I have no right to add to her problems.* "This way." He rose, took Quatar from Kyla and headed for the door. Tphah followed with Peri cradled in her arms. Kyla walking at her side.

Shashtah led his family to the Common Lodge where he purchased a bed for each of them for a copper a head. He staked out a readily defensible corner of the hostel and gestured for Tphah to lay Peri on a bed by the wall as he settled Quatar onto the one next to him. As Shashtah turned to Kyla, he realized that she was standing exceptionally still, staring at the boys. "What's wrong?"

"Could they leave if they wanted to?" Kyla whispered. "Could I?"

"Yes," Shashtah said, "but things didn't go very well when I left them in the King's Camp nor when they left me inside Mount Paradin. I doubt anything better would happen here."

"You seem nice enough. But you're a Prophet of the Light—"

"And I glow in the dark. Which makes you wonder if you should be within a thousand wingspans of me," Shashtah finished for her. "Fair enough. My god's priests have done nothing to make you trust them, and I'm not exactly on the list of Dragonriders people most want to be around."

Kyla glanced at Tphah—who was staring at her like an adder. She instinctively tried to hide behind Shashtah. "I'm sorry! I didn't mean to say anything disrespectful about your Rider."

Shashtah inclined his head toward his Prophetess.

Tphah rolled over on the bed she had claimed, turning her back on him.

Shashtah sensed his Prophetess's displeasure, and he was fairly certain Kyla wasn't its target. Gently, he pulled Kyla out from behind him and settled her onto her own bed. "You've had five years of mistreatment, and I'm about to throw you into a culture that is completely different from the one in which you've lived. You have every right to feel confused and scared." He crouched down to her eye level. "I'll do the best I can. I can't promise I won't make mistakes. Please, tell me if I'm doing something you think is wrong. I'll listen to what you have to say, and then make the best decision I can. I expect such decisions to be obeyed, whether you understand them or not. In return I'll share my water and food with you, see that you are provided for when I'm on the frontline, and train you in the profession of your choice. I'm a military man. My time is not my own. If you ever want to leave me, I'll take you anywhere you please the next chance I get. Deal?"

Unexpectedly, Kyla giggled. "Tphah said it's impossible for you to stop trading."

Shashtah smiled at himself. "She's right. What do you say we visit the armorer in the morning and see if we can find you a sword to practice with?"

"A sword?" Kyla echoed.

"Unless you'd prefer another weapon."

Kyla grabbed his hand and kissed it. "Thank you."

"Get some sleep. Tphah and I will take turns keeping watch." Shashtah waited until she crawled under the worn but serviceable blanket. Then he unsheathed his scimitar and sat cross-legged on the wooden floor, the blade balanced easily across his knees, wondering exactly how much Tphah had told Kyla about him when he hadn't been around.

Shashtah spent every heartbeat of the remaining days of their leave with his family, showing them all the secrets of Krillion he remembered from his childhood. He listened as Kyla told Quatar tales of their parents and her life in the Great Woods before they died. He almost forgot Peri was there, so quiet and unobtrusive the mutant was as Quatar learned about the sister he had never known. Tphah kept her arm possessively around Shashtah most of the time, and he delighted in the contact with her. He could tell that she wanted to spend more time alone with him, but there was nothing to be done about that in the bustling city in the heart of the land of the Dragonslayers.

By the end of their stay in Krillion, Shashtah grew concerned about the sheer bulk of food Treigo had amassed for him to convey from the City of Thieves to Dumnonia. He couldn't imagine how he was going to transport the piles of dried fruit and vegetables, sacks of grain, and preserved whole carcasses of cattle, pigs and sheep that lay in a somewhat haphazard fashion around the base of the ramp to the city.

Tphah shifted to her dragonform, stretched her great Bronze wings in the light of the setting sun and roared at the crystal-blue sky. :*Kashon's on his way with enough Riders to help.*:

Peri shifted to his moldy green trueform just before Kashon and most of his century blurred into the air above them.

Kyla hid behind Shashtah at the sight of so many Dragons, all of them far larger than Tphah.

Katrell set down near Tphah, and Kashon slid to the grass.

Shashtah gaped at the skill with which they managed the maneuver without destroying any of the piles of food.

Kashon saw the expression on Shashtah's face and laughed. "All that practice landing on battlefields finally came in handy!"

Quatar put a protective arm around Peri's neck, warily eyeing the Dragonlord.

Kashon spotted Kyla. "Another stray?"

"Quatar's sister," Shashtah said. "I couldn't just leave her—"

"Most people collect something other than children." Kashon teased. "I'm surprised you aren't taking all of the orphans of Tor back to the King's Camp."

"Her name is Kyla, just like the War Goddess, so you two worship the same deity," Tphah declared loudly in ClearTalk, distracting Kashon as Shashtah flushed. "She wants to be a warrior, so my Rider offered to teach her. She's very smart and used to not eating much. I think she'll be able to adjust to Dumnonian ways quickly. The best part is that she'll be able to take care of Quatar and Peri while we are fighting so they won't bother you."

Both boys nodded vigorously.

Kashon favored Shashtah with a suspicious look. "Since when has Tphah become such a cicada?"

Shashtah sent a wave of gratitude to Tphah for giving him the time he needed to pull himself together. "Since she's been living with a five-winter-old Daethian and a Hatchling for a rotation."

Kashon rolled his eyes skyward. "Imagine what she'll sound like when you become king and have hundreds of Hatchlings to look after!"

Kyla stepped out from behind Shashtah so she could get a better look at him. "You're going to become king?"

"That's what the Dragons tell me," Shashtah said. "Personally I'm not convinced."

"You will!" Tphah prophesied.

"'oo 'ill!" Peri confirmed.

Kashon smiled affectionately at the Hatchling's attempt at ClearTalk. "He's quick. About, what, sixteen winters ahead of Tphah?"

The Prophetess cracked her tail in annoyance but instantly grew still as Katrell bugled a warning at her.

Shashtah took the opportunity to introduce his newest fosterling. "Kyla, this is my Dragonlord, Kashon. His Dragon is Katrell. You do whatever either of them tells you to do when they tell you to do it, or it's my hide. Understand?"

Kyla nodded as she gave Kashon an appraising look. "I don't have a Dragon. How do I get to Dumnonia?"

"You can fly with me," Kashon offered.

Shashtah saw the look of delight on Kyla's face and made a mental note to warn her about Kashon's preferences the next time he had the chance.

"The Dragons and their Riders are ready," Katrell informed Kashon.

Shashtah surveyed the field.

The Dragonriders had gathered as many of the perishable items as they could into piles in front of their Dragons, ready for them to lift. The rest of the supplies would have to wait for a caravan.

:*Why don't we always transport things this way?*: Tphah asked. :*It's so much faster than caravans.*:

Shashtah pulled his keffiyeh out of his belt and tied it onto his head with his leather thong. :*It's too dangerous to open warps between places like this and the King's Camp. I'm surprised Kashon agreed to it at all. If the Dark One's forces found out*—: He stopped midthought as he felt Tphah's guilt seep through their Bond. He narrowed his eyes and stared at her. :*Kashon doesn't know where the order came from. He thinks Shaharadesh gave the command, but it was you. You told Katrell what was needed, and he simply relayed the message.*:

:None of the Dark One's forces are here.: Tphah crouched low, preparing for him to mount. *:And what Kashon doesn't know won't hurt him.:*

:What Kashon doesn't know can get him hauled before the Council of Ancients again!: Shashtah snapped. *:They've tortured him before for making this exact error. The next time they could kill him!:* He saw Kashon studying him, visibly aware that he and Tphah were fighting. Shashtah took a deep breath and controlled himself. He picked up Quatar, climbed onto Tphah's muzzle and let her boost them to her neckridge. He visually checked her harness, placing Quatar on his right thigh.

Kashon helped Kyla mount Katrell. Once in place he eased the frail Daethian girl onto his right thigh. He glanced around to make sure everyone was ready, then thrust his left fist in the direction of the King's Camp.

Tphah leapt into the air, sending them soaring with beat after beat of her great wings.

Shashtah hugged Quatar close and made sure Peri was in formation off Tphah's right wingtip. *:Tell Katrell we're ready.:* He called to mind the image of the King's Camp as seen from the air. After a heartbeat, two images blurred with his, and they burst into the blistering skies of Dumnonia as the sun prepared to set yet again on the same day.

Shashtah and Kashon
before the War Goddess

Chapter 9:

Battle Dance

As a unit, the coordination between Dragon and Rider surpasses the expectations of their designer. The telepathy between them appears to be almost instantaneous. The weakness in Dumnonian defenses seems to lay in the relay of commands between the Dragonlord and his Dragon to the other Dragons in the century, with the subsequent translation of the orders to the Dragonriders. This link is subject to all of the corruptions of the spoken word. Rare indeed are the Lord and Rider who can think almost as one, let alone act in unison.

—from *Report on the Dumnonian Bronzes*
by Maelor of Daethia

SHASHTAH HAD TO WAIT most of the next day before he was allowed to see Shaharadesh. With the preparations for the Feast of the War Goddess, the king had little time to do much more than deal with his support personnel as they inventoried the new supplies and prepared the immense banquet that would be required to feed the abnormal number of celebrants who were in Camp. Shashtah considered himself lucky to be granted an audience at all, and he spent the interim candlescars settling his family into the tent they would occupy for the next rotation and making certain that Kyla and the boys knew how to draw on his account for water from the Tribal Cistern, supplies from the king's officers and necessary services from the camp personnel. When he had assured himself that his ever-growing menagerie was unlikely to precipitate another disaster on either Kashon or Shaharadesh and Tphah took Peri hunting, Shashtah ordered Quatar to run errands for Katrell and contrived to spend some time alone with his foster daughter.

Kyla looked far more comfortable in the trousers, shirt, boots and headscarf of a Dumnonian warrior than in an orphan's tunic or even the elven clothing she had replaced it with. The desert clothing suited her as if she'd worn it all her life. The sword he'd purchased for her hung at her left hip as she lounged easily on an embroidered dark blue cushion at the foot of the throne-like couch in the center of the tent. Even at a distance he felt Tphah's concern about leaving him alone with such a nubile virgin. An improper smile curled across his face as he reassured his Prophetess that Kyla held no such attractions for him.

"Dragon trouble?" Kyla asked perceptively.

Shashtah laughed. "She'll get used to you. She's just wanted me to herself for so long that she still can't believe she got her wish."

Kyla returned his grin. "I understand."

Shashtah sobered, shifted his scimitar out of the way and settled onto one of the other pillows that were scattered on the rugs. The tent of a lowly Dragonrider felt more than a little cramped now that it had to accommodate two young boys and a teenager in addition to its normal occupants and furnishings. He supposed he should count himself lucky he had a tent provided for him at all. There were many Riders in Camp this rotation who had to sleep out on the dunes because they were not officially on duty. Realizing that Kyla was growing uncomfortable as she misinterpreted his daydreaming, he asked, "How old are you?"

"Seventeen." Kyla cocked her head slightly, a quizzical look on her face.

"I suspected as much. You are a young woman with a woman's wants and needs. I saw the way you looked at Kashon outside Krillion."

Kyla averted her eyes. "Do you think he thinks of me as anything more than a sack of grain?"

"Oh, considerably more than a sack of grain, but," Shashtah paused as he watched her brightening expression cloud, "I thought I should tell you that Kashon is mated to his Dragon just as I'm mated to Tphah. Not all Dragonriders are that way. Kashon happens to prefer male Dragons. I prefer my Prophetess. But many Riders prefer non-Dragons, and you might be able to find several who would be willing to take you into their household if you find mine not to your liking."

Kyla favored him with an uncertain look. "So even here I'm a brood mare?"

"Fertile Dumnonians and Dragons are expected to mate whenever our monarch orders us to do so. You don't need to worry about that, though. You are Daethian and under no obligation to help Dumnonia with its population problems. You can do or be whatever you want, as long as you are earning your place in our society or someone like me is earning it for you."

"So here I can be a warrior instead of farmer's wife?"

"How can the Daethians not let you fight for them?" Shashtah marveled. "We would have vanished from Centuria millennia ago if not for our women. Several of our Dragonlords are female, and Dragonlord Kassandra is probably the best warrior in Dumnonia. You could learn a lot by watching her."

Kyla laughed. "This new life is going to take some getting used to. Are you sure aren't going to fade away like a dream?"

Shashtah smiled ruefully. "I'm more likely to blow myself up."

Kyla studied him for a heartbeat. "Quatar and Peri don't understand, but I can guess how much taking care of us is costing you. Why are you doing this?"

Shashtah considered his answer carefully. "It was my fault Peri was born. It was my fault you were sent to Tor."

"And Quatar?"

"I saved his life. That made me responsible for him." Shashtah shook his head slightly, scattering his memories of the past and returning his attention to the present. "So, given my horrible, mean, and totally unnecessary restrictions, do you wish to stay with me or would you prefer it if I found somewhere else for you to live?"

"Tphah's right. You think better with your heart than with your head. Why wouldn't I want to stay with you?"

Dragons on the brain!

This time Shashtah recognized the voice as his mother's. *No, Mother. I have Dragons in my blood. And you knew it.*

Kyla arched her eyebrow but this time kept her speculation about his silence to herself.

"You want me to agree to what?" Shaharadesh exploded in a voice that could probably be heard through half the Camp.

Makara's humanform, wearing a chador of white samite and glittering with jewelry from the Tribal Hoard, lounged on embroidered red silk pillows to the king's right, staring with grim satisfaction as Shashtah tried not to squirm.

Shashtah knelt before his king's throne in the traditional pose of a supplicant. His untouched cup of qaffah sat on the rug to his left as he tried to concentrate on his monarch. "I want one caravan to run to the Elven Kingdom with magic items, and then come back here with food. I want another to take sand to the Galantites where it will pick up magic items and take them to the Elven King, then take trade goods from the Elven Kingdom to Krillion where they will be exchanged for food and supplies, and come back here—along with information about the Dark One's forces from the Krills. And I want one caravan to take spices, salt, and whatever else we can afford to Tor and exchange them for offerings of food to take to Krillion. The Krills will swap out that food for what the temples actually need, which the caravan will take back to Tor. Then that caravan will come back here."

A vein throbbed angrily on Shaharadesh's temple beneath his brilliant white keffiyeh. "Come back here with what?"

"Daethian orphans," Makara supplied.

Fury flashed in Shaharadesh's eyes. "The first caravan would be slaughtered in a heartbeat if the Dark One's forces discovered what we were doing. The second caravan would be gone for almost a year, when it could normally make three runs for goods that we desperately need. And the third caravan—are you out of your mind? Dragonriders trading goods to Dragonslayers for the Light knows how many orphans!"

Makara smirked. "About fifteen hundred."

Shaharadesh gaped at her. "Fifteen—?" He rounded on Shashtah. "The Council—!"

"The Daethian clerics are the ones who requested the trade," Shashtah persisted. "Some of the orphans would be settled in the Great Woods--"

"Most of them would come here," Makara interrupted.

Shashtah hung his head, admitting the truth.

Shaharadesh made an inarticulate sound. "Where are you going to find Riders who are willing to care for Dragonslayers?"

"I'm not expecting the Riders to care for them," Shashtah replied. "I'm expecting them to become caravaneers and supply personnel."

"They aren't adapted to desert life the way we are!" Shaharadesh thundered. "They'd use up water and food we need for the Dragons, and none of them could ever be Riders! I won't ask the Council to allow such a thing. I'd be turned to a pile of ash on the spot. The answer is no!"

Shashtah drew his breath sharply. "What about the other two caravans?"

"Talk to the traders, and stop wasting my time!" the king roared. "Get out!"

Shashtah rose and, with an elaborate salaam, backed out of the tent.

Outside he swore a silent oath, then trotted off toward the section of the Camp where the traders had gathered, hawking their wares.

An extraordinary number of caravans had arrived for the Feast of the War Goddess, and with them came the mercenaries, centaurs, giants, and assorted other marvelous beings, including the occasional copper or silver dragon and the even rarer miniature dragon, who followed the dragonless warriors of Dumnonia.

Shashtah's mood lightened considerably as he lost himself in the happy chaos of friendly rivalries, the swirl of vibrant colors, and the babble of countless languages that had surrounded him throughout his youth. He soon located two of the most daring traders he knew: Reisel and Pali. All he had to do was listen for the loudest bellows issuing from the most garish combination of colors and surrounded by the most improbable collection of followers. Since Shashtah's father had taken his place Leader of the Council of Ancients, Reisel and Pali had emerged as the uncontested champions of the trade routes. Uncontested, that is, except as far as each other was concerned. Between themselves they argued constantly about everything from who had the best wares at the lowest prices to who knew the best oases on the run from Daethia to the basecamps to the Valley of Ancients and back again.

To Shashtah's delight soon after his arrival the argument degenerated into not whether the traders would make the illicit runs to southern Daethia but which run would be made by who.

"I've been using racing camels for decades!" Reisel propounded. "I could make the second run three times before you could get there once!"

"Yes," Pali admitted, a wicked gleam in his dark amber eyes. "If I didn't know where the better warps are!"

Shashtah laughed as Reisel turned a deep shade of bronze. "Let Pali have the short run. Treigo is offering twenty percent on the Krillion leg, which means you will clear the tithe you are missing when you leave town and earn a handsome profit."

Both traders gawked at Shashtah in disbelief.

Pali found his voice first. "Impossible. What will we be carrying besides food?"

Shashtah lowered his voice. "Information about where the camps of the Dark One's troops are."

"W-what?" Reisel spluttered. "By caravan? Are you suntouched?"

Shashtah shook his head. "The caravans regularly travel between Daethia and oases near the basecamps. The Dark One's troops know that. That's been going on for millennia. If Dragonriders suddenly started traveling regularly between Krillion and the King's Camp, the Cinnamarians will know we were up to something. But if caravans carry the information to the supply personnel for the basecamps, the Dark One's forces will suspect nothing."

"At what price?" Pali asked.

Shashtah grinned. "Fifty percent."

The sahibs' eyes widened larger than Shashtah thought was possible. They fell to arguing all over again. The sun had almost set by the time they agreed that Pali would take the long run and Reisel would try to make the run to the Elven Kingdom three times before his fellow trader returned, with ten percent of each other's profit as the wager.

Shashtah bought passage on Pali's caravan for his three fosterlings, promising to take them off the trader's hands at the end of his rotation on the frontline no matter where they happened to be. "Tphah will find them. Peri will tell her where you are." That settled, he returned to his tent, slipped into his ceremonial robes and escorted Kyla to the feast.

Tphah, wearing the aba and veil of a Priestess of the Mother, threaded her way through the seated Dragons and Riders, Quatar and Peri in tow. She grimaced as she joined Shashtah and Kyla, who were in the front row of Kashon's century. "I don't think I'll ever make a feast on time!" She shoved one boy into each of Shashtah's arms and slipped in between Peri and Kyla. "They're your foster sons! You deal with them!"

Shashtah eyed the boys warily.

Quatar, dressed in a white aba and turban, looked smug, and Peri was so frustrated his humanform was turning almost the same shade of green as his trueform beneath his shapeshifted desert robes.

"What's wrong now?" Shashtah demanded.

Peri harrumphed. "I told Quatar how Tphah and I brought back three water buffalo for the feast, but he won't tell me what he did while we were gone!"

"Secret business of the Dragonlord!" Quatar declared importantly.

Shashtah glanced at Tphah, who rolled her eyes.

Kyla giggled, leaned across Tphah, and shielded her face with the drape from her headpiece as she whispered something in Peri's ear. "Now you and I have a secret to keep from Quatar."

Quatar squawked in indignation.

"That didn't help," Tphah informed Kyla.

"Stop it, all of you!" Shashtah growled. "This is a feast to celebrate fights against the Dark One, not to have ones among ourselves!"

The contrite children grew still in the light of the campfires that dotted the sandy plain.

Shashtah balanced a boy on each knee.

Tphah repositioned herself behind him, allowing Kyla to move back into place. The Prophetess dug her powerful fingers into Shashtah's neck and shoulder muscles, trying to ease the tension she could feel in him. "I'm sorry. I should have resolved that squabble before we got here."

Shashtah waved aside her concern. "That's not the real problem. I'll explain later."

The Dragonlords, their ceremonial robes billowing around them, strode to the center of the enormous circle. Amasiah, Genna, Tirhaka, Xia, Zofar, Kassandra, Corban, Harabi and Kashon—the names alone sent shivers through Shashtah.

"What are they doing?" Kyla asked.

"Drawing lots to see who will have the challenge of dancing the Ban-kai to ask for the War Goddess's blessing upon the Dumnonians for another year," Tphah explained.

Shashtah was at as much a loss as his three charges were when it came to understanding the bizarre ritual. He knew the moves of the Ban-kai stretches, but Garesh had always arranged for his caravan to be in Krillion during the Feast of the War Goddess. As a result, Shashtah had absolutely no idea what the actual Battle Dance looked like.

"A Dragonlord will dance with his or her Dragon's humanform," Tphah elaborated. "If they can make it through the entire performance with sufficient ease and grace, the king will declare that we have the Goddess's blessing for another year."

"What happens if they don't make it?" Peri asked the question Shashtah dared not pose.

"Then," Tphah declared in her scariest voice, "we get to blame everything that goes wrong in the War on them for the next year."

"I take it the lot did not fall to Dameth much," Shashtah commented drily.

Tphah stopped rubbing and slapped him between the shoulder blades.

"Hey!" Shashtah protested.

"Unwise to speak ill of the undead," Tphah hissed.

Shashtah's retort was cut off by her startled yelp. "What's wrong?" He half turned to see if someone had hurt her.

"Katrell says the lot fell to Kashon!" Tphah whispered.

The other Dragonlords, Amasiah leading the way, retreated to their positions in the circle as a groan started to rise from Kashon's century.

Tphah took a sharp breath. "He wants you to join him."

Shashtah spun to face her, nearly dumping Quatar and Peri onto the sand. "You said his Dragon was supposed to dance with him!"

"I—," Tphah glanced at the children, then bent slightly to address them. "The most difficult form of the Battle Dance is when two Riders try to dance it together with the Dragonlord calling the sequence of moves to the other Rider through their Dragons. The honor is so great that, if they succeed, the Goddess may manifest."

And if they fail?" Quatar asked.

Tphah swallowed. "Then all of the gods will withdraw their favor from us until we can earn it back at each of their respective Feasts."

"Wouldn't that take a year?" Quatar puzzled.

"At least a year. If," Shashtah let the word hang in the air, "we're lucky. Tphah—"

"We're supposed to join Kashon and Katrell in the center of the circle," the Prophetess interrupted. "Now."

"You will both sit with Kyla," Shashtah instructed his foster sons in his most deadly voice. "You will not move until I personally tell you to, even if you have to wait for me to get back from Cinnamar to do it. Do I make myself clear?"

The boys both nodded as they promptly sat down.

Kyla glowed in the warmth of her foster father's trust.

Shashtah took Tphah's arm and escorted her toward the center of the circle. :Is Kashon sunstruck?:

:I don't think so. Katrell and I are so close we can practically think each other's thoughts. That will allow us to relay the sequence of the moves to you rapidly enough for you to keep up with Kashon.:

:What moves? I've never seen the Battle Dance!:

:It's just the Ban-kai stretches, only faster,: Tphah assured him. :All you have to do is follow Kashon's orders.:

:How much faster?:

:A lot faster. The drummers will keep the time.:

:Kashon could have warned me,: Shashtah groused.

:I told Katrell you'd been practicing regularly with the children, just not to speed. He seemed to think that was good enough. How do you feel?:

:Too scared to think!:

:Good. *You aren't supposed to think. You're supposed to obey.*:

Kashon greeted them sheepishly. "Katrell says you've never seen the Battle Dance."

Shashtah glanced at Tphah. "Tattletale."

"Stop it," Katrell growled. "This is deadly serious. The drummers are in position. We have to make this official."

Kashon spread his hands, palms up in supplication. "It's your choice, Shashtah. Katrell and I could dance successfully, but you know as well as I do what the reaction to that would be. I think you and I can do this. You're unfamiliarity with the Battle Dance is actually useful. Look at it as a symbol of a Dragonlord's control in battle. I'm telling my Dragon to tell your Dragon to tell you what to do. You know the moves, but you do not know how I want them put together. Katrell's been giving Tphah commands for almost six winters, and she's used to relaying his orders to you because of the Training. What do you say?"

"You're a wise man," Shashtah conceded. "Which is more than I can say for me. What do you want me to do?"

Kashon clapped his friend on the shoulder in thanks. "You wearing anything under that aba?"

Shashtah nodded.

"Then strip down to your trousers, lose your boots, and I'll minimize the moves where your legs have to bend." Kashon shed his excess clothing.

Whispers swept through the crowd as Shashtah copied Kashon's example. He wriggled his bare toes in the sand. "Where do you want me to start?"

Kashon playfully shoved him into position.

Their Dragons collected their Riders' clothes. Katrell executed a very military turn and marched with Tphah to a spot a few dagger lengths in front of Shaharadesh. The Dragons turned in unison and sat cross-legged on the ground, discarded clothing in their laps, in an attitude of complete concentration on their Riders.

Kashon took his own position and nodded to the drummers.

The pounding mimicked Shashtah's pulse—which was hammering altogether too fast for his liking.

Kashon gave one final glance at his friend, then nodded at Katrell.

:*Hatchling Rising!*: Tphah's voice rang in Shashtah's head.

Shashtah moved, in time with the drums, even before he thought about what he was doing.

Kashon's movements mirrored him exactly.

:*Turn left low! Flying Dragon!*:

Shashtah spun close to the sand and came up in the Flying Dragon pose even as the next instruction rang through his head:

:*Rider Mounting!*:

Shashtah felt a thrill surge through his chest as the spray of sand from his foot hit the spray of sand from Kashon's presicely between them.

:*Double tumble forward! Spring!*:

As Shashtah found himself in midair exactly at the same level of Kashon's shoulder he began to believe that maybe they could really meet the challenge.

:*Dragon Landing.*: Tphah's voice flitted through his brain, yanking him like some insane puppet on a string. :*Up, arabesque! Shoulders up with wings! Repeat with stride three times! Up, arabesque! Dragon Spinning! Dragon Landing reversed! Sandstorm Rising! Reverse! Triple backflip! Pause! Double Dragon Spinning! Rider Fighting! Rider Dismounting! Dragon Springing! Dragon Twining! Reverse! Pause! Breathe, Dragonheart! Dragon Arching! Sandstorm Swirling! Rider Fighting! Split to ground! Fly up to full stance!*:

Somewhere in the back of Shashtah's brain, behind the beat of the drums, behind Tphah's voice as it directed his muscles, he thought he heard a growing cheer.

:*Don't think! Salute and Rise! Dragon Fighting! Dragon Falling! Rider Landing! Leap forward, arabesque, look left!*:

Shashtah noted the grin of sheer pleasure on Kashon's face and realized that the same smile was plastered on his own.

They twined and twisted, thrust, dove and rolled together as perfectly as lovers in a dream.

Somewhere in the middle of the dance Shashtah sensed that they were acting out the story of how Bahakesh avenged the death of Tphah's ancestor, Tchang, the member of the Council of Ancients who had been slain by Tardyz of Daethia.

:*Stop daydreaming!*: Tphah's voice ordered. :*Rider Stalking! Rider Slashing! Rider Falling! Sand Dune Shifting! Storm Clouds Rising! Dragon Rising! Dragon Gliding!*:

Shashtah felt himself thrilling at the joy of flawlessly executing the moves with the most perfect partner he could have imagined. If Kashon had been a woman, Tphah might have had competition that night, and he imagined that his Dragonlord was having similar fantasies about him . . .

:*Stop daydreaming!*: Tphah's voice growled again, her hysteria growing. :*Rider Tumbling!*:

Shashtah lost himself in the blur of call and response. The sense of sheer power, delight and comradery surpassed anything he had ever felt with anyone besides Tphah and only then when they were sharing the Mother's Dance.

:*Salute! Freeze!*: Tphah's familiar chuckle preceded her next command: :*I told you to breathe half a candlescar ago, Dragonheart! Breathe!*:

Shashtah sucked the dry desert air into his lungs. Sweat drenched his entire body and soaked his trousers. He glanced at Kashon, who was beaming at him like a djinn freshly freed from a lamp.

That was when Shashtah realized a strange woman, twenty dagger lengths high and clad in a magnificent chain mail suit of pure Galantite, was standing about halfway between him and the edge of the circle. She bore a shield emblazoned with a crow, and her right hand rested casually on the hilt of the most deadly sword Shashtah had ever seen.

"Why can't all Dumnonians be like you two?" she asked serenely.

Maybe it was not the best idea on Centuria to plant his face in the sand when he was still trying to breathe, but it was the only action that occurred to Shashtah.

Divine laughter rolled across him like a cool zephyr in the midday heat. "Father says I must return. You have my blessing."

In the roar that followed Shashtah heard his name being chanted along with Kashon's. He felt someone pick him up by the shoulders and brush the sand from his face. "If you weren't mated to Tphah . . . " a husky, female voice mused.

"Touch him again, and you're dead!" the Prophetess declared as she grabbed Shashtah from Dragonlord Kassandra. "Dragonheart!" She planted a kiss on his lips that probably set the entire Camp to blushing, but he had earned it.

Shashtah let Tphah help him back into his clothes as Katrell dressed Kashon. Then he leaned on his Prophetess's arm as she guided him through the crowd of excited Dumnonians to his fosterlings. Before he could hug his half-smiling, half-terrified children he was set upon by everyone in his century.

" . . . Never seen anything like it! . . . "

" . . . miracle! . . ."

" . . . Now, that's what I call a goddess! . . ."

Shashtah only half heard the praises of his fellow Riders and their Dragons. The power of his Bond with Kashon still clutched his mind, making it even harder for him to think that it usually was. He started to snake his arm around Tphah he felt her stiffen. "What's wrong?"

"Kashon's really angry." Tphah twisted slightly in Shashtah's grasp. "And Katrell won't tell me why."

Shashtah spotted his friend in the throng.

Kashon, flanked by Dragonlords Corban and Kassandra, was literally yelling at his king, but the words were lost in the noise of the crowd.

Shaharadesh sat mutely, letting his Dragonlord rage, an understanding but resolute look on his face.

Kashon's fury, unable to ignite a response in his monarch, finally burned itself out. He bared his throat in submission, then gestured at Makara and demanded something of her that Shaharadesh accepted with a curt nod.

Dragonlords Xia, Harabi, Genna and Tirhaka also nodded their approval of Kashon's demand. Amasiah and Zofar simply looked ill.

Makara curled seductively against Shaharadesh.

Shashtah saw Kashon clench his jaw at the gesture. The Dragonlord turned abruptly and scanned the crowd. Anguish contorted his handsome features as he spotted Shashtah and Tphah. He quickly glanced away, noticed Salene, and descended on her like a ten-winter storm.

Salene immediately saluted, listened to his orders, and saluted again. She worked her way through the crowd to Kyla, Quatar and Peri.

Kashon took a deep breath, and then marched slowly toward Shashtah like a man about to order the execution of his best friend. "Let's go to your tent," he said in a deadly quiet voice.

Shashtah stilled Tphah's question, knowing they would receive no answer until they were alone with Kashon. He led her after the Dragonlord, dimly aware that Katrell was talking agitatedly with Garesh and Tlee.

The instant they were inside the small tent, before Shashtah could even offer his friend the traditional cup of qaffah, Kashon let loose with a string of explicatives that did credit to his command of most of the major languages on Centuria. He tore off his aba and dumped it on the opposite side of the flap from the brazier.

Tphah slipped Shashtah out of his aba and dropped it atop Kashon's.

Kashon ran his hand through his damp hair. "You'd better sit down." He waited until Shashtah and Tphah settled onto their throne, and then turned to look at them. The simple act sent him into a fit of profanity all over again.

Shashtah draped his left arm across Tphah's shoulders and hugged her close to him. "What have we done now?" he asked quietly when Kashon paused to breathe.

A final, exasperated oath exploded from Kashon's lips as he crouched in front of them. "It's what Tphah hasn't done that's the problem." He reached out and put his hand on her knee. "I should've insisted that you Breed before you were Bonded. I didn't because most females don't start laying eggs until they are at least two winters older than you are. I still think you're too young, and I've watched Katrell Breed with someone he doesn't care for so many times I'd hoped to spare you that. But Shaharadesh has ordered me to order you to Breed before you rotate up to the frontline. The bloodline of Tchang must be secured."

"Breed?" echoed Tphah.

Shashtah sensed her growing disquiet. "Is there time?"

Kashon nodded. "If she mates tonight, she will clutch the day before we leave for our basecamp. I think it is positively ludicrous to ask a newly Trained Pair to take the frontline the day after the Dragon has lain eggs for the first time, especially when she isn't even of Breeding age. But my opinion apparently doesn't matter. If you take Tphah on leave directly from the frontline, her eggs will hatch while she's gone. The Hatchlings won't have a mother around so they can be taught to look to Shaharadesh, and Tphah will lose her attachment to them before she's confronted with them in the King's Camp."

"And if one of them isn't another Prophet or Prophetess?" Shashtah ventured, increasingly disturbed by Tphah's silence.

"Then I'll have to order you to do this all over again in the Fast of the Lost." Kashon's words sizzled almost visibly in the air.

"We have no choice, then," Shashtah said softly.

Kashon rose and spread his hands helplessly. "There is one choice: that of the Breeding partner. There are over three hundred fertile Bonded males in Camp because of the Feast, seventy-three of whom are Bonded to female Riders if it would be easier for you to be doing the Mother's Dance with one of them while the Dragon mates with Tphah. Or there are the Priestesses of the Mother."

Shashtah dismissed the suggestion with a shake of his head. "Forget about me. All that matters is what Tphah wants."

Kashon took a deep breath and let it out slowly. "Of the UnBonded fertile male Dragons only two are willing to offer themselves." He stared at them, his face unreadable. "And then there's always Katrell." Both Shashtah and Tphah started to protest, but Kashon silenced them with a wave of his hand. "Hear me out. Your odds of getting a Prophet or Prophetess in the first clutch are better if you go with one of the two UnBonded Dragons: They both have strong factors in their favor. But Katrell at least cares for Tphah, and he was her Teacher. Plus, I've been through the effects of his breeding so many times, I could help you through any unpleasantness."

"Who are the UnBonded Dragons?" Tphah whispered, fingering the scarab at her throat.

"Tlee and Garesh," Shashtah answered before Kashon had a chance to respond.

Kashon nodded. "Tlee is a member of the House of Tchang, so there's a good chance the inbreeding will produce a Prophet. Garesh," he gestured at Shashtah, "is the only living male who has proven he can sire a Prophet, other than Tphah's father, who vanished even before she Hatched."

Shashtah forced Tphah to look at him. "I want you to do whatever is easiest for you."

Tphah pressed her ear against his breast, listening to the wild beating of his heart. She focused her amber eyes on Kashon's face.

Kashon stared back, trembling with rage.

Tphah reached out, took his left hand in hers and pressed her lips to his ring. "You have always been kind to me. I'm afraid I'm about to be unkind to you."

Kashon adjusted her veil. "Be as unkind as you like. I'm being nothing but cruel to you now."

Tphah bit her lower lip, then straightened up, pulling away from Shashtah. "Stay with my Rider, Lord. He will need your experience."

Kashon bared his throat to her.

Tphah touched Shashtah's cheek, pulled her veil around her face and fled into the Dumnonian night.

Shashtah stifled an urge to run after her. "She chose Katrell?"

Kashon settled onto the pillows where Tphah had been, trying to compose himself. "I have no idea. I told Katrell to take Garesh and Tlee to meet her outside Camp, so all three of them are together."

"You once said that you saw mating Dragons better if you were alone."

"I have no intention of leaving, unless you ask me to go."

Shashtah felt fear wrap around his heart. "Shaharadesh just looks a bit distracted when Makara mates. You practically bend a dinner plate in two. What will happen to me?"

Kashon draped his arm protectively across Shashtah's shoulders. "I don't know. It's different for everyone. Let's just hope you don't start glowing."

Shashtah smiled at the weak joke. Then dread almost paralyzed him as he remembered his nightmare in Tor. "Do you think I might?"

"I don't know," Kashon repeated. "I do know that Tphah's the jealous type. What about you?"

"I've never thought about it," Shashtah admitted. "I've Bonded with two Breeding Females, but Tkai was so old and Tphah is so young . . . " He lowered his eyes. "The thought of Tkai doing the Mother's Dance with anyone was laughable to me—until the Dark One forced her to bear his son. I was alone and in wolfform when she bred. I have no idea how I reacted." He shook his head slightly, trying to rid it of the image of Tkai's corpse on the cell floor deep inside Mount Cinnamar, her blood on his hands. "I've known that Tphah would eventually have to mate with someone besides me. I knew someone else would sire her children because I can't." He shrugged. "Like everything else in my life, I've never thought about it!"

"Easy," Kashon crooned in the same voice Shashtah would have used to quiet a spirited horse. "You don't have to know. I was simply curious about whether or not I should be ready to pin you to the rug."

"Pin me to the—?"

:It begins,: Tphah's voice whispered in Shashtah's head.

Confusion flashed across Kashon's face. "Four love potions? Why does she need four—?"

"That's not what I meant by whatever is easiest for her!" Shashtah gripped a pillow so hard the fabric threatened to tear.

"What's she doing?" Kashon whispered. "Katrell's too confused to give me a straight answer."

"Diving for Tlee's throat!" Shashtah screamed. He threw the pillow at the rug as hard as he could as he lunged to his feet, blurring between his human- and dragonforms.

Kashon rose with him and gripped his shoulders. "Control yourself! She needs you to stay in control!"

Shashtah's knees buckled under him, and he sank to the rugs atop a pattern of a Bronze Dragon locked in mortal combat with a winged demon. "What's she doing? That's a death grip, not a lovemaking hold!"

"A death grip?" Kashon echoed, horrified. "Talk to her! Promise her anything you have to, but don't let her kill Tlee!"

Shashtah closed his eyes, draconic instincts warring with human emotions within him. "Sounds easier than it is!"

"Concentrate!"

Shashtah screamed his frustration. "You of all people know I can't concentrate!" Yet he tried. :Tphah! You're hurting Tlee!:

:But he's hurting me!:

:He's trying to help us. If you don't want his help, release him!:

"Katrell's too flustered to separate them," Kashon interjected, "but I think I got him to pass the order along to Garesh."

Shashtah suddenly felt as if jaws had closed around his own throat. Part of him realized that Kashon was restraining him. Another part felt Tlee shudder violently as Garesh separated the breeding Dragons and forced Tphah onto her back. The Ancient Dragon out-massed the young adult too many times for her struggles to be of any use. Garesh wrapped his tail around hers and used his powerful legs and forearms to press her wings gently, but firmly, to her sides where they would not be injured. He extended his own wings and fluttered in a feigned attempt to pull away from her as Tlee shifted to his humanform and backed off, rubbing his throat. Garesh was efficient, brutal, and quick in performing the task set for him. Tphah ceased her struggles and became perfectly limp.

Kashon let out a squawk of dismay. "No, Katrell!"

Shashtah dimly sensed that Katrell was trying to take Tphah from Garesh. The Ancient Dragon slipped away, and Katrell took his place. The smaller male simply lay on top of the Prophetess, hissing at the two Councilors. Garesh lost interest, shifted to his humanform and turned to check on Tlee.

Kashon still had Shashtah pinned tightly to the rug. "I can't stop him. She's already mated with the other two; she doesn't need to mate with him. It must be the potions."

The picture of Katrell lying on top of Tphah, flicking his tongue in and out just above her muzzle, blurred with the sight of Kashon's handsome face, which was hovering a handspan from Shashtah's own. "What is he waiting for?"

"Sometimes I think he has fewer brains left than a handful of sand!" Kashon swore.

:*It's all right*,: Tphah's voice reassured Shashtah.

:*You Dragons have a very strange sense of what is "all right."*: Shashtah wondered if his Dragonlord was seeing a Dragon or a Dumnonian reflected in his eyes.

:*Katrell wants me to know that I can trust him, that even though the potion is making his body want mine his soul only wants Kashon. He wants to know if I will satisfy the needs of his dragonform so he won't injure Kashon. What should I tell him? He's awfully upset, but so are you. He'd let me go if I asked him, but I would feel terrible if he accidentally hurt Kashon.*:

Shashtah felt himself blur and wondered if Tphah should instead be worrying about whether *he* was going to hurt Kashon. :*Do as you please. You have already done what was required.*:

Kashon's expression grew concerned as he saw Shashtah slipping into his half-dragonform. "What is my beloved nit doing to your poor Dragon?"

"The same thing the other two did. Only he's making her love him for it."

"Sands, Shashtah!" Kashon whispered. "I'm sorry!"

Shashtah shook his head, trying to get the vision of the breeding Dragons to separate from the world around him. All he succeeded in doing was bringing

Kashon's face into sharper focus. He felt his forked tongue flick out, caressing his friend's lips.

Kashon's eyebrows raised in surprise. A thousand thoughts flashed through his amber eyes. He slid his hands from Shashtah's shoulders to his neck. "No shifting!"

Shashtah immediately blurred wildly between his dragon- and his humanform, completely disobeying Kashon. "Gripping . . . my throat . . . is not . . . helping!" He wrapped his arms around Kashon and pulled him firmly to his breast. He threw him to his left and landed on top of him. Shashtah pressed his left ear against Kashon's chest and listened to the powerful heart that beat inside. He closed his eyes as tightly as he could. "Don't let go!"

"I won't," Kashon promised. He heaved Shashtah to the right and lay heavily on top of him.

Shashtah twisted, trying to pull away.

Kashon pinned Shashtah's elbows to the rug and knelt with his legs on either side of his friend's hips, using his desert boots for traction. "Hold your shape! A Dragon is not your trueform. Half of you is Dumnonian."

"Half of me is not!" Shashtah fought to keep his nails from blurring to talons as he tried to lift his arms. "I don't want to hurt you!"

"Then you won't."

Shashtah screamed, arching his back.

"I have you. Hold your shape!"

Shashtah stiffened halfway between his dragon- and his humanforms, and then collapsed as the vision of the Dragons vanished. He let himself fall against the rug. He took several deep, slow breaths, settled back into his trueform and opened his eyes.

Kashon released him slowly. He relaxed into the landing position for Speedflying. He wiped the sweat from Shashtah's face licked it from his hand. He spread-eagled himself on his back on the rug beside his friend. He put his right hand against his forehead and started to chuckle softly.

"What's so funny?" Shashtah demanded.

"You're a lot more trouble than a dinner plate. Are you all right?"

Shashtah ran his free hand through his damp hair. "That depends."

"On what?"

"On whether you want an answer from the Dumnonian or the Dragon half of me." Shashtah glanced at his friend.

Kashon laughed so hard he made no sound.

Shashtah swiveled into a sitting position. "I'm sorry! Breathe!"

Kashon let Shashtah help him sit up. "Does this mean you forgive me?"

"There's nothing to forgive. I'm grateful to you. I can't think of anyone else in Dumnonia who had a chance of wrestling me into submission."

Kashon's face relaxed into a relieved smile. "Shapeshifting I know how to handle. Glowing—that is probably out of my league."

Shashtah rose and helped Kashon to his feet. "Well, at least we know I won't destroy the King's Camp every time Tphah has to mate. As long as you are around to keep me in my trueform, anyway."

Kashon blushed.

Katrell pushed aside the tent flap and stepped inside, Tphah tucked carefully under his left arm like a fragile vessel he was afraid would break. "I'm sorry. I had to. I knew it was me—"

Kashon quickly crossed the tent and stopped his Dragon's babble with a kiss.

Shashtah matched him step for step. He took Tphah from Katrell and engulfed her in a firm embrace. He put his lips close to her ear. "You are mine!" he whispered.

Katrell melted against Kashon with a sigh of contentment that made Shashtah's heart ache.

Shashtah met Kashon's stare over Tphah's shoulder.

Kashon searched for an answer in Shashtah's eyes that he did not find. "I'll see you in the morning. Salene will watch your fosterlings until then." With that he grabbed his aba and keffiyeh and led Katrell outside.

Shashtah guided Tphah to their throne. He sat and pulled her down beside him. He held her close. "That was a bit risky: giving love potions to three males and taking one yourself. They could have killed each other, not to mention you."

Remembered pain flooded across Tphah's face. "I'm the one who almost killed Tlee. I don't know what happened. I was angry but not at him. I just closed my jaws on his throat and—" She twisted in his embrace and placed her ear against his chest, tears spilling from her eyes. "Thank the Mother your father stopped me!"

Shashtah rocked her gently. "He didn't have to be so rough about it."

"Yes, he did. I couldn't have handled tenderness from him." She sniffled. "I wonder how many of my children will be your half-brothers or sisters."

Shashtah wiped away her tears and pressed the moisture to her lips. "Just consider this to be a bad dream that will fade away in time."

Tphah licked at his fingers. "I don't think Katrell's going to fade anywhere," she said quietly. "Were we too hard on you and Kashon?"

"I didn't burst into a miniature sun on him, if that's what you mean. Just a bit of shapeshifting. Nothing he couldn't handle. We'll be fine." Shashtah took a chance on a joke. "I'd much rather be with him than with Salene or Shaharadesh."

Tphah gave a small laugh. "I'd much rather have you with Kashon than with either of them." She ran her fingertips over his face, outlining his features. "I'm sorry about Katrell. But he was my Teacher, and we do have something like a Bond. That's going to be difficult for you, isn't it," she said with no hint of a question in her voice.

"Not as difficult as it will be for Kashon. It's a good thing he's used to wrestling with Dragons." Shashtah tickled her.

Tphah yelped in mock protest.

"You are so beautiful," Shashtah said as they stretched out beside each other.

Tphah smiled, love glistening in her eyes. "You make me this way. I take my image from your heart."

Shashtah cupped his hand along her jaw. "My precious Prophetess."

Tphah shut her eyes and relaxed into his love.

First Battle

Chapter 10:

Battle Nerves

The problem with sending Dumnonians into battle is not getting them to fight but rather getting them to fight as something resembling a cohesive unit. Once engaged in combat, the Dragonlord's prime responsibility is simply to keep the Dragons from accidentally killing each other and their Riders.

—from *The Dragonlords' Handbook*
by Corin of Daethia

THE ROTATION OF DUTY IN THE KING'S CAMP passed too quickly for Shashtah. Days and nights became reversed in an effort to escape the scorching desert heat and to prepare the Bonded Pairs for the constant fighting they would endure on the frontline.

Shashtah's nights began with a cherished candlescar just before sunset of teaching his fosterlings new moves to the Battle Dance and practicing the stretches they had already learned while Tphah dozed peacefully on the dune he had opted to share with her. With eggs growing inside her she preferred to sleep in her dragonform, and she craved his presence.

When Tphah awoke shortly after sunset, she would take Peri hunting, passing along what she remembered of the Training she had received while in Shaharadesh's care. Shashtah took advantage of her absence to train Quatar and Kyla in the use of the scimitar and sword. At midnight he permitted his charges a small meal, then sent them off to help the king with his Hatchlings while he reported to Kashon. In exchange for being spared watch duty while Tphah was carrying eggs, Shashtah helped Patch arrange for the supplies that would support them on the frontline and took over whatever duties he could from the seriously overburdened Katrell. When Shashtah's schedule permitted, he talked with the Riders of other female Bronzes who were currently in Camp. He knew he should have spoken with Shaharadesh, who had by far the most experience in handling a clutching female, but the argument over the caravans followed so closely by the Dragonking's order for Tphah to Breed had left Shashtah more than a bit leery of his monarch.

Tphah would return with Peri near dawn, deposit their kills with the butchers, and promptly curl up atop her dune as the young dragon practiced his ClearTalk by detailing exactly how much game the Prophetess had managed to devour against his philanthropic protests.

As the sun rose, easing the growing ache in Tphah's sides with its warmth, Shashtah would share the main meal with his fosterlings, then deliver the boys into Kyla's care and disappear beneath the shade of his Prophetess's wing.

The dawn Tphah snapped at Quatar for getting too close to her, Shashtah knew her time was near. Kyla quickly ushered the baffled boys into the Camp while Shashtah took his broody Prophetess to the massive whaleback dunes near the Valley of Ancients that served as the traditional clutching place of the Dumnonian Bronzes.

Upon their arrival Tphah immediately burrowed into the warming sand and declared :*I'm not going to lay my eggs! If I don't lay them, no one can take them from me!*:

Shashtah felt the tips of his ears burning. :*Tkai gave birth to Peri instead of laying him as an egg, and look what happened to her! I'm not about to lose you the same way!*:

:*You won't! Tkai was trapped in humanform when Peri was born. I'm in dragonform. There's plenty of room inside me.*:

:*For one dragonette or even two,*: Shashtah conceded. :*But Makara usually lays three or four eggs, half of which are mutants. If you're trying to hold that many dragonettes inside you, what is your reaction time going to be like on the frontline? How many magic blasts are we going to get caught in? Do you want all of your children to be mutants? Look at the torture I had to go through to keep Peri alive. How many times do you think I can survive that? And if you don't lay your eggs, then you will still not have produced an heir, a Bronze Prophet or Prophetess, which is what started all this trouble in the first place!*:

Tphah threw up her head and gave a cry of distress that sent Shashtah's hands flying for his ears.

:*Tphah!*: Shashtah sat on the side of the dune, removed his keffiyeh and ran his hand through his hair in a vain attempt to control himself. :*If Kashon or I become king, then we can figure out how to transport dozens of mutant eggs to Mount Paradin and leave them in the Galantites' care. But until that time comes, just lay your eggs so we can go up to the frontline and fight the Cinnamarians like we're supposed to!*:

Tphah brightened. :*That's a good idea! We'll take the mutants to Mount Paradin!*:

:*If it will get you to lay those thrice damned eggs, I'll take your mutants to the Afterlife!*: Shashtah tied his keffiyeh back into place with his leather thong. :*You've made your nest. Now, lay the eggs, and let's go!*:

Tphah clambered onto the edge of the depression she had scooped in the sand.

As Shashtah had been instructed, he slid into the nest, noting as he did so that the first egg was already halfway out of her ova duct. He reached up and caught the leathery shell as she squeezed it into his hands. :*Pure Bronze*,: he called as he quickly set the egg in the sand near his feet.

:*Tkell*,: a voice whispered in his head.

:*What'd you say?*: Shashtah asked.

Tphah craned her neck up toward the sky as she strained to deposit the second egg, oblivious to him.

Shashtah caught the next egg and settled it beside its sibling. :*Another Bronze. You are doing perfectly!*:

:*Garal*,: a voice rumbled inside him.

:*What was that?*: Shashtah asked again.

:*More!*: Tphah grunted.

Shashtah grabbed the third egg and gently laid it beside the other two. :*Bronze again! Looks like we won't be making a trip to Mount Paradin after all!*:

:*Katrina!*: a high voice called.

Shashtah wondered if he was hallucinating from the desert sun. Then he noticed that Tphah was trying to lay another egg. :*Four?*: He caught the precious shell and lowered it lightly to the sand.

:*Kchang!*: The word rang in his head.

:*Did you hear something?*: Shashtah asked before he realized Tphah was laying yet a fifth egg. :*Five? What are you doing? Going for the all-time record?*: He grasped the egg.

The shell—blue, black, bronze and silver—sparkled in his hands.

:*Achates.*:

Tphah rolled off the rim into the warm sand. :*A mutant?*: She hung her armored head over the edge of the nest.

:*Should've stopped at four.*:

:*You promised!*:

:*The penalty for stealing eggs is death, Tphah.*: Shashtah tried to keep the thought reasonable, but he could hear the panic underlying it.

:*You haven't let the last egg touch the sand. No one will believe that I laid more than four eggs.*:

Shashtah considered the four Bronze eggs at his feet. :*No one will believe you laid four eggs and no mutant.*:

Tphah cracked her tail angrily against the sand, narrowly missing the nest and eggs. :*Why not? I'm a Prophetess!*:

Too tired to debate the matter any further, Shashtah relented. :*All right. Stay put. Move a muscle, and I'll bring the egg back!*: He launched himself into the air as he shifted to his dragonform and, gripping the mutant egg carefully in his talons, willed himself high in the air above the entrance to Mount Paradin. He circled down slowly to the slope, watching the guards. His jaws split into the draconic version of a grin as he spotted Makkaba on duty. He landed near her and resumed his humanform. "Thank the Light!"

Makkaba scowled at him. "You left without being dismissed."

"Sorry. Here." Shashtah handed Tphah's egg to her.

"Another one?" Makkaba rumbled.

"No time to talk. The Light be with you!" Before Makkaba could object, Shashtah shifted into dragonform and plunged off the side of the mountain. He caught the air under his massive wings, hurling himself upward as the orb of his god topped the Dragon's Back Mountains. He called up the memory of Tphah near her nest and warped himself back to the Valley of Ancients. He remembered to change back to his humanform just before he landed in the footprints he had left heartbeats before. :*Your egg is safe.*: He climbed out of the nest and leaned against her shoulder. :*I'm exhausted. Carry me back to Camp?*:

:*You're exhausted?*: Tphah nudged him affectionately. :*Climb up.*:

Shashtah mounted her, thankful for the rule that Dragons must wear a real harness while on duty.

"The harness simply vanished when I was halfway up her side!" one Rider unlucky enough to have his Dragon clutch while they were on leave had lamented. "It would have been nice if someone had told me they can lose control of their shape when they're in pain!"

Shashtah shoved the thought to the back of his mind, brought his right fist to his left breast and gave Tphah the command to rise. He felt her groan as she leapt into the air and thrust downward sluggishly with her wings. A frown of concern distorted his handsome features as his image of the King's Camp blurred with hers. :*Tell Makara where the nest is. Shaharadesh will defend it.*:

Tphah begrudgingly did as she was told. After a short flight she landed at the edge of Camp, waited for him to dismount and shifted to her humanform. Her fingers played nervously with the scarab at her throat.

Shashtah caught her in his arms as she burst into tears. :*Hey, now. You're going to have me all to yourself for a full rotation. Let's put my menagerie on a caravan so we can take advantage of my tent while I still have one.*:

Tphah dried her tears and kissed him. :*You are the most wonderful Rider a Dragon could ever have!*:

Shashtah practically preened himself in the glow of her love. "Come on." He twined his arm around her waist and escorted her toward the Camp.

"But I want to ride a horse like Kyla!" Quatar protested in response to Shashtah's instructions to Pali that his foster son be mounted on a camel at all times while the caravan was in motion.

Tphah rolled her eyes skyward. :*Not again.*:

Shashtah hid a smile as he recalled his own petulant cries to his father. He knelt and stared into Quatar's dark brown eyes. "Kyla doesn't want to be a Dragonrider. She wants to be a warrior. Dumnonians who want to ride Dragons learn to ride camels, not horses. If you would rather learn to ride a horse than a camel, then you can't be a Dragonrider."

"That's not fair!" Quatar insisted, stamping his foot.

Pali glowered. "If he keeps that up, I'm not taking him."

Shashtah glanced at the trader and knew instantly that the sahib meant the threat. He rose and roared at his fosterling. "You will learn to ride camels, or I will take you to Tor and put you in an orphanage!"

The threat had the immediate effect Shashtah had hoped for. Kyla and Peri each took one of Quatar's arms and leaned in close.

"You don't want to go to an orphanage!" Kyla glanced at Shashtah. "Can I learn to ride a camel instead of a horse?"

"No," Shashtah ruled. "Daethian warriors ride horses."

Kyla turned back to her brother. "See? He won't let me do what I want, either."

Tphah looked skeptically at Shashtah. :*Are you sure this is going to work?*:

"I'll ride a camel with you," Peri offered. "That way we'll both know how to do something Kyla doesn't know."

The storm in Quatar's features visibly subsided. "Can Peri ride a camel?"

"No!" Shashtah declared. "Quatar rides a camel. Kyla rides a horse. And Peri flies in dragonform."

:*The frontline is going to seem like leave after this.*:

Quatar and Peri bared their throats to Shashtah, and Kyla regarded him thoughtfully.

"Now, listen to me. I'm giving Pali the right to kill any or all of you if you misbehave in any way. Tphah and I will be fighting on the frontline, and we will not be able to come rescue you if you mess up. There will be no whining, no temper tantrums, and no disobedience. Pay attention to these caravaneers. They can teach you more about surviving in the desert than you will ever learn in the King's Camp. You will do your share of the work, and you will only eat or drink what you earn. Do I make myself clear?" Shashtah watched as all three heads nodded.

:*This is a sunstruck idea.*:

:*Quiet, Dragon!*: Shashtah took Kyla's hand and led her to one side. "I'm counting on you to protect the boys. Quatar almost lost his hand the last time I was away. I can't worry about something like that happening while I'm trying to fight."

Kyla stood a full fingerwidth taller. "I'll take care of them."

Shashtah smiled. "I know you will." He turned to the boys and heaved Peri into his arms. "I told Pali that you're a good hunter and that you can help feed the caravan."

Peri nodded. "I will."

Shashtah handed the dragonboy to Tphah.

Peri cuddled against the Prophetess. "I'll miss you."

Tphah smiled at him and kissed his check. "Tell me at once if anything goes wrong."

"I promise," Peri assured her.

Tphah set him down.

Shashtah lifted Quatar. "Be good so I can be happy when I return to you."

Quatar threw his arms around Shashtah's neck. "I wish you could come with us." He looked at Tphah. "You, too," he said as an afterthought.

Shashtah laughed as Tphah bristled. "We have to be on the frontline fighting so you'll be safe. Think about where you want to go when I'm on leave this time." He set Quatar down, giving him a slight shove toward the nearest camel. Satisfied that there would be no repeat of the incidents that had disturbed his Training, he led Tphah back to their tent.

Kashon was waiting for them. "How are you, Tphah?" he asked when the Prophetess refused to meet his gaze.

Shashtah put his left arm protectively around her shoulders and answered for her. "Tired. A little queasy from having the insides of her dragonform rearranged. More than slightly upset at having her eggs taken away from her."

Kashon nodded. "I thought as much. Tphah, if you don't feel up to fighting this rotation, any of the centuries currently on duty in the King's Camp or on leave would be happy to have you transferred to them. Kassandra in particular has been asking me about you. She's an excellent Dragonlord."

Tphah gave a small cry as she felt Shashtah's dismay.

Shashtah quickly caressed her cheek. "Forget about me. Are you well enough to fight? Should we transfer?"

Tphah leaned against him. "No. I'll be fine as long as I'm with you."

Kashon eyed her closely. "The king wanted me to ask, just to make sure. He said he's never known a Dumnonian Bronze to breed true. Four eggs! All Bronzes! Katrell says Makara is turning copper from embarrassment!"

Shashtah didn't dare take his eyes off Tphah's face, but no hint of their deception flickered in her features.

The Prophetess smiled weakly at Kashon. "Do I have time to rest before I take my Rider to the frontline?"

"Of course!" Kashon replied, a little too heartily. "Do you need to see a Healer?"

"No. I'm just exhausted. Nothing rest and food won't cure." Tphah glanced at Shashtah's concerned face, then blinked her eyes slowly at Kashon. "I know you have a million things to do, and I know you need help. But would it be possible for you to excuse my Rider from his duties until sundown? I think I need him with me right now."

Kashon clapped them both on their upper arms. "Certainly! Salene has already offered to cover for you. I did even better than I thought when I traded for her. Fosterlings in safe keeping?"

Shashtah nodded. "I put them on a caravan. Peri will fly cover so Quatar and Kyla will be safe. They won't bother you this rotation."

Kashon grinned his approval. "Patch needs to clear this tent. Should I tell her to wait or will you two be more comfortable on a dune until we're ready to leave for our basecamp?"

"A dune sounds wonderful," Tphah said.

Shashtah smiled. "The Prophetess has spoken!" He dropped in a salaam to his friend and felt Tphah bend with him.

"Don't worry," Kashon said. "You'll do fine."

Shashtah waited for Kashon to leave. He held Tphah at arm's length. "You're sure?"

Tphah nodded. "I'm sure."

'Okay." Shashtah adjusted her veil, and then led her to the sands at the edge of the King's Camp.

Tphah promptly shifted and made another nest.

Shashtah took his dragonform as well and settled beside her. He coiled around her, letting her feel the brush of his scales against hers. He felt the warmth of his god's orb surround them as he wrapped Tphah's mind with his love, and within a few heartbeats his equine ears detected her quiet snore.

:*Good morning, Dragonheart,*: Katrell's amused voice filtered through his dreams. :*Or should I say good evening?*:

Shashtah opened his eyes and yawned, revealing his impressive fangs. "Finally! I'm not upside down!"

Katrell flicked his talons in a movement that was too fast to follow.

Two large smoky hands with golden armbands, such as Shashtah expected to see attached to a rather large djinn, materialized, grabbed his dragonform by the back legs and hauled him into the air.

Shashtah, completely unaware that Katrell had any of Kashon's skill with magic, roared with laughter. As Tphah startled awake he took his humanform, slipped from the hands' grasp and dropped to the ground, tucking and rolling as he hit the sand. He spun to his feet and executed a salaam to Katrell as the Dragon grinned and dismissed the hands with a wave of his forepaw.

Tphah rose slowly, stretching her wings.

Katrell, who had been avoiding them for the entire rotation, fidgeted beneath Tphah's wary gaze. "You seem all right," he ventured in ClearTalk. "My Rider wanted me to make sure: Makara can do little more than curl up on a dune for half a rotation after laying four eggs."

"I'm not Makara," Tphah retorted.

Katrell inclined his head to the Prophetess. "Thank you for your gifts to the Tribe and for your generosity toward me. My behavior toward you was inexcusable."

"Yes!" Tphah slapped her tail against the side of the dune.

Shashtah dusted himself off and straightened his keffiyeh. "Give her something to fight other than you, Katrell. The Elven Lord suggested long ago that we throw tempers like hers against the Dark One."

Katrell briefly bared his throat to Shashtah, and then raised his head and bugled at the darkening sky, signaling the Riders of Kashon's century to mount.

Shashtah scrambled up to his perch behind Tphah's neckridge.

Katrell launched himself into the air and bugled again.

Tphah leapt after him.

Shashtah suppressed the thrill of seeing a hundred Dragons and their Riders rise into the light of the setting sun. :*Where's Kashon?*:

:*Already at the basecamp.*: Tphah gave him an image.

:*I don't recognize it.*:

:*Katrell says to imagine Kashon standing on a seif dune, staring up at us. That should be enough with the image he gave me.*: Tphah presented Shashtah with another picture, this time with the added detail of their Dragonlord, standing boldly atop an enormous dune, proudly awaiting the arrival of his century.

Shashtah imagined Kashon pacing fitfully atop the same dune, staring at the sky. He stifled a nervous laugh as the images blurred together and his fanciful scene proved to be more accurate than the version supplied to Tphah by Katrell.

Kashon, his eyes narrowed with concern, watched his century land. "All Dragons to humanform!" he bellowed. "Line up on me!"

Katrell, looking as confused as everyone else, dutifully passed along the instructions.

Too slowly the individual Riders and Dragons of the century took up their positions.

Patch, who was standing a few paces behind Kashon, shook her head in dismay.

Shashtah noted the tiny lines of fear at the corners of Kashon's mouth. :*What's wrong?*:

Tphah gave a mental shrug. :*Katrell's complaining that we're not together. But we are together. I don't understand.*:

:*I do.*: Shashtah stepped forward and saluted Kashon. "Permission to speak, Lord!"

Kashon favored him with a dubious look. "Permission granted."

"Permission to lead the century in the Ban-kai stretches while you meet with the other Dragonlords and finalize tonight's battle plan!" Shashtah shouted.

Kashon cocked his head slightly. "Approach!"

Shashtah trotted over to Kashon, Tphah trailing after him. He came to a clean stop and saluted again. He hid a sigh of relief as Tphah mimicked him perfectly.

Kashon leaned his head close to Shashtah. "Do you think you can pull them together? Last time I thought it was because I had just taken over from Dameth. I was hoping they would be better this time after drilling for a rotation."

"They know I can dance. The question is: 'Can I lead?'" Shashtah joked.

The left corner of Kashon's mouth twitched briefly as he suppressed a grin. "Well, they can't get any worse than they are now. Keep it simple. Carelessness is bad enough. I don't want anyone dying out there tonight from fatigue." He signaled for Shashtah to turn and face the century. "Dragons kneel!"

Some quickly, some far too slowly, the humanforms of the Dragons knelt. Tphah was the slowest of all.

:*I'm sorry!*: Shashtah apologized silently. :*Are you up to this?*:

:*Better than drilling maneuvers.*: Tphah folded her hands in her lap and prepared to relay his instructions. :*At least all I have to do is think.*:

" . . . and you will do what he instructs until I return!" Kashon was barking when it occurred to Shashtah that he should probably pay attention. Kashon slapped his friend on the back. "They're all yours." He motioned for Katrell to shift to his dragonform.

Katrell complied. He waited patiently for Kashon to mount, and then leapt into the air.

Shashtah removed his cloak, shrugged out of his shirt, pulled off his boots and waited for the rest of the Riders to do the same. :*Ready?*: Shashtah asked Tphah when the last warrior had handed her clothing to her Dragon.

Tphah nodded.

:*Hatchling Rising on three,*: Shashtah ordered as he struck the opening pose—crouched close to the sand, hunched over with his face against his knees and his arms wrapped tightly around his shins—and waited for the other Riders to mirror him. :*One, two, three!*: He slowly uncoiled and thrust himself upward in time to his count. He balanced on the balls of his feet, back arched, head tilted back, arms extended, and palms angled toward the sky.

Twelve Riders hit their mark in time with him. The rest came in halfheartedly at best.

:*Flying Dragon!*: Shashtah rotated his palms downward and slowly stretched his arms down to his sides, then brought them back up. :*Again!*: he repeated the maneuver. :*Again!*: He grimaced as roughly a quarter of the Riders were in time with him by the third repetition. :*Again!*: he ordered, :*and tell them that we are going to keep repeating this one stretch until everyone does it at the same time!*: After what seemed like more than a thousand heartbeats, Shashtah noticed boredom and discomfort starting to work their effect. Each time he repeated the exercise, additional Riders moved in unison. Shashtah waited until all the Riders performed three perfect repetitions, then commanded, :*Dragon Fighting! Dragon Landing! Rider Dismounting!*: He stopped, straightened and rubbed his forehead with his left hand as he surveyed the mess before him.

With a set of simple dance steps Shashtah had managed to do what the forces of the Dark One could not: Kashon's entire century lay in a tumble of arms and legs on the sand.

Shashtah felt Tphah's wince through their Bond. :*They're complaining that there's a reason most Dragonlords don't try this with someone else at the Feast of the War Goddess.*:

:*Yes. They don't practice*,: Shashtah growled. "My three fosterlings can do better than this, and they don't have Dragons to warn them what's coming next!" He watched as the Riders and Dragons bristled at the insult, and then instructed Tphah, :*Tell the Dragons that I fear for the lives of their Riders, that they may accidentally kill each other's Bond Partners in the air just as they knocked them down on the sand.*:

Shashtah covered his ears as Tphah dutifully relayed the message and every Rider in the century swore at the combined distress cries of their Dragons.

:*Have everyone stand up, and we'll try this again.*: Shashtah waited until the Riders returned to their starting positions, their Dragons kneeling at their sides. :*Hatchling Rising!*:

The majority of the Riders hit their mark at something approaching the same time. The stragglers were soundly berated by their Dragons and hit their marks accurately when Shashtah ordered everyone to repeat the maneuver.

By the time Kashon returned Shashtah had the Riders spinning easily through the simpler moves of the Ban-kai stretches. Kashon watched them for a few heartbeats, impressed. He dismounted, and Katrell shifted to his humanform.

Shashtah brought the Riders to a concluding pose.

Kashon waited for Shashtah and the other members of his century to dress, and then turned to Katrell. "Give the order to mount."

Tphah took her dragonform, revealing her harness.

Shashtah had barely started to clamber onto her back, when he felt a hand close on his leg.

Kashon smiled his thanks as Shashtah looked down. "You do realize that you just appointed yourself 'Exercise Master.'"

"'Exercise Master?'" Shashtah echoed. "That's a rank?"

"It is now. I like what I see, and I can envision the benefits of the entire century joining together to perform the stretches for a candlescar before fighting every night." Kashon released Shashtah and stepped away from Tphah. "Take position off Bahktarah's right wing."

Shashtah saluted and swung up onto Tphah's back.

Kashon mounted Katrell and gave the command for the century to rise.

Tphah sighed heavily beneath her Rider as she brought them into position.

:*Tphah, are you sure you can do this? Kashon will let us stay in camp tonight if you need to. We can transfer to another century in the morning.*:

:*No. I just don't want you to die.*:

Shashtah patted her neck affectionately even though he knew she couldn't feel the gesture through her armored hide. :*How can I become king someday like you are always nattering on about if you lose me in battle tonight?*:

:*Prophecy can work in strange ways, Dragonheart. So can magic.*: Tphah gave him the image Katrell supplied of an oddly shaped dune off Mount Cinnamar.

Shashtah provided her with the matching image, and they flew through a warp.

Immediately the enemy was upon them.

:*Up right!*: Shashtah called the alert as his desert adapted eyes picked out the shadows of demons flying on winged terrors against the stars.

Tphah angled up smoothly, moving in unison with the rest of the century. :*Katrell says you just earned first pick of the treasure!*: she purred with pride as her extraordinary wings carried them into position to attack.

:*First we have to win! Let me know if you lose contact with Katrell and I need to take over giving you instructions. Otherwise I'll make myself useful letting you know when to duck!*:

:*Deal!*: Tphah added her war cry to the sound of every Dragon in the century challenging the creatures of the night.

"Eternal Death to the Dark One!" the Riders screamed.

The century blazed into battle, magical bursts of light flashing through the desert sky and casting eerie shadows over the sands.

Tphah cracked her jaws, breathed, raked with her claws, battered barely-seen foes with her wings, and slapped wildly with her tail as Shashtah prayed and did his best to hang on.

:*Down left!*: Shashtah warned.

Tphah arced into a dive. She sent a blast of light crackling over six demons who had made the mistake of flying in almost a straight diagonal between the Dragonriders and the sand.

:*Back right!*: Shashtah held on as Tphah tucked, barrel rolled, and straightened out, spraying her stench into a particularly thick clump of black-winged hell horses and the wraiths that clung to their backs.

The fiendish mounts, oblivious to their riders' frustrated shouts, neighed their disgust, turned and fled, shaking their heads and trying to rub their muzzles against their shoulders and forelegs.

Almost as soon as it had begun, the battle was over. Kashon gave the command for his century to land.

That was when Shashtah realized that literally hundreds of corpses littered the sand. He felt his stomach twist at the sight. :*Land where?*:

Tphah ignored him and set down wearily atop the charred and mangled remains. Demons, devils and vampires disappeared in wisps of mist or piles of ash, which were scattered by the desert winds. Broken cadavers of other horrors lay where they had fallen.

In all the carnage two sights disturbed Shashtah most. The first was a Dumnonian standing atop a beheaded, snake-haired gorgon with no Dragon at his side as he keened his grief at the moonless sky. The second was the corpse of a red dragon that looked distressingly like a Bronze in the darkness of the desert night.

Tphah waited for Shashtah to dismount, then shifted to her humanform and rushed into his arms. :*Three dead. One Dragon and two Riders. Kashon's gone to the Valley of Ancients to identify the bodies. We're supposed to distract everyone by having them search the dead for valuables.*:

:*You start on that. I have another problem to tend to.*: He released her and moved toward the howling Dumnonian. He stopped a pace from the grief-stricken man. He had no idea who the Rider was or what was supposed to be done with someone who had clearly just lost his Bond Partner and had not been transported to the Valley of Ancients with his Dragon's body. He stepped forward and embraced him. "What was your Dragon's name?"

"Ysel!" the Dumnonian wailed.

Shashtah held the man tightly, closed his eyes and prayed. Suddenly he heard someone speaking and recognized the voice as his own. "Let Ysel rest until you can join her in the Light. She waits for you with the other Riders she has lost. She greets them now, but your sorrow keeps her distant from them. As you love her, grieve softly at a separation that can only be for a short while as Dragons measure time. Be patient as she has been patient, and she will bless the day that you can join her once more."

The man's sobs did not completely abate, but they did quiet at Shashtah's words.

Shashtah glanced up, reassured himself that Tphah was slowly organizing something that resembled a systematic search of the dead, and then led the grieving man away from the battlefield.

A Healer appeared seemingly out of nowhere and took the Dumnonian from Shashtah.

Shashtah watched the two figures struggle into the darkness, oblivious to their surroundings. His thoughts finally tumbled back into the present and he looked around for Tphah. He located her providing security over a growing pile of treasure that made his blood pound. Nothing like what the haul two rotations earlier must have been and nothing to justify the loss of a Dragon and two Riders—three fighting Pairs—but certainly more than enough to ease the raw nerves of the survivors. He made his way over to Tphah and slipped his arm around her waist. "See anything you like?"

Tphah leaned her head against his shoulder. "Just you."

Shashtah grinned and kissed the top of her head. "Then you won't mind if I choose the agate necklace atop that crossbow for my first pick and give it to that poor fellow who just lost his Dragon so he'll have enough funds for a rotation or so until he decides what he wants to do?"

Tphah gave a small cry of astonishment. "You are the most wonderful Rider I could ever have Bonded with!"

Kashon suddenly returned with Katrell. They landed near Shashtah and Tphah. The usually graceful Dragonlord dismounted awkwardly. He carried his cloak instead of wearing it.

Katrell shifted to humanform the instant Kashon's feet touched the sand and rushed toward him.

Kashon waved Katrell away.

"What's wrong?" Shashtah whispered to Tphah.

:*Shaharadesh ordered Kashon to take a lash for each death in his century.*:

Shashtah clenched his teeth against the oath he wanted to swear. :*I take it Dameth didn't lose many Dragons or Riders.*: He watched Kashon walk stiffly yet determinedly toward him.

:*No. In that at least he was a good Dragonlord.*:

Shashtah suddenly felt her fear wrapping around his heart. :*Tphah?*:

Tears glistened in the Prophetess's eyes. :*Dameth always had the Healers tend to him at once.*:

:*And?*: Shashtah pressed.

:*Kashon is not Dameth,*: Tphah answered. :*Katrell's thoughts are one long shriek of protest. I can barely understand him. All I'm sure of is that Kashon doesn't plan to have himself healed.*:

:*I don't know which of you is more infuriating: You Dragons or him!*: Shashtah turned as Kashon came to a stop near his elbow.

The lines at the corners of Kashon's mouth were set hard against his pain. "See anything you like?"

"Just you," Shashtah choked. He rotated until their right shoulders were almost touching. "You are as much of a sunstruck nit as your Dragon."

Kashon gritted his teeth. "I don't see you performing any miracles, so that means we do this the old-fashioned way: by tradition."

Shashtah saw the distressed look on Katrell's face. "Let a Healer help you."

"No!" Kashon said sharply.

"It's not your fault," Shashtah reasoned. "We were riding for a disaster with a major victory followed by a rotation of leave followed by what has to be the easiest rotation in the King's Camp within living memory—Dumnonian or Dragon."

Kashon collected himself. "I know. You spared me the brunt of what I feared. I thank you for that." He turned to face his century as they piled the last of the loot near his feet. He dropped his cloak to the sand and threw his keffiyeh on top of it. "I cry the praises of Ysel, Paresh, and Cadai with my blood!" He stripped off his shirt to show them the three vicious lash marks on his back. Kashon spun in place slowly so all could see the price he had paid for their loss.

Shashtah stifled a gasp.

The marks cut deep into Kashon's shoulder muscles, nearly to his bone.

What in the names of all the gods did they hit him with? No whip did that. Shashtah, a thousand questions in his eyes, stared in horror at his friend.

Kashon pulled his shirt back on. He clenched his teeth as the fabric made contact with his torn skin. "Bataq and Djar are in the care of the Council. The Healers have claimed Haran. Since Dragonrider Shashtah spotted the enemy first, I leave him in charge of the distribution of tonight's treasure. Following the division, you may do as you please until sundown, then I want you all to report to the west side of camp so our Exercise Master can lead you in the Ban-kai stretches prior to tomorrow night's drills."

Shashtah picked up Kashon's keffiyeh and cloak and handed them to him.

Something unreadable flashed in Kashon's dark amber eyes. "Thank you." He turned toward his Dragon. He paused, eyes unfocused, and then he bellowed, "Katrell!"

Katrell reluctantly shifted to dragonform.

Shashtah locked stares with the magnificent Bronze. He could see the madness in Katrell's eyes. *Lend him your strength as you did the last time the Council tortured him.* He had no idea if Katrell could hear his thoughts, but he watched grimly as the great Dragon helped Kashon to his perch so he would not have to climb.

Katrell launched himself smoothly into the air and glided away from the battlefield, bearing his beloved prize.

Tphah clutched Shashtah's left arm. :*Look.*:

As Shashtah glanced around him, the entire century—Dragons and Riders alike—was prostrated on the sand. :*Damn him. The last thing we need out here is a martyr.*:

:*Then give them something else.*:

:*Like what?*: Shashtah appealed to the stars. *Why do people always want me to think when they know I'm dreadful at it?* He scanned the horizon in the direction Katrell had flown off with Kashon. :*Someone will challenge him for favoring me if he keeps this up, especially when they know he is too injured to fight.*:

:*Someone,*: Tphah hissed, :*will challenge him eventually no matter what he does. He's a walking target, and he knows it. Use the power he has given you to help him.*:

Shashtah watched the Bonded Pairs pick themselves up off the sand for the second time that night. The vision hit him so hard he nearly fell. He saw himself and Tphah leading a century against seemingly countless red dragons with dark riders. :*Damn him! He wants it to be me. He wants me to challenge him! You and I aren't ready for that. We can barely tell which way is up.*: He stared at the silent century.

All the Pairs kept a respectful distance as they could tell he and Tphah were arguing.

Shashtah knew he had to do something. He raised his hands as if to deliver a blessing and was thoroughly delighted when, for once, nothing happened. "To the survivors!" he promptly dedicated the treasure in a voice that carried easily over the dunes.

"To the survivors!" a hundred and ninety-two throats cried.

Shashtah gestured at the pile. "Take one piece each! Riders first!" he ordered, claiming the agate necklace. He knew he had reversed the traditional order of Dragons first. He had no idea why. *Perhaps they will think I'm flustered by what happened to Kashon.*

Whatever they thought, the members of the century obeyed his orders. Rider after Rider and Dragon after Dragon advanced slowly, taking one piece from the pile after another.

When they finished, he motioned for Tphah to pick up a piece, wondering why the Prophetess had not taken her share of the treasure earlier.

Tphah chose an exquisite fire opal necklace. "For Kyla."

Shashtah smiled his approval. "Again." He selected a pair of matched throwing daggers. "For Peri and Quatar."

The Riders and Dragons approached the pile a second time.

After everyone else had had their turn, Tphah chose a pouch that Shashtah suspected was like Kashon's: able to hold far more than it should. "For Patch."

"Again!" Shashtah called. He picked up a finely-crafted belt. "For Patch."

When all the Riders and the Dragons had claimed their third reward, Tphah snatched something from the pile and pocketed it before Shashtah could see what it was. "For Katrell."

Shashtah quickly divided the remainder of the spoils into five piles. "For Bataq!" he intoned over the first pile.

"For Bataq!" the century shouted.

Shashtah held his hands over the second glittering heap. "For Djar!"

"For Djar!" the century confirmed.

"For Haran!" Shashtah consecrated the third mound.

"For Haran," the Dragons and their Riders agreed.

Shashtah dropped the agate necklace on the third pile and moved to the fourth. "For the Tribe!"

"For the Tribe!" came the answering cry.

Shashtah paused over the fifth. "For our Dragonlord?"

"For our Dragonlord!" the century thundered, almost deafening him.

"Go!" Shashtah ordered. "Do as our Dragonlord has commanded!"

A scattering of sand and a whir of wings served as his response.

Patch trudged across the sand to join him, tears sparkling in her amber eyes. "Go. I'll see that the rest of the treasure gets where it belongs."

Shashtah studied her closely. "A Dragonlord to die for, eh?"

Patch bit her lip, then nodded once. "As long as he doesn't get himself killed first."

"Yes," Shashtah hissed. He handed her the belt. "This is for you."

Patch started to protest.

"I said I owed you when we finished our Training, and I pay my debts," Shashtah insisted.

Tphah pressed the magical pouch into the aide's hand as well. "We both do."

Shashtah motioned for Tphah to take her dragonform before Patch could object.

Patch saluted him. "It is an honor to serve with you, Dragonheart."

Shashtah returned her salute. "The honor is mine, Patch. The honor is mine."

Peri and Quatar

Chapter 11:

Blood Ties

On some level all Dragons know the identities of their draconic parents and simple logic reveals to them that other Dragons of a similar age are likely to be their siblings. This knowledge, however, should be de-emphasized so that their ties to all Dumnonians and all Bronze Dragons can be strengthened, since these are the loyalties that will one day allow them to Bond with Riders.

—from *Handbook for the Dumnonian Rulers*
by Corin of Daethia

AFTER THAT FIRST NIGHT THE ROTATION DISSOLVED into a nightmare that would not go away. They slept, drilled, fought, divided spoils, tended to the wounded, drank, ate, trained Fledglings, and prayed that no one else would die.

No one else did. The entire century flew with an excess of caution bred from a common desire to protect their Dragonlord. As a result, while they suffered no more losses, they won no great victories either.

The only time Shashtah saw Kashon or Katrell was in battle. The Dragonlord claimed his century after the evening stretches, did his job, and left Shashtah in charge of the cleanup. Through it all Kashon moved with an awkwardness that suggested that he was far from well.

Bahktarah guarded Kashon's tent flap like a Dragon protecting a hoard, permitting only Patch to pass. While Salene handled most of the Dragonlord's administrative duties, she had no better access to Kashon than Shashtah did. "They're treating him like a Trainee at the Anvil," she complained after her own Dragon had once more refused to let her enter Kashon's tent.

Shashtah found himself agreeing. "There are some days I think I'll never understand Dragons! I don't know what is going on in the Council's collective heads, but incapacitating our Dragonlords is no way to fight a war."

:*Peace, Dragonheart,*: Tphah crooned silently from where she lay out on the dunes, waiting for him to join her for their midday sleep. :*Katrell has everything under control.*:

The response only increased Shashtah's concern. He couldn't reconcile the image of the personally involved Dragonlord he knew Kashon was with the distant recluse he had become. Nor did he have any notion what the hopelessly rattled Katrell could possibly mean by "under control".

So it was that at the end of the rotation Shashtah couldn't decide whether to be worried or relieved when Kashon summoned him and Tphah.

This time Salene, instead of Bahktarah, was on guard. She gave Shashtah an apprehensive look as she let them pass and closed the tent flap behind Tphah.

In contrast to Dameth's opulent court, which Shashtah remembered from his childhood, Kashon's tent was as Spartan as that of any Dragonrider. A few dozen embroidered, blue silk cushions for guests were scattered along the outer edges of tent in front of the large, ebony couch. Some cooking utensils and a brazier slightly larger than Shashtah's were tucked neatly to the left of the entrance. A few more pillows and a stack of five rectangular objects that Shashtah recognized as spellbooks were stored neatly at the very back of the tent. Other than that, and the pack of Kashon's personal belongings that was stashed behind his throne, the tent was bare—so a guest's attention was immediately drawn to the magnificent rugs that covered the floor and the tapestries that hung on rods against the sides of the tent. All were rich, but tasteful, and decorated with legends of Tchang executed in jewel-tones. The trader in Shashtah could practically hear the haggling that must have gone on for Kashon to obtain such treasures. He had no idea his friend was so wealthy. Or at least had been wealthy before he bought the tapestries and rugs.

:*Kashon's been collecting them for years,*: Tphah commented with the thrill of someone finally able to reveal a long-kept secret. :*I'm so happy he finally has a proper place to display them.*:

Kashon sat stiffly on his throne, Katrell standing a little too near him in a deceptively relaxed stance.

Shashtah's brow furrowed with concern as Kashon did not rise to great him. *Why is he being so formal?* He crossed the seemingly-vast expanse between him and his Dragonlord, Tphah gliding like a shadow behind him. He dropped into a salaam.

Instead of mimicking Shashtah, Tphah stepped between him and Katrell, baring her throat to the older Dragon.

Shashtah's eyes shifted to the Dragons. *She thinks Katrell might hurt me?*

"Qaffah?" Kashon's voice sounded like an echo of the one that had once boomed commands over the dunes.

"No, thank you, Lord," Shashtah responded, using the ceremonial form of address. He startled at how loud his own voice sounded.

Tphah declined the courtesy with a simple shake of her head, baring her throat to Katrell once more.

Tradition satisfied Kashon lowered his eyes and stared at an image of Bahakesh astride Tchang on the rug beneath Shashtah's feet. "Thank you for tending to so many of my duties this rotation. I had no right to ask that of you."

"You're my Dragonlord," Shashtah reminded him. "You can order me to do anything you want. Besides, I owe you more than one favor. The Light knows how many times you've scraped me off the sand."

The corner of Kashon's mouth quirked into a slight grin. "What would I do with my life if I didn't have you to look after?"

Shashtah pursed his lips as he studied his friend. "You tell me." He half expected Tphah to stamp on his foot the way Tkai would have done, but she remained motionless.

Kashon shifted his eyes, staring past Shashtah into space. Or time.

"Kashon," Shashtah said. "Look at me."

Kashon hesitated another heartbeat, then obeyed.

The Dragonlord looked dreadful, even in the dim light. Lines of pain and stress etched his face. The fiery glint in his eyes had dulled almost beyond Shashtah's ability to make it out. His usually immaculate clothing looked rumpled, as if he had spent the entire rotation lying down.

Which he probably has. Only once had Shashtah seen Kashon look worse, and that had been after another disastrous encounter with the Council of Ancients. *He needs to be around someone besides a barely sane Dragon for a while.* "You look like something that crawled out of Cinnamar. Dragonlords don't have to stay in Dumnonia all the time, do they? Why don't you come on leave with us?"

Kashon made a small sound that wasn't quite a "yes" but wasn't a "no" either.

"You sound like Patch," Katrell observed.

In response to Shashtah's puzzled look, Kashon elaborated. "Our capable supply officer informed me that she has commandeered my Fledglings for this rotation to help move and restock our basecamp. She made it quite clear that I was to give them no other responsibilities during this time, which was her way of relieving me of my duties."

Shashtah raised an eyebrow. "Sounds like Patch fixes broken Dragonlords as well as broken supply lines."

Kashon stared at the rug yet again. "She's the real Dragonlord in this camp. Dameth's century would have fallen apart years ago if it hadn't been for her."

"It's your century now." Shashtah stepped forward, took Kashon's left hand and kissed his ring in the traditional gesture of fealty. "You have the scarring back to prove it."

Kashon yanked his hand away from Shashtah. "The marks on my back just mean I'm incompetent."

Fed up with whatever game the other three were refusing to let him in on, Shashtah threw decorum to the desert winds. "The marks on your back mean that you take responsibility for the lives of the Dragons and Riders under your command. That's better than Dameth could ever claim. There isn't a Rider or a Dragon in the entire century who doesn't love and honor you for breaking Dameth's reign of tyranny. We can't believe our luck in having you for a Dragonlord, so we're all overreacting. But if every one of us is busy trying to keep you from being hurt, we are totally useless as a fighting unit."

"The Council expects the Dragonlords to have themselves healed," Katrell snarled.

Shashtah danced out of the way as Kashon surged to his feet and rounded on Katrell. "And you know precisely why I can't do that!"

"Kashon!" Shashtah barked. *I've never heard him speak to Katrell like that! Tphah keeps saying that they fight, but I thought she was talking about the way they wrestle like mating Dragons! What is the matter with them?*

Tphah put her hand over Katrell's heart. Magic flashed from her fingertips.

Katrell seethed but remained where he was. "He spends too much time reading."

Shashtah studied Kashon's eyes and found terror rather than anger in them. *What is he afraid of? Katrell?* "Pretend for a heartbeat that I'm dumber than sand and that I haven't spent years living with you the way Tphah has. Why can't you let a Healer help you?"

If anything, the fear in Kashon's eyes redoubled. "My magic," he whispered.

"Your magic?" Shashtah echoed, thoroughly lost.

Kashon glanced at Tphah. "You didn't tell him?"

Tphah gave a slight shake of her head.

Kashon cocked his head slightly. Calculations tumbled behind his eyes.

"Kashon," Shashtah called softly, redirecting his friend's attention to him. "I can't help if I don't understand what's going on."

Kashon shifted his focus to one of his tapestries.

Shashtah followed the Dragonlord's stare. Bronze and sapphire threads twined together in the shape of Bahakesh flying high above the Anvil on Tchang.

"I share a problem with Bahakesh," Kashon murmured just loud enough for Shashtah's sensitive ears to hear him. "Healing spells cause me harm."

Shashtah wasn't sure he'd heard correctly. "Is that how Dameth nearly killed you during the Training?"

Kashon nodded. "Dameth figured it out, but the Council doesn't understand even though Katrell has repeatedly tried to explain it to them. My magic is like that used by the Wizards of Corin. It conflicts with Dumnonian magic."

Tphah stared pointedly at her Rider. :*How do the Daethians slay Dragons?*:

Oh, sands! Shashtah's nightmare gripped him once again. *But then why didn't the magic in Tor affect her? Or Peri? Or Tkai?* He knew the answer before he finished the thought. *Dragonprophets. They must be immune to the effects of conflicting magics. But I'm only a Dragonheart, so it conflicts in me. Kashon has Wizard's magic, though. Why hasn't being Bonded to Katrell killed him?* He noticed Kashon eyeing him nervously. *Oh! It IS killing him. As a Rider he had enough power to slow the process down. But as a Dragonlord--.* The Prophecy came into focus. *I have to get him out of here.* "Come with me."

"I don't want to cause trouble," Kashon said. "If your boys are still intimidated by me—"

"I'll order them not to be." Shashtah felt himself growing as stubborn as one of his father's camels.

Worry filled Kashon's eyes. "Kyla—"

Shashtah cut him off. "I've talked with her. She understands about you and Katrell."

Kashon glanced at Katrell again. "What about Tphah?"

"What about me?" Tphah snapped. She instantly bared her throat to Katrell yet again.

"Will Katrell's presence make you uncomfortable?" Kashon asked.

"You should ask Katrell if my presence will make *him* uncomfortable," Tphah grumbled.

"Forget about me for once," Katrell growled. "You need to be around Shashtah."

Kashon hesitated for a few more heartbeats. Finally he said, "We'll go with you."

Katrell gave a relieved sigh.

"How long will it take you to get ready?" Shashtah asked.

Katrell strode over to the spellbooks, picked them up and shoved them into his Rider's backpack. He slung the strap over his shoulder. "Done."

Kashon laughed affectionately as he saw the stubborn look on Katrell's face. He turned to Shashtah. "How about you?"

Shashtah spread his arms. "The joys of being a shapeshifter. I don't have to worry about losing my clothes anymore."

"How many times did you wind up naked in the desert before you learned to change shape?" Kashon teased.

"I lost count," Shashtah admitted.

Tphah's eyes unfocused. "Peri says they're at an oasis. It looks like Karaif's."

"That can't be right," Shashtah said, perplexed. "Karaif's is less than half a rotation out of the King's Camp by caravan."

The look in Katrell's eyes grew distant. "Tphah's right. It looks like Karaif's. I don't see Kyla or Quatar, though. Or the caravan."

Shashtah hit the tent flap at a dead run, sending Salene bounding out of the way.

Tphah followed on his heels with Kashon moving after them at a slightly slower pace under Katrell's watchful eye.

Tphah shifted to her dragonform as she reached the edge of the camp and waited for Shashtah to mount. She lunged into the air and beat her wings less than three times before she gave Shashtah her image of the oasis combined with Peri's.

Shashtah provided her with his own view and saw the pictures blur together.

They burst into the air above the crystal blue water.

Tphah banked in a circle until she spotted the moldy green lump on the sand. :*There!*: She dove.

Kashon and Katrell flew out of a warp above them and glided after her.

Shashtah slid from Tphah's back and was running toward Peri almost before her talons touched the sand. "Peri?" he cried as he fell to his knees beside the mutant.

Peri pulled his head out from beneath his left wing and buried his muzzle in Shashtah's stomach. "I tol' Quatah not ta worree," he declared in ClearTalk. "I tol' hin I coul' take care o' hin an' Kyla until you coul' find uss an' fiss ev'ythin'."

"'Fix everything?'" Shashtah echoed as Katrell landed with Kashon. "What do I need to fix? What's wrong? Where are Kyla and Quatar? Where's Pali? What happened to the caravan?"

"Peri!" Kyla's imperious voice sounded from under the mutant's right wing. "Let me out!"

Peri complied.

Kyla scrambled to her foster father and threw her arms around his neck. "Finally! I tried to make Peri call you sooner, but he said you said you couldn't come rescue us while you were on the frontline!"

Shashtah returned his foster daughter's embrace. "Calm down. What happened? Where's Quatar?"

"Under Peri's left wing." Kyla nodded at the hiding place.

"Is he hurt?" Shashtah asked, trying to pry up the wing without injuring Peri.

"Not exactly," Kyla replied.

Shashtah's alarm deepened. "What 'exactly' then?"

"Quatar and I had been sleeping under Peri's wings," Kyla explained quickly. "I was almost in place so nothing much happened to me. Quatar was making a final check of his camel when we were attacked. He scrambled back to us as fast as he could, but some kind of magic must have hit him or something. He got older really fast and split out his clothes and—"

"Tphah!" Shashtah ordered, no longer listening to Kyla. "Tell Peri to raise his left wing!"

Tphah roared at Peri, who promptly lifted his wing, revealing a dark-haired Daethian of about twenty, naked except for the magical ring on his left hand and a leather thong tied around his head. He sat hugging his knees to his chest with arms that boasted muscles almost twice the size of Shashtah's. A few bristles of hair grew from his chest and legs, and the beginnings of a very unDumnonian beard jutted from his jaw.

"Great sands!" Shashtah released Kyla and scrambled under Peri's wing. He took off his cloak and draped it around the Daethian, realizing upon closer inspection that the headband was formed from the remains of a belt. "Quatar?"

"Peri said you'd fix me," Quatar rumbled in a deep baritone, vaguely reminiscent of Farador's voice.

Kashon poked his head under the wing, and, to his credit, registered his surprise only by a slight widening of his eyes. "There's been a battle out here. From the looks of things, everyone on the caravan was slaughtered along with the horses and camels. Something disposed of the corpses. Everything they were carrying is gone as well. What are these three doing alive?"

"Peri spit something at our attackers and told them that if they didn't leave us alone his father would punish them," Kyla volunteered. "They didn't bother us after that."

Kashon glanced at Shashtah, and both Dumnonians snickered at a shared joke.

"It's not funny!" Quatar protested.

Shashtah hugged him. "We're not laughing at you. We're laughing at how stupid some of the Dark One's forces can be. Can you stand?"

Quatar nodded curtly. "Peri insisted that we keep practicing the Ban-kai stretches every day," he explained as he crawled out from under the mutant Dragon's wing and stood up.

Shashtah's eyes widened farther than he thought possible.

Uncoiled and on his feet, Quatar was easily half a head taller than either Shashtah or Kashon.

Kashon helped Shashtah rise, leaning close enough to whisper, "I don't think there's any fixing this."

Shashtah signaled for Kashon to keep still. "Peri, please take your humanform."

Peri complied, taking the shape of a Dumnonian of about fifteen. His magical cloak resembled a short cape.

Shashtah touched Peri's cheek. "I thought you looked too big to hang on my leg anymore. Kyla said you spit something at your attackers. What was it?"

Peri shrugged. "All kinds of things. I just opened my mouth, and they came out."

Kashon ran his fingers through his hair. "Hatchlings don't breathe anything. The King's Camp would have burned to ash millennia ago if they did."

Shashtah gestured at Peri. "Look at him. He's no longer a Hatchling any more than Quatar is five. They've both aged about fifteen winters."

"I don't want to be twenty, papa!" Quatar objected.

Shashtah placed his arm across Quatar's massive shoulders, feeling the awesome power in the lad and hearing the panic of the child he should be in the voice of the adult he had become. "Sure you do," he soothed, not knowing what else to say. "Kashon, would you and Katrell please go find something big enough to fit this young giant?"

"I'm not a giant!" Quatar howled.

"I'm sure Patch has something he can borrow." Kashon walked quickly over to Katrell, looking more like someone trying desperately to escape from an awkward situation than an errand boy. He let Katrell help him up to his perch.

As soon as the Pair blurred out of sight, Shashtah released his hold on Quatar and stepped back, admiring him. "You've become quite the impressive warrior!"

Quatar sank to his knees. "I don't want to be a warrior yet! I want you to pick me up and hold me and tell me everything is going to be all right!"

Shashtah pressed Quatar's shaggy head against his breast. "Everything is going to be all right."

"Yeah," Kyla grinned, catching onto Shashtah's tactic. "You're just my big brother instead of my little brother now. You can protect me and watch out for me, and I no longer have to babysit you."

Quatar snuffled. "I'm not a baby!"

Shashtah stroked Quatar's dark hair into place as best he could. "Of course, you're not. You've been very brave, going through this with only Kyla and Peri around. It must have hurt a lot to have your body grow so quickly."

Quatar shrugged. "It did. But Kyla cleaned all the cuts my clothes made, and the warm sands have stopped my joints from hurting."

"There, you see?" Shashtah said a little too loudly. "You don't want to go through that pain all over again. You won't have to keep retraining your muscles to use different sizes of swords as you grow, and the other children in the King's Camp won't pick on you for being a Daethian because you'll be so much bigger than they are." :*Give me the pouch,*: Shashtah commanded.

Mystified, Tphah complied.

Shashtah pulled out the two sheathed daggers he had taken from the treasure and handed one to Quatar.

Quatar drew the dagger slightly and blinked at the blade. He resheathed it and looked at his aba. "Where do I put it?"

"It might fit on your leg," Shashtah suggested.

Quatar looked at the straps skeptically but accepted the present anyway. He fastened the sheath just above his ankle while Shashtah bestowed the matching set on Peri.

Tphah pulled out the fire opal necklace and offered it to Kyla. "For you."

Kyla gasped. "I couldn't!"

"Nonsense!" Tphah laughed as she hooked the jewels around Kyla's neck. "There. That will keep it safe until we get to Krillion. Then you can trade it for something you really want."

Mercifully Kashon chose that heartbeat to return with the clothes Shashtah had requested. The Dragonlord had selected a large aba and keffiyeh and an adjustable leather agal to keep the head cloth in place. Atop the pile was a pair of sandals. "Patch thought these would work best until you can have some trousers, shirts and boots made." He deposited his gifts on the sand at Quatar's feet.

Shashtah helped Quatar into the unfamiliar clothing. He gave his fosterling an appraising look. "You are impressive enough to be a sahib!"

Quatar appeared unconvinced.

"So," Kashon drawled, "how are you going to get Quatar out of here? I can possibly manage Kyla, but I can't handle Quatar, and he's too big to fit on Tphah with you."

"You're thinking like a Dragonrider, not like a caravaneer," Shashtah said as Kyla offered to show her brother how to use his new dagger to shave—a skill the beardless Dumnonians had never needed to master. "First, I become a racing camel—"

Kashon held Shashtah at arm's length. "A racing camel?"

"Yes," Shashtah continued, wincing as Quatar nicked his cheek with the sharp blade and Kyla volunteered to finish the task for him. "Quatar rides me. You carry Kyla on Katrell and fly cover. Tphah and Peri scout ahead for Reisel. Second, we try to catch up to his caravan. He doesn't know the short cuts to the Elven Kingdom that I do, so he should only be about five days' ride from here. When we hook up with Reisel we stash his load and fill his packs with sand. Then I guide him through the warps to Mount Paradin. With my help, we should be able to make the runs from the Galantites to the Elves, up to Krillion, and return to the Elven Kingdom. There we can pick up the food we need on our way back to the King's Camp. Once we're gone, Reisel can return for the stashed goods and make the run he'd originally planned."

"All in one rotation?" Kashon asked skeptically.

"Yes," Shashtah insisted in a voice that suggested he didn't have the slightest idea if his plan would work.

"And what," Kashon asked, "makes you think Reisel is going to go for this sunstruck idea even if we do catch him?"

Shashtah grinned like a Dragon dreaming of a hoard. "Profit. He'll pick up Pali's cut as well as his own. He'll do it." He gripped Kashon's shoulder gently. "When I asked you to come on leave with me, I didn't say I'd be spending it lounging beside a puddle in the sand. You can still change your mind."

Kashon gave a genuine laugh. "No. This way I won't have to find out about your latest fiasco secondhand. Besides, I've never flown cover for a caravan. Sounds interesting."

"All right," Shashtah said, accepting the deal. "Let's see if we can talk Tphah and Katrell into making a shelter for us until nightfall."

The task proved easier than Shashtah had anticipated. Apparently the Dragons had reached some sort of understanding about their relationship, because neither of them balked at the suggestion that they lie nose-to-tail, left wings extended to shelter the Dumnonians and Daethians.

Kashon ducked inside.

Shashtah sent Kyla and Quatar after him, and then focused on Peri, who was doing his best to fade into the shadows on Tphah's offside. "Come here."

Peri ran to Shashtah and fell at his foster father's boots. "Tphah says you're angry. What did I do wrong? You told me not to contact her unless it was really important."

Shashtah hauled Peri to his feet. "You Dragons drive me crazy! If an entire caravan getting wiped out by the Dark One knows what forces isn't important, and if you and Quatar getting aged fifteen winters isn't important, will you please tell me what you do think is important?"

Peri cringed away from him. "I didn't mean to let Quatar get hurt! I kept him and Kyla safe! Don't be mad!"

Shashtah lifted the struggling boy into the air so his feet couldn't touch the sand. "Settle down! I'm not mad at you. I'm just . . . surprised. I thought I was going to have a while longer with you both as children so I could teach you everything you need to know. We can still spend that time together; you'll just be a bit bigger than I thought you'd be while we're doing it. All right?"

Peri nodded slowly.

Shashtah lowered Peri to the ground. "Now, in the future, if you or Quatar or Kyla or anyone you are with gets attacked by anyone or anything, you will tell Tphah at once. Understood?"

Peri nodded again.

"All right then. Let's get some sleep." Shashtah led Peri under the Dragons' wings and settled him near Kyla, who'd already drifted off. *She probably hasn't slept much for the better part of a rotation. None of them has. Neither has Kashon. Maybe we should go sit beside a puddle instead of chasing mirages across dunes.*

Kashon lay on his stomach, his head cradled in his arms, pretending to doze.

Quatar, his keffiyeh and agal in a pile at his side, huddled against Tphah's flank as far away from the Dragonlord as he could get.

Shashtah lowered himself to the sand beside Quatar. "Problem?"

"I don't see why he has to come with us," Quatar brooded.

"He almost didn't because he thought you'd act this way," Shashtah said quietly. "He needs companionship, not rejection. I thought maybe you could understand that."

"Well, I don't," Quatar retorted.

"Dragonlord," Shashtah asked, "would I be overstepping the bounds of our friendship if I asked you to show Quatar your back?"

Katrell let out a small cry and stuck his massive head under his wing.

Kashon opened his eyes, sat up, and carefully studied his friend. He lifted his shirt gingerly and turned so the scarring lash marks were visible.

Quatar gasped, pressing closer to Shashtah. "Did a demon do that?"

Kashon lowered his shirt and lay down again.

"No," Shashtah answered in a flat voice. "Our king had that done because two Riders and a Dragon in our century were killed. Our laws dictate that our Dragonlord bear that pain for their deaths. You should be honoring him instead of causing him grief."

Quatar scrambled to his knees and dropped in a salaam so low next to Kashon that his nose almost touched the sand. "Forgive me, Dragonlord."

Kashon opened one eye. "Only if you stop looking at me as if I'm about to sprout three heads."

Quatar smiled weakly. "I'll try."

Kashon raised up slightly and grasped Quatar's forearm. "Someday you will do more than try." He released the boy and lay back down. "Get some sleep. You have a long ride ahead of you."

Quatar settled so that he was lying with his head in Shashtah's lap. "Could he really grow three heads?" he whispered. "I don't like things with three heads."

Kashon curled up in a desperate attempt to stifle a snicker.

Shashtah ignored his Dragonlord. "No one will grow any extra heads. We're all having more than enough trouble with the ones we have. Now, go to sleep."

Quatar rolled onto the sand.

Tphah's voice rumbled in Shashtah's head. :*Quatar's not that big. I could carry both of you.*:

:*You will do nothing of the sort! He's bigger than I am. If we over balance, I could lose my grip and drop him. His ring may not work if we're in a nonmagic zone.*:

:*I could turn into a camel and run with you.*:

Shashtah sent a sigh of exasperation through their Bond. :*Sands, Dragon! Will you think? I have two sons of the Dark One who are now fifteen winters older than they should be, and that's awakening powers in Peri that he's not ready for. The Light only knows what this has done to Quatar. I need you to keep an eye on Peri while I keep an eye on Quatar, and we're leaving Kashon and Katrell out of this mess. We've already caused them more than enough trouble.*:

:*Kashon probably could have fixed this if his parents had sent him to train as a Wizard instead of keeping him in the King's Camp,*: Tphah said sleepily. :*He's the only Dumnonian who's any good at magic.*:

:Parents?: It had never occurred to Shashtah that Kashon might have family members who were still alive. *:Who are his parents?:*

:You were practically sitting on top of his father at our Bonding Feast,: Tphah replied as she began to nod off.

Shashtah tried to recall anyone else at the head table besides Katrell, Makara, and Shaharadesh—and failed. *:That's not possible.:*

:What's not possible?: Tphah asked, stirring slightly.

:That Shaharadesh is his father. He assigned Kashon to Dameth!:

:Dameth took Kashon,: Tphah corrected him, *:and Shaharadesh did nothing to stop him. Still, we could use a Wizard in Dumnonia who can actually leave a Tomb. Kashon could do it. He doesn't have to become king.:*

Shashtah tried to wrap his head around the idea that in any other land his friend would have been the Crown Prince. *Another Juel. Another Treigo. And I'm displacing him. Or is that exactly what he wants? If being a Dragonlord is killing him, would becoming king kill him even faster?* Shashtah felt his head start to ache. He shoved the puzzle to the back of his mind and forced himself into a dreamless sleep, desperately hoping that somehow things would be better when he woke up.

Shashtah, in the shape of a racing camel, gamboled easily over the desert sands, somewhat comforted by the weight of Quatar on his back.

Tphah flew high overhead with Peri, teaching the Hatchling to pace runners on the ground. Katrell soared above them in gentle sweeps as Kashon balanced Kyla easily on his right thigh and indicated the geographic features that were visible from the air.

By the dawn after the fourth night Reisel's camp was in sight—or at least the miniature, coppery-red dragon flying cover above it was. Midmorning found the travelers safely in the company of the caravaneers. Reisel proved as amenable to Shashtah's proposal as he'd hoped. The trader was elated to have the personal protection of a Dragonlord after hearing the grim details of the attack on Pali's caravan and seeing the results of that attack on Quatar and Peri.

They spent the better part of the day stashing Reisel's magic items and filling the packs with sand. Shashtah took the opportunity to swap Peri's too small cloak for one that was more his current size. The magical power would be the same to the Elven King, and the properly-fitting cloak would go a long way toward making Peri feel comfortable in the presence of others. As they continued toward Daethia, Quatar mounted a real camel, and Shashtah resumed his perch on Tphah.

Reisel could hardly contain his glee when, under Shashtah's expert guidance, they reached the banks of the Sterrefyr five days later. The Dragons proved instrumental in convincing the camels that crossing the swiftly-flowing water at a shallow ford was a good idea, and the travelers spent the next day camped well into Daethia on the southern bank of the Ripon. They reached Mount Paradin without incident. Fearing that Tphah might let a hint of her mutant egg's existence slip to Katrell if they stayed in the Galantite Kingdom too long, Shashtah completed the trade of sand for magic items in record time.

Gaining access to the Elven Kingdom proved more difficult. Shashtah ordered Tphah to land in a clearing when they were still several candlescars' walk from the gates to Farador's stronghold. Kashon continued to fly cover on Katrell with Peri's help, the darkness of the night hiding the color of the little dragon's hide. Shashtah grabbed a set of reins from one of the caravaneers and ordered Tphah to assist Reisel's half-elven Priest of the War Goddess who was also trying to lead two camels. Quatar and Kyla did their best to help as well, but they were largely inexperienced at coaxing camels through a forest. The intractable beasts hated walking through the Great Woods with their sensitive feet, but Shashtah had never found another way to get a caravan to the Elven Kingdom.

An elven patrol started to shadow them shortly after midnight, and by the time they reached the gates at dawn, Shashtah knew the caravan was completely surrounded.

"Lani!" Quatar called, once again recognizing the elf on duty at the gate. This time, however, as the Daethian rushed forward, aba billowing around his legs and head covered by his keffiyeh, he found a sword leveled at his breast instead of his friend's open arms. "What's wrong?"

"Who are you?" demanded the elf.

Before Quatar could answer, Shashtah stepped forward. "Shashtah Dragonheart with one of the caravans I promised the Elven King. This strapping young fellow is Quatar, Elven Ward. We had a bit of trouble getting out of Dumnonia, and some of the Dark One's forces scared a few years off my fosterling's life." Out of the corner of his eye he saw Peri land and quickly shift to his humanform.

Katrell also set down and, waiting just long enough for Kashon to dismount, followed Peri's example.

"Kashon, Dragonlord of Dumnonia, to see the Elven King!" Kashon identified himself.

Lani's eyes lingered on Peri's strange green eyes and magical cloak, which was of elven manufacture. "Then you'd better go back to Dumnonia and attend the Feast your king is throwing in my king's honor."

Shashtah blinked at Kashon.

Kashon scratched his head. "He's right. I'd forgotten. The Feast of the Elven King follows the second rotation after the Feast of the War Goddess."

Reisel pushed his way forward to join them. "Now what?"

"Shashtah!" Juel Elven Lord called as he stepped out the trees and into the clearing. Blood still spattered his Galantite armor. He strode toward them as his warriors carried the night's wounded through the Elven Kingdom's gates. "Just in time! You can—oh!" He spotted Peri and realized that there could be no other boy in Shashtah's company with that precise shade of putrid green eyes. He shifted his attention to the massive Daethian-in-Dumnonian-clothing at the Dragonrider's side and raised an enquiring eyebrow. "Quatar?"

Quatar turned back to Lani. "See? He recognizes me!"

Juel removed his helm and let out a low whistle. "Ouch."

Shashtah favored Juel with a sidelong glance. "You won't guess the half of it. Help us get this caravan inside so they can begin trading, and I'll fill you in."

Juel ordered the guards to let the caravan pass with a simple nod of his head, and then pulled Shashtah to one side. "I knew there was a reason we didn't let warriors go to the frontline until they'd gotten their full growth."

"That's the scary part," Shashtah said. "They weren't on the frontline. They were on a caravan deep inside Dumnonia. Everyone else died, including the animals. All of their tack and goods were destroyed as well. If the War Goddess hadn't smiled on me during her Feast, I suspect my fosterlings would have also been killed."

"What could do that?" Juel asked.

Shashtah shrugged. "From the tracks that were left we think it was about half a century worth of dragons under the command of someone who knew exactly what he was doing even if his Riders did not."

Juel frowned. "The Dumnonians have a renegade century?"

"No," Shashtah said slowly. "But we do have an exiled Dragonlord who was last seen trying to train a red dragon how to fight like a Bronze. With the help of the Dark One's magic, he may have succeeded."

Juel's frown deepened. "Where would this Dragonlord find Riders?"

Kashon, satisfied that their companions had the caravan under control, joined them and answered the question. "We haven't been able to recover the bodies of every fallen Dragonrider. Those who become vampires or other types of undead do not return to the Valley of Ancients when they're slain. If it's Dameth, he could easily have enough Riders for several centuries from the Dumnonians lost in my lifetime alone."

"Undead Riders mounted on red dragons and led by a Dragonlord." Juel scowled. "Not good. What are the Dumnonians doing about it?"

"We can warn everyone—especially the Krills—to keep an eye out for them," Shashtah suggested. "But until we find their basecamp, we're in as much danger as everyone else."

"More," Kashon corrected him. "Dameth knows too much: who flies in which century, how every Dragonrider in our century fights, what our rotations are for this year and who will be on duty where, what our holy sites are and when to avoid them, where we keep the Tribal Hoard and the Tribal Cistern. Everything."

"He doesn't need a basecamp. All he has to do is hit you where it hurts each night, then duck back inside Mount Cinnamar by day. With the mobility dragons can give him and the power of the undead—" Juel let the thought hang in the air like the prelude to a ten-winter storm.

Kashon set his mouth in a grim line. "Plus, someone is using Time Magic. Someone who is flying with Dameth. I don't know who, but you saw Peri and Quatar. Dragons live for over a millennium, so they wouldn't notice if Time Magic hit them. Dragonriders may have long lifespans, just like the elves, but we don't know. I don't think anyone has ever seen an elderly Dumnonian. We all get killed before we reach Life's Winter." He rubbed his temple as if he had a headache. "What if those spells hit the basecamps or the King's Camp and we wind up with hundreds of Fledglings or Hatchlings who age too fast? If the Bronzes come into their powers before we are able to teach them how to control them, they could wipe us out as easily as protect us." He lowered his hand, started to say one thing, and then asked something else. "Once we fall, how long will it take a century of red dragons to burn the Great Woods to the ground?"

Juel watched Reisel lead the last of the camels into one of the magical trees. "We're ground troops. Our archers can only hit dragons if they fly low enough, and it would take a lot more than one arrow to bring a dragon down."

"Hit the riders," Katrell advised as he joined them.

That's actually a good idea. Since when does he have those? Shashtah glanced around for Tphah, but she and his fosterlings had already entered the Elven Kingdom.

"If they are flying high enough, it would take a very lucky shot even for one of us to hit a rider. We'd have to figure out how to get them closer to the ground before our arrows could do any good." Juel's mind raced behind his solid violet eyes, and he did not like the picture his thoughts were painting. "Once the Cinnamarians stop worrying about you, they'll come for us. They just have to fly high over our heads and then hit the forest. Gran'da's magic will only protect the woods for so long before his power runs out. What can we do?"

"Send us back with lots of garlic," Shashtah suggested only half in jest.

"How many caravans do you think you can get through before you collapse?" Juel asked.

"I've already talked with our king. He told me to deal directly with the traders. That worked this time, but after they hear about Pali . . . " Shashtah gazed up through the tree branches at a dragon-shaped cloud, calculating. "Reisel will make enough profit to volunteer for another run. I can probably talk Ulah or Ciaphah into taking over Pali's route. We can only alter the paths a little without losing rotations of time: There are just so many fixed warps that we know about within easy riding distance of each other. If we lose one caravan each time, at say six runs a year, we're probably looking at about five years before we won't have any traders left who are willing to take a bribe. We might be able to stretch that a little longer if I send my fosterlings with one caravan every time: That will alert us if that particular caravan is attacked. I can spend my leave guiding another caravan over whatever terrain they haven't covered by the time I finish my frontline duty. Once the caravans stop, I figure we have maybe six rotations with the Dragons foraging before we exhaust the land. So call it six years before what's left of the Dumnonians and our Dragons will be crowding inside Daethia's borders with the rest of you. I'm sure the Dragonslayers are going to love that." He could see fear once again cloud Kashon's eyes.

"And, without Corin's Tomb," Kashon wondered aloud, "how long after that before the last Bonded Rider dies?"

Shashtah's soul shivered as he saw the problem.

"We don't need Time Magic to kill us. If Dameth destroys our young—" Kashon met Juel's troubled stare. "The Dumnonians are going to cease to exist very, very soon if we continue to fight. Unless the Lord of Daethia and the Elven Princess get busy creating that Great Wizard who is supposed to seal creatures like Dameth away from us and figure out how to raise and Train their child—" He looked from Juel to Shashtah. "It'll take too long. We're already out of time."

"Time." Juel echoed. "Maybe we have more than we think. Tor."

Shashtah followed the elf's thought.

"The White Wolf's lab," they said at the same time.

Juel nodded. "As soon as Gran'da returns, I'll tell him about the problem.

Maybe he can change the spell so Time runs faster instead of slower. Or maybe Balkar can. Or maybe the information is in our library or in Shane's spellbook. Someone has to know how to do it. I'll stay in Tor and fight with Criton and Adrial. Once the spell is altered, I'll lock them in the thrice damned room if I have to. I'm not going to let anyone else die because they're afraid of a Prophecy." He motioned for the Dumnonians to follow him into the Elven Kingdom.

"What are you two talking about?" Kashon asked as he fell into step beside Shashtah, Katrell following a pace behind.

"There's a room in the School of Corin," Shashtah explained in a low voice, "where time is almost stopped. The White Wolf created it."

Kashon's eyes sparkled with curiosity. "How?"

"As if I know," Shashtah said. "The White Wolf has taken himself out of the war, but he left us his lab. Perhaps he knew we'd need it."

"Perhaps he did," Katrell said softly as he followed Kashon and the others into the magical tree.

Shashtah absently toyed with his shirt collar as he watched Kashon.

The Dragonlord sat at the other end of the table from him in the Elven King's dining hall, completely oblivious to the juices that congealed around the blood-rare steak in front of him. His gaze darted from one platform to the next, paying more attention to their construction than to their occupants. He'd spent the entire day ensconced in the library, scanning text after text after text while Shashtah had worked with Quatar and Kyla on their swordplay in the meadow and Tphah and Katrell had disappeared with Peri, presumably instructing him on things a Dragon needed to know. The feverish, half-mad look of a starving man who had just been presented with a mountain of food shone in Kashon's dark amber eyes.

I wonder why Katrell's never brought Kashon here before. The nit clearly knows his way around the place. He found the magic pools faster than Quatar could. He knows how much Kashon loves this kind of magic, and he doesn't have to worry about it conflicting with anything. Why avoid the Elven Kingdom? Shashtah watched Katrell busily polish off Tphah's ice milk, stack her bowl atop his and reach for Peri's bowl, which the mutant bemusedly shoved at him. *Maybe he forgot how to find it. He seems to have forgotten about ice milk until Quatar reminded him.*

Quatar sat beside Peri, babbling to Kyla about the magical world where he had grown up.

Shashtah could tell that Kyla's elvish had no hope of keeping up of the stream of words that poured forth from her brother. His own elvish was barely up to the task, and he'd spent more of his life around elves than around Dumnonians.

"I'm sorry!" Quatar squealed in Dumnonian as Katrell's eyes practically crossed at the onset of a dragon-sized headache.

Tphah quickly pressed her fingertips to Katrell's temples. Magic flickered. She lowered her hands. "I don't know how you can stand that stuff. Even a Hatchling could tell eating more than a taste of it would make a Dragon sick!"

Kashon tore his attention away from a spot in the grain of the wooden wall where an elf had just emerged carrying a plank stacked with Elven Bread. He rose and hauled Katrell to his feet. "Come on, you nit. Time for bed." He turned to Shashtah. "Where are we supposed to sleep?"

Quatar pressed his hands together and looked imploring at Shashtah, silently mouthing "Please, please, please, please, please!"

Shashtah turned a laugh into an awkward cough.

Peri and Kyla exchanged a curious glance while Tphah smiled triumphantly behind the folds of her veil.

Kashon tilted his head and narrowed his eyes. "I know that look, Tphah. Which of your traps did I step into this time?"

Shashtah threw up his hands. "All right! We'll spend the night in a guest suite."

"Yes!" Quatar leapt to his feet, nearly tipping over the wooden bench. He grabbed Kyla and Peri by their hands. "Come on! You have to see this!" He half dragged, half carried his sister and foster brother out of the dining hall.

"We'll have to bring you along every time we're on leave." Tphah said as she swayed to her feet. "My Rider would never dream of forcing his Dragonlord to sleep on the grass."

"Dragons sleeping on grass?" Kashon asked incredulously.

"What's wrong with that?" Shashtah knew he sounded like a defensive Stripling, but the words were out of his mouth before he could stop them.

Kashon shook his head in disbelief. "Didn't Tkai teach you anything about Dagons?"

Shashtah looked perplexed. "Before she died, she transferred her memories to me. I couldn't quite handle them all, but she told me not to worry, that I would know what I needed to know when I needed to know it."

Kashon froze. "She said what?"

"She said I would know what I needed to know when I needed to know it," Shashtah repeated.

Kashon started to burst into a string of explicatives but settled for an unintelligible roar. "No wonder you never know any of the basic things you should about Dragons! She changed the spell! What was Corin thinking when he created Dragons and Dumnonians with absolutely no ability to understand the type of magic he used?"

"That the lack of such knowledge would keep them from changing his spells," Katrell observed absently. "He never considered that ignorance would cause the same thing to happen."

Shashtah and Kashon stared at Katrell and then at each other. :*Did Katrell just make sense about complicated magic?*: he asked his Prophetess silently.

Tphah ignored him. "So where are these guest suites Quatar is so excited about?"

Shashtah dropped in a partial salaam, gesturing toward the entrance to the hall. "Allow me to show you what the elves call a 'bed'."

Kashon raised an eyebrow but made no comment as he let Shashtah guide them into a twisting hallway, Tphah following silently at their heels.

The guest rooms in the Elven Kingdom were everything the Galantite guest rooms were not. The wood of the magical tree branched out to form a comfortable space that resembled a fox's den. A very, very large fox's den. Shashtah doubted that there was a straight line anywhere in the quarters. Wooden mosaics with magic runes covered the floor, and a reddish brown ceiling curved above their heads like a bole in an ancient oak.

At the far side of the room Quatar gleefully bounced up and down in the center of something that looked like a nest. Every spring sent him soaring high into the air where he performed flips and somersaults like a Dragon in battle. The ceiling politely shifted out of the way every time his adult body came too close.

Kyla stood to one side, watching her brother, looking as if half of her wanted to join him and the other half thought he'd been struck by a pixie's arrow.

Peri's head bobbed up and down as he watched Quatar's acrobatics.

Kashon stopped in the doorway so suddenly that Tphah nearly ran into his injured back before Katrell could tug his Bond Partner to safety. Despair darkened the Dagonlord's face. "I'll never be able to work magic like this!"

"Even Shashtah can work the magic in here," Katrell teased.

Shashtah approached the wall to their left and gestured as if he were pulling something out of the floor.

A large, shallow, wooden bowl-like structure that looked similar to Quatar's grew out of the mosaic.

Shashtah launched himself into the center of the nest.

A nearly invisible membrane caught him and tossed him into the air.

Shashtah twisted slightly until he looked as if he were lying on the ground, propping himself up with his elbow. His bouncing ceased, and the membrane shaped itself to conform perfectly to his body.

Kashon cocked his head, looking for all the world like a hound who had just encountered a lizard for the first time.

Shashtah grinned. He made a swirling motion with his left hand, and the nest became large enough for Tphah.

The Prophetess cautiously stretched out next to him.

Kashon thrust his head forward like a tortoise peering out of his shell.

Shashtah laughed. "Any size you like. Anywhere you like. The membrane adjusts itself to whatever the most comfortable position is for you. It's almost as if the stuff can read your mind."

Kashon raised both eyebrows. He stepped to the other side of the room and mimicked Shashtah's gesture. He straightened with curiosity as another nest rose out of the floor.

Katrell touched the edge of the opening to the hall, sealing them inside. He lunged for the center of the nest Kashon had created.

"No!" Kashon ordered far too late.

Katrell spun like a Dragon in midair. He landed on his back and folded his hands behind his head. "It's been centuries since I've slept on one of these!"

Kashon looked from Katrell to Quatar to Shashtah.

Shashtah jerked his head toward Katrell. "Go on. Your back will be okay. It's impossible to hurt yourself on these things. Whoever invented them must've had injured warriors in mind." He glanced at Quatar who showed no sign of calming down. "Or maybe children."

Kashon tentatively joined Katrell. The membrane gently applied pressure to the uninjured parts of his body.

Katrell curled against his Rider's chest and sighed with content.

Kashon, enchantment with his Bond Partner shining in his eyes, gently brushed Katrell's hair away from his face with his fingers.

Shashtah watched them, thoughtfully. *This is where they belong. The strain between them lessens here.*

Quatar increased the size of the nest so Peri and Kyla could join him.

"Let me guess," Tphah teased as she cuddled against Shashtah. "You acted just like that until your father made you go sleep with the camels."

Shashtah's skin turned the color of molten bronze. "Eavesdropper."

"I don't have to eavesdrop to know what terrors Prophets can be as children." Tphah kissed Shashtah's cheek. "They'll settle down eventually. Sleep while you can."

Perhaps it was the bed or the magic of the room, but Shashtah found himself slipping away from consciousness almost before she finished the command.

About a candlescar later Kashon roused Shashtah and led him into the corridor. "We need to talk. Alone."

Shashtah nudged Tphah partially awake through their Bond. :*Kashon needs to talk with me, and he doesn't want anyone else, especially Katrell, to hear what he has to say.*:

:*Finally! I thought he was never going to get up the nerve. Katrell's in a deep sleep. I think Kashon cast a spell on him before he left. I'll let you know if he wakes.*: With that she settled into a watchful sleep and withdrew her presence into a private corner of Shashtah's mind.

Satisfied that they would not be interrupted, Shashtah deftly guided Kashon through the maze of oak paneled halls to the elven springs.

They found a cavern that was unoccupied, and Kashon paused at the entrance to cast a spell. Before he could drop his keffiyeh to the deck and pull off his boots, Shashtah had stripped and was floating lazily in the steaming water.

Kashon studied his fallen keffiyeh. "I didn't want to say anything in front of the others, but something occurred to me when we were talking with Juel. I don't think Katrell's able to make any sense out of what's bothering me, but can you stop Tphah from telling other Dragons if something upsets her?" He turned his head enough so he could see Shashtah.

"Tphah can keep a secret, if that's what you mean. It seems as if I'm always finding out something she learned while training under you that she has neglected to tell me."

Kashon bit his lower lip, and then made a decision. "Only your three fosterlings survived the destruction of Pali's caravan. Absolutely nothing else was left. No bodies, no trade goods, no tack. Nothing except scorched sand. I assumed that red dragons caused all the destruction. But what if something else happened? Peri said all sorts of things came out of his mouth when he breathed at their attackers. What if—?

Shashtah half rose out of the water. "Are you suggesting that Peri killed the caravaneers while driving off their enemies?"

Kashon flexed his fingers, eyeing the ring that marked him as a Dragonlord. "You know as well as I do that battlefields are never that neat." He eased himself into the water and waded over to Shashtah. He gently gripped his friend's shoulder. "You can't let Peri take dragonform unless he is well away from anyone or anything else. Not until you're sure he can control his powers. That's why we take Striplings into Cinnamar to teach them in their dragonforms: It's too dangerous to train them in Dumnonia."

Shashtah shrugged off Kashon's hand. "Are you saying that I wiped out Pali's caravan by sending Peri with it?"

"You had no way of knowing this was going to happen. How could you? Peri should still be a Hatchling. He's breathing to attack, though. That means he's been aged to be at least as mature as our Striplings." Kashon took a deep breath, bracing himself against what he was about to say. "The Council is very unforgiving when it comes to the deaths of Riders and Bronzes. What if it hadn't been caravaneers who were killed? What if it had been a Rider or a Bronze?"

Shashtah felt a look of horror spread across his face.

"You can't take that chance with Peri ever again," Kashon warned. "If he kills a Rider or, Goddess forbid, a Bronze, the Council will kill him—and your father won't be able to stop them. And then they'll order Makara to lash you."

Shashtah's heart shivered at the depth of the bitterness in Kashon's voice. "What can I do? Tkai made me swear to save Peri before I killed her. He's my responsibility."

"To save, yes. But that doesn't mean you have to keep him with you constantly."

Shashtah gave a harsh laugh. "I didn't keep Tkai with me. You know how well that turned out."

"The Dark One may have captured Tkai and forced her to conceive Peri even if you had been together. Tkai herself prophesied her death. She also prophesied that she would be your first Dragon, so she knew you'd have a second one. It's not unusual for a Dragon to Bond more than once, but it's almost unheard of for a Dumnonian to do so, especially to a full Bronze. No one had ever heard of anyone Bonding with a second Dragonprophet until you came along. I'm certain that Tkai's Prophecy is the only reason such a thing was allowed. Tkai's Prophecies, and the fact that Peri is a mutant instead of a Bronze, are the only reasons he's still alive. But if Peri kills a Bronze, even accidentally, Tkai won't be there to champion him."

Just like she wasn't there to champion you. Shashtah shook his head helplessly. "I don't know how to teach a Stripling."

"None of us knows how to teach Peri. He's a mutant. We don't know how fast they mature because all the mutant eggs laid in the Valley of Ancients have been destroyed."

No, they haven't. Shashtah bit his lower lip, grateful Kashon could not read his thoughts. They are about to hatch, and if you think the Council is upset about one mutant, just wait until they learn what I found out and didn't tell them.

Kashon paused, choosing his next words carefully. "We have to get your fosterlings Bonded, Trained and out of Dumnonia as soon as we can. We can't risk having them around."

"You mean I can't risk having them around."

"I meant what I said. I'm your Dragonlord, and I'm not going to tell the Council what I suspect. I Trained Tphah, which makes me the only Dumonian with any experience teaching a Dragon with extraordinary abilities. But if something goes wrong and Peri kills a Rider or a Bronze, the Council will almost certainly pass the same sentence on me that they pass on you because I didn't demand that you get rid of them."

Shashtah gaped at his friend, appalled. "But it won't be your fault!"

"I'm your Dragonlord," Kashon repeated, "and everything that happens in my century is my fault."

"I can't send the boys into exile. They're bastards of the Dark One who still have the minds of children. We don't know what their powers are. The elves and Daethians don't know how to Train Bronzes let alone mutants. Surely the Council will understand that."

"The Council understands what is good for the Bronzes, and that doesn't include having two uncontrolled bastards of the Dark One in Dumnonia."

"What do you want me to do?" Shashtah whispered.

"Send them to the White Wolf."

Shashtah backed away from him. "How sunstruck are you? The White Wolf would hack me to pieces with his battleaxe for even suggesting such a thing!"

"The White Wolf's power comes from a different source than the Elven King's," Kashon explained. "He was able to teach Shane of Corin. He'll know how to teach Quatar and Peri. He'll see the need, and he'll understand that there's no other choice."

Shashtah stared at the surface of the water.

Several heartbeats passed before Kashon asked, "Why haven't you tried to drown me yet?"

Shashtah blinked at him. "Why would I do that?"

"Because I just tore apart the family you've been trying so hard to build around you to replace the one you lost," Kashon said softly.

Shashtah nodded slowly, acknowledging the truth in Kashon's words. "You're right. That's what I've been doing."

Kashon settled cautiously onto an underwater ledge. "Dragonriders don't have families the way caravaneers do for a reason, Shashtah. It's too hard. We can't fight and raise Dragons and Train each other and care for children and have mates all at the same time. It drains us physically and emotionally just as surely as using magic drains the Elven King. That's why we foster our children to non-Riders."

"Just as our king fostered you?" Shashtah asked a little too viciously.

Kashon stiffened. "Who told you I'm Shaharadesh's son?"

"As Tphah has wisely observed many, many times, even a daydreamer like me can figure out some things if the details are shoved under my nose often enough."

"And that doesn't bother you?" Kashon pressed.

Shashtah settled onto the ledge beside Kashon. "Why should it?"

"Most people back a thousand wingspans away from me once they find out. After all, how could our king possibly treat me the way he does if I'm his son? I must have done something terribly wrong."

Shashtah rolled his eyes. "What could you have possibly done wrong? Tphah says you succeeded at a ridiculous number of Dragonquests before you were allowed to Bond. You survived Bonding with Katrell, which I'm told very few Riders have managed. You lived through the most horrific Training in Dumnonian history. You've kept Katrell under control longer than anyone thought possible. You raised Tphah. You've saved my life. Multiple times. You got rid of Dameth. You pieced a broken century back together. You made a goddess manifest! I know what Shaharadesh's problem is with me: My power overrides him every time I disagree with our traditions. He thinks I'm an even bigger danger to our people and our way of life than I am to Tphah. But you? How can he possibly find fault with you? You follow every tradition, obey his every command. Why isn't he proud of you?"

Kashon stared at the ripples on the water. "He wants to break my Bond with Katrell, but he can't do that while I give him no cause."

"Why does he want to break your Bond?" Shashtah spluttered.

"Will you look at Katrell?" Kashon studied the glowing moss on the roof of the cavern without really seeing it. "He's even more dangerous than Peri. One heartbeat he's scaring the Council halfway into the Afterlife, and the next he's a puddle, vanishing into the sand. We're a terrible Pairing as far as Shaharadesh is concerned. He fears that if I become king, Katrell and I will repeat the same disaster Dumnonia had with Bahakesh and Tchang."

"That a Dragonslayer will kill Katrell?"

"Didn't your father teach you anything about Dumnonia?"

Shashtah felt the tips of his ears burning at the honest question.

"Tchang wasn't slain by Tardyz of Daethia. That's just what the legend says because it sounds better. Bahakesh broke his Bond with Tchang on purpose."

Shashtah, certain he'd misheard, frowned. "He what?"

"You can't resign the kingship of Dumnonia the way a Dragonlord can lose a Challenge Fight." Kashon stared at the rising steam as if he were looking into the past. "The only thing that will remove a monarch from office and leave both you and your Dragon alive is a Bond Break."

"But why would Bahakesh do that?"

"Tchang couldn't handle being a king's Dragon. The Council includes the monarch in their meetings to remind them of the Dumnonian point of view. But Bahakesh and Tchang were backward. Bahakesh thought like a Dragon because he was a Wizard, and Tchang empathized with the Dumnonians so much he might as well have been one of them. Their magic conflicted, but Bahakesh could handle that as a Dragonrider. As a Dragonlord—" Kashon shook his head, banishing the thought. "Then, instead of letting Bahakesh lose a Challenge Fight and return to being a Dragonrider, the Dragons made him king. Unlike Tphah, who is too young to see more than general patterns of what may be, and Tkai, who could see exact details in the far future, Tchang could see the immediate consequences of every decision made in his presence. The heartbeat Bahakesh became king, Tchang's life turned into a constant nightmare. He felt the fear and pain of every Dumnonian the Council found guilty of anything as if they were his own Rider's, and neither he nor the king could overrule the Ancients."

Shashtah saw the tale taking a sickening shape. "And Bahakesh was a Dragonheart. He could have ruled for a millennium."

"Or longer. It's already hard to kill a Dragonheart, as you well know. The Dumnonian monarch is so closely protected that there was little chance of Bahakesh dying of anything other than extreme old age. He would've had to watch Tchang suffer for century after century after century . . . " Kashon's voice trailed off.

"So Bahakesh took the only logical way out of the dilemma he could see," Shashtah finished for him. "He broke their Bond."

Kashon nodded slowly. "What he didn't realize was that by doing so he would also break Tchang's heart. Tchang couldn't understand that Bahakesh was still alive. He went mad, flying mission after mission to avenge the Rider he thought he'd lost. No longer able to speak telepathically with Tchang, Bahakesh retired alone to the cottage in the Great Woods where he'd planned for them to live out their lives together. He spent his days alone, writing down every one of Tchang's Prophecies he could remember until he received word from Dumnonia that his Dragon had been killed. He sent his book back with the messenger, and then died of sorrow over what he'd done to the Dragonprophet whom he loved." He shook his head, rousing himself out of the story. "Theirs is a cautionary tale for me. That's why I collect those rugs and tapestries. I'm ruled by my head, and Katrell's ruled by his heart. If I become king—" He let the words hang. "Shashtah, it can't be me. Katrell can't handle it anymore than Tchang could."

"I'm the one who everyone is swearing will follow Shaharadesh," Shashtah reminded him.

Kashon's eyes flashed. "Prophecy is a tricky thing. I might be a king caught between the two of you."

"Neither Tphah nor I see that happening."

"But it could! Plus there's more to being a king's Dragon than serving on the Council. The king's Dragon must Breed as often as possible in exchange for being spared duty on the frontline. How could I be the one to order Katrell to do that?"

Shashtah tried not to look horrified—and failed. "The Council wouldn't ask that of you!"

"You think not? I had to order Tphah to mate when they willed it. Do you think I'd win that argument about Katrell?"

Shashtah remained silent.

Kashon lowered his eyes. "I'm going to lose another argument even sooner. One that's going to tear Katrell's heart to pieces." He held his breath for a heartbeat. "I'm a Breeding Male."

Infertile himself because of the amount of dragonblood he carried, Shashtah had never thought about Kashon being fertile. The differences between his own lithe build and his friend's powerful body were obvious, but he'd always attributed that to Kashon's habit of wrestling with Dragons. "What difference does that make?"

Kashon slapped the water, sending a spray away from them. "All the difference on Centuria! Just as something in Katrell's bloodline makes him extremely valuable, something in my bloodline makes me vitally important. It can't be Shaharadesh. He wasn't even a Dragonlord. He only became king because of Makara and her ability to lay large clutches of eggs. It must have something to do with who my mother is."

"Who is she?" Shashtah asked before he could stop himself.

"A Priestess of the Mother," Kashon answered helplessly. "I don't know which one. She must be powerful. I wasn't fostered just anywhere. I grew up with the Hatchlings of the king before Shaharadesh. I barely saw him. I don't even remember his name. When I ask Katrell about him, he just says that past's past and that only Shaharadesh matters." He gave a small laugh. "My beloved nit still hasn't figured out that he wasn't even being considered as my potential Bond Partner. I suspect he had over thirty Riders before I came along, perhaps many more than that: Sometimes he calls me by the wrong name when he's muddled. Every time his Bond was Broken he immediately returned to the Valley of Ancients and demanded another Rider. He'd had a Bond Break not long before I presented myself to the Council, and he just couldn't get it through his head that I wasn't the next Rider destined for him. That was fine by me because I took one look at his humanform and couldn't see any other Dragon as my Bond Partner." The hint of a smile played across Kashon's lips. "He could have taken his humanform from my deepest dreams."

Shashtah felt the same smile curl across his own lips. "Tphah told me once that the Dragons do that."

"The Council ordered Shaharadesh to send us through the doors of Corin's Tomb. Me Bonding with the most unpredictable Dragon in Dumnonia, the one who holds the dubious honor of having had the most Riders killed— Shaharadesh was sickened at the very thought. Yet Katrell and I were Bonded, and I took my place under Dameth." Kashon shook his head briefly as if trying to rid it of yet another terrible memory. "I fully expected to be killed our first rotation on the frontline, yet I lived. And I continued to live. Then I was assigned to Train Tphah. It didn't make any sense. Me? Shaharadesh hates me. Why would he choose me to Train the Prophetess? That's when I realized it had nothing to do with me. It was Katrell. For some reason he needed to be Tphah's Trainer, and the Council thought he'd improved enough to be able to handle her. Perhaps he had." Kashon took a deep breath and settled back beside Shashtah. "But if I'm forced to breed against my will—"

"Surely Katrell has had Riders breed before."

"None like me. He didn't feel the same way about the others. You've seen what happens to me when he breeds. Reverse it."

Shashtah felt his heart grow cold. "How out of control is he?"

Kashon closed his eyes against remembered pain. "The night I reported to the Valley of Ancients because of the Riders and Dragon our century lost, Katrell knew what was coming even though I didn't. I'd read what to expect in *The Dragonlord's Handbook*, but for some sunstruck reason I thought Shaharadesh was going to intercede with the Council on my behalf the way he had when a Rider was killed while I had you in Training. I was still the newest Dragonlord, and Dameth had left me with a huge mess. It's our king's responsibility to make sure the Council takes such things into consideration. What I didn't realize was that once Tphah's Training was complete, the Council no longer cared whether or not I stayed Bonded to Katrell." Kashon opened his eyes and watched nightmares dancing in the wisps of steam. "When I went to the Valley, I identified the dead and presented myself to the Council for judgment. My fault, they decided. My fault. Shaharadesh said nothing in my defense. The Council can't upset all of the Dragons with their magic every time a Rider or Dragon dies, so *The Dragonlord's Handbook* said I was to take a lash for each Rider or Dragon I lost. I thought that meant someone was going to flog me with a whip. Then I heard Shaharadesh order Makara to lash me with her tail."

"Shaharadesh did what?" Shashtah surged to his feet, sending water sloshing everywhere.

Kashon turned his head to one side and closed his eyes hard against the memory. "Katrell fell completely apart. He was blurring between his human- and dragonform like a hysterical Hatchling. It took four Councilors to restrain him." Kashon opened his eyes and ran his hand lightly over the surface of the water as if trying to quiet the ripples. "No one can stand alone against a blow from a Dragon's tail, and Katrell was in no shape to brace me. Your father took his humanform and steadied me while Makara carried out my sentence."

Shashtah held his tongue, knowing that this was why Kashon had desperately needed to be around someone who was a Dumnonian and not a Dragon. *He needs someone who can understand how inhumane that sentence was.*

"As soon as it was over, they let Katrell come to me. I could barely think, and I couldn't give him directions. He knew a Healer couldn't help me, but he thought you could. So he took me to you instead of to our basecamp. His fury that your magic didn't do anything had Tphah paralyzed. It flattened the rest of the century. I don't know why it spared you. Maybe he was still hoping you would fix me." Kashon ran his fingers through his hair, brushing it away from his face. "Tphah recovered enough to talk him into taking me back to our basecamp where I was supposed to be." Kashon bit his lip for a heartbeat. "That's when Bahktarah figured out that I had to heal like a Trainee with Katrell caring for me. He let me out long enough each night to control the century in battle, but then I had to return to my tent so Katrell could tend to my injuries . . ." He let the thought trail off. "If you were king, would you have let the Council carry out that sentence without even trying to come to my defense?" He looked for an answer in Shashtah's eyes.

"If I were king, you would not be asking that question."

"That was not an easy question for me to ask. I deserve something better than an easy answer."

"Come here." Shashtah pulled Kashon close until they were standing chest to chest, hip to hip. He placed one of his arms around his Dragonlord's neck and the other across the small of his back, bracing him. "I'm not afraid of you. I'm not afraid of Katrell. I'm not afraid of the Council, and I'm not Shaharadesh. I'll always defend you and protect your Bond with Katrell, and I'll never force you to take responsibility for something that's not your fault."

Kashon held onto him like a Trainee clinging to the face of the Anvil. "What am I going to do when I'm forced to breed? I won't be able to concentrate well enough to restrain Katrell. An adult Bronze out of control in the King's Camp—" He dropped his voice so low that Shashtah could barely hear him. "That will be a thousand times worse than anything Peri could do."

Shashtah pressed his head against Kashon's. "When you had me in Training, you gave Katrell a string of orders just as absently as you would have told Patch to do a million things at once, and you expected him to carry them out. Do you remember how happy that made him? Tkai always said that you underestimate your Dragon. Tphah's told me the same thing. "

"I'm not a Dragonheart like you. If Katrell loses control . . . The punishment for that could get me killed. If I die—" Kashon pulled slightly free from Shashtah. "Swear to me that you'll protect Katrell if I can't."

Shashtah grabbed Kashon's hand and kissed his ring. "I will always protect him."

Kashon refused to let go of Shashtah's hand. "The very valuable Prophetess Bonded to an out of control Prophet, and the very valuable king's son Bonded to an out of control Dragon."

"Two sides of the same coin," Shashtah agreed, "and Shaharadesh has no idea what to do with either of us. Our Dragons aren't the problem. We're the terrible match." He punched him playfully in the shoulder. "You're the only reason I didn't wind up as a smear on the sand long ago. The Council and Shaharadesh can simply deal with it. I'm not about to let anyone separate me from you."

Kashon smiled sheepishly. "You do have a talent for trying to get yourself killed."

Shashtah chuckled. "Fortunately, you have a habit of making sure I don't die."

Kashon splashed water at Shashtah then heaved himself onto the deck. "Let's cool down, then try to get some sleep while we still can."

"Sounds like an excellent plan."

Shashtah, Shaharadesh,
and Kashon

Chapter 12:

Divisions

I tell you and tell you and tell you to Train the Bronzes and their Riders to attack a single goal, and not a one of you listens to me! You divide and win individual victories against a thousand nameless evils, and yet you are losing the War! What does it take to make you understand? You are the Light! I send you to attack the Darkness, and you scatter to the Eight Winds like the desert sands! One ruler fears you will cease to be yourselves without the Darkness to define you. Another fears that by destroying the Darkness you will take its place and become the new evil in the world. Imbeciles! I am not asking you to wipe the Darkness from the face of the planet. I am asking you to set Dumnonia on fire before a random puff of wind blows out your last spark of flame!

—from *Tirades from the Tomb*
by Shane of Corin

"ARE YOU SUNSTRUCK?" GARESH ROARED at Shashtah.

Tphah and Peri instinctively stepped between the outraged Council Leader and Kyla and Quatar.

Shashtah felt the tips of his ears turning red as he confronted his irate father. "I haven't been back in Camp long enough to have done anything wrong yet!"

Garesh pointed at Quatar, whose head came far closer to the ceiling of the tent than Shashtah would have liked. "You brought a Dragonslayer into the King's Camp! It was bad enough when you had one of their whelps running around, but now you return with one of their warriors?"

Quatar backed up until he was in the family space behind Shashtah's throne as Kyla joined Tphah and Peri.

"That's Quatar!" Shashtah bellowed, well past caring if the entire Camp heard him. "He was hit with some sort of magic when Pali's caravan was wiped out!"

Garesh pulled himself up short. "Pali's caravan was wiped out?"

Shashtah felt his heart quake as he realized he had blindly stumbled down the path he didn't want to take in front of the one being on Centuria besides Tphah who could catch him in a lie.

Kashon burst into the tent. He rushed forward, nimbly dropping into a deep salaam to Garesh. "Time Magic, Council Leader."

Katrell surged through the tent flap behind him.

Tphah lunged into her fellow Dragon's path, her hands flickering with magic as she intercepted him.

Shashtah sensed the shock as the power of the two Dragons collided, and he saw his father's eyes narrow.

Katrell subsided, but a look of terror remained on his face.

"Someone is using the forbidden spells of Time Magic," Kashon repeated, drawing Garesh's attention back to himself.

"Why didn't you report this at once?" Garesh challenged the Dragonlord.

Kashon rose and spread his hands, making himself entirely vulnerable to the furious Dragon. "I couldn't be sure until I consulted with the elves. You know Dumnonians don't understand this type of magic, and I didn't want to raise an unnecessary alarm if I was wrong. I was on my way to report to the king when I heard you arguing with Shashtah. I had no idea you were in Camp, or I would have sought you out immediately. This is far too big a problem for two Dumnonians to try to deal with it on their own. We need your guidance."

Shashtah did his best to control his features. He was fairly certain Kashon was lying through his fangs.

:*Don't think, Dragonheart!*: Tphah warned silently. :*Trust.*:

"How long have you known about the Time Magic?" Garesh demanded.

"I guessed several days ago," Kashon replied, careful not to say how many days. He gestured at Quatar. "I had to get the boy to the Elven Kingdom so they could examine him to make sure I was right, and I wasn't in any shape to carry him on Katrell." He waited for Garesh to remember why he was injured before pressing on. "Once the elves confirmed what I feared, I ordered everyone back here so we could handle our own problem instead of having the elves and Daethians decide what we should do for us."

Garesh studied Kashon carefully.

Shashtah had never learned to read his father's face any better than the hundreds of traders who had ever dealt with the wily caravaneer.

:*Keep your mind blank!*: Tphah ordered.

The command was unnecessary. Shashtah was far too terrified to think.

"Report to the king. Now." Garesh waited for Kashon to bare his throat and head for the tent flap.

"Stay here," Kashon begged Katrell as his Dragon made a move to follow him.

Katrell started to protest, but light flickered from Tphah's hands again, and he remained where he was.

Garesh's sharp eyes caught the flash. He shifted his look from Quatar and back to Shashtah. Without another word, he followed hard on Kashon's heels.

After several candlescars Kashon returned unscathed from the meeting with Shaharadesh. He silently collected Katrell and hurried off.

Before Shashtah could follow him, Patch appeared. "The Dragonlord wants extra security on the supply caravans. Take your Dragonslayers and mutant with you. They'll be of more use there than here." With that, she left.

:*Katrell has given me the location,*: Tphah said before Shashtah could ask. :*Peri can fly. Salene and Bahktarah will carry Kyla while you and I handle Quatar.*: "You heard her. Everyone grab your packs." She picked up Shashtah's backpack and handed it to him. :*This is the farthest away Kashon can get us from the King's Camp while keeping us on duty.*: Tphah lay her hand on his arm and steered him out of the tent. :*He's doing everything in his power to buy you as much time as he can. Your fosterlings can stay on the supply caravans, learning what the caravaneers have to teach them, and Peri can tell me where they are if he needs to. We're to take the three of them to the Elven Kingdom whenever we're on leave and teach them whatever else they need to know there.*: Tphah nodded her greeting to Bahktarah and Salene as they reached the edge of the Camp. She took her dragonform and waited for Shashtah to mount. :*Dragonslayers helping to guard our most secret caravans! Katrell's having a fit and rightly so. Bahktarah has agreed to protect your secret for now, but if he's put in a position where he has to tell the Council, then you, Kashon and Salene will all be worse than dead. The sooner we get Quatar, Kyla and Peri trained and out of Dumnonia, the better for all of us!*: When Quatar had settled onto Shashtah's thigh and Kyla had joined Salene astride Bahktarah,

Tphah took to the air without waiting for him to give her the command.

Shashtah clenched his teeth as Bahktarah and Peri took their positions. The image of an oasis, surrounded by camels and fantastical creatures of the desert took shape in his mind. He knew the spot well and gave Tphah the answering image.

A heartbeat later she carried them through a warp.

Shashtah was not on watch the night the dragons came. He was busy ignoring the macabre rituals that surrounded the Feast of the Dark One by teaching Kyla and Quatar how to perform a double parry, twist, backthrust. He'd spent several rotations popping between the supply caravans, the Elven Kingdom, and the Border, and he honestly had no idea where on Centuria he actually was. *Could be in the middle of Cinnamar, for all I know,* he grumbled to himself. His holy scimitar flashed in the red light of the Dark One's moon as he bore down on the siblings.

Quatar's and Kyla's eyes widened as he attacked them with an uncharacteristic ferocity.

Shashtah twisted—and tripped over a small plant. He landed inelegantly on the rocky soil between the two massive seif dunes that shielded them from the caravaneers' curious eyes. *Not Cinnamar.* He surged to his feet and kicked the offending plant. *If I were in Cinnamar I wouldn't have stumbled over you!*

Quatar and Kyla partially lowered their weapons and backed away.

"Dragon trouble?" Kyla ventured.

Shashtah stared at his left hand. His knuckles were white where his fingers gripped his scimitar's hilt, and he was quite literally trembling with rage.

Peri dropped out of the sky directly behind the siblings and scooped them close to him with his wings. He hissed at Shashtah.

Shashtah felt dragonfangs lift him by his collar. He had no time to panic before Tphah deposited him at the base of her neckridge and instantly took to the air again.

":*Katrell's under attack!:*"

:*Where?:* Shashtah sheathed his scimitar and braced his feet in her harness.

:*At the Anvil with the new Trainee!:* Tphah's wings caught a current.

:*Why does that sound familiar?:* Shashtah gave her the appropriate image of Katrell near the immense plateau.

Tphah's picture blurred with his.

Suddenly they were in the middle of the most confusing battle Shashtah had ever seen.

:*How many centuries did that nit call up?*: Shashtah tried to take some sort of count in the dim light of the blood-red moon.

:*Just the three on rotation in the King's Camp.*: Tphah shot a blast of magical light through the wings of an ancient red dragon. :*The frontline is already engaged in skirmishes. Shaharadesh is waiting for Katrell's next report before calling for the centuries who are on leave.*:

:*Up left!*:

Tphah sent a spray of her scent into a particularly thick clump of crimson dragons and their riders.

:*Sands!*: Shashtah swore as the dragons kept coming. :*Scent isn't working. Send word to Katrell to tell everyone to stick to light attacks!*:

Kashon, magic glittering around him as Katrell carried him into position, waved his hands in the air. He mouthed the words to a spell and sent several bursts of light toward the oncoming dragons. Sixteen dragons and riders fell from the sky.

Shashtah watched them crash onto the sand, hoping none of them were Bronze. :*It's Dameth, isn't it,*: he declared, no question in his voice.

:*Not just Dameth. Dameth and someone who knows how to use a Dragonlord.*: Tphah scraped a vampire from the back of an adult red. She screamed in dismay as the undead creature turned into a bat and flew back to rejoin its mount.

:*It's okay!*: Shashtah reassured her with a confidence he didn't feel. :*Wish we could get some of the archers from the caravans out here. We could herd the dragons toward them. Holy arrows through their hearts ought to slow down some of these undead things. Uck! That looked like a rotting Dumnonian!*:

:*It was.*: Tphah lashed out with her tail, sweeping an unwary vampire from his perch. :*Katrell's sent for the archers, but even on racing horses they won't get here for candlescars.*:.

:*We need to add some of those elven wizards who can create warps to our ranks.*: Shashtah felt Bonds Breaking all around him as Dragons and Dumnonians died. The adrenaline surging through him kept his panic and pain at bay, but he dreaded what would happen when the fighting stopped. Somewhere behind him he heard a scream of rage. He glanced over his shoulder to see Katrell and an ancient red plummeting toward the sand, their wings fouled.

Kashon's scimitar flashed in the wine-colored light as he fought to free himself and Katrell from the death grip. He tore off his cloak to give him more range of movement and sent it fluttering to the ground. It landed on the Anvil.

With a sudden chill, Shashtah recognized the red dragon's rider. :*Dameth!*:

:*Down left!*: Tphah called, distracting him.

Shashtah gasped.

Easily a hundred hyenas were attacking the Bronze on the sand like starving ants swarming over a dying lion. Exhausted from the Training, the Dragon had done all he could to defend himself. He'd curled up, placed his head under his wing with his Rider, and prepared to die.

Shashtah glanced up in time to see the ancient red dragon crash onto the Anvil, crushing Dameth's body beneath it. :*Where's Kashon?*:

:*Busy!*: Tphah screeched as she swooped down, skewered four hyenas with her talons, snapped one in two with her jaws and scattered several more with her tail.

Shashtah could feel the incredible strain on her wings as she climbed higher and higher, then leveled out and dropped the four, shrieking hyenas she had impaled.

The beasts plummeted toward the sand and landed with satisfying splats.

Their fellow hyenas ignored them and continued to attack the bleeding Dragon.

:*They'll kill the Trainees!*: Tphah swiveled to her right and slapped her tail at the rider of a younger red.

The vampire lost her grip, fell, then turned into a bat and flew back to her mount.

Tphah screamed her frustration to the desert winds. She arced around to make another pass at the Anvil and backwinged with surprise.

Peri's dragonform was perched on the shoulders of the injured Bronze, spitting burning liquid light at the hyenas. The substance seemed to stick to the animals' fur, rubbing off on their companions and setting them aflame as well.

Quatar and Kyla, back to back, sword and scimitar flashing in the eerie light, stood on the sand, fighting to protect the wing that covered the Trainee. What Quatar lacked in skill, a magically glowing blade Shashtah had given him made up in quality, and what Kyla's blade lacked in quality, she more than made up in skill. Together the siblings methodically slew anything that got within reach of their weapons with a grim proficiency that did credit to Shashtah's teaching and their own prowess.

:*How did they get here?*:

:*I'm sure I don't want to know! Back right! Up!*: Shashtah called, then braced himself as Tphah somersaulted and tried to climb toward the flailing body of a Dumnonian that was plunging toward the ground.

The Prophetess roared in exasperation as her talons just missed the Rider.

Shashtah watched in horror as the Rider bounced on the sand and then lay still.

Beginning at a ring on the Rider's left hand, the magic of Corin glittered around her corpse, and the body vanished.

:*Who was it?*: Shashtah asked.

:*Dragonlord Xia! I couldn't catch— If I had only— She—*: The abortive thoughts trailed off into an inconsolable wail that quickly transformed into a cry of utter distress that was echoed by every surviving Bronze in Xia's century.

:*Tphah!*: Shashtah tried to shock her out of her hysteria. :*You did the best you could! You—*: He suddenly saw the problem and screamed himself.

Xia's Dragon, Ishaiah, out of control with grief, was diving toward them, slaughtering friend and foe alike as he sought the Rider he would not find.

Zofar, the third Dragonlord assigned to the King's Camp, tried to intercept the distraught Male with his own Dragon, Onycha.

Ishaiah neither recognized them nor slowed, slamming full speed into Onycha's side, breaking her right wing and knocking Zofar from his perch.

From above the Anvil Kashon sent a bolt of magic toward Zofar as Onycha instinctively attacked the source of her pain, taking Ishaiah's throat between her fangs in a death grip.

Zofar's fall slowed, and he started to drift just as Quatar had floated down while wearing his magic ring after slipping from Peri's grasp. Then the massive bodies of the two Dragons crashed into the Dragonlord, adding their combined weight to his and bearing him with them to the sand.

Shashtah heard Katrell's screech over the din of the battle. He watched in horror as Ishaiah's enormous, armored frame crushed Zofar beneath him

Onycha, insane with pain and grief, dispatched her fellow Dragon before dying herself.

Corin's magic flared again, and the gruesome pile of corpses faded through a warp.

The surviving Dragons in Zofar's century lost all semblance of discipline. Their Riders, too busy trying to hold onto their harnesses to direct their mounts, were at the mercy of any enemy who could get close enough to them. Several never saw the flaming blasts that killed them. Bronzes screamed mindlessly, the soul shredding sound of blade scrapping against blade, and turned on anything that came too close in futile attempts to protect the Riders they had already lost.

One vampire separated himself from the confusion and aimed his dragon at Tphah.

Shashtah had never seen the Vampire King, the one who had terrified Garesh into slaughtering everyone on his caravan. He had never been able to figure out how anything could strike such fear into his father's heart. But one look at the abomination that was Eschlend, and everything fell into place.

The Dumnonian king before Shaharadesh, the one whose name no one dared to speak, stared at Shashtah through undead eyes.

No wonder he wanted Dameth! :Pull up!: Shashtah instructed, then changed his mind as he saw another vampire slam his smaller red dragon into a Bronze, repeating the catastrophe of Zofar's death with one exception: The vampire shifted to batform mid-fall and flew away. *:Tphah! Warp!:* Shashtah gave her an image of Katrell off the Anvil.

Instincts took over. Tphah gave Shashtah the answering picture just as she had during their Training, and they blurred a fraction of a heartbeat before Eschlend struck them.

They came out of the warp practically touching Katrell's right wing.

Katrell shielded Kashon from a red dragon's fiery blast.

Tphah twisted right, backflipped and came up on the other side of their opponent as Katrell rolled out of her way. Her talons fastened on the shoulders of the vampire. She plucked him from his perch, broke the dragon's wings with her tail, and climbed high above the battle. She tore the undead monster in two and sent the remains plummeting toward the sand.

:Tell Katrell to tell Kashon to snap out of it! We need a Dragonlord in control out here, and he's the only one left!: Shashtah watched his friend's face contort with anguish as the message was relayed.

Katrell soared above the Anvil, bugled and backwinged to hold himself in place.

:Katrell says we're to form up on him.: Tphah climbed still higher.

Shashtah was about to instruct her to obey when he saw Eschlend aiming his ancient red at Kashon. He took a firm grip on Tphah's harness. *:Eschlend! Speedfly! Breathe light! Don't slow down! If we hit him, we hit him!:*

Tphah angled toward the ground.

Shashtah drew a deep breath and roared, ":*Eternal Death to the Dark One! Dive!:*"

Tphah plunged toward the ground.

Shashtah kicked his feet out behind him as soon as he felt the air catch his chest. He gripped Tphah's backridge between his powerful thighs and used his muscular legs to ease the strain on his hands and arms.

Tphah leveled out. Skyfire crackled around her armored hide as every hair on Shashtah's head stood on end. *:Close your eyes!:* she warned as a bolt of pure magical light shot from her open jaws, striking, point blank, at Eschlend's chest.

Shashtah snapped his eyes shut as the Vampire King disintegrated with an unearthly shriek.

Tphah carried Shashtah through the space where Eschlend had been.

Shashtah felt his Prophetess weaving to avoid hitting other Dragons and their Riders. *:You can slow down now.:*

Tphah's body undulated wildly. Finally, she settled into a glide.

As soon as Shashtah felt her extend her wings, he brought his knees up tightly to his chest and thrust himself away from her deadly spikes. He opened his eyes as he felt her land on something hard and flat.

:*The kavir,*: Tphah supplied. :*Are you all right?*:

:*No.*: Shashtah felt blood dripping from his chin onto Tphah's armored hide. He noted with an absurd sense of detachment that his fingers had almost been severed by her harness. He shivered, feeling a familiar pain lance from the back of his neck, dash over his brain, and stab toward his eyes. His world wavered. Then a blackness trimmed in gold shot through his skull and along his spine, as he began to fall . . .

Shashtah had no intention of waking up ever again, but, somewhere in the silent darkness that enveloped him, an annoying whine insisted that this was no time for him to take a nap. He screamed in protest, feeling the growing pain in his head as he flinched away from consciousness and tried to slip back into the comforting nothingness into which he had fallen.

:*Dragonheart*!: the voice commanded. :*You must wake up!*:

Shashtah drew a deep breath and gagged as the reek of the salt flats mingled with the stench of the battlefield. He felt a hard surface against his back, but he could not for the life of him tell which way was up. He opened his eyes.

The worried face of Tphah's humanform whirled into view. Behind and above her, the battle continued, bursts of light and flame flashing against the starry sky.

Shashtah winced. :*Ouch.*:

Tphah lay her hands along his broken jaw, took a deep breath and closed her eyes. Light leapt from her fingertips, enveloping his skull.

Bones shaped themselves back into their proper forms. Tendons, muscles and skin secured them in place.

Suddenly Shashtah heard the cacophony of the battle above him, the distant thunder of hooves, and the unmistakable singing of arrows in the air. :*What are the archers doing out here already?*:

:*You've been out for a while.*: Tphah magically reattached his fingers to his hands. :*We're also a lot closer to the King's Camp than where we started.*:

Shashtah struggled to his feet and glanced around.

Centaurs from the caravans had joined the archers who rode fleet desert horses. Blessed arrow after blessed arrow pierced the hearts of any enemy whose dragons flew too low, and the undead horrors landed in broken piles on the sand, prevented from either rising or shapeshifting by the sacred wood.

Shashtah smiled with grim pleasure as one after another of the foul creatures stayed where they fell. :*Where's Kashon?*:

:*Still at the Anvil, directing the battle.*: Tphah rose.

:*We'd better obey that order we ignored.*:

Tphah nodded and shifted to dragonform.

Shashtah hauled himself up her harness and onto her back with a helpful nudge from her armored head. He wrapped his right leg around the spike at the base of her neckridge, brought his right fist to his left breast and thrust it toward the Anvil.

Tphah sprang into the air. Her magnificent wings quickly carried them high above the fray.

Shashtah noted that the Dragons and their Riders were slowly herding the forces of the Dark One toward the Dumnonian archers. *That's how we do it. The Dragonriders herd the Dark One's forces toward the elves.* The thought vanished as he ducked a blast of flame.

As Tphah positioned herself beside Katrell, Shashtah wondered absently what was bothering him about the solitary body of the ancient red dragon that lay dead atop the Anvil.

:*Katrell says it took us long enough to obey his last order.*: Tphah circled into formation above the plateau.

:*Tell him I'll try not to die faster next time.*: Shashtah noted that Quatar and Kyla guarded either side of the Trainee's injured Dragon and that Peri screamed defiantly from the Bronze's back at anything that approached.

Tphah let Katrell lead her over the wadi and into a glide high above the kavir. :*Hold on,*: she cautioned as they rejoined the other Dragons and Riders.

Shashtah gave a sharp laugh and gripped her harness firmly with his newly-healed hands as he felt her twist, soar and dive. :*As if I'm going to do anything else.*: He clung to her back, glancing behind him occasionally to make sure all of their enemies were still in front of them and watched with cheerless satisfaction as the archers did their work.

Finally, the remaining forces of the Dark One disengaged and fled south.

Tphah, under Katrell's direction, flew after them, tearing with her claws and fangs, lashing with her tail, battering with her wings, and shielding Shashtah from the dragons' fiery breaths with her armored hide.

Shashtah shouted in relief when the three centuries from the Border flew out of a warp and into formation above them.

:*We're to go back to the Anvil,*: Tphah informed him as she broke off the pursuit. :*The other Dragonlords will take it from here.*:

Shashtah gave her a picture of the Anvil with the corpse of the ancient red dragon draped over it.

Tphah presented him with the answering image, along with the added detail of Quatar, Kyla and Peri still defending the Trainees.

The pictures blurred, and they burst into the almost empty sky above the Anvil.

The all-too-few survivors of what had been three centuries joined them and ordered their weary Dragons to settle onto the blood-soaked sand.

Shashtah was about to ask Tphah to join them when he noticed Dameth standing next to the red dragon's body atop the plateau, howling his amusement at the stars. :*But he's dead!*:

:*Apparently he didn't stay that way.*:

Shashtah drew his scimitar from its jeweled sheath as Tphah landed near the former Dragonlord. "Dameth!" he screamed, flourishing his blade. The etched symbol of his god flashed with an Otherworldly light. "Eternal Death to the Dark One!"

Dameth laughed harder and gestured at the pitifully few survivors who searched the immense battlefield for wounded Dragons and Riders. His mirth quieted into an obscene giggle. "More like 'Countless Deaths for the Dark One!' tonight, don't you think?" He sniggered. "Glad I'm not the Dragonlord responsible for this mess. I might have been, but that abomination took my century and my magnificent Tlee away from me. He's welcome to this!" He gestured at the piles of dead that littered the dunes. "I wonder how long he'll live when the Council gets their talons on him."

Shashtah felt a chill grip his heart, and he tightened his leg around Tphah's neckridge. "What are you blithering about?"

Dameth drooled. "My Lord tells me not to bother with the abomination, that his pain won't last long enough to be of any use. But it will last long enough for me because you will make sure he dies knowing that Dameth, Dragonlord of Dumnonia, has claimed his revenge!" With that, the undead obscenity collapsed into a puff of smoke and blew away on the desert winds.

Shashtah searched the empty sky and found no sign of Katrell. :*Where's Kashon?*: He sheathed his scimitar and brought his right fist to his left breast, then thrust it skyward, giving Tphah the command to rise.

Tphah leapt wearily into the air. :*The Valley of Ancients,*: she finally responded, giving him the proper image with Shaharadesh standing on the rim above Corin's Tomb.

Shashtah glanced down just long enough to spot Quatar tending to the injured Dragon and Trainee while Peri, in humanform, helped Kyla, her chain mail spattered with gore, make sure that every enemy that looked dead on the battlefield stayed that way. Then he gave Tphah his own image of the Valley with the bodies of several Dragons and Riders lying on the sand. He felt the Prophetess carry them through a warp as the pictures blurred.

Neither image was remotely accurate, Shashtah noted with dismay as they burst into the air high above an impossibly large pile of carnage. The bodies of easily one hundred and fifty Dragons littered the ravine floor, the sand invisible beneath their bloody armor plates. The corpses of almost half again as many Riders lay entwined with them. Most of the Council members perched along the rim of the gorge, trying to control the screeching Dragons who had lost their Bond Partners. Garesh stood practically on top of Katrell at the Valley's mouth, restraining the smaller male, who was blurring to shape after shape after shape as he screamed in abject terror at his fellow Dragons.

Shaharadesh watched silently from atop the cliff at the far end of the gulch as Kashon's lonely figure struggled through the corpses, trying futilely to sort through the dead.

Makara, tail twitching with agitation, crouched beside the king.

:*Dive!*: Shashtah ordered.

Tphah obeyed.

Shashtah leapt from her back a few paces from Kashon. :*Help Garesh with Katrell!*:

The Prophetess promptly returned to the air and swooped toward her target.

Kashon, oblivious to the precipitous arrival of his friend, stood among the dead, scales and scars blurring hopelessly before his tear-filled eyes.

Shashtah struggled over to him. "Kashon," he said quietly as he reached out and touched him lightly on the arm.

The Dragonlord raised his head at the sound of his name but failed to focus on Shashtah, unable to see anything but the slaughtered Dragons and Riders. He shook his head in utter denial of what his eyes were telling him. "There can't be this many! I don't know even half of their names!"

"You can't do this, Kashon," Shashtah said in a low voice, sensing the turn his friend's thoughts had taken. "You can't take responsibility for this many dead. Not even for the ones in your own century. There are too many. It would kill you. That's what Dameth wants. He wants you to be beaten to death by the same laws that exiled him. He's forgotten to take Shaharadesh into account. Your father knows Dumnonia can't afford to lose a third Dragonlord in one night. Throw yourself on your father's mercy. He'll convince the Council to grant you mercy."

"No! Someone has to pay for this! I knew what I was doing! I took command! That makes me responsible!" Kashon stared blindly at the dead bodies around them. He dug the palms of his hands into his eyes as if somehow the pressure would make the nightmare go away.

Shashtah grabbed his friend's wrists and pulled his hands away from his face. "Kashon, listen to me! You did everything you could. I doubt even a Great Wizard could have kept two Dragons and a Dragonlord aloft with that spell."

Kashon yanked his hands out of Shashtah's grip. "Controlling one century strains Katrell's abilities. I know that, and I asked him to control three!"

"Someone had to do it! We were killing each other out there without Dragonlords in control! You saved the lives of dozens of Dragons and Riders. You and Katrell are heroes!"

Kashon gestured at the twisted corpses and snarled, "This is not the work of a hero!"

"You're right. This is the work of a traitor, an undead monster who wouldn't spit on a parched Bronze to save its life, who called up uncountable perversions in the name of an unholy king, all to kill a half-dead Trainee. And you know what? That monster is Dameth, not Kashon!"

Kashon pounded his chest with his right fist. "I *am* Kashon, Dragonlord of Dumnonia, and I am responsible for those who die in the centuries I command! Even if I don't know who they are . . . " He rubbed his brow as if he had a headache. "If I could just get Katrell to give me a clear picture of each Rider's scars—" He started to shake violently and clutched at his head.

Shashtah quickly pressed his hands over Kashon's. Light sparkled from his fingertips, bathing Kashon's temples in a soothing glow. "Stop it! You're fraying your Bond by trying to accept responsibility for too much. Listen to your poor Dragon. He's going to burst his heart he's so sure his inadequacies have killed you. He thinks that if he were still as smart as he was with his first Riders he wouldn't be about to lose you now." The light from Shashtah's hands glowed brighter as he watched Kashon pick out Katrell's plaintive wail above the screeches of the other grief-stricken Bronzes. "Tell him he's wrong! Tell him he's the most magnificent Dragon who's ever lived! He did exactly what you asked him to do. He controlled three centuries and routed the enemy by relaying your orders. Tell him this is not his fault and how proud you are of him and how much you love him!"

Kashon closed his eyes and swayed dangerously. "I should never have challenged Dameth."

Shashtah slapped Kashon hard across the face. "Then we'd all be dead!"

"Dragonrider Shashtah!" Shaharadesh boomed. "Is it your intention to challenge Dragonlord Kashon for control of his century?"

Shashtah blinked up at his king in disbelief.

Katrell whimpered in confusion.

Shashtah glanced at where Tphah was coiled around Katrell. *Neither of them are in any shape to serve as Seconds. Do I fight Kashon without Seconds? Or do we do something else?* He glared at his father. *Why didn't you teach me anything I needed to know about Dumnonia? So I'd only have my instincts to rely on at times like this?*

Garesh stared back, the face of his dragonform as unreadable as the face of the trader he was in humanform.

:*Tphah! Tell Katrell what a splendid Dragon he is, the best Dragon his Rider could ever have! Tell him how much Kashon needs his support right now, and how confident you are that he, out of all the Dragons in Dumnonia, will be able to give it to him!*:

:*I am?*:

:*Lie through your fangs, Dragon! I don't want their Bond to Break! Tell Katrell I'm here, and I'll fix everything!*:

:*I don't think you can fix this, Dragonheart.*:

:*I'm not going to lose a third Dragonlord in one night without a fight!*: Shashtah made eye contact with his king and realized that Shaharadesh was still waiting for an answer. *All I have to do is take Kashon's century away. They can't punish him if he's not a Dragonlord. If the Council decides to lash me in his place, I can survive this. The Demonlord Yapada tried to beat me to death and couldn't. Makara can't succeed where Yapada f—*

Kashon's right fist caught Shashtah's newly healed jaw, sending him reeling.

:*Dragonheart!*: Tphah's voice screamed through his head.

Shashtah tripped over a corpse and sprawled face first into the gore.

Kashon grabbed him from behind. The Dragonlord roared as hauled Shashtah to his feet.

Katrell's matching scream echoed off the canyon walls.

Kashon turned out the sound.

Shashtah pulled free and spun to face his friend.

Madness shone in Kashon's dark amber eyes.

Shashtah's own eyes widened in horror. He crouched and brought his arms up in the Flying Dragon with Wings pose. :*Tphah! Do something about Katrell! He's going insane and taking Kashon with him!*: Shashtah hurled himself forward, wrapping his arms around Kashon. His momentum carried them both tumbling into the bloody heap, wrapping them together in his cloak as they rolled.

Kashon's fingers closed on Shashtah's throat in a death grip.

Arms pinned to Kashon's body by the cloak, Shashtah threw himself to the right. He glanced away from his friend's face just long enough to spot the base spike of a dead Dragon near his left hand. He forced his hand as far away from his body as he could and thrust the cloak down on the spike.

The fabric tore.

Shashtah felt his form start to blur.

"No shapeshifting in a Challenge Fight," Shaharadesh roared.

If Shashtah hadn't been trying so hard to breathe he would have laughed. Somewhere in the back of his mind, he heard the night fill with battle-sounds once more. :*Tphah! I don't want to hurt Kashon! Do something about Katrell!*: He thrust his left hand through the tear in the cloak and up between Kashon's elbows. He wrapped his fingers around his friend's throat in imitation of the draconic lovemaking hold. He fought to keep his nails from growing into talons.

Kashon released his grip on Shashtah. He tried to pry the fingers from his throat with his right hand as his left fist landed a solid blow on Shashtah's right ear.

:*Tphah! Are you listening to me?*: Shashtah slipped his left hand out of Kashon's grip and punched the Dragonlord in the ribs.

Tphah's voice crackled through his head like skyfire. :*Do you want me to listen to you or do something about Katrell?*:

Shashtah shoved Kashon away from him, ripping the cloak in two. He staggered to his feet and sucked air repeatedly into his lungs as he watched Kashon rise.

The Dragonlord's chest heaved as he struggled to gain his footing on the pile of the dead. He clenched his fists and prepared to attack again.

Shashtah's own words haunted him: *I'm not going to lose a third Dragonlord in one night. Maybe I'm wrong. Maybe I'm not supposed to take his century away. Maybe I'm supposed to establish his right to keep it.* He thought he saw of flicker of sanity in Kashon's eyes and bared his throat in submission.

Kashon halted mid-lunge as instinct took over. He threw his head back and roared in triumph at the blood-red moon.

The simoom of sound clashing around them suddenly ceased.

Shashtah felt himself settle fully into his humanform. He tried to wipe away the blood that was dripping from the corner of his mouth, but he only succeeded in smearing it across the growing bruise on the side of his face.

Kashon, still taking deep, rapid breaths, looked at him with unseeing eyes.

Shashtah matched his breathing to Kashon's.

Just as in the Battle Dance, their pulses started to beat as one.

Shashtah willed his pulse to slow and watched in fascination as Kashon's did the same. :*Tphah, I want the senior surviving Pair from Xia's and Zofar's centuries out here. Now. And tell Makara to get Shaharadesh down here. Immediately.*:

Apparently the orders were relayed because Makara leapt from her perch and carried the king to a spot near the combatants.

Two Dragons from the other centuries, with their Riders, landed beside Shaharadesh.

"Sire," Shashtah said quietly, never taking his eyes off Kashon, "I think we've all had enough Bond Breaks for one night. Could you, please, prevent another one?"

Shaharadesh glanced quickly from Shashtah to Kashon then carefully picked his way over the bodies to his son. Gently, he wrapped his arms around the bloodied Dragonlord and pulled him into a firm embrace. "Kashon . . . " he called softly.

A magical glow surrounded them for a heartbeat, then Kashon collapsed, sobbing, into his father's arms.

Shashtah waited until he was sure Shaharadesh had control of Kashon and then staggered toward the other Riders. "Each of you, figure out who's alive, who's dead, who's Bonded and who's Bond Broken in your centuries. I'll try to—" He stumbled and nearly went down.

An Ancient Dragon detached himself from the canyon wall and glided swiftly to the Valley floor. He shifted to his humanform. Dameth's former Dragon, Councilor Tlee, put a steadying arm around Shashtah's shoulders. "I know the scar and scale patterns of all who served under my former Rider. I'll help you sort the bodies."

Shashtah accepted Tlee's offer with an absent nod. "Thank you, Honored Ancient." He leaned heavily against the dragonman and slowly began to count the dead.

What seemed like candlescars later, Shashtah staggered over to where Tphah was nuzzling Katrell, who had finally settled down. Sticky with half-dried blood, Shashtah collapsed to the sand and leaned heavily against his Prophetess's side. :*Forty-seven Bonded Pairs left in our century, including us and the Trainees. Twenty-one in Zofar's; twelve in Xia's.*: He swallowed hard and watched the grieving Dragons on the Rim. :*Fifty-nine Dragons with Bond Breaks. How many*

Dumnonians with Bond Breaks has Peri found on the battlefield?:

:None. And I doubt all of the dead Riders are here. Many are probably undead.: Tphah's mental sigh held a world of despair. *:What are we going to do? Dameth was right. We can't survive this.:*

:I know.: Shashtah watched Shaharadesh and Kashon struggle through the corpses to the mouth of the Valley.

At the sight of his Rider, Katrell shifted to humanform and ran to intercept him.

Shaharadesh half-guided, half-shoved Kashon into Katrell's arms, and then stumbled over to Shashtah and slumped beside him. "What are we going to do?"

Shashtah favored his king with a sideways look. "That is indeed the question." He surveyed the Dragons on the rim. "We can't afford any more Bond Breaks. We have to keep every surviving Pair alive. Since you're our spokesperson, I suggest you inform the Council that we're in absolutely no shape to injure any more Dragons or Riders—especially our Dragonlords. The centuries on the frontline need to follow the example of the Daethians and the elves and stay put on our Border until we clean up this mess. The Pairs on leave need to be called to duty to protect the Valley and the King's Camp until the rest of us get back on our feet. Then we need to figure out which Dragons are willing to Bond and get as many of them matched up with Dumnonians—even if those Dumnonians haven't completed their Dragonquests—and stick the new Pairs into the Training as fast as we can."

Shaharadesh closed his eyes, leaned his head back against Tphah's armored side, and gave a hopeless laugh. "You haven't given this any thought at all, have you." There was no question in his voice. He gestured at the doors to Corin's Tomb. "So you would throw most of our traditions to the desert winds."

"I don't think we can fill even part of the hole Dameth just tore in us unless we do precisely that."

Shaharadesh glared at him. "Our traditions are what bind us."

Shashtah ran his hands through his gritty hair. He absently noted that his keffiyeh and the leather thong Tphah had given him were missing. "There is no 'us' to bind, unless you aren't staring at the same Valley I am. You know as well as I do that we were already a dying race. The elves, the Galantites, even the Krills—everyone can tally the ledger, except, apparently, us." He waved his hand at the pile of corpses. "We can't replace that fast enough. It takes too long to raise and Train a Dragon. It's too hard to qualify a Dumnonian to Bond. With what we have left, we're going to be nothing more than half-forgotten memories in a storyteller's tale if we keep sticking to our traditions!"

"Dragonheart, we're already dead." Shaharadesh unpinned the flame-shaped brooch from his shoulder and dropped his cloak on the sand. He turned the brooch in his fingers, studying it carefully. "Every ruler of our allied peoples wears one of these. It symbolizes the Light that binds us. Our part of that light just sputtered out." He threw the brooch away from him.

The piece of gold landed at Kashon's feet.

The Dragonlord looked down at it. He released Katrell, bent and picked it up. He looked over at Shashtah and Shaharadesh as if suddenly noticing they were there. Slowly, he walked toward his king, Katrell following close behind. He offered the brooch to his father with a salaam.

Shaharadesh took the brooch from him. "What's the point?"

Kashon glanced at Shashtah. "We aren't dead yet." He met Shaharadesh's stare. "And I don't want to die." He held out his hand.

Shaharadesh bit his lower lip. He took Kashon's hand and let him help him stand. He clapped his son on the shoulder. "And I don't want you to die."

Kashon flashed him a quick smile, and then released him. He offered his hand to Shashtah.

Every muscle in Shashtah's body screamed as Kashon pulled him to his feet.

"Still alive?" Kashon asked.

Shashtah tightened his grip on his friend's hand. "So my body tells me. The question is for how long." He looked for an answer in Kashon's eyes.

"Until we kill the Dark One?" Kashon suggested.

Shashtah nodded his head slowly. He let go of Kashon and trudged to the edge of the carnage. He looked up at the Council of Ancients, who had all returned to their perches.

The Council gazed down at Shashtah as if waiting for something.

Shashtah drew his holy scimitar and thrust it skyward. "Eternal Death to the Dark One!"

"Death!" The echo thundered through the Valley and rolled across the surrounding whaleback dunes.

Garesh nodded his armored head in approval at his son. He cracked his jaws and sent a bolt of magical light at the bodies of the dead.

The other Ancients and Makara joined their light to his.

Shashtah felt the light surge toward him. The blast flowed into him, through his veins and ignited a flame in his heart. He felt the sacred fire within him flare. The different forms of magic mixed and exploded outward.

The corpses that littered the Valley erupted with magical fire, and then crumbled into ash.

The power flowed toward Corin's tomb, seeped under the doors and drained into the darkness beyond.

Shashtah froze, wondering why he hadn't blown himself into the Afterlife. He was fairly certain he was still glowing. At least the light along the blade of his scimitar had not flickered out.

A hand closed on Shashtah's shoulder.

Shashtah turned to see Shaharadesh standing next to him, his cloak pinned firmly back into place with his brooch. "Sands," Shashtah swore, lowering his scimitar. "Why doesn't that ever happen when I'm in battle?"

The corner of Shaharadesh's mouth twitched. "Because your power is not of Darkness and death; it is of Light and life." He stood straighter as he confronted the Council. "Dragonlord Kashon won the Challenge Fight!" he declared. "Albeit a little unconventionally," he added to Shashtah in a low voice. He raised his voice again. "By tradition," Shaharadesh threw a quelling look at Shashtah, "he remains in command of his century." He raised his hands toward the Council and spread his arms as if to embrace the Valley. "I suggest that you don't kill him so we only have to replace two Dragonlords."

The Councilors looked at Garesh, who, after a heartbeat, nodded. "So ruled."

Shashtah flashed a quick grin at Kashon, who smiled weakly.

"Whom do you name as the new Dragonlords?" Shaharadesh asked.

"Shashtah!" the Council thundered as one.

Shashtah gave a mental shrug as he returned his scimitar to his scabbard, sheathing its light. :*Didn't really think I was going to get out of that one,*: he observed philosophically to Tphah.

"And the other Dragonlord?" Shaharadesh queried.

This time the Council took a bit longer. "Salene!" they finally declared.

Shashtah's brow furrowed. :*She's a good choice, but what made them think of her?*:

:*I did,*: Tphah confessed. :*They asked me what I saw, and I said I saw Salene with Kashon.*:

Kashon stepped up to Shashtah's right side. "I'm going to miss our leaves together," he said quietly.

"Me, too," Shashtah confessed, knowing that the odds were against them sharing the same tour pattern again.

Bahktarah landed nearby, and Salene slid to the sand. She looked uncertainly at Shaharadesh. "Now what?"

"Draw lots for the centuries," Shaharadesh instructed.

Salene smiled worriedly as she took Shashtah by the arm and led him out of earshot of the others. "Whoever gets me is going to be disappointed."

Shashtah smiled. "Only until they realize how wonderful you are."

Salene bent down and selected a black and a white stone from the Valley floor. She removed her belt pouch, emptied the contents onto the sand and dropped the stones inside. "Black for the twenty-one; white for the twelve?"

"Agreed." Shashtah averted his eyes, reached into the pouch and closed his fingers around a stone. He pulled it out and looked at it. White shone from the palm of his hand. "Wish me luck." He held the stone up to the twelve remaining Pairs from Xia's century. "I claim the century of Xia, Dragonlord of Dumnonia!"

The Dragons and Riders of Xia's century screamed his name in elation as the survivors in Zofar's century groaned.

Salene dumped the black stone into her hand. She raised it to the sky. "I claim the century of Zofar, Dragonlord of Dumnonia!" She squatted, dropped the stone at her feet, returned the original contents to the pouch, and fastened it to her belt. "What did I tell you?"

Shashtah let his stone fall beside hers as she rose. "Just wait till those nits figure out that you are the only Dragonrider in Kashon's century who could put the fear of the gods into me." He dropped into the salaam that he usually reserved for Shaharadesh. "Congratulations, Salene, Dragonlord of Dumnonia. I look forward to serving with you."

Salene's century belatedly raised a cry in her honor.

"Let's get our orders." Shashtah let her help him back to Shaharadesh.

"I'll hold your Installation Feast at sundown." The king smiled sadly at his new Dragonlords. "Customarily you wouldn't have to assume your duties until the next dawn, allowing time for your aides to resettle the households of the previous Dragonlords and prepare for the transition of power. I think, however, it might be wise if you meet briefly with your Pairs and check the tents of the dead Riders to see how many Striplings no longer have someone to look after them. You might want to look in on your Fledglings as well."

"I forgot about the Fledglings!" Shashtah started to run toward his Prophetess.

"For the love of the Light," Shaharadesh swore as he grabbed Shashtah by the arm. "Tphah, get him cleaned up before he goes charging around, shocking all the children!"

Kashon glanced down at his own blood-soaked clothes. He waved his hand, and the grime vanished from him instantly.

Shashtah pulled himself free from his king and shook his finger under Kashon's nose. "You are going to teach me that trick or I'll—!" The threat faded into an inarticulate roar.

Kashon laughed and repeated the same gesture, cleansing Shashtah. As an afterthought, he made his way over to Salene and Shaharadesh and cleaned them off as well. He motioned for Katrell to shift to his dragonform. "Ask Patch to work you into my schedule."

"You insufferable—" Shashtah tried to lunge at Kashon.

Shaharadesh and Salene caught him as he almost fell.

Kashon made a rude gesture at Shashtah, mounted Katrell and gave his Dragon the command to rise.

Katrell obeyed—making sure that he hit only Shashtah with a spray of sand.

Salene laughed, released Shashtah and mounted Bahktarah. "Those two are going to be the death of me!"

Shashtah felt his soul shiver as Bahktarah carried her into the sky. He glanced at Tphah, who was staring at him, her eyes wide with fear. :*I know. Prophecy. We'll worry about it later.*: With a gentle prod from Tphah's snout, he climbed to his place on her neckridge. He brought his right fist to his left breast, then drove his hand up toward the canyon rim as what was left of Kashon's century took wing and melted into the starlit sky. He tried unsuccessfully to swallow the lump in his throat as Tphah landed and the twelve surviving members of his century, all the Dragons in their humanforms, prostrated themselves on the sand before him. He dismounted near the first Pair.

Shashtah bent down and helped the Rider to her feet as he signaled for the dragonwoman next to her to stand. "You are?" he prompted.

"Jeri," replied the Rider as she took her Bond Partner's hand. "And Annakah."

Shashtah acknowledged them with a nod. "Did either of you lose anyone special?"

Jeri shook her head.

"Just friends," Annakah responded for her Rider.

Shashtah reached out and touched Jeri's face. "There's no such thing as 'just friends.' Check the tents of the Riders you knew to see if there are any problems I should know about."

Jeri reverently dropped into a salaam. "We'll do what we can to ease your burden."

Shashtah turned to the next Pair. He talked quietly with each of them, taking care to lay his hand on every Rider. He could feel his power bind them to him, though the connections were nowhere near as strong as the Bond he shared with Kashon. He spent as much time as each individual needed in spite of Tphah's fretting that he was further exhausting himself. The conversations fueled his dread. Half of the Dragons had lost preferred mates. All of the Riders had lost friends, seven had lost siblings, and three had lost lovers. Erchiah, the eldest, had lost his son.

Shashtah waited until his century had mounted, launched themselves into the air and disappeared through warps on their way to carry out his orders before he let Tphah help him onto her back once more. As she leapt skyward, he looked down at the Councilors, who were still regarding him inscrutably. He glanced over at where Salene stood next to Bahktarah, surrounded by a circle of kneeling Dragons and Riders. :*I'd tell you to take us home, but I haven't the slightest idea where in the King's Camp that is.*:

Tphah's warm reassurances flowed through their Bond. :*Peri does.*: She gave him a picture of the King's Camp from the appropriate angle.

Shashtah called up the answering memory and watched the images blend together, resolving into a reality of confusion and sound that confirmed his fears that they may have won the battle but they were definitely losing the War.

Kyla of Daethia

Chapter 13:

Responsibilities

If a Stripling is assigned to a Dragonrider who is killed, the Dragonlord may reassign the youngster to someone who is able to fill the teacher's place. In the event that no suitable Trainer can be found, the Stripling remains the responsibility of the Dragonlord.

—from *The Dragonlords' Handbook*
by Corin of Daethia

PERI, QUATAR AND KYLA MET Shashtah and Tphah at the edge of the King's Camp. Shashtah suspected that his Prophetess had summoned his fosterlings and drew a breath to protest, but Quatar and Kyla scrambled onto Tphah's head, grabbed him and lowered him to the ground before a sound passed his lips.

"Papa!" Quatar gasped.

Shashtah grimaced as brother and sister joined him on the sand. "I'm all right," he lied.

"You," Tphah growled in ClearTalk, "can barely stand!"

"Yes, I can," Shashtah lied again as he almost fell.

Quatar caught him. "Right." He threw a glance at his sister.

The Daethian siblings braced Shashtah between them.

Peri suddenly found the toes of his shape-shifted desert boots fascinating.

Shashtah gripped his Daethian fosterlings' necks and waited until Peri looked at him. "I'll say it once, and then I'll never mention it again. I was exceedingly glad for your help out at the Anvil. By protecting Kashon's Trainee you gave him the freedom he needed to salvage that battle for us. But I never want to find out how you got out there so fast nor how you got back here, nor do I ever want you to attempt such miracles again. Understood?"

Kyla and Quatar nodded glumly, but Peri burst into tears, ran forward and hugged his foster father.

Shashtah released his Daethian fosterlings and clasped Peri to him. "Hush! Don't tell me!" he insisted, already knowing the truth. "I don't have the strength or the heart left to be angry at any of you tonight. Just promise me you'll take better care of Quatar and Kyla from now on."

Peri nodded.

Shashtah kissed him on the head. "Good. Now, I've just been promoted to Dragonlord to replace Lord Xia, and I need every bit of help you can give me."

Tphah shifted to her humanform. :*You need someone to knock some sense into you.*:

:*Kashon already tried that. It didn't work.*:

:*Falling flat on your face from pain and exhaustion is no way to make a good impression on your new century.*:

:*That was no small crash we had on the kavir. You've taken care of the worst of my physical injuries, but you haven't done anything about my remaining problems, which tells me you're drained. That little "light show" out at the Valley of Ancients was of the soul, not the body, so it did nothing about the fact that I'm in need of at least a rotation of leave. The Healers have their hands full with patients who are much worse off than I am, and I'm now a Dragonlord. My needs just got trumped by those of our century. So, if you can't figure out how to help me, then, please, don't fight with me!*:

Tphah rolled her eyes but remained silent.

A young scamp trotted out of the King's Camp and jogged toward them. He thrust a vial of something at Shashtah, completely ignoring everyone else. "Here."

Shashtah released Peri, took the potion and eyed it suspiciously. "What's this?"

"Something to keep you on your feet until you tend to your survivors," the rakish knave proclaimed. "The king ordered the Chief Healer to prepare one for each of the Dragonlords in Camp. He wants you to have your centuries organized by dawn, and he figures you can't do that if you're all lying prostrate on your rugs. Although, if it were my decision, I'd have asked the Chief Healer for something to put the lot of you to sleep for half a rotation. Patch and Peg will have their centuries under control soon, and I've already done everything I can with ours." His face darkened. "I didn't have as much to do."

"And who might you be?" Shashtah tried to get his brain to work, but he felt as if he were thinking through Daethian mud.

"Will, Camp Aide and Supply Specialist, at your service, Dragonlord." He bent into an appropriate salaam.

"'Will?'" Shashtah unstoppered the vial and drained the contents. He gave the lad an appraising look. "Are you Dumnonian?"

Will straightened and grinned, though his solid amber eyes were red-rimmed from recent tears. "So I'm told," he chirruped. "My mother was a Priestess of the Mother. My father was, well . . . " He finished the sentence with a shrug.

Shashtah, already feeling the warmth of the restorative draught spreading through him, nodded his head in understanding. He handed the empty vial and stopper to the aide. "How did you get such a non-Dumnonian name like 'Will'?"

"Where there's a Will, there's a way!" the lad piped as he recorked the vial and dropped it into his belt pouch. "Besides," he confessed with a mischievous smile, "it's easier to bellow 'Will!' than 'Ahithophel!' when you need me."

"You have a point," Shashtah chuckled. "All right, Will, talk to me. When you say you have our century under control, does that include everyone at our basecamp as well as those who are here? Dragons, Dumnonians, Striplings, Fledglings, support personnel and . . . anyone else I don't know about yet?"

Will raised an eyebrow, impressed. "One of the Riders on leave popped down to our basecamp and had a look around for me. Lots of people are mourning their dead, but most of those who are still at the camp are dragonless and are being pretty sensible about everything."

"The Fledglings?"

"Thirty-one who looked directly to Lord Xia." Will choked on his former commander's name but pressed on. "I'll have their files for you by dawn. I've confined them to their communal tent and sent some support personnel to watch over them, but that might be an unnecessary precaution. They seem to be handling the disaster fairly well. There are a few budding Prophets among them who are reassuring the others that you are the next best thing to a warm, dry nest in a flash flood, so most of them are rather curious and eager to give you a chance."

"Prophets?" Shashtah prompted, stilling the wave of conflicting emotions that surged at him from Tphah.

"Kchang, Katrina and Tkell," Will replied promptly. "And then there's Garal. We're not sure what he is."

Shashtah shot Tphah a warning glance as he recognized the names of her children. :*Not a sound out of you. Shaharadesh is too busy with his Hatchlings right now to give a thought to our Fledglings. Let's keep it that way.*: "I'll have to spend some extra time with them as soon as things calm down. They sound useful."

"You have to watch out for them," Will cautioned. "Shaharadesh tried putting them in with the Hatchlings for a while, but it didn't work. Their powers are far too advanced for their apparent age. He's worried that they might have been caught in some kind of Time Magic at the Valley of Ancients before they hatched, though no one can figure out how that might have happened. The king thought they'd be safer with our Fledglings than his Hatchlings, so he transferred them to us."

"What about the Striplings?" Shashtah asked.

Will removed his turban and turned it absently in his hands. "As you can hear, the Camp's a bit of a mess. I've told the households of our century that you," he nodded at Shashtah and replaced his headpiece, "have ordered everyone to stay in their tents until things calm down. Most of them are too grief stricken to do anything anyway. There were thirty-four Striplings assigned to Riders; only five were assigned to Riders who survived. Nine Pairs agreed to take an extra Stripling into their tent until you decide what to do with them."

Shashtah saw Quatar reach involuntarily for Peri's hand. "Ask the Pairs to take care of them until we have new Pairs to assign them to. If any Striplings would rather be transferred to another century, let me know at once."

Will nodded, accepting the orders.

Shashtah rubbed his forehead. "So I have twenty Striplings who are sitting alone in tents, scared halfway into the Afterlife about what I'm going to do with them."

"That about sums up the problem."

"I take it I have a couple of unoccupied tents somewhere that are big enough to hold a dozen or so cots each?" Shashtah asked.

"I've emptied the tents next to yours," Will confirmed.

"All right, Kyla and Quatar, you go with Will and help him set up cots. Kyla will be in charge of one tent; Quatar will oversee the other. Tphah and I—"

"What about Peri?" Quatar interrupted.

"For now," Shashtah massaged his temples, wishing his head would clear, "Peri will join me to help Tphah escort our unattached Striplings to the new tents. When they're settled, . . . " He waved his hand in the air. "We'll figure out what disaster we have to tend to next."

Will did his best to look as if a Dragonlord asked him to work with Dragonslayers every day. "Yes, Lord."

Shashtah grinned at his aide, impressed by the lad's unflappability.

Tphah snaked her arm around Shashtah. :*How do you think he got the job?*:

Will noticed the silent exchange but chose not to comment on it. "Our century is assigned to columns eleven through twenty. I'd give you the precise list of which Striplings are supposed to be in which tents, but it will probably be faster if you just walk the rows and check the tents as you go."

Shashtah nodded. "That's probably best. Off with you, now."

Will honored him with a salaam and led the Daethian siblings into the King's Camp.

Shashtah draped his arm across Tphah's shoulders as they walked toward the tents with Peri. He was surprised at how much, in spite of the restorative effects of the potion, he had to use her to steady himself.

"You can't serve as a conduit for that much magic and assume a simple potion will put you back on your feet," Tphah complained aloud now that Will was gone.

Peri matched their pace on Shashtah's other side. "Why do you keep expecting him to have good dragonsense? He's never had any, and he never will."

Shashtah smiled at his foster son. "You will make some Rider a fine Dragon someday."

Peri averted his eyes. "I don't want just any Rider, papa. I want Quatar. Do you think the king will ever agree?"

Shashtah considered the thought carefully, as if he had not spent almost every day since he had taken the two fosterlings into his care asking himself the same question. "Don't worry. It will happen."

Peri beamed, hope replacing uncertainty on his face. "Prophecy?"

"Perhaps." Shashtah stopped and stared at the deserted aisle between the first two columns of tents. "Now, please, concentrate for me. We have twenty Striplings to find and convince that I'm not some ogre out of Cinnamar." He cocked his head slightly as he listened for sounds coming from the tents as Tphah guided him down the aisle.

Some tents stood ominously dark and silent.

Voices hushed with grief signaled that some of the brazier-lit tents contained occupants who did not share Bonds.

Peri pulled aside the flap of the first quiet tent that glowed with lamplight.

A dragonboy of about sixteen sat on the carpet, staring at the empty throne and hugging an embroidered red pillow to his chest. He took one look at the intruders and dashed the tears from his cheeks. "Lord Shashtah?"

"You are?" Shashtah prompted.

"Makel," the youngster supplied, setting aside his pillow, rising and bending in an appropriate salaam. "May I offer you qaffah on behalf of my—" His voice faltered.

Shashtah stepped forward, put his hand on the Stripling's shoulder and gently forced him to straighten. "Thank you for the offer. You do your Trainers honor. I—"

"Dragonheart!" The teenager lunged forward and embraced the startled Dragonlord.

Shashtah frowned. "Do I know you?" He suddenly remembered another terrible night when the King's Camp had been in a similar disarray and he had paused to quiet the fears of a Hatchling in humanform. He wrapped his arms around Makel, not unlike the way he had held the frightened boy so long ago. His power bound the Stripling to him just as it had with the Riders.

Makel's only answer was to grip Shashtah harder.

"You're safe," Shashtah assured him. "This is Peri. He'll take you to a tent beside mine. I'll watch over you personally until I can find someone who is worthy of you."

"Yes, Dragonlord."

Shashtah eased Makel into Peri's arms, then waved his foster son out of the tent with his charge. :*One down*.:

:*Nineteen to go*,: Tphah reminded him.

Shashtah slipped his arm around her waist. :*If they're all that easy, I might actually get some sleep before the feast*.:

:*Don't count on it*.: Tphah escorted him outside.

Shashtah soon discovered, however, that Will had been better than his word. His aide really had done a brilliant job of getting everything under control after Xia's death. Seventeen of the lone Striplings were in their tents and readily let Shashtah hand them over to Peri or Tphah, who in turn guided them to where Quatar and Kyla settled them onto cots and watched over them as they pretended to sleep. Two more were located by Riders on their visits to their slain friends' tents. The final Stripling, whose humanform suggested that she was almost old enough to Bond, turned up on her own in response to the telepathic urgings of her draconic friends.

:*Hands off!*: Tphah commanded as she hauled Shashtah away from the stunning Lahshah before he could touch her.

:*You know you're the only Dragon who interests me*,: Shashtah vowed as they entered Xia's tent.

The jealous fire in Tphah's eyes confirmed that she knew no such thing.

Shashtah glanced around, noting that the carpets and tapestries were worn, but still serviceable. The main rug depicted scenes from the tale of how Shantaclezad had slain Tabo, Thief of Eggs, one of Shashtah's personal favorites. Secret knowledge curled his lips into a smile as he focused on the image of Shantaclezad's Bond Partner, his own father, Garesh. Djinn, efreeti and other mystical creatures cavorted along the edges and across the other rugs and tapestries. Qaffah simmered on the brazier should he require it, and his personal belongings were neatly piled behind the throne-like couch in the middle of the tent. The pillows that covered the throne were a garish yellow, and Shashtah made a mental note to ask Will to scavenge something a little easier on the eyes. At least he wouldn't have to clear out all the coffers, potted palms, statues, hammocks, musical instruments, and assorted bits of gaudy décor that Kashon had had to sort through when he had taken over from Dameth.

A bound manuscript that someone, probably Will, had placed conspicuously on his throne caught Shashtah's attention: *The Dragonlord's Handbook* by Corin of Daethia. He stifled a groan, pushed the pillows onto the floor, and stretched out on them, the book in his hands. "What did Katrell say when we were Training? Something about Kashon having to go through his own Training of sorts when he became a Dragonlord?"

Tphah took the manuscript from him and flipped through the pages. "You can read, can't you?"

"Every trader worth his salt can read. You have to learn, or the Krills will steal you blind. I just don't enjoy the pastime the way Kashon does."

Faster than a summoned demon, Katrell threw aside the flap and glanced at Tphah.

Tphah let out a yelp, dropped the book onto the throne and rushed outside.

Shashtah pushed himself into a sitting position on the rug. He gave Katrell a beleaguered look. "She's a Dragonlord's Dragon now, Katrell. Could you please show her a little respect?"

Katrell dove at his chest.

Shashtah instinctively closed his arms around him.

"Play along!" Katrell begged. He pulled Shashtah into a passionate kiss, just as Makara rushed into the tent.

Shashtah's eyes widened with surprise more at being kissed by his friend's Dragon than at the appearance of the Dragonqueen, but the effect was the same. He broke the embrace with Katrell. "Makara!" he shouted indignantly.

Makara gawked at them, open-mouthed. "You—! But—! I—!" A wicked smile spread across her face, and she slipped outside.

"Makara, no!" Katrell howled convincingly at her departing back. As soon as the flap settled back into place, he rolled away from Shashtah and lay panting on the carpet. "I'm sorry. There wasn't time to warn you. My Rider told me that you'd promised to take care of me if he couldn't. Did I hurt you?"

"No," Shashtah said, suddenly thinking to check. "Where's Kashon?"

Katrell coiled into a sitting position. "Trying to figure out how he and Salene are going to mate without both of them dying from embarrassment."

"Tonight?" Shashtah surged halfway to his feet.

Katrell waved him back down. "I took him to her myself as soon as I forced the restorative potion down his throat. Patch and Peg can handle things long enough for them to do the Mother's Dance. Tphah went to rescue Bahktarah before Makara puts two and two together and goes to find him."

Shashtah rubbed his forehead, desperately trying to put two and two together himself.

Katrell's mouth twisted into something resembling a smile. "We just lost almost a third of all the Dragonriders in Dumnonia," he said slowly, as if to a child. "In a few candlescars at the feast to honor you and Salene, the king is going to order all breeding Dumnonians to mate so that the gap in the population can be replaced in about a quarter century."

"And Salene's a Breeding Female," Shashtah said, beginning to understand.

Katrell nodded. "She doesn't want a bunch of Breeding Males charging at her anymore than my Rider wants a bunch of Breeding Females charging at him. If they've already Danced before Shaharadesh gives that order, then neither of them will have to worry about it. This way is much better for everyone concerned." Katrell pulled at a piece of loose thread in one of the smaller rugs.

Shashtah absently recognized that Katrell was unraveling a picture of Tchang. *That's more words than Katrell's ever said directly to me in all the time I've known him. He sounds rational, almost calculating. How can that be? Just candlescars ago he was blurring worse than a Hatchling in the Valley of Ancients.* Kashon's words forced their way to the surface of his memories: *Reverse it. An adult Bronze out of control in the King's Camp* . . . "Katrell, do you remember what happens to you when one of your Riders Dances? Is it safe for us to stay here, or should we be out on the dunes in case I have to change into something bigger to sit on you?"

Katrell gave a small laugh. "I'll stay in my humanform. I wanted to have more time to reassure you, but I wasn't planning on running into Makara."

Shashtah tried not to let his concern show on his face. *What makes him so certain he'll hold his shape? Kashon has no faith in his ability to do that, and I've seen why.* He recalled Tkai's comment yet again that Kashon seriously underestimated his Dragon. He reached out and touched Katrell's arm. "You're definitely not the nit your Rider thinks you are."

Katrell looked up, genuinely horrified. "Don't tell him! Please! I Bonded with him so soon after I lost my last Rider I was pretty much an imbecile for the first rotation or so. By then I was his 'nit,' and I realized I rather enjoyed the way he treated me when he thought of me like that. I—" He doubled over, grabbing his head. "Sands!" Anguish clouded his amber eyes. "What have I done?"

Shashtah panicked. *He's going to lose control! What would Kashon do?* The answer followed in the next heartbeat: *Talk himself hoarse.* He pushed himself to his knees and gathered Katrell into his arms. "Come here." He sat back, cradling him. "You have done what very few Dragons could ever do. You enabled your Rider to command three centuries! That's amazing! Makara couldn't handle even one century on a good day. She's great at laying eggs, but she's pretty useless when it comes to anything else."

"That's why the Dragons chose Shaharadesh for king. We need more eggs."

Shashtah smiled sympathetically as he saw the shadows of Kashon's forced mating flash in Katrell's eyes. "You're a wonderful Dragon, and I'd be envious of Kashon if I didn't already have Tphah. Always what the Dragons need or what the Tribe needs; never what Katrell needs. Your Rider is not 'The Giving One,'" he said, translating Kashon's name into the Daethian language. "You are."

"I'm not 'The Giving One'. He is. I'm 'The Extreme One!' " Katrell howled. "I can't lose him again. I waited so long! So long . . . "

"Again?" *What's he talking about? What happened to that Dragon who was making sense just a few heartbeats ago?* Shashtah's brow furrowed as his unreliable sense of time tried to straighten itself out. "How old are you?"

Katrell shuddered. "Too old . . . "

"Old enough to be on the Council?" Shashtah asked. "Tkai once said something to me that made me think you were older than she was, but you're too small."

"Too old," Katrell repeated. "Too muddled. Too many Bond Breaks. Too many dead Riders. He was always Bonded to someone else before I could—" He screamed. "I'll lose him! I can see it! I waited so long! I can't wait that long again!"

Shashtah arched his eyebrows. "Are you a Dragonprophet, Katrell? Is that why they keep breeding you? Is that why the Council insisted that you be the one to Train Tphah?"

Katrell suddenly collapsed in hysterical tears. "Don't tell Kesh! Don't tell him! I'm his nit! That's all I am! His nit! Don't tell him!"

Shashtah tightened his grip on Katrell as Kashon's words floated through his mind. *"Sometimes he calls me by the wrong name when he's muddled."* "Hush! I'm not telling anyone anything you don't want me to." He rocked him as he would a Hatchling. *"Katrell." "The Extreme One." It's a description, not a name. Who is he? What is he? A Dragonprophet? One older than the Council of Ancients?* "We can't tell how far into the future we're seeing with our Prophecy," Shashtah repeated the phrase he had heard Tkai and Tphah use so many times.

Katrell whimpered. "But I used to know before Bond Break after Bond Break after Bond Break, searching for him! He's my Reward! My Divine Gift! I didn't do anything wrong! I can't lose him again!"

"Easy," Shashtah marveled that the distressed Dragon, the one who was famous for falling apart, showed absolutely no sign of blurring. *Did Kashon put a spell on him to keep him from shifting like the one he used on me during the Training?*

"Sands! How can he still love me after all this time?" Katrell despaired. "I'll never agree to Dance with anyone else ever again, no matter how much we need more Dragonprophets! I'd forgotten how horrible it is for the Bond Partner!"

Shashtah braced him. "Hush. I'm here. I'll take care of you. I promised." He suspected, though, that Kashon was wrong: No one needed to take care of Katrell. Katrell had spent millennia taking care of the Dragons and their Dumnonians. *But if he's as old as I think he is, why is he so small?* His own heart suddenly lurched, distracting him. He sensed Tphah allowing Bahktarah to pin her dragonform to the sand.

Katrell felt him stiffen. He looked up and recognized the expression in Shashtah's eyes. "I'm sorry! Tphah was willing, but I should've given you the choice. Just once I wanted to make it through a feast without being forced to Dance with Makara. Kesh deserves that much tonight!"

There's that wrong name again. Who is "Kesh"? I've never heard stories about him. It's another description. "The Gift." Shashtah held Katrell tightly, trying to quash his own urge to shapeshift. "You need to calm down. Kashon needs your support. Even a nit like you can see that. Your secret will be safe. No one else will find out you're a Dragonprophet. No one will force you to lead the Council. Tphah and I will lie through our fangs to protect you."

"Kesh needs me . . . " Katrell whispered. He twisted until he was staring into Shashtah's eyes. "Tphah needs you, too." He cupped his hand firmly along Shashtah's jaw.

This time Katrell's kiss caused power to surge through Shashtah and into Tphah. Shashtah had never felt anything like it, even when doing the Mother's Dance with his Prophetess. The magic was ancient and strong, almost primal.

Katrell subtly shifted their position until Shashtah was lying on the rug beneath him.

The power continued to flow through Shashtah, almost as if Katrell was breathing life into him.

Or magic. Shashtah felt the power coil around the forces within him, setting up a Bond between him and Katrell that was completely unlike anything he shared with Tphah and Kashon. Soul met soul. The magic flared, then twined into the shape of a Dragon within his heart.

Katrell's face suddenly turned the color of molten bronze. He broke the kiss and settled into the landing position for Speedflying. "I'm sorry," he whispered. "I shouldn't have used you like that."

Shashtah gaped. *If that was just kiss, . . . ?* "Are you a Priest of the Mother? Are you why Tphah became a Priestess?"

Katrell ignored the question. He touched Shashtah's bruised cheek. "A Dragonheart can live a very long time. If both of our Bond Partners die first, I would be honored to Bond with you, to help you carry 'Eternal Death to the Dark One!'" His voice rose to a hysterical pitch as he half-shrieked the Dumnonian battle cry.

Shashtah blushed as Tphah finished mating with Bahktarah. "It would be my honor to be your Bond Partner, Katrell, but I love my Prophetess and you love Kashon, and I don't see either of us ever Bonding with anyone else." His words rang true in his heart, stunning him. *Prophecy . . .* "I'll never let anyone nor anything take your Rider away from you."

Katrell gasped, scrambled to one side and prostrated himself before Shashtah. "I'm not worthy of such a boon!"

Shashtah felt his skin prickle. He got to his feet and forced Katrell to rise. "If you're not worthy, I don't know who is."

Kashon quietly slipped inside the tent flap and stood with his head bowed.

Shashtah turned Katrell so he could see his Rider.

Katrell gave a small cry. He rushed forward, took Kashon's jaw in his hands and gave him a kiss that sent yet another blush over Shashtah's face and brought a smile to Kashon's lips.

Kashon broke the kiss and gathered Katrell into his arms. He glanced sheepishly at Shashtah. "Sorry about that."

"No apology necessary," Shashtah assured him as he sank onto his throne and studied his friend. *What on Centuria is he Bonded to? A Dragonprophet who's also a Priest of the Mother? One who's old enough to lead the Council of Ancients even though he's far too small? One who's more than half mad from too many Bond Breaks? No wonder the Council is terrified!*

"I'm never going to lose you!" Katrell declared happily as he returned Kashon's embrace.

The tent flap pulled aside again. "Prophecies of Tphah," the Prophetess shuddered as she stepped inside. "I babbled too much as a child." She dropped in a half-salaam to Katrell. "I thank you for your Wisdom."

"If Katrell's thinking the best out of the lot of us, we're all in serious need of some sleep." Shashtah waved his hand toward the tent flap. "Get out of here, you two nits! I don't want to see either of you again until the feast!"

Kashon grinned his thanks and led Katrell out of the tent.

Shashtah held out his hands to Tphah.

The Prophetess swept silently across the carpet and placed her hands in his.

Shashtah pulled her gently down beside him. "I'm sorry," he whispered, leaning his head against hers. "I didn't see that coming."

"No reason you should have. You're a Prophet of the Light, not of the Mother." Tphah kissed him soundly, setting his blood pounding all over again. She broke the kiss and sighed. "I shouldn't have done that. I'm too exhausted to follow through on that promise."

Shashtah picked up his *Handbook* to move it out of their way. He stared at the manuscript. "All new Dragonlords really have the time and are alert enough to read this thing?"

Tphah laughed and took the book from him. "I doubt it." She set the manuscript on the rug and curled up atop the pillows on the throne. "I promise not to be so much trouble about my eggs this time."

Shashtah stretched out beside her. "What would I do if you ever stopped being trouble?" He brushed her cheek with his hand. "I get the feeling Katrell has been playing us all like a Master Bard plays a qanun. I know he's not a nit. I'm not even sure he's a Bronze. Is that why none of you have ever left me alone with him before?"

The Prophetess nestled into his embrace. "You've fought a battle, fought Kashon, channeled the Mother only knows how many different types of magic, become a Dragonlord, . . . That's more than enough for one night. Let's sleep."

Realizing he was not going to get an answer out of her, Shashtah rolled onto his back. "You're going to be the death of me, Dragon."

"No," Tphah said. "I'm going to be your life."

Shashtah awoke to Tphah's gentle nudge, feeling mostly alive again.

"I've healed you," the Prophetess informed him.

"Thanks," Shashtah said as he rubbed the sleep sand from his eyes. "Am I still a Dragonlord?"

Tphah laughed. "I'm afraid so. Get dressed. We've been summoned to the feast."

Shashtah heaved himself off the throne and donned the new white aba and keffiyeh Will had provided for him. As he reached for the golden agal to secure the keffiyeh to his head, he realized that the leather tie Tphah had given him was there instead. "Where'd you find it?"

"I didn't. Kashon did when his century was cleaning up the battlefield. I have no idea how."

Shashtah picked up the bit of leather and tied his keffiyeh into place. "I have a feeling that he knows a great deal more magic than he lets on."

The Prophetess smiled cryptically and shifted into her aba and the veil of a Priestess of the Mother. "They've divided the treasure among the survivors with Bond Breaks." She melted against him and pressed her lips to his.

"Wicked Dragon!" Shashtah laughed when he could breathe again. "You're going to make me late for my installation!"

Tphah dropped into an apologetic salaam, mischief twinkling in her eyes.

Shashtah sighed with genuine regret.

The Prophetess unsealed the tent flap—then whirled nimbly out of the way as over three dozen Fledglings in humanform poured inside and swarmed over Shashtah, carrying him to the ground.

"See?" a little dragongirl declared imperiously as she pounced on his chest and peered intently at his eyes. "I told you he was a Dragonheart!"

Two small boys tried to pull her off Shashtah. "Come on, Katrina," one urged. "We know what he is. Let someone who doesn't know see."

"But Tkell—!"

The second boy cut off her protest by picking her up and draping her over his shoulder like a sack. He threw an exasperated look at Tkell.

"Kchang! Put me down!" Katrina ordered, but her eyes strayed warily to a third boy who clung to Tphah like a Trainee on the Anvil as the Prophetess balanced him on her hip.

Shashtah's Prophecy stirred. He let Tkell help him to a sitting position only to be knocked flat again as the rest of the children pressed forward.

Will burst into the tent. "Sands, Lord Shashtah! I'm sorry!" He began hauling children off the Dragonlord, enlisting the aid of the teenagers among them with a single threatening glance. "Not a one of them has the brains the Mother gave a sunstruck she-lizard! They got away from the aides at the basecamp and transported to the Valley of Ancients before transporting here. Garesh warned Annakah that they were on their way, but he had his talons too full with the Bond Broken Dragons to stop them."

Shashtah finally managed to stand, children clinging to every handspan of his hem and sleeves. He scowled at them. "How could these be our Fledglings? They must be in their tent at our basecamp where they belong. They never dreamt of disobeying Lord Xia. Certainly they've accorded me the same respect."

Will shrugged helplessly. "Well, Lord, I'm afraid these are our Fledglings."

The children, sensing Shashtah's displeasure, released him and backed away.

"Sit down at once!" Shashtah hid a grin as even his Prophetess and aide obeyed. "Will, count noses! If there's even one Fledgling missing," he continued as his aide stood up and began to count, "I want you to tell the king I'm sorry, but I won't be able to attend my installation because I'll be facing the Council of Ancient for punishment."

"What?" Will gasped and stopped counting as Tphah and the dragonchildren squawked in distress.

"The Council punishes Dragonlords for allowing harm to come to Dragons and Riders under their command," Shashtah thundered. "What do you think they'll do if I endanger even one Fledgling who's assigned to me?"

Kchang sulked. "Katrina said you'd be happy to see us."

Shashtah crouched until he was the same height as Kchang. "I wanted to be."

"Prophets!" a teenager sniffed as Kchang's lower lip began to tremble. "There's a reason Hatchlings don't share tents with Fledglings."

Shashtah stood up and motioned for Will to continue counting.

"Yes," a dragongirl of about fifteen agreed. "We should have known better than to listen to one who isn't old enough to know which future she's reading!"

Katrina stuffed most of her fist into her mouth to keep from crying out.

"This is all your fault, Katrina!" Kchang snarled, his disappointment turning into rage.

Tkell glowered at his sister. "We finally get to see Papa, and you make him mad at us!"

The boy in Tphah's lap sighed and reluctantly left the comfort of her embrace.

Shashtah searched through his memories for the name of Tphah's fourth child.

:*Garal*,: Tphah supplied.

Garal dropped into a salaam before Shashtah. "I'm sorry, Dragonlord. They're sorry, too; they just don't know it yet." He turned on the Fledglings. "Stop blaming Katrina for something that's your own fault."

Kchang and Tkell grew still, and even the older Fledglings shifted uncomfortably. Katrina brightened slightly at the promise of support from this unexpected quarter, but she still regarded Garal with caution.

Shashtah shot a glance at Tphah, wondering if she had any idea what it was about his half-brother that seemed so odd and that obviously had the other dragonchildren completely intimidated.

The Prophetess looked as puzzled as Shashtah felt.

Garal put his tiny fists on his hips and continued, "Every one of us was sunstruck enough to transport not once but twice without a Rider supervising us. That makes it our error—even if Katrina did give us the idea. This is not the Dragonlord's fault. He is not officially responsible for us until he's installed. We can't let him take the blame for our mistake. That means each of us needs to be responsible for his or her own error!"

Katrina hugged herself, patently unhappy with the way her brother's judgment condemned her at the same time it absolved her.

"All the Fledglings are here," Will informed Shashtah.

Shashtah barely heard his aide, he was so busy gawking at Garal.

"What sentence do you impose on us for undertaking a sunstruck action that could have resulted in our deaths?" Garal asked.

Shashtah blinked at his half-brother, and then turned to Will. "Does he always talk like this?"

Will gave Shashtah an apprehensive look. "He does more than talk."

The Fledglings prostrated themselves.

Garal looked nervously at them before shifting his attention to Shashtah. "*The Dragonlord's Handbook* says that we should be brought before the Council of Ancients for judgment."

Shashtah glanced from Garal to the Fledglings to Will. "Is he right?"

"Lord Xia never found a time he wasn't," Will responded, a strange tone in his voice. "It's as if he hatched with the entire content of Dumnonian Law in his head—and the magic to enforce it."

Shashtah shifted his attention back to Garal.

The dragonboy fidgeted but held his ground, awaiting the Dragonlord's command.

Shashtah felt his head starting to hurt again. "There's no way I'm taking anyone out to that Valley so soon after—".

"So be it," Garal proclaimed. "The punishment will happen here." He extended his hands and a wave of magical light swept over the Fledglings, avoiding Will, Shashtah and Tphah. "We feel true grief," he intoned quietly.

Shashtah froze as he recognized the modified opening to the ritual words of a judgment by the Council of Ancients. :*What's he doing?*: he asked Tphah silently.

Tphah shrugged her ignorance.

"We make no excuse," Garal continued. "We seek no mercy. We admit our error. We understand what is needed. We entrust ourselves to the wisdom of our Law. It is decided. Our punishment for endangering our lives now begins." Light flashed from Garal's hands. He gave a small yelp and pitched forward onto the rug, convulsing as the magic ripped through him.

Shashtah gasped as every Fledgling contorted with quite real pain.

Within a few heartbeats all of them were blurring between their dragon- and humanforms. Most of them were stifling shrieks, and all of them were crying.

Shaharadesh is going to kill me! "Stop! Stop it now!"

The light vanished.

Shashtah finally recovered from his shock enough to haul his whimpering half-brother into his arms. Will's words reverberated through Shashtah's memory. *"Then there's Garal. We're not sure what he is."* Having felt the effects of that spell himself, Shashtah had a horrible suspicion that he knew exactly what his half-brother was. "Garal, I of all people understand what it's like to have magic you can't control, but we have to do something about this!"

Garal sniffled and curled miserably against Shashtah's chest. "Lord Xia said I had to use the power that's been given to me."

"I'm not Lord Xia." Shashtah spat the name. "I do not expect a child to take on the responsibilities of an adult, let alone those of a member of the Council of Ancients!"

Garal looked confused as the other dragonchildren began to settle into their humanforms. "Are you mad at me?"

"Sands, no!" Shashtah assured him. "I'm saying you're barely old enough to take responsibility for your own actions without making everyone else take responsibility for theirs."

Garal brushed a tear from his cheek and licked the moisture from his hand. "Does that mean I can go back to Mother now?"

Shashtah caught the look in Tphah's eye, which threatened all sorts of unsavory things if he did not hand her son over to her at once. He promptly released Garal, who ran to the Prophetess. Shashtah helped a girl of about seven to her feet.

She threw her arms around his legs. "Dragonheart! I'm sorry! I'll try not to be bad ever again!"

"I know," Shashtah said. "That's all I ask of you."

"Can we go to your installation?" a boy of fifteen asked.

"Of course you can!" Shashtah decreed, having absolutely no idea what the protocol was in this situation—or if there even was a protocol. "Will, please escort our Fledglings to the campfires where our century is gathered."

Will acknowledged the order with a salute and moved to the tent flap, holding it open for the children.

Shashtah took the time to hug each Fledgling before he passed them into Will's care. As Shashtah released Tkell, the dragonboy walked over to where Tphah sat holding Garal. "You're right, Garal." Tkell made a face. "As always."

"Yeah," Kchang confirmed as he broke away from Shashtah and strode over to his brothers. "Come on, Garal! Let's go to the feast. We get to sit with you because you're our nestmate."

Garal squirmed out of Tphah's lap and let his brothers put their arms around him. He watched Katrina contritely as Shashtah gathered the dragongirl into his arms. "Katrina . . . "

"She's sorry, too," Tkell said.

"Yeah," Kchang confirmed, flashing a quelling glance at his sister.

Katrina wiped her nose on her sleeve. "G-garal," she stammered.

Shashtah rocked her gently. "Hey, now," he crooned. "Are you planning to misbehave again?"

"Never!" Katrina promised, honestly meaning to try.

Shashtah smiled, wiping the last of the tears from her face and licking the moisture from his hand. "Good." He lowered Katrina to the ground. "Now, off with you. I'm certain I'm supposed to be doing something, and I'm equally certain it isn't this."

Katrina raced across the tent. If Kchang and Tkell hadn't been supporting Garal, brother and sister would have sprawled on the rug as Katrina tackled him. "You're amazing! How do you work those spells?"

Tkell and Kchang herded a far happier Garal and a gushing Katrina outside before the dragonboy could respond.

"The Light forbid he's ever able to explain it to her!" Will shuddered as he took his leave of Shashtah with a flourish and scampered after the Fledglings.

Tphah rose quietly, staring at the flap.

Shashtah felt a shiver run along his spine. "Council Magic? At his age? At least my powers waited to start using me until I was an adult!"

"Dragonprophets show our powers as soon as we hatch. I've never heard of anything like this, though."

Something finally settled into place that had been lurking at the back of Shashtah's mind. He cocked his head. "Listen."

Tphah tilted her head as well. "What am I listening for?"

"That's just it," Shashtah said. "I don't hear anything unusual. If Garal was using Council Magic, why isn't every Dragon between here and Mount Cinnamar screeching? Council Magic upsets the Dragons. That's why Kashon was lashed when we had those deaths in our century instead of being subjected to the Council's punishment spell. Come to think of it, I have the feeling that this has happened before. Why don't you and I know about it?"

"Maybe Shaharadesh knows." Tphah panicked as soon as the words passed her lips. "You can't ask him! He'll take my children away!"

"Don't worry," Shashtah said as he wrapped his left arm around her and he straightened her veil with his right hand. "I won't ask."

Tphah leaned her head against his shoulder. "When you're king, you'll not leave those with uncontrolled magic without support. You'll be a great king."

"Let's see what kind of a Dragonlord I make first," Shashtah chuckled as he escorted her toward the circle of campfires on the dunes at the edge of Camp.

Shashtah Dragonheart, former trader and twice-Bonded Dragonrider, joined Dragonrider Salene before Shaharadesh to be installed as a Dragonlord of Dumnonia. Behind him he sensed Tphah, his beloved Prophetess, glowing with pride. Councilor Bahktarah stood behind Salene, an equally pleased grin on his face. The other Dragonlords—Kassandra, Harabi, Amasiah, Corban, Genna and Tirhaka—and their Dragons were stationed in a double semicircle behind them. Katrell had positioned himself beside, rather than behind, Kashon. From where he glared defiantly at everyone, daring anyone to suggest that he abandon his Rider and resume his proper place with the other Dragons.

Will had enlisted the Striplings and surviving Dragons and Riders of Shashtah's century to hold the Fledglings, ensuring that the youngsters would stay out of trouble. Will himself held Katrina while Garal cuddled in the lap of the eldest Stripling, Lahshah. Makel sat to Lahshah's right restraining Kchang while Jeri, who had settled onto the sand at Lahshah's left, had a firm grip on Tkell.

Makara stood beside Shaharadesh, holding two rings of office on an elaborately-embroidered pillow.

Shashtah felt absurdly glad that the Council of Ancients was still caring for the Bond Broken Dragons. If the Councilors, his father leading them, had taken their traditional positions behind Shaharadesh, Shashtah doubted that he could have concentrated on anything his king was saying.

Shaharadesh motioned for the two new Dragonlords to kneel.

Shashtah flashed a nervous smile at Salene as they both fell to their knees before their king.

Shaharadesh took a ring from the pillow and approached Salene first. "Salene, Dragonrider of Dumnonia," he intoned as he placed a ring shaped like a Bronze Dragon onto the third finger of her left hand, "I give you Lord Zofar's century, with all the privileges and responsibilities of his command."

Salene grabbed Shaharadesh's right hand and kissed his ring of office.

The king smiled at the gesture, then took a second ring from the pillow and turned to Shashtah. "Shashtah Dragonheart, Dragonrider of Dumnonia," he chanted as he slid a similar ring onto the third finger of Shashtah's left hand, "I give you Lord Xia's century, with all the privileges and responsibilities of her command." He leaned closer so Shashtah could hear him over the crowd's thunderous roar. "Garesh, citing the Wisdom of Tchang, says the Council has ruled that having to argue constantly with Tphah about disciplining her four hellions is a more fitting punishment for letting them endanger themselves than my reassigning them to a different century would be. I trust the Council is correct?"

Shashtah nodded, lowering his eyes. :*Your Fledglings are ours to raise as long as I'm a Dragonlord. Either my father holds a lot more sway with the Council than I think he does, or Tchang himself has risen from the dead to plead my case.*:

:*Perhaps he has,*: Tphah replied, deliberately making it unclear whether she was talking about Garesh or Tchang. She helped Shashtah to his feet and steered him after Shaharadesh and Makara to the Festival Tent.

As the Dragons ate their fill from the adequate, if not abundant, feast Shaharadesh had spread before them, Shashtah searched for the faces of the other Dragonlords in the clouds of abas and keffiyehs that billowed around the Dumnonians. He spotted Katrell hovering over Kashon in a corner at the back of the tent, refusing to leave his Rider for a heartbeat, even to eat. The other faces failed to resolve into any recognizable features. His stomach rumbled.

Tphah slipped him a date under the cover of a kiss. :*You're starving. Chew.*:

I need to conjure myself some manna before I attend feasts, Shashtah thought, wondering why the idea had never occurred to him before.

:*You're starting to think,*: Tphah teased. :*Kashon must be rubbing off on you.*:

:*And you're eavesdropping,*: Shashtah accused. He shifted his attention back to his friend. Katrell's insistence that Kashon was going to die still bothered him. *Why don't I sense such a tragedy? Because it's too personal? Or too far in the future? Or is Katrell simply muddled and remembering something that's already happened to someone else? Something that happened to "Kesh"?*

Around midnight Shaharadesh called the Dragonlords together in his private tent and gave the order to breed that Katrell had predicted. The king smiled with surprise at Kashon as Salene, resplendent in her stylized Galantite keffiyeh, vouched that she had already Danced with her fellow Dragonlord to set an example for the other Dumnonians.

Kashon stretched like a great cat on a set of pillows beside where Shashtah had settled.

"That Dragon of yours," Shashtah said in a low voice as he watched the other Dragonlords protest the order, "is worth his weight in Galantite ore."

"I think so," Kashon rumbled happily, pleasure with his Bond Partner almost driving the concern from his eyes.

"At least Tphah has also complied," Shashtah said. "I can't imagine what our century is going to think when I have to give that order and they figure out I'm a mule."

Salene overheard and knelt beside him. She put a comforting hand on his arm. "They are going to be as disappointed as I am." She smiled and kissed him chastely on the cheek. She glanced at Kashon. "I hope we didn't upset Katrell too much."

"No," Kashon said. "In fact, he has been so attentive to me ever since that I'm thinking about offering myself to you as a permanent stud."

:*What's wrong?*: Tphah's confused voice suddenly sounded inside Shashtah's head. :*Katrell just got a funny look on his face and took off toward the King's Tent like a bat out of Cinnamar!*:

Shashtah guffawed as Kashon scrambled to his feet. :*Don't worry. Kashon's just teasing him.*: He watched Kashon make a hasty excuse to Shaharadesh and duck outside.

Salene laughed. "He really is marvelous." She lowered her voice so Makara couldn't overhear. "I wonder if the Dragons will choose him for the next king."

Shashtah shrugged. "Shaharadesh isn't dead yet, and the way Kashon always seems to be in the thick of things, our present king has a good chance of outliving him."

"I don't know about that," Salene said, winking conspiratorially at him. "That was a pretty big light show you put on out at the Valley of Ancients in his defense. With that kind of support, he might survive."

"If it pleases the Light," Shashtah said softly. "If it pleases the Light."

Peri and Quatar were waiting outside the tent flap when the king and his Dragonlords emerged.

Shashtah kept his face expressionless as his foster sons bent in salaams before Shaharadesh.

"We want to Bond," Quatar announced.

Peri put a quieting hand on Quatar's arm. "As son of Tkai, former Leader of the Council of Ancients, I request that the king of Dumnonia allow me to Bond with Quatar, foster son of Shashtah Dragonheart, Dragonlord of Dumnonia."

Shaharadesh gaped at them, appalled. "Now?"

Kashon, Katrell at his side, joined them. "Why not? Quatar is only a Daethian. We shouldn't expect him to go on a Dragonquest when all he wants to do is Bond with a mutant who should have been killed long ago."

Shashtah started to object but held his tongue when it struck him that neither boy had reacted to Kashon's negative tone.

"Besides," Salene said, "Shashtah won't have time to run after them now that he's a Dragonlord."

Shashtah sensed a conspiracy swirling around him. :*Have they planned this?*:

Tphah gave him a warning glance and remained silent.

Amasiah, immaculate in his white robes, pushed forward. "You can't expect Shashtah to learn to be a Dragonlord, rebuild an almost obliterated century and put a Dragonslayer and a mutant through the Training all at the same time. Exile them."

"Who says Shashtah can't do it?" Corban challenged, brushing a fold of his keffiyeh away from his face and looking generally uncomfortable in his ceremonial garb. He deftly moved his foot out of the way before Kassandra could stomp on it.

"Mutants shouldn't be allowed to live, let alone Bond." Genna's white silk veil fluttered slightly as she tossed her head in annoyance. Alone among the female Dragonlords she eschewed masculine dress. Somehow that small bit of defiance made her seem irresistibly attractive even if her personality did not.

"Corin decides who Bonds," Kassandra snapped. She looked even more out of place than Corban in a hastily donned white djellaba that did nothing to hide the fact that she was still dressed for battle beneath her vague attempt at ceremonial robes. "We can decide what to do with them after they come out of the Tomb, but they must go through the Training. We don't need any more unTrained Pairs wandering around Centuria." She glared at Shashtah, causing

him to back a step away from her. "Shashtah's century has too few Bonded Pairs
to take frontline duty next rotation. He might as well stay here and Train them.
My century will take his place on the frontline for this rotation. Corban and
Amasiah can join me so Kashon and Salene can stay here, too. They need to
Train as many newly Bonded Dumnonians and Bronzes as we can find. Genna,
Tirhaka and Harabi are assigned to guard the King's Camp next rotation. And
we'll all be back here for the Feast of the Mother to figure out what we are going
to do after that."

Shashtah blinked at her, wondering why in the name of the Light the Dragons
had not chosen her as Queen.

:*We need her to fight*,: Tphah supplied.

Harabi, visibly impressed with the practicality of Kassandra's observation,
abruptly stuck his hands in the sleeves of his aba. "Besides, who knows what is
'old enough' for a mutant and a Dragonslayer?"

"Dragonslayers have much shorter lifespans than we do," Tirhaka agreed, her
eyes twinkling with a deadly light beneath her well-worn keffiyeh. "Maybe they
can become Riders faster."

Amasiah bared his throat. "As long as they are only mounted on mutants."

"You sound like the Council of Ancients," Shaharadesh grumbled. "Why am
I even here?"

"To fight with the Council," Shashtah reminded him.

Shaharadesh took a deep breath, let it out slowly and nodded. "So be it." He
faced Quatar and Peri. "I will allow you to attempt to Bond at dawn on the
condition that once you complete the Training you withdraw to Daethia where
you belong. Getting the Council to approve the Bonding will be hard enough.
There is no way I'll get them to permit a Dragonslayer mounted on mutant to
fly in our centuries."

Shashtah took a heartbeat to absorb his king's words. He wondered if
Quatar and Peri realized that they had just been banished from Dumnonia for
the rest of Shaharadesh's life. "It will be all right," Shashtah assured them,
although his rousing Prophecy insisted it would not. "This is what you've always
wanted." *Or what Kashon wanted . . .*

Quatar's eyes widened as he suddenly understood what everyone else already knew.

Peri quickly stepped on Quatar's foot with better aim than Kassandra had
had with Corban. An unspoken Prophecy glittering in his putrid green eyes, he
bent in an elaborate salaam to Shaharadesh, forcing Quatar to do likewise. Then,
without a word, the mutant Dragonprophet fled with his Chosen Rider in the
direction of Shashtah's tent.

Shashtah was about to escort Tphah after them when he spotted Makara maneuvering toward Kashon and Katrell.

Katrell tightened his hold on his Rider.

Tphah spun elegantly into the Dragonqueen's path. "Katrell's already done the Mother's Dance with me," she declared, careful not to say when. "He should not be forced to breed again so soon."

"You Danced with Bahktarah," Makara snarled.

Tphah refused to bare her throat. "I'm a Priestess of the Mother. I can worship her as many times as I please. I've lain eggs by three different sires in the same clutch. When have you ever done as much?"

Shashtah was preparing to pull Tphah away from the Dragonqueen when Kassandra latched onto Makara's arm.

"I was so hoping you'd consent to Dance with Farral," the lethal Dragonlord said sweetly, "since Corban's Dragon is already carrying fertilized eggs. They're preferred mates, you know, but I can't imagine that she'd have any objection to Farral doing the Mother's Dance with you. As long as he has to breed with someone, I'd like it to be with the best."

As if on cue, Farral, in humanform, charged out of the festival tent, sprinted over to them and fell on his knees at Makara's feet. He took her hand and kissed it. "Would you do me the tremendous honor of accompanying me to Karaif's?"

Shashtah noticed Kassandra subtly shift her grip from Makara to Shaharadesh as a look of consent spread over the Dragonqueen's face.

Farral rose, wrapped an arm possessively around Makara and led her away from the Dragonlords.

Shaharadesh moved to protest, but Kassandra restrained him.

Shashtah doubted that he had ever seen anyone look as completely terrified as Shaharadesh did at the touch of the formidable Dragonlord. He almost felt sorry for his king. Almost.

"Come," Kassandra crooned. "We need to return to the feast." She steered Shaharadesh toward the Festival tent as Katrell swiftly dragged Kashon in the opposite direction.

Tphah placed her hand on Shashtah's arm, preventing him from following the other Dragonlords. "Will suggested that it might be wise for us to take our dragonforms and curl up on the dunes outside Camp with our Fledglings."

Shashtah smiled. "I suppose Will already has them waiting out there for us?"

"So my children tell me."

Shashtah laughed. "He truly is remarkable."

"Worth his weight in Galantite ore."

Shashtah and Kashon

Chapter 14:

Full Circle

Perhaps the hardest time in a Rider's life after the Training is the day an assigned Stripling becomes an adult and must either Bond with a Rider or go off to live on its own. The wise Dragonlord will have another Fledgling ready to supply for such Riders, for the new responsibility, while never taking the place of the old one, tends to ease the pain of parting just as caring for a Rider tends to compensate the female Dragon for the loss of her eggs.

—from *The Dragonlords' Handbook*
by Corin of Daethia

SHASHTAH, SURROUNDED BY THE OTHER DRAGONLORDS and clutching Tphah's hand, watched Shaharadesh, who alone still wore his ceremonial robes, greet Peri and Quatar at the doors of Corin's Tomb. "Come out over the Valley," Shashtah had instructed Peri as he walked the length of the sacred canyon with them. Tphah and Kyla had exchanged hidden grins at Shashtah's attempts to arm his fosterlings against the real and imagined dangers of the Tomb. Kashon and Katrell were a little less successful at concealing their amusement.

Kashon rubbed Shashtah's neck beneath his keffiyeh with a sure hand. "Relax They'll be fine."

"I've done this twice!" Shashtah snapped. "Corin scared me halfway into the Afterlife both times!"

"It's not that way for everyone," Kassandra, looking far more at ease in her trousers and shirt, reassured him. "Bonding with Farral was as easy as taking a stroll across the dunes."

"We thought we were walking through the desert for the better part of a rotation. Without water. Unable to find the King's Camp. Or Daethia. Or the Northern Wastes. Or Cinnamar. Or anything else," Farral elaborated in a low voice.

Katrell scowled at his fellow Dragon. "I'm sure that makes him feel so much better."

The Tomb doors opened, and Peri and Quatar stepped through the portal. The doors closed, sealing the boys inside.

Tphah stifled a whimper as Shashtah practically crushed her hand. She half-shifted to her dragonform. :*Let. Go. Now.*:

Shashtah abruptly released her. :*Sorry.*:

The Prophetess resumed her humanform. "They're adults. They'll be fine."

"They only look like adults!" Shashtah protested. "They're just children!"

"Not in those bodies," Kassandra observed, causing Farral to glance imploringly at Corban. "You just like him because you're his Dragon's preferred mate."

Corban chuckled, unoffended. He draped an arm comfortably across Kassandra's shoulders. "Talons in. We've all had enough fighting for one rotation."

"I'll never have enough fighting!" Kassandra declared, bloodlust shining in her dark amber eyes.

Shashtah noted the reflection of that look in Kyla's eyes.

Kyla, glitteringly beautiful in her chain mail, smiled as she noticed his scrutiny.

Shashtah was so busy returning Kyla's grin that he failed to see the grief-stricken Rider descending on them through the crowd.

Tphah spotted the intruder first and pulled Shashtah back next to Kashon.

The Rider and a massive Dumnonian warrior, who could only be a Dragon in humanform, scattered the Dragonlords into a circle.

"Sands!" Tphah whispered.

Shashtah ignored her, trying to remember who the Rider and Dragon were.

"I, Rahab, Dragonrider of Dumnonia," the man bellowed, "demand the rite of Challenge!"

Amasiah, who apparently was the Rider's Dragonlord, shook his head in flat denial at the accusing looks he received from Genna and Tirhaka. "I didn't put him up to this! I'm not a fool!"

"And I am?" Rahab barked.

Amasiah looked miserable. "I didn't mean that!"

"Of course you did," Kassandra said too sweetly, smiling as she rested her hand lightly on the hilt of her scimitar.

"Do something!" Harabi appealed to his annoyed king.

"Dragonrider Rahab," Shaharadesh half-roared in exasperation, "is it your intention to challenge a Dragonlord for command of a century?"

"It is," Rahab said solemnly.

"That wasn't what I meant," Harabi muttered to no one in particular.

"By tradition," Shaharadesh intoned, ignoring his irate Dragonlords, "you will fight for yourself with your Dragon acting as your Second." He turned and faced the dragonman. "Darkon, you may intervene if at any time you fear for your Rider's life. As soon as you enter the fight, the judgment will go against your Rider. Is that understood?"

Darkon nodded. "Understood."

Shaharadesh pegged Rahab with a chilling gaze. "If the judgment goes against you, you may resume a position under the command of any Dragonlord who will have you. If you cannot bring yourself to do this, or if no one will accept you, you must withdraw beyond the borders of Dumnonia and stay there until your Bond is broken. Do you understand?"

"I understand!" Rahab spat.

"Whom do you choose to challenge?" Shaharadesh indicated the nine Dragonlords.

Rahab stabbed his finger at Kashon. "You!" he roared. "I challenge Kashon, Dragonlord of Dumnonia!"

Katrell bristled.

Kashon lay a quieting hand on his arm. "It will be all right," he lied.

"Too afraid to challenge me?" Kassandra snarled.

Salene edged closer to Kashon. "This is nonsense!"

"Lord Kashon just fought me a few candlescars ago!" Shashtah protested. :*Who came up with these sunstruck traditions?*:

"Easy," Tphah murmured.

Kashon gripped Shashtah's shoulder with his left hand while maintaining his hold on Katrell with his right. "The man is half mad with grief. Let him be."

"I see no fresh stripes on his back!" Rahab proclaimed, still glaring at Kashon. "He shouldn't be alive!"

"Cause a death in a Challenge Fight," Shaharadesh warned, "and you and your Dragon shall both die!"

"Haven't we had enough death for one rotation?" Harabi asked.

"I don't need to kill him," Rahab said. "I just need to take away his century so no more Dragons or Riders will die because of his incompetence! He'll have to leave Dumnonia in disgrace!"

"No!" Shashtah barked. "We can't afford to lose any more Pairs. If the judgment goes against Kashon, he can serve under me!"

"Or me!" Kassandra agreed.

"Or me!" Salene echoed.

All the other Dragonlords repeated the cry.

The survivors of Kashon's century murmured their concern.

"We don't want another Dragonlord!" one of them called.

"Silence," bellowed Shaharadesh. "If Dragonlord Kashon is defeated, you will obey your new Dragonlord as you have obeyed him!"

"As if that will happen," Kassandra sniffed. "We'll have open rebellion."

Shaharadesh glared at her.

Kassandra glared back, completely unrepentant.

"Let me fight for you!" Katrell begged. "It's your right to choose me as your champion. I can defeat him."

Kashon rejected the offer with a shake of his head. "No. I will fight. My Dragon shall be my Second."

Katrell paled as Shaharadesh declared, "So be it!"

The king stepped to one side of the circle in a flurry of robes, escorting Makara out of harm's way.

Shashtah reached up, unfastened the brooch at Kashon's neck and removed his cloak. "Let the fool win," he whispered. "That's been your plan all along, hasn't it? To have someone take away your century?"

Kashon set his jaw stubbornly. "My Riders and Dragons can't stand to see me slink off to hide under your wing when they've just watched so many others die under my command."

Shashtah gently squeezed Kashon's upper arm, feeling the powerful muscles that lay beneath his friend's skin. "They can't stand to see you die, either."

Kashon favored him with a lopsided grin. "Then I'd better not die."

"'I stand with you in the Valley of Death,'" Shashtah whispered the words from *The Book of the Light*.

Kashon's eyes glistened. "'I have no fear.'" He turned to Katrell and kissed him gently. "You will not interfere." He strode to the center of the circle and faced Rahab.

Shashtah glanced at Tphah. His Prophecy screamed through his veins. He knew he was glowing, but he doubted anyone could tell in the glare of the morning sun. :*You heard Kashon. Stand where you can grab Katrell if something goes wrong. I think Kashon's afraid Katrell might kill someone.*:

Tphah moved closer to Katrell.

Kashon stared over Rahab's head at the doors of Corin's Tomb.

Rahab circled him, feinting, testing the Dragonlord's defenses.

Kashon remained motionless.

"What is this?" Rahab taunted. "You agreed to fight me!"

"I agreed to let you challenge me," Kashon said in a too-quiet voice.

Rahab bellowed his fury and lunged at Kashon's chest.

Kashon bent his knees, letting Rahab's weight carry him onto his back.

Katrell screamed.

Distracted, Kashon missed the timing of the roll that should have spun them over once more and landed him on top of Rahab. Instead, there was a sickening crack.

Rahab's hands closed around the Dragonlord's throat—

The Dragonrider scrambled backward as he realized Kashon's neck was broken.

Silence more complete than anything Shashtah had ever heard filled the Valley.

Kashon's body sprawled obscenely on the sand.

Shashtah dropped Kashon's cloak and ran to his friend.

"No," Rahab mouthed silently, then glanced at his horrified Dragon. "That wasn't supposed to happen!"

Katrell's soul-shredding keen echoed off the Valley walls.

Tphah and Bahktarah grabbed the distraught dragonman.

Two Councilors flew to the ravine floor. They shifted to humanform, took Rahab and Darkon by their upper arms and forced them to kneel before Shaharadesh.

Some part of Shashtah heard the king sentence the Pair to death.

Katrell continued to wail, a cry of unfathomable sorrow that would have deafened everyone in the Valley if he had taken dragonform.

Shashtah ignored the sounds as he knelt in the sand and gathered Kashon's limp body into his arms. He pulled his friend's corpse to his breast.

Kashon's head lolled grotesquely against Shashtah's shoulder.

"No . . ." Shashtah whispered to ears that could no longer hear. He closed his eyes and prayed to his god for a miracle that did not come. *What's the good of all this power if I can never do anything with it?*

Suddenly something shifted inside Shashtah's head. He stood on an endless plain.

The War Goddess appeared before him as she had after the Battle Dance. All of the greatest heroes and heroines of Dumnonia were ranked behind her.

All but one.

That one hesitated between Shashtah and the goddess.

Kyla, Goddess of War, sword in hand, saluted Kashon as she welcomed him. She spotted Shashtah and demanded, :*Why are you here? You belong to the Light, not to me!*:

:*I come for Kashon!*: Shashtah declared. :*You granted us your blessing!*:

The goddess nodded. :*Yes, I did. That is why I claim his soul now. He is mine. The Dark One shall never hurt him again.*:

:*Dumnonia still needs him!*: Shashtah cried. :*Kashon, come back with me! Come back to Katrell!*:

Kashon's shade turned. :*Shashtah?*:

:*Katrell cries for you!*: Shashtah shouted. :*Can't you hear him?*:

The shade cocked his head as if, perhaps, he could hear the heartbroken Dragon's scream. :*Katrell?*:

:*Eternal Death to the Dark One!*: Shashtah shrieked at the goddess. :*Not to Kashon! Not to Kashon . . .*: He held out his hand to his friend. :*Dragonlord of Dumnonia, come back with me! Don't leave Katrell! He needs you. We need you. Both of you. Together. Not apart.*:

Kashon stared through him with sightless eyes. :*And I don't want to die . . .*: He hesitated, then turned and made a deep salaam to the goddess. :*You know what glory we can bring you if we remain together. Please. Do not separate us. Not again.*:

The goddess closed her eyes and raised her face toward the eternal sky. :*Someone with my name prays!*: She opened her eyes and pointed with her sword. :*There!*:

Shashtah felt his heart tremble as he saw his foster daughter materialize less than a wingspan from them.

Kyla of Daethia knelt before the goddess whose name she bore. :*For a man who will never show me physical love, I foreswear all love but love of War! For a man I will never intentionally see again, I pledge all of my heart in the pursuit of the Dark One's death! For these oaths, jealous goddess, will you, for the lifetime of the Dragonheart, grant Dumnonia the life of Kashon?*:

:*Oh, Kyla!*: Shashtah choked.

:*No, Kyla . . .*: Kashon whispered. :*You don't know what you give up.*:

Kyla turned and smiled at Kashon. :*I care not what I give up because I know what I gain.*: She turned back to the goddess. :*Give Kashon to the Dragonheart, and you can have me.*:

:*So be it!*: declared the goddess. :*I release all claim on this hero. If he would return to me, he must earn the right again.*:

Shashtah gasped and opened his eyes as he felt Kashon's dead body stir in his arms.

Light such as Shashtah had never seen enveloped them. It shone like polished Galantite, shooting sparks and rainbows everywhere.

The neck that had been broken became stiff once more.

The light flashed and vanished.

"Ouch . . ." Kashon whispered as he opened his eyes and squinted at Shashtah as the magic faded to normal sunlight. "Where—?"

Shashtah kissed Kashon full on the mouth, tasting the sweet breath of his life, and then buried his face against the Dragonlord's shoulder and sobbed happily. "Kashon!"

"KASHON!" The entire Valley echoed with Katrell's roar as he broke away from Tphah and Bahktarah and tackled the two Dragonlords.

"Katrell! Be careful!" Shashtah squirmed out of the way as Katrell latched onto Kashon. "I think we're fresh out of deities who are willing to grant us miracles this rotation."

"I can't hear you!" Katrell shrieked.

"Hush, you nit." Kashon pushed himself into a position where he could get a better hold on his lover. "It's just a Bond Break. You've had them countless times before."

"I've lost so many!" Katrell sobbed. "Not you! Not you! I've waited so long—"

"Katrell! I'm not dead!" Kashon put his lips close to Katrell's ear. "We can reBond. As soon as Quatar and Peri are out of Corin's Tomb, Shaharadesh will send us right in and Corin can reform our Bond." He tried to rise. "Come on. Let me stand up."

"No!" Katrell pulled him back down. "I'm not letting go!"

"No one is asking you to. Please." Kashon pressed his fingers to Katrell's lips. "Let's wait by the doors of the Tomb so Shaharadesh can send us in as soon as Quatar and Peri come out."

Katrell twisted so he could get a firmer hold on Kashon. "We're not supposed to touch in the Tomb! I'll have to let go of you! I won't do it!"

Kashon's eyes pleaded with Shashtah for help.

Shashtah appealed to his king.

Shaharadesh shrugged. "I can heal frayed Bonds, but the only way to form one is by sending the Pair into the Tomb."

Shashtah frowned at Kashon and Katrell, trying to think.

Kashon was getting absolutely nowhere with Katrell.

Shashtah reached out and tried to help the Dragonlord to his feet. As soon as he touched Kashon, magic shimmered along the Bond he shared with his friend. This time the light felt familiar. *King's magic . . . And something else.* Shashtah closed his eyes and sensed his power join with Kashon's. He pulled the Pair erect and embraced them. He sent golden, glittering light through the jagged edges of Kashon's Broken Bond and toward Katrell. He threaded their souls back together like a weaver repairing a torn tapestry. As their Bond grew stronger, he sensed them growing toward each other and away from him. He released them and staggered backward, leaving them locked in each other's arms.

"SHASHTAH!" The cry began as a whisper and ended as a roar that rattled the doors of Corin's Tomb.

Kashon turned to Shaharadesh as the blinding light faded once more to the usual glare of the Dumnonian day.

Rahab gaped at Kashon. "What are you? Undead?"

"In this sunlight?" Kashon laughed. "I doubt it. I'm a Dragonlord. I think." He glanced at Shaharadesh. "I'm not sure this is covered in any of our Handbooks."

Shaharadesh stood before his son for a heartbeat. "I don't think it is." He dropped into a salaam.

Kashon waited until Shaharadesh straightened, and then released Katrell and bent in his own salaam to his king.

The Dumnonians and Dragons prostrated themselves on the sand at the gesture.

Shashtah felt completely forgotten—which suited him just fine. Although he was thrilled his friend was alive, he was terrified about what would happen once the Dumnonians and Dragons fully realized what he had just done. *First, I raise Kashon from the dead using the War Goddess's magic. Then I create a Bond without sending the Pair into the Tomb . . . by using the magic of the Light? The King's magic? Something else? Wizard's magic? None of that matches. It all conflicts. Why didn't I just blow everyone to ashes?*

Tphah swayed to her feet and put her hand on the small of his back.

Shashtah felt the tingle of her power along his spine, restoring him even before he realized how completely drained he was.

Kashon rose as the others picked themselves up.

Kassandra snatched Kashon's cloak off the sand and draped it across his shoulders.

The two Councilors who flanked Rahab glanced at each other, nodded at the no longer dead Dragonrider, and then scanned the canyon walls for the other Ancients.

"The Council," Garesh declared from his place on the rim, "recognizes Kashon as a Dragonlord of Dumnonia and grants him the lives of his executioner and the condemned Dragon to do with as he pleases."

Kashon turned to Rahab and Darkon. "Since I'm not dead, I see no reason you should die. You may take a place in my century if you like, or I have no objection to your returning to Lord Amasiah's century, if you desire and if he'll have you. Or you may join any other century, if the Dragonlord will have you."

Rahab scrambled to Kashon, grabbed his left hand and kissed his ring of office. "I give my life and the life of my Dragon to you as members of your century. Command us!"

"Gather your belongings, and ask my aide to assign you a tent," Kashon ordered.

Rahab let Darkon help him to his feet. He bared his throat, and then led his Bond Partner through the crowd.

The Dumnonians and their Dragons hissed at the Pair as they passed.

Katrell took Shashtah's face in both his hands and kissed him chastely on the lips. "My soul is yours for this. What would you have me do?"

"Just keep him happy, Katrell." Shashtah absently caressed the magnificent scimitar Kashon had given him what seemed like a lifetime ago. He was a trifle amazed he still had it. "He is the sword we need to wield against the Dark One. I don't want him breaking when we need him most."

Kashon's hand closed on the scruff of Shashtah's neck. "I'm all done breaking, thank you. Next time you're the one who gets to die."

"I think I'm doomed to live." Shashtah scanned the crowd. His eyes settled on Kyla. She stood not far from where he had last seen her, studiously averting her eyes. He danced out of the way as those near him converged on Kashon and Katrell. He stopped before his foster daughter and hugged her. "Thank you."

"Small payment for everything you've done for me." Kyla stiffened as she saw something above the Valley, over his shoulder. "Look!"

Shashtah squinted at the sky and saw Quatar astride Peri, riding the young mutant the way a Daethian warrior would ride a horse.

The new Pair circled toward the Valley floor. The scattered Dumnonians and Dragons enough for them to land.

"What's going on?" Quatar asked as he dismounted.

Peri shifted to his humanform. "Papa's been working miracles again."

Shashtah released Kyla and faced Quatar. "Will you submit to the Training under me, Quatar of Daethia?"

Quatar bent in a salaam. "As if I would dream of asking anyone else!" He straightened and pulled his sister into his arms. "It worked!"

"I'm so happy for you and Peri!" Kyla exclaimed. "I'm sorry I'll miss your

Bonding Feast," she added hastily. "I have a caravan I need to escort to Tor. I'll see you in Daethia after you finish the Training." Before Quatar could respond, she broke away from him and disappeared into the rising wave of Dumnonians.

"What's wrong with her?" Quatar asked.

Shashtah smiled after Kyla as Tphah finally found her way to his side. "Nothing. Nothing at all. She's perfect."

"Papa," Peri murmured in Shashtah's ear, "Corin says 'Yes, the mutants can be Trained and Bonded,' and 'Daethians might not look like Dumnonians, but whether they can be Dumnonians is up to the Dragons.' Does that make any sense to you?"

"Some." Shashtah smiled as Shaharadesh joined them.

The king looked gravely from Shashtah to the new Bond Partners. "My Camp is in too much disarray for me to hold a Bonding Feast for a Dragonslayer and a mutant. What would you say if I gave you all permission to go wherever you please until sundown to celebrate? I think Will can handle your century until then."

"I'm sure he can," Shashtah said. "Peri? Quatar? Shall we share a bowl of ice milk as big as the two of you put together with the Elven King?"

Peri laughed as Quatar flushed.

"How about just enough for all of us to have a taste?" Quatar suggested.

"That sounds fine," Tphah laughed.

Shashtah considered Kashon and Katrell, who looked decidedly as if they'd rather be just about anywhere other than where they were.

Shaharadesh followed Shashtah's gaze. "Things might calm down around here a bit faster if you take the two of them with you. I'm sure Patch can handle things while you're gone."

"The camp aides are the real Dragonlords," Shashtah said, echoing Kashon's words to him long ago. "I'm sure she can." He saluted his king, and then forced his way through the frenzied crowd toward his friends.

Shashtah floated like a crocodile in one of Farador's hot springs, watching Kashon remove his boots. Eyes barely above the level of the water, limbs hanging downward and spine trying not to blur into a tail, the Prophet drifted, staring through the steam. The cavern was empty except for the two of them. Every elf in the kingdom seemed to have turned up in the dining hall for the Bonding Feast, and Shashtah suspected that somewhere there was a very upset, volatile elven chef.

Tphah had volunteered to keep an eye on Quatar, Peri and Katrell so the two Dragonlords could retreat somewhere quiet to discuss how on Centuria Shashtah was going to put a mutant and a Daethian through the Training, which had been designed with Bronzes and Dumnonians in mind.

Shashtah, however, was contemplating a more violent encounter with his fellow Dragonlord.

Kashon stripped off his shirt, revealing his scarred back. He slid out of his trousers and eased his aching body into the water beside Shashtah. He rubbed his neck absently as the heated liquid surrounded him. "Remind me again: Why did I let you convince me that returning from the dead was a good idea?"

Shashtah surfaced and settled onto the submerged ledge beside Kashon. "Will you, please, let the elven Healers take a look at you? I'm not used to channeling the War Goddess's magic, even with Kyla's help. I have no idea whether I put you back together right."

Something dark flashed in Kashon's amber eyes. "I figure I wouldn't be breathing and have Katrell fretting himself halfway into the Afterlife inside my head if you hadn't."

Shashtah reached up with his left hand and massaged the place where Kashon's neck had been broken only candlescars before. "So what now? Too many people saw me resurrect you today. You can't just dance back into the King's Camp as if nothing happened."

"I know." Kashon leaned into Shashtah's touch.

Shashtah applied both hands to the problem as he felt the tension in Kashon's shoulders. "You can't keep facing Challenge Fights every time you turn around. There's going to be a simoom of Bonding as we try to replace the Riders and Dragons we lost. We need you to help train the new Pairs."

Kashon closed his eyes. "I know. And I know Katrell is in no condition to help me run a century, never mind Train new Pairs. And I'm well aware that the entire Council will not be able to sit on him hard enough if something bad happens to me again."

Shashtah sighed. "You might as well be permanently on leave."

Kashon slapped the water, undoing any good Shashtah's hands had done. "What do you want me to do? I'm a Dragonlord! I can't just take off and leave a decimated century without a leader. I'd have to lose a Challenge Fight to someone, but Katrell will go mad simply at the thought of me facing another opponent. Even supposing that I could get the Council to replace me without a fight because Katrell is unfit to be a Dragonlord's Dragon, they'll never let me take him permanently out of Dumnonia, which is where we really both need to be. He's too valuable!"

"We need a new tradition," Shashtah observed softly.

Kashon spun and gaped at him. "That is the one thing I was certain you would say we could do without."

Shashtah turned Kashon around and dug his fingers firmly into his friend's muscles once again. "Kassandra's on the right track. She's already shown us how to get ourselves back to full strength: The devastated centuries simply stay on rotation in the King's Camp until we're able to replace enough Pairs for them to rotate up to the frontline. But it's going to be a massive task to Train all of those Pairs, and someone needs to coordinate it. You're the only one of the Dragonlords with enough brains to do it." When Kashon didn't object, he plunged ahead. "You created an office when you made me Exercise Master. Ask Shaharadesh to create an office for you now. Dragon Trainer, or something like that. You could spend your days torturing Trainees instead of taking all the risks that go along with running a century. When you aren't personally needed, you could post a guard over the Trainees, like you assigned Salene to keep an eye on me, and take Katrell out of Dumnonia until the guard calls you back."

"Assuming that my father would even go for such a sunstruck idea, how does that keep me from being attacked?"

"No one attacked me when you named me Exercise Master because no one wanted the job."

"It's a sunstruck idea, Shashtah."

"Maybe. But if you don't keep Katrell off the frontline he is going to have the biggest meltdown in the history of Centuria, and now you know how much more dangerous that will be than simply having an Adult Bronze out of control in the King's Camp." Shashtah suddenly grabbed Kashon in a choke hold, wrapping his left arm around the Dragonlord's throat and his right arm around his waist. He pulled him firmly against his breast and put his lips close to his ear. "You know who he is. You know what kind of power he has. You were dead just a few candlescars ago. I held your body in my arms. You are alive now, not undead. And you can't keep acting as if that's normal. You can't keep acting as if he's normal!"

Kashon tried to twist away. "Stop it!"

Shashtah shifted to his half-dragonform and coiled his tail around Kashon. Even so he could barely maintain his grip on the powerful Dragonlord. "Can't you hear the questions everyone is asking? Why could I bring you back to life and not the Dumnonians and Dragons they loved? Why could I fix your Bond Break without sending you into Corin's Tomb? I know the answer. You know the answer. The Dragons already know about him, but if anyone else finds out, that will expose him to precisely the danger you've been trying to protect him from."

"Stop it!" Kashon screamed again.

:*What are you two nits doing?*: Tphah's voice whispered through Shashtah's mind softly enough that the question would not distract him. :*Katrell's turned as white as the ice milk he's been devouring and broke a chunk off the edge of one of the Elven King's tables.*:

Shashtah ignored her. "You heard the War Goddess agree to Kyla's terms that your life be tied to mine. I'm a Dragonheart. If I don't get myself killed, that's going to be centuries, maybe millennia. That will give you the time you need to stabilize him and give him back to us. But that's going to come at a price. Everyone is eventually going to wonder why you don't die."

Kashon heaved himself upward. "Stop it!" he shouted a third time.

Shashtah clung on. "You've come back from the dead again and again and again to find him and fix your mistake. When you were reincarnated, no one noticed and your past lives were lost to you. But this time you were resurrected, everyone noticed, and you've retained your memories. There's only one Dumnonian who's ever been close to being a Wizard. You know who 'Kesh' is. You know who Katrell is. You know why the Councilors defer to him. You know why he had to be the one to Train Tphah. He's a Dragonprophet. The first Dragonprophet. Perhaps the greatest Dragonprophet of them all. My father shouldn't be leading the Council of Ancients. Your Dragon should."

"He can't!" Kashon roared. "He's no longer the Dragon he was. He's had too many Bond Breaks!"

"Just as he had it Broken today when you died." Shashtah's voice, as quiet as a dagger, slipped between the ribs of his unwary opponent and stabbed him in the heart.

Kashon's inarticulate shrieks of horror echoed off the cavern walls.

Shashtah disentangled himself from Kashon, turned so they were chest to chest and braced him, letting him scream.

After what seemed like an eternity the earsplitting cries gave way to hysterical sobs. Eventually deep, ragged breaths took their place, and Kashon let his head fall limply against Shashtah's shoulder.

Shashtah dropped back into his humanform. "Listen to yourself. You're as bad as he is. Neither of you is in any shape to fight. If you don't like my idea, fine. But we have to find a way to keep people from trying to kill you so no one figures out that it can't be done. In the meantime, you need to let the elven Healers make sure that mixing Divine Magic, King's Magic, Wizard's Magic and whatever else was pumping through me didn't turn you into something you shouldn't be."

Kashon hesitated, and then gave his consent with a nod. "I'll let them look," he said in a barely audible voice. "But I've been so many people over so many centuries. . . Whom do you think they'll see?"

Shashtah eased Kashon slightly away from him and studied his face. Image after image after image of a Rider—one time a king—reflected in Kashon's dark amber eyes, and Shashtah knew that he had managed to reawaken the memory of at least the most important past life in him. "They'll see my friend, Kashon, Dragonlord of Dumnonia."

Kashon was silent for several heartbeats. "You know, the story is wrong." He stared into the steam. "I didn't fully Break our Bond. I used the Wizards' Magic, not the King's Magic. I couldn't bear the thought of not being able to hear him in my head. That's why he's never had a successful Bond with anyone else. He's always been partially Bonded to me. He's not the nit. I am." He absently drew an outline in magical light on the surface of the water that Shashtah belatedly recognized as the image of Tchang.

Shashtah instantly felt himself blown away from Kashon as if he'd been hit in the chest by a Dragon's magical bolt. Power surged around them, filling the cavern with a radiance that didn't come from the Elven King's magic. Everything disappeared into that glare, and Shashtah had the disturbing sensation that he was floating in a world of pure light such as he'd always imagined served as the home for his god. He hung there for a heartbeat, then fell back into the pool, slid beneath the water's surface and promptly began to drown.

Shashtah heard the headache pounding in his ears before he felt the blinding pain behind his eyes. His lungs coughed up water onto the Elven King's deck, and each heave made him wish that someone would take mercy on him and chop off his head.

Firm, loving hands gripped his temples, pressing back the pain. :*Breathe, Dragonheart,*: Tphah's beautiful voice soothed.

Blessed, fresh air finally replaced water, and Shashtah opened his eyes.

Farador stood beside the pool, drying the last of the water from his clothes with a wave of his hand.

Kashon squirmed futilely nearby where Katrell had him efficiently pinned to the deck.

Katrell's stubborn expression declared quite plainly that he was not going to allow Kashon to go anywhere anytime soon.

Shashtah almost laughed until he saw Katrell's look mirrored on Tphah's face.

"An out of control Prophet and an out of control Wizard," Farador said. "The Dark One doesn't need to fight us. We're going to blow ourselves up for him. I haven't seen anything like this since the White Wolf brought Shane to Daethia." He stroked his chestnut-colored beard. "What am I going to do with the two of you?"

"Nothing," Kashon growled. "We are Children of the Desert, not of the Great Woods!"

Shashtah grunted. "What is the purpose of having allies if we keep trying to do everything alone?"

Tphah looked at Katrell. "I say we dunk them both in the cold pool until they come to their senses."

"They have no senses to come to!" Katrell refused to take his eyes off Kashon. "I'm sick to death of losing you. I'm not going to do it again! The elves are going to make sure you are truly in one piece. Then they'll teach you how to keep you and Shashtah from nearly destroying our world every time you get together. After that the only place I will take you is to the Anvil so we can deal with our Trainees. You will not set foot in the King's Camp or anywhere else until I'm convinced no one will lay a talon on you. And you are not going to argue with me about any of that!"

"What about our century?" Kashon protested.

"Patch has kept things running smoothly for decades, even under Dameth." Katrell cocked his head slightly as he saw continued resistance in Kashon's eyes. "I'm serious. I will not let you up until you swear you will do exactly as I say!"

Shashtah glanced from Katrell to Tphah. :*Where did that Dragon come from?*:

Tphah stood up and helped him to his feet. :*He's always been there. He's just hard to see these days.*: "Katrell, let Kashon up before you break him. I swear we won't let him go anywhere you don't want him to go."

Katrell hesitated, then stood and helped Kashon rise.

Tphah dropped in a salaam to Farador. "Our humble apologies. We're new to this type of magic. Katrell is the only one of us with any real experience, and even he didn't know this would happen."

"Dumnonians think with their hearts, not with their heads," Farador said.

"And the Wizards of Corin thought with their heads, not with their hearts!" Katrell snarled.

Shashtah's narrowed his eyes as he studied Katrell, trying to see the Dragonprophet Tchang he knew lurked within the shapeshifted humanform. "Which means that someone around here had better figure out how to do both at the same time if we're ever going to win this War."

Kashon looked as if he had the same headache Shashtah did. "I'll see the Healers. Then I'll let the elves teach me how to control my magic so it doesn't mix with anyone else's. But that's all I'll agree to for now. I have a Pair in Training, a century to run, a war to fight—" He took a deep breath. "We need time, and we don't have it."

"Criton's stuck in the past," Farador said. "I can barely manage the present. The only being I know who was ever any good at Time Magic is the White Wolf, and he insists that the safest place for him is in the Northern Wastes where none of us can find him."

"I found him once." Shashtah's shoulders slumped. "I hate the snow," he said to no one in particular.

Katrell shrugged. "It's just another kind of desert. Only colder."

Farador sighed. "I need to return to the dining hall before someone comes looking for me. Try not to blow up my kingdom while I'm gone." He strode out of the cavern, still shaking his head.

Shashtah pulled on his clothes, absently noting that Kashon was doing the same. *Bahakesh Dragonheart, King of Dumnonia, "The Divine Gift" . . . Not anymore. He has become something else. He has become "The Giving One". He has become Kashon.*

"Healers. Now!" Katrell ordered, as he marched his strangely meek Rider out of the cavern.

"Please tell me that you are not going to drag me around the Northern Wastes the way Tkai did," Shashtah groaned.

"You know I never do anything the way Tkai did," Tphah replied, a secretive smile on her face. "Besides, we aren't going anywhere until we Train Peri and Quatar."

Shashtah nodded. "One disaster at a time." He took a deep breath, let it out slowly and escorted her back to the dining hall.

Shashtah spent the rest of the day watching his pregnant Prophetess gorge herself as Quatar and Peri cavorted shamelessly with the elves. Adrial, her hair finally arranged in the intricately-braided style of an elven matron, popped down briefly from Tor to congratulate Quatar and to have a private word with her father. From the look of resignation that settled over Farador's face, Shashtah guessed that the Elven Princess had finally managed to conceive Criton's child, an act of creation that sounded her own death knell. When Juel showed up to summon his troops for the night's fighting, Shashtah took the opportunity to give the Elven Lord a message for Jochia. "Please tell the Galantite king to tell Balkar that the mutants can be Trained and Bonded like the Bronzes."

"I'll let him know," Juel promised as he herded his army through the dining hall doors.

When Kashon and Katrell returned, Tphah sstood. "We should be getting back. I'll collect the boys."

"No," Shashtah said. "This is their Bonding Feast. Let them enjoy it. Tell them to meet us at the edge of the King's Camp at dawn—our time."

Tphah saluted only half seriously and slipped off to deliver the message.

Shashtah scratched his head as he watched her go. "You still have a Trainee at the Anvil. Where do I send Quatar?"

"To the Anvil," Kashon replied. "We all go there. It gives us something in common. We just need to settle Peri out of reach of the Bronze. It's generally no worse than trying to get two females to nest on the dunes at the same time."

"If you think that's bad, just wait until the end of the rotation," Katrell grumbled. "Tphah only has one day head start on her eggs from all the others who bred last night."

"Oh, thank you so much for pointing that out!" Shashtah rubbed his forehead, feeling his headache return. "Try to remember not to mention that little detail to my Prophetess. She had a fit the last time and then she was alone. I don't want to think about what she'll be like with other broody females around!"

Kashon punched him playfully on the shoulder. "I'll meet you at the Anvil. I'll work with my Trainees and help you with Quatar and Peri until we figure out how I can walk back into the King's Camp without someone trying to break my neck again." He slid out of Katrell's embrace. "Let's go."

Shashtah watched them leave, Katrell hard on Kashon's heels, clearly not at all happy about following him rather than walking at his side.

"Katrell is going to explode," Tphah said quietly as she rejoined Shashtah. "I just can't see when."

Shashtah nodded. "All I see is sand around him when it happens. That could put them anywhere in Dumnonia—or Cinnamar. At least it won't be in the middle of the King's Camp." Shashtah stared proudly at his fosterlings for a heartbeat. "I want to check on our Fledglings and Striplings."

Tphah took his arm and leaned her head against his shoulder. "You are going to be positively insufferable when you wind up with hundreds of Hatchlings."

"I know." Shashtah laughed at himself. "I know."

At dawn, Shashtah and Tphah set out to find Quatar and Peri at the edge of Camp. They located them quickly, Quatar snoring peacefully in his dragon's forearms.

A twinkle in his darkened amber eyes, Shashtah shifted to his dragonform, grabbed Quatar by the ankles and hauled him into the air.

Tphah and Peri both disintegrated into giggling fits at Quatar's inarticulate protest.

Shashtah shook his foster son unceremoniously out of his desert boots and onto the sand.

Quatar's dagger, which had been strapped to his ankle, pulled lose and fell onto the seif dune.

Shashtah resumed his own form and picked up the dagger.

"A simple 'Good Morning' would have sufficed," Quatar pawed the loose sand from his hair.

Tphah cracked her jaws in the draconic version of a grin. "That's 'Good Morning, sir!' to you, Trainee!"

"Good Morning, sir!" Quatar shouted as he saluted the Prophetess and his Dragonlord.

"Where's your sword?" Shashtah demanded as he slid the dagger into his belt.

Quatar frowned his puzzlement. "I left it with Will. I didn't think I'd be needing it—"

"You won't. I take it you'll never forget where the Anvil is?" Shashtah asked.

"No, sir!" Quatar barked with a nervous glance at Peri.

"I'll meet you there with water at midday," Shashtah promised. "And no transporting!"

"But—!" Quatar started to protest.

"Peri will fly cover as you run," Shashtah said. "Don't be late!" He took Quatar's boots and headed back to Camp.

Tphah caught up to him and slipped her arm through his as they strolled through the tents. "They'll make it," she assured him as they heard Peri take wing and Quatar start running across the dunes.

"That's not what worries me," Shashtah confessed. "I'd like to get at least a few more candlescars of sleep, but, with my luck, those two will be the first Trainees in history to make that run before midday!" :*Why didn't you tell me that*

Katrell is Tchang and that Kashon is a reincarnation of Bahakesh?:

:*Would you have believed me?*:

:*No.*: Shashtah sent a wave of love through their Bond, pulling their hearts and minds as close as he could. :*You know me too well.*:

Tphah laughed, matching her magic perfectly to his.

From the shadows beside a tent, a dragonman honored Shashtah with the salaam usually reserved for the Dumnonian king. :*Thank you for my life and that of my Rider.*:

"Did you say something?" Shashtah asked Tphah as the dragonman, whom he belatedly recognizes as Darkon, straightened and slipped into the next aisle.

"No," Tphah replied. "I was just thinking that you are going to make a marvelous king."

"I need to learn how to be a Dragonlord first."

"You'll do fine."

"Prophecy?" Shashtah teased.

"What else?" Tphah smiled proudly as she kissed him and led him back into the King's Camp.

Acknowledgements

I have dedicated this novel to Scriptorium 101, a writing group that met at my home for many years. The three most faithful members were Sue and Carl Flaherty and Nancy Hubbs-Chang. I want to take this opportunity to thank them for the countless hours they spent reading, commenting on, and editing this work.

Many thanks are also due to my dear friend, Kendra Hosseini, who is co-President of the Mercedes Lackey Fan Club, Queen's Own, where she is known as Healer Adept Moonstar. As my beta-reader she has given me much valuable advice, particularly in respect to developing my female and LGBT characters, which I greatly appreciate.

Thanks also to Zane of the Ever-Changing Name for helping me with material about Middle Eastern cultures and with LGBT characters from an Arab perspective.

I am tremendously grateful for the support and advice of Dr. Ken Atchity, who was my Creative Writing professor at Occidental College and who is now helping me publish my books through Story Merchant Books.

A huge thank you to my illustrator, Laura Cameron! We first worked as a team in the 1990s when I was publishing stories in Mercedes Lackey fanzines. Laura has always had a knack for taking what is in my head and putting it into drawings. I greatly admire her skill and thoroughly enjoy working with her.

As to everyone else who has been part of the process of taking *Dragon Sun* from creation to novel, you have my deepest gratitude. A thousand apologies if I have failed to mention you by name. Know that I am eternally grateful to you all.

Dear Reader

In *Dragon Sun*, the second book of the Dragonlords of Dumnonia series, I have continued to explore ideas and issues that are dear to my heart: the interaction between religion and politics, speculation about what a tolerant Arab culture might look like, and human rights. I have also attempted to present the difficulties of allies trying to fight a war against a common enemy when everyone is not on the same page. While these are all topics that are currently of interest in the real world, I have chosen to deal with them in a fantasy setting, which I hope has given you the opportunity to consider these problems from the perspective of these characters as they interact with their own world rather than from a personal perspective of our modern times.

I hope you will return to spend time with old friends and to make new acquaintances as you follow their adventures in their magical world. Please take the time to tell others about the *Dragonlords of Dumnonia series*, be that by word of mouth or by writing a review on Amazon.com or elsewhere on the Internet or in print. Join our Facebook page for updates on future releases and to discuss the works that have already been published.

May the Light be with you! Or, as Shashtah would say, "Eternal Death to the Dark One!"

About the Author

Dr. Linda A. Malcor is a folklorist and comparative mythologist who specializes in the traditions of King Arthur. She is the co-author, with C. Scott Littleton, of *From Scythia to Camelot*, a nonfiction work that has been translated into several languages. She served as the researcher for the movie *King Arthur* (2004), which was inspired by her publications. She has written many articles, short stories, and other works of fiction and nonfiction. She lives in Southern California, where she is known in fan circles as Herald-Mage Adept Danya Winterborn, co-president of the Mercedes Lackey fanclub Queen's Own (Yes, she really can do stage magic!). She is an ordained elder in the Presbyterian Church (USA), through which she has engaged in many human rights activities. Her particular passion is LGBT issues, though she has recently become an advocate for Freedom of Expression in the Middle East. *Dragon Sun* is her second novel in the *Dragonlords of Dumnonia* series, which began with *Dragon Heart*.